THE
HOUSEWIFE
NEXT
DOOR

BOOKS BY LYNDEE WALKER

The Pastor's Wife

The Housewife Next Door

LynDee Walker

THE HOUSEWIFE NEXT DOOR

bookouture

Published by Bookouture in 2026

An imprint of Storyfire Ltd.
Carmelite House
50 Victoria Embankment
London EC4Y 0DZ

www.bookouture.com

The authorised representative in the EEA is Hachette Ireland
8 Castlecourt Centre
Dublin 15 D15 XTP3
Ireland
(email: info@hbgi.ie)

ISBN: 978-1-80550-198-5
eBook ISBN: 978-1-80550-197-8

For my mom, who taught me not only what it means to be a good mother, but how to avoid getting tangled in family secrets and drama.

PROLOGUE

Present Day

Ainsley died a week before her twenty-second birthday, with the sunshine on her beautiful face. But her last words were about the dark.

"It's too scary." She grasped one of my hands in both of hers, her eyes glassy and skin blotchy from fever, pulling her whole torso up off the simple white rail twin bed her father and brother had carried somberly outside into the pink rays of dawn as her sisters sobbed, huddled around the kitchen table. Her mother stood in the corner of the great room, watching everything with a flat, stoic look that seemed out of place in the chaotic house.

"Meg, you," Ainsley coughed before she gagged, her throat closing up on itself again.

That was the first thing I'd noticed: she'd spit water all over my leg. Was that just yesterday? We were playing gin rummy after dinner and she'd taken a swig from her glass. Nothing out of the ordinary.

Her eyes had popped wide, and the water sprayed out at

first, then sort of trickled down her chin as her mouth gaped open, her hands going to her throat. I had dropped my cards and called for help. Ainsley's family was huge, there were always people around. Four, maybe five of them had come running.

Eighteen hours later I knelt by her bed, set carefully in the front yard where she could see the rising sun. Ignoring the gravel biting into my knees, I held her hand as she tried to talk.

"It's okay," I whispered. "You're going to be okay." I knew it wasn't true, but it was all I could say. My heart flat refused to accept the truth of the horror unfolding in front of my eyes, never mind trying to make my brain put words to it.

Yesterday, Ainsley was a bubbly, kind, clever girl who loved the sun, her people, and a good glass of lemonade on a warm day. She had a big heart and the brightest, kindest smile of anyone I'd ever known.

Looking at the pale, sweaty shell twisted in the bedcovers as the sky brightened around us, I couldn't seem to force my brain to acknowledge that they were one and the same. Like I was looking at someone else—a sad, unfortunate stranger instead of my friend. Maybe that's how I'd escaped the sorrow that seemed to have such a grip on everyone else. I'd rather believe that than wonder if I had just seen too much death. I knew this day would join the others that haunted me, knew I would miss Ainsley's shy smile and kind heart. I just didn't want to think the things I'd seen and done before I came here had broken me in some horrifying, fundamental way that meant I wouldn't feel a loss this profound the way I should. The way she deserved for me to feel it.

Ainsley's eyes narrowed as she managed to haul in a deep breath. "Don't lie, just listen," she snapped. "You see the dark, don't you? You can help. I didn't help her."

I didn't take my eyes off her face, the sweat shining in the pink light such that her skin seemed to be glowing from the inside. "We're in the sun. Can't you feel the sun? It's not dark."

Her head fell back to her pillow, the blue flowers on the case almost mocking in their cheerful innocence. She sighed.

"It's always dark. For years now. Always dark in the garden."

My brow furrowed and I reached to smooth hers.

"You ought not touch her," her brother said from a watchful post about four feet behind me.

"I heard the doctor tell your mother this isn't catching," I said over my shoulder. "It's something that happened to her a long time ago, just lurking inside her." Like Ainsley had lived her whole life on borrowed time. I swallowed hard. I would not cry. We had a deal, Ainsley and me. We'd seen terrible things, both of us, but we didn't cry. We had learned early on how to handle life's messes.

"If you believe the doctor." Her brother's tone said he didn't.

"Do you need to be right there, right now?" I asked instead of arguing.

His hands disappeared into the pockets on his overalls to halfway up his forearms. "Momma said stay out here with her."

I twisted my neck to glare at him and he backed off ten yards or so, slouching against the base of a massive old tree. He grabbed a stick and pulled out a pocket knife.

Ainsley squeezed my hand, her grip crushing my fingers. I pulled in a sharp breath, going still when I looked back at my friend.

Her face was... hers, but somehow also not. I blinked, scrubbing at my eyes with my free hand.

Maybe I so desperately didn't want her to die that my brain was just going to refuse to watch it happen.

Or maybe her big, stupid brother was right and I had caught whatever this was. I mean, the doctor had said Ainsley was losing her mind—in the middle of the night, before they'd carried her outside, she kept talking about the little girl in her garden no matter how many times we'd repeated that her sisters were all safe in their beds. Her mother had left the room then, crying into a linen handkerchief. She'd lasted longer than anyone but me and the doctor—the men had all vacated hours before.

"It's just us," I had said, stroking the back of her hand. "Nobody's in the garden. Just rest so you can get better."

"Hallucinations are common." The doctor had shaken his head, closing his bag and patting my shoulder. "Near the end. Such a shame."

He'd left, too.

Back aching, I'd kept myself folded onto a milking stool next to Ainsley's long, narrow metal-framed bed for hours. The air grew thicker with each chime of the big clock in the front hall, and by the time light peeked through her blue drapes I could almost see sweat and sickness floating around us, so warm I was half convinced her fever was roasting us both in the shoebox of a bedroom.

That's when Ainsley really started screaming about the dark. I'd been relieved when her mother swept back in, ordering her father and brother to carry her, bed and all, out into the breaking daylight.

Now I was seeing things, too, right out in the fresh air.

I knew logically that I was still looking at her glowy, fevered face, but I saw something else entirely—a different being than the sick, ebbing shell on the relentlessly adorable blue-flowered sheets.

I saw Ainsley laughing as she splashed me in the creek last summer.

I saw her riding her favorite horse, her long dark hair streaming behind her when he took off at a gallop.

I saw her working on an old wooden baby puzzle with my son, her patience a never-ending well of laughs as he chewed on one piece while he threw another across the room.

"I am so thankful for you," I said, swallowing tears despite my best efforts to keep smiling for her. "Every day of my life, I will be thankful that you were part of it. That you saved us that first day we met, and every day since." The words tasted bitter and felt thick, but I wrestled them out anyway. I had to make sure she heard them before...

Well. She had to know.

I couldn't feel my fingers anymore, but somehow I knew she was squeezing them even tighter. Maybe I heard a bone crack through her labored, wheezy breathing.

The last of her strength.

It didn't even occur to me to call out to her family. I knew, without her saying, that she didn't want them anywhere near us, like something of her had crawled inside my skin and could whisper to me without her lips moving.

"Yes. That first summer you came here. It's dark. So dark in the garden, ever since then," she whispered, her brow furrowing like she was frustrated. I leaned closer. "No. Under the garden. Under the garden, in the dark. The cold. I couldn't help her, Meg. Remember. You have to find her. Promise. Save her. Get her out of the dark."

Ainsley choked on the last word, her chest heaving twice more before it went still.

Her bumbling brother hollered behind me.

I stayed there with my knees in the gravel, pain rocketing up my arm when feeling returned to my hand as her grip fell slack.

A little girl. Not in the garden. Under the garden.

Dear God.

Her family swarmed around the bed, sobs breaking the silence.

I stood and backed away. I wasn't family. Didn't belong there.

Not that I'd ever belonged much of anywhere.

I watched Ainsley's father use his thick fingers to close her eyes for the last time, her mother pressing on the side of her thin neck looking for a pulse. She shook her head as the sun crested the front barn's tin roof, confirming what everyone in the yard already knew.

Ainsley was gone.

And I was the only person who knew that she'd used her last seconds on earth to tell a secret.

A terrible secret.

The thing I didn't know, standing there watching grief settle over her family, heavy and hot in the cool late summer sunrise, was whether or not it was true.

But it sure seemed like I owed it to Ainsley to find out.

PART ONE

Found Family
Two Years Earlier: The First Summer

ONE

Ainsley
June

"Snake!" My voice sounded shrill as I screamed, the young woman surveying the blackberry bush about a hundred paces in front of me dropping a small metal pail when she jumped, both her arms closing around the infant on her hip as her head swiveled, first toward me and then all around, looking for the danger.

"He's in the bush," I called, hurrying over the hilltop. "Just take a few steps backward."

She moved quickly, but with careful steps, then turned to me with a small smile, shifting the baby to the other hip—the one furthest away from me.

"Thank you," she said, her voice carrying away on the wind such that I couldn't say for sure if I heard those first words or simply saw her lips move.

I jogged the last few steps in my heavy skirts, the June sun warm but the breeze ruffling the grass on the hillsides cool enough to make it a nice day. I stopped a few feet from her, smiling again and bending to pick up her pail so she didn't have to do that while holding the little one. Up close, the little boy was a cutie in his tiny blue sailboat onesie and chocolate brown shorts, his bare toes begging to be tickled as he kicked his feet while hiding his face in her shoulder.

"I didn't mean to scare you." I held the pail out to her. "I just spotted the snake as I was coming over the hill and wasn't sure if you saw him."

She took the pail and waved it in the general direction of the massive blackberry bush that covered this section of the hilltop, fed by water runoff from the higher stretch of the hill and nearly the full day of sun this time of the year. "I still don't see it, but you sounded real sure, so I took your word for it."

I stepped carefully toward the bush, its branches heavy with fat, ripe berries, scanning between the berries and leaves close to the ground until I spotted him. "There," I pointed. "See the triangle-shaped head? That's a copperhead. We get them around here in the summertime, he's just the first one I've seen this year."

She backed further away. "He can just have the blackberries. I don't need to eat a whole pie anyway."

"He's not after the blackberries," I said, smoothing my frizzy, escape-artist hair back toward the bun on the back of my head. "He's hiding in the shade and waiting for whatever might want the blackberries."

She flinched and I laughed. "I don't think he could eat one of us, but a prairie dog or a barn rat would keep him full for a few days. The problem is that they bite humans when they feel threatened. And maybe just out of spite, if you ask my papa. He says copperheads are the whole reason 'mean as a snake' is a saying."

"How did you see it?" she asked. "I mean, I was practically standing on it and I didn't notice."

"I grew up here," I said. "There are nearly always snakes in this blackberry bush. So I knew to look for one." I looked her up and down and smiled at the baby. "No disrespect, but nobody around here takes kindly to trespassers, and you're on private property. The state park stops just the other side of that next hill."

"No, I'm..." She glanced at the ground and then raised her eyes to meet mine. "I didn't come from the park. I'm Meg. I moved in a few months ago."

"You live here?" I looked toward the house, then back at her. "Like here, here? Since when?"

"We bought the place in March. Been getting settled and exploring when there's time. Little buddy and me came for a walk today and I spotted the bush when we were about halfway up the hill. I thought it was a blessing, you know? I mean, all this fresh fruit just sitting here in the sun. So I went home and got a pail. And then the bush tried to kill me." She laughed, but it wasn't a joyful noise.

Technically, it was the snake that could've hurt her. But I annoyed people at home by saying stuff like that out loud, so I kept it to myself and smiled. "Well then, I'm glad I came to get blackberries for supper. Maybe my snake-spotting skills are enough for you to forgive me for trespassing on your land?"

"Trespassing. On my land." Something soft lit her face as she repeated the words, like she was testing them out almost. But she didn't say anything else, just kissed the baby's head and stared at the horizon with a look on her face I couldn't make out.

"I was just making a joke. You know, because I warned you about this being private property and then it turned out to be yours..." I let the last words trail, swinging the empty pail at my side. "I'll have to tell Momma the Lesters' blackberry bush has a new owner, she needs to add them to her list for the market."

I watched Meg's face, but her expression didn't change for probably twenty seconds after I stopped talking.

Huh.

It wasn't until I turned back for my side of the hill that she seemed to return to the here and now.

"Wait," she barked a little too sharply, making my head snap back around to look at her. "I didn't get your name."

"Ainsley," I said, stopping and walking back toward her a few feet. "Ainsley Godfrey. I live on the next farm over."

She laughed again, an entirely different, happy sound, like little bells chiming. I felt my face light up as I joined in.

"Well, Ainsley Godfrey, I think you're the best snake spotter in the county. Maybe in the world, and me and my buddy sure are appreciative of that. I believe saving us today earns you all the blackberries you can carry." Her face spread into a lovely smile, her cheekbones high, her eyes wide and pretty with long, thick lashes. The grin faded when she eyed the copperhead. "I, uh… I don't suppose you have snake-wrangling experience, do you?"

"They're easily fooled," I said, looking around for a rock. I lined up my aim and landed it in the tall grass just a few feet to the left of the bush, away from Meg and the baby, then ran to the spot in a wide arc, watching my feet as I rustled the same grass.

The copperhead shot out from under the blackberry bush and streaked toward the grass. I hurried back the other way, meeting Meg's eyes with a smile just as she shuddered.

"They're so creepy."

I didn't want to argue with her before we were even friends, so I kept all the facts I knew about why snakes were cool to myself. After years of being told that know-it-alls were irritating, I was trying to learn how to be better at getting along with other folks. Just in case I decided to leave the small rural county that raised me someday.

The grass rustled again as a bird chirped nearby, and we watched the snake chase it further up the hill, away from us. The bird took to the air before the copperhead could reach it.

"Shall we?" I swung my pail toward the bush.

"Lifesaving guests first." Meg smiled, and I started picking, showing her as I went how to tell good berries from bad ones and warning her about the bush's thorns.

She struggled, holding the baby with one arm as she tried to pull berries and get them into her bucket with the other hand. When she sighed and stepped back after a few minutes, I put my pail down and took hers, filling it quickly.

"You're good at this," she said when I handed it back.

I popped a berry in my mouth, closing my eyes for a second when the sweet taste of summer burst across my tongue. "I've been picking them since I wasn't much bigger than him." I tweaked one of the baby's bare toes with my little finger and he laughed, watching me with an adorably curious knit to his little brows. "When you grow up the eldest of six, you get chores quick."

The baby started to fuss, and she checked his diaper and made a face. "I need to change him," she said, taking a couple of steps back down the hill. Maybe it was wishful thinking, but I could swear I heard something in her voice. Something that said she didn't want to go. I didn't want her to, either, but it would be rude to ask if I could follow her home.

I hadn't had a friend in so long. Watching Meg back down the hill with the baby's cries getting louder, a desperation rose in my chest until I almost couldn't breathe at the thought of letting this chance slip away. I might not get another.

"You could do that while I finish picking berries and then come over to our house." The words were out of my mouth before I could swallow them, and the way her face lit up, I couldn't take them back.

"We'll be so fast, won't we, bitsy?" she cooed at the baby as she turned to run down the hill, her beige cotton shorts making that far easier than it was for me in my skirts.

Momma said women didn't have any business wearing pants. Pants were for men.

Momma wouldn't like Meg.

Me and my big mouth—I'd tried so hard, and here I'd still managed to cause trouble. But there was nothing for it now.

Meg was coming to my house. Whether Momma liked it or not.

TWO

Meg
June

I had flat out lost my mind.

Isolation was the entire point of moving here—well, most of the point, anyhow—and I hadn't lasted three full months and now I was going on social calls? What in the blue hell was I thinking?

In another life, in a universe with no dark secrets or dead people in my past, I would've smiled and joked and chatted with Ainsley. I would've been glad to meet her. I would've agreed to go back up the hill and over to her house once little buddy had a clean diaper.

Somehow, for a few crucial minutes, I'd convinced myself that was the life and universe I was part of. And now I didn't know how to get out of it.

Here's the really weird part: even as I walked through my front door and plunked my pork chop down on his changing table, I didn't want to get out of it. I knew it wasn't my true reality, but for those few minutes, it felt so nice to breathe, to smile, to talk to someone who had a full set of teeth and knew how to talk back.

I knew I could just stay put—Ainsley'd figure out I wasn't coming back and go home eventually. But that was mean. She'd looked just as excited to see me, and I hadn't rescued her from anything.

Or had I? There weren't many people near our age around here. She had to be younger than me, but I wasn't sure by how much, exactly—I guessed her to be probably between eighteen and twenty.

I knew better than most people that a snakebite couldn't hurt as much as some kinds of loneliness. They were two different kinds of poison, really: one might stop your heart, but the other could devour your soul.

"What do you think?" I blew a raspberry on the baby's belly after I fastened his clean diaper in place. He giggled, my heart lurching in my chest. He was growing so fast, and I was still amazed at the physical responses I had to his noises. That giggle would forever be my very favorite sound in the world. I had learned the difference between a hungry cry, a tired cry, and a "help me" cry, but all three made me feel like I wanted to climb out of my own skin, the need to fix his problem overwhelming in its power and ferocity. "Has Mommy lost her marbles? Do we need a friend?"

He scrunched up his little forehead and cocked his head to one side like he was seriously considering his answer. I copied his expression, tipping my head the other way and managing to hold a straight face for thirty seconds or so. When I smiled, he busted into a fit of laughter that made my heart sing—cheesy, I know, but I had no other words for it. This tiny human was my world, and he made me happy every day.

Watching him laugh before I picked him up, I realized maybe I wasn't as dumb as I thought.

I walked through the house and picked up the only two

photo frames, stashing them in a drawer just in case Ainsley was of a mind to come looking for us.

Nothing else in the house would give away our past. To everyone here, we were just a young mother with a new baby and a sad story, and I had to make sure it stayed that way.

For months, everything in my life had revolved around this little boy. I had been happier than I could recall ever being before. Standing on the hill, I'd been grateful for Ainsley, because she saved me from the snake. Because she saved *us* from the snake.

I had also noticed, without fully realizing it in the moment, that my baby had warmed up to her like butter hitting a hot skillet.

Back at the house with a minute to think, I understood that I liked Ainsley because he liked her.

Keeping to myself was safe, and I'd done just fine with it for the whole spring. Back in the house alone, it was easy to think I didn't actually need a friend for myself.

But I would do anything for my son.

Even call on the neighbors and make a new friend because my baby had smiled at the girl who lived on the next farm.

THREE

Ainsley
June

"Four hundred and seventy acres," I said, sweeping one arm at the farm from the top of the hill between our house and Meg's. "Firefly Grove, we call it—give the weather another two weeks and you can see why every night at dark. The name's not quite as old as the farm is, but it goes back, to maybe my great-grand-mother. It's all ours, as far as you can see. Probably farther, actu-ally, unless your eyes are better than mine."

I laughed as Meg's eyes widened, her eyebrows lifting almost to her hairline as she looked down at the sprawling black-shingled roof. "Is that... your house?"

"It used to be the barn." I waved for her to follow as I hurried down the hill, swinging a silver pail brim-full of ripe blackberries at my side. "But my parents needed room for more kids, so they made the old house into an office and turned the biggest barn into the house." I pointed, "The wings Papa added have our bedrooms. And that big oak over there to the side is more than three hundred years old. Funny to think that generations of my family have grown up climbing that thing."

"You really have five brothers and sisters?" Meg hurried to keep up, the baby bouncing on her hip, so I stopped to tie my skirts around my legs and let her catch me.

Running down the hill toward home was one of my favorite things in the world. Nothing else made me feel so free and so safe in the same breath, my legs churning, heartbeat picking up, my feet crashing into the packed earth of the hills that had surrounded my family, protecting us for five generations.

But today, I had special reason to be slow. Because today, I had made a new friend.

New friends—new people at all, really—were about as rare as unicorns in our little pocket of southern Kansas.

I hadn't so much as talked to a soul I didn't share a bloodline with since last fall, which was how I missed that the old Lester place had sold. I wasn't shocked—I knew what the land was worth to anyone who wanted to work it. Having someone happen along who both wanted a farm that was wasting back into the hills and had the means to buy it off the state on account that Old Man Lester hadn't had any kin at all when he died—that was always the problem.

"I can't tell you how glad I am that you wanted blackberries," Meg said as I picked up the pail and started walking, shortening my steps to match hers. "I did climb the hill, just once, right after we moved in, but I don't know if I ever would've gotten brave enough to bother y'all." She looked around as we hit the bottom of the hill and stepped into the main garden. "Wow, I've never seen a garden like this except on the TV. You don't have your own blackberry patch?"

I pointed to the tomato plants, already nearly knee high with varying shades of green and red fruit hanging from the stalks. "They don't get on well with the tomatoes," I said. "Draw the wrong kind of bugs. And the wild patch on your side of the hill has always produced more than an army could eat, even when Old Man Lester was still spry enough to get himself up there and pick his own."

"We're happy to share, aren't we, buddy?" Meg kissed the baby's dark curls and he squeaked, kicking his chubby legs, the cute little rolls on the thighs poking out of his shorts stretching out before they resettled against her side.

"How old is he?" I asked, waving her up onto the porch Papa and my brother had built along the front of the house last summer. The pine columns still smelled like fresh-milled wood. I breathed deep as I walked past, like I always did. The feel and smells of outside, of the hills that raised me, were like a balm for my soul. Whenever anything was too much for me to bear, all I had to do was go outside to make it right again.

I wondered sometimes if other girls my age—ones who grew up in the city, or in some cute little house Papa liked to call a "cracker box" with a fenced yard and a neighborhood swimming pool that smelled of chlorine and hot dogs on long summer days—ever felt like I did in darker moments.

Like under the crushing weight of secrets and expectations, and the pressure of dreaming dreams too big to chase, life itself was just too much. Wonder was as far as I'd ever gotten, though—it wasn't like I could ask my sisters, who were all younger than I was. And I wouldn't dare ask Momma. But now... what if I could have a real friend? Maybe I'd finally have someone to ask.

"Eight months," she said, tipping her head to rest her cheek on the baby's downy hair.

I wanted to ask how old she was—she didn't look much older than me, so I couldn't tell for sure if the baby was her brother or her son—but that felt rude. Intrusive, or presumptive, just yet, anyway.

I reached a hand toward him, offering her a smile "May I?"

The baby grabbed my middle finger before she got the "of course" out of her mouth. His whole little face lit up like a star, and he pulled my finger toward him as he flailed his legs again and squealed through a grin.

"He likes you." She smiled with so much genuine joy it was downright infectious.

"The feeling is mutual," I said, setting the pail on the wide bench by the front door and tapping the baby's cute upturned nose. He opened his mouth and tried to catch my finger, and Meg and I both dissolved into giggles.

Before I had myself under control, the front door opened.

"Ainsley!" Momma's eyes crinkled at the corners with a small smile as she dried her hands on her blue apron. "My goodness, it's nice to hear you laugh." Her eyes flicked to Meg and the baby. "I see you found the new neighbors. Are those berries for supper?"

"Yes, ma'am," I said, pointing to the bucket. "There were plenty."

"Ainsley saved us from a snake," Meg said. "I was happy to share."

Momma didn't speak.

I watched Meg shuffle her feet as Momma stood there blocking the door, examining the berries but not moving to invite us into the house. Like I said, outsiders were rare. And not always welcome, even when they were brought over as guests.

"Momma?" I prompted finally, when she pulled a third leaf from the pail and commented on my sloppy picking technique.

"What?" she snapped, a little too sharply even by her own estimation, evidenced by the way she smiled with no teeth and shook her head. "Forgive me."

"Of course," Meg and I said in unison.

Everyone always forgave Momma.

Even when she didn't deserve it.

FOUR

Meg
June

Chaos poured from the wood-paneled walls of Ainsley's gigantic house. We'd scarcely stepped inside before a shrill chorus of screams lanced through my eardrums, announcing the arrival of a whole passel of girls in different sizes and shapes, running in from a long hallway to my left.

"Momma, make Ainsley come home and take—" A slender girl of probably thirteen, with pitch-dark hair and green eyes as big and round as teacups stopped short in both her steps and her speech when she spotted us. That caused a pileup, eardrum-rattling shrieks ricocheting off the rafters as two smaller girls knocked the first one down and collapsed into a heap on top of her. The one little girl still standing, the smallest of the bunch, cackled at them from the doorway, her dark gold ringlets bouncing as she laughed.

Before anyone could speak, my son kicked both feet and squealed, grabbing a handful of my black T-shirt as a grin spread across his face at the sight of other small humans. As the girls disentangled themselves, the smallest one ran to hide behind Ainsley's mother's long skirts while the other three turned big eyes on me.

"This is Meg." Ainsley packed more fanfare into the words than I would've thought possible—or warranted. I almost felt like I ought to bow or curtsey or something. "She lives over the hill at the old Lester place. I met her picking blackberries for supper." She turned to me, "Meg, these are my little sisters—"

"Can I hold your baby?" the dark-haired tallest of the bunch interrupted, taking a small step forward. "I love babies, and we haven't had one in a long time."

Whatever she'd wanted Ainsley to do was apparently less interesting than my son.

I glanced at Ainsley and her mother. Ainsley smiled and gave me a small nod. Her mother's face pinched like she was in pain.

"Is there a place you could sit down with him?" I asked.

"Yes, ma'am." Her face lit up as she turned and waved for me to follow her.

"May I?" I directed the question in the general direction of Ainsley's mother. She ducked her head, the soft sunlight glinting off a few gray strands in her dark hair, though I would've only guessed her to be about thirty-five. I glanced at Ainsley when the silence stretched to the edge of uncomfortable.

"Of course." Ainsley swept an arm toward the doorway her sister had disappeared through as her mother shrugged, running her fingers through the soft spun-gold hair of the little girl clinging to her skirt with both fists.

I tugged my shorts down in the front as I walked, more aware of my clothes than I could recall being in a long time. Everyone here was wearing a plain, earth-toned top with long sleeves and a high neckline, and these ankle-length brown or blue skirts that looked like they escaped from an episode of

Little House on the Prairie. I loved the show, but seeing the wardrobe on my neighbors made me feel like I didn't belong in this place I'd chosen to make a home for my little one.

The doorway was tall and arched, set in an angled wall that came off the hallway and then turned slightly past the archway into the massive wood plank and stone wall the front doors faced, which was decorated with the heads of four twelve-point bucks, hung in pairs flanking two long rifles. Somehow they managed to look both out of place and perfect for the space, all at once.

Hunting trophies as a decorating choice have always puzzled me. Might've been my granny's fault: my daddy made noise about having one made when I was about nine, and my granny had told him right quick he'd better find himself another home to hang it in if he did.

Maybe she'd set my opinion for me that day—Lord rest her soul, the prickly old woman who raised me had always been the closest thing I had to a true north—or maybe I just thought it was creepy. Either way, the hair on my arms stuck straight up and I avoided looking at the glass eyes staring out of the animal heads as I scurried after the girls. All but the smallest one had trooped off, chattering about how cute the baby was.

"Bethany is very good with the little ones." Ainsley caught up with me as I stepped through the arch, her voice low in my ear. "She's small for fourteen, I know. But when Momma and I are busy, she's the one who takes care of the girls, so she knows more than you'd think. Just so you don't worry."

I nodded a thank you, my breath catching as I stepped into Ainsley's living room for the first time.

It was huge, but also cozy and welcoming, with such an overwhelming feeling of home I felt my shoulders relax reflexively as I looked around.

A U-shaped sectional that could've held a whole football team dominated the center of the space, surrounding a furry rug with an oak-footed glass coffee table on it. The sofa was framed in gleaming dark wood, with thick cushions upholstered in soft beige suede.

One entire wall was a stone fireplace so big I could've stood up in the center of it, under a long wood mantel stuffed with so many framed photos I couldn't even count them from across the room.

In the corners opposite the sofa, a pair of oversized, over-stuffed chocolate leather recliners faced the doorway—and the kitchen, which stretched behind me, sunshine filtering down through skylights onto a granite island as big as my childhood bedroom.

"Wow." I couldn't keep the word in, and Ainsley smiled.

"I don't remember the last time we had company. I guess it's a lot, isn't it?"

Everywhere I looked there was something else that gave me pause, from the heavy beams supporting the soaring paneled ceiling overhead to the walls, which looked like they were faced with old, weather-beaten wood, to the rug, which I noticed when I got closer still had a bear head attached to it on the other side of the coffee table.

"It's..." I hunted for a word. "Magnificent," I said finally. The rug was kind of gross, but it wasn't enough to discount the glory of the rest of the room.

"That's very kind of you," Ainsley's mother said behind me, her voice still flat. It was plain that she didn't want me there.

Before I could think of something to say that might make her brighten up, the front door opened and closed, a pair of boots thudded to the floor, and a big man with broad shoulders and thick blond hair covered by a straw cowboy hat rounded the corner, pausing in the doorway to take stock of the room.

Smiling, he nodded to me, his kind green eyes crinkling at the corners in the only notable sign that he was much older than I was. "I didn't know we had company," he said, dropping one large hand on Ainsley's mother's shoulder. She leaned her cheek against his fingers, and he wiggled them slightly, caressing her face. She smiled and turned her head, dropping a kiss on his knuckles before she jumped, her hips flinching, and squealed. "Burt! What in the world?"

"A man has the right to pinch his own wife's backside in his own house, don't he?" He winked as she spun to face him, clearly pleased with his mischief. I glanced at Ainsley, who was watching them from hooded eyes, a soft smile playing around her lips.

It was nice, I thought, that Ainsley seemed amused by her parents acting like teenagers in love. A lot of kids would holler and cover their eyes—especially when Burt planted a kiss on his wife that could've started a fire on a winter day—but Ainsley just looked happy.

"Baby, baby, hi there, buddy." Ainsley's sister Bethany drew my attention from her parents, turning around from her post in one deep corner of the sofa.

Little buddy kicked and squealed again, throwing his entire torso toward her with his arms reached out.

I gasped as I caught him just before he wriggled himself right onto the shiny golden wood-planked floor. "My goodness, Bubba, we're going." I hurried over and delivered him to his new friend, beaming as he squeaked with joy, his huge, curious, impossibly blue eyes taking in each of the children who crowded around in turn.

The girls were clearly enamored. My boy was completely enchanted.

And I felt... at peace. Which was so alien for me it took a minute to recognize it. Standing there next to Ainsley watching her sisters play with my baby, I felt a kind of calm I wasn't sure I'd ever known—the sort of rock sure and sudden confidence that everything is just right that makes you a little dizzy when it hits all at once.

Maybe we really had been led here. Just when I was starting to think I'd made yet another downright foolish mistake.

By the time I looked back at Ainsley's parents, her mother's neat bun was mussed, her eyes glassy and her lips rosy. Burt, looking quite pleased with himself and the state of affairs, tipped his hat in my direction. "I'm afraid I have work to do and the daylight won't last, ladies, but I wish you all a nice visit." He got water from the kitchen in a huge silver thermos and disappeared just as quickly as he'd come in.

Ainsley's mother cleared her throat and straightened her blouse, smoothing her hair back. "That man," she said in a tone that seemed to indicate she was glad he was hers. My son screeched and I looked back at the couch as Ainsley put one hand on my arm watching the girls coo over my little sunshine.

"He'll be happy as can be for a bit." Ainsley tugged me toward the kitchen. "Can I get you a glass of iced tea? Or some lemonade?"

"Can I mix them?" I asked.

Her eyes brightened. "That's my favorite." She looked over her shoulder. "Momma, would you like to join us?"

After prodding the blonde toddler with the impossibly wide eyes who was still hanging on her skirts to go join the other girls by gently pulling the fabric from the child's grip, then squatting to talk to her, Ainsley's mother shook her head.

"I still have five sets of sheets to change and launder, bread to bake, and supper to cook."

"I'll take care of supper," Ainsley said.

"I'll make the butter," a strawberry-blonde little girl who looked about six or seven chirped from the sofa, not taking her eyes off my son. "That's my job, the butter."

"Thank you, Daisy bug." Her mother ruffled her hair as she walked past the sofa toward what looked like a mudroom, sun streaming through the windows in the top of a door that led outside.

I watched Ainsley watch her mother go, her forehead creasing and her teeth closing over her lower lip.

"If you need to help her, please don't mind us," I said. "That sounded like a heck of a chore list."

"No, no." The frown vanished in half a blink and Ainsley turned a smile on me. "She won't let anybody help her with the sheets, and I am such a menace with bread she gave up trying to teach me for a while." She opened a white refrigerator with levered handles that reminded me of the ancient Frigidaire in my granny's trailer, except of course Ainsley's fridge wasn't old. It was new and shiny made to look old—a rich-people fixation I couldn't understand. Ainsley pulled fluted glass pitchers of tea and lemonade from the cavernous fridge, then got glasses from an overhead cabinet and filled them with ice from the kind of old-fashioned metal tray that had a handle sticking up to crack the cubes loose with.

With the exception of the appliances, Ainsley's kitchen could've been plopped here straight from the 1940s.

"Please sit," she said, waving a hand at a long row of stools lining the island, as well as a shiny, dark wood picnic table that stretched along five windows in an alcove opposite the island.

I chose the table, perching on the end of one matching bench. "This is okay?"

"Perfect." She sat across from me and sipped her drink. I did the same, my eyes widening at the flavors. "This is amazing." I held the glass up in the light. "Is the lemonade fresh squeezed?"

"Is there any other kind?" Ainsley's brow furrowed and I wasn't sure if she was kidding or not, so I just smiled.

"It was really nice of your mom to invite me in," I said. "Are your folks always like that? Like they're dating still?"

"Isn't everyone?" Ainsley's forehead puckered more than it had about the lemonade—enough so that I picked up genuine lack of understanding. "Everyone who's married, anyway?"

It wasn't my place to shatter her illusions, so I just nodded, looking at Ainsley with a different kind of curiosity. The self-assured girl who knew everything about blackberry picking and babies and farm life who'd saved us from a snakebite and immediately invited us to see her incredible home looked dreamy and distant as she considered her parents' love story.

"Everyone who's that much in love, I suppose," I said. "It's really adorable."

"I'm very proud of them," Ainsley said. "I guess maybe it's weird for me to be proud of my parents, you usually hear that the other way around. But we do things our own way out here, and I am all the same."

I waited for her to say why, but she didn't, and it was too soon for me to be nosy.

"I think that's amazing," I said, pointing out the window behind her. "As is that—truly some garden y'all have."

"The garden makes up forty-two acres," she said. "We grow just about everything you can think of, from apples to zucchini."

"Except blackberries." I smiled and sipped my tea.

"Except blackberries," she repeated. "And I've never been so glad. Welcome to Firefly Grove, Meg." She smiled at me, raising her glass. "Here's to new friends and long summer days."

I raised my glass.

I had spent my time here so far thinking I didn't need friends.

But sitting at Ainsley's kitchen table as summer started to take hold in the valley, I realized how much I wanted someone to talk to. How downright jealous I was of her big, loud family with children running all over and multiple beds to change and suppers that were a massive team project. Her mom was a little strange, but not strange enough to make me less envious of a house filled with so much love you could feel it in the air just sitting at their kitchen table in the sun.

It couldn't hurt anything, really, me making a friend. We'd

been here for months without so much as a glance from anyone. Everything bad in my life was well and truly in the past.

Surely.

Ainsley would only ever know this version of me: Meg, the nice young mom who was trying to make a go of farm life. That was all there was to know now, and I'd make sure it stayed that way. I hadn't spoken to a soul in Kansas except the real estate lady, the feed store owner, and the folks at the bank. I could be anyone I wanted to be.

"Where'd you move from?" Ainsley asked.

"Utah," I blurted so quickly I surprised myself, committing the lie to memory.

"Have you ever seen the Great Salt Lake?" Ainsley leaned forward on her bench. "I've seen pictures in books, I've always wanted to go."

"Oh sure," I said. "It's really big. And… salty."

I gulped my tea as she tipped her head and stared at me for a second before she burst out laughing. "I imagine so." She reached across the table and grabbed my hand. "You're funny, Meg."

Warmth radiated up my entire arm from where her fingers rested over mine, with a quiet peace that said I'd found my place in the world after everything I'd done.

I didn't trust anyone. But I trusted Ainsley. It was so immediate and deep I didn't even think to question it.

From the next room, my baby squealed and laughed, and Ainsley's sisters giggled, the littlest one clapping.

This right here was the life I'd searched all my days on this earth to find.

Whatever Ainsley wanted in a friend, whoever I needed to be to fit in with her family—that's who I'd become.

FIVE

Ainsley
June

I'd never once finished my morning chores as fast as I did the day after I met Meg. By the time the sun was high enough to see over the front barn, I'd made my bed to Momma's crisp-corner standards, retrieved a dozen eggs from the chicken coop, milked all six cows, and cooked the bacon for breakfast.

I was adding flour to the bacon grease still sizzling in the skillet to make gravy for the biscuits my sister Bethany was cutting on the island when Papa came in the back door.

"Morning, girls," he said.

"Morning, Papa," we chorused, everyone pausing her chore to curtsy.

Our menfolk deserved our respect because they protected and provided for us, and every one of us learned from the time we could walk that curtsies and "yes, sirs" and putting care in our housework were good ways to show it.

Daisy sliced a massive bowl of strawberries, picked fresh from our garden, while Claire perched on a stool, feeding two-year-old Francine her applesauce because Momma had long ago lost patience with letting toddlers make a mess of their food.

"Smells good in here." Papa kicked off his field boots by the door and walked over to the stove, snatching a piece of bacon off the platter I had just filled and grinning when I raised an eyebrow at him. "Perfect as usual, Ainsley." He filled a cup with water after he gobbled the thick slice up.

"Thank you, sir." I watched the beige roux in my skillet for bubbles, whisking it quicker when they started to form.

"That was some excitement yesterday." Papa refilled his coffee mug. "The new neighbor?"

I bit my lip, reaching for the cream to add to the skillet when the roux was ready. "Yes, sir."

"The little guy was awfully cute. Hers?"

"I didn't reckon it was polite to ask, but I think so," I said, whisking the gravy faster with one hand as I sprinkled in pepper with the other.

"Husband?"

"He was probably busy. Not like a farm takes care of itself this time of the year."

Papa sipped his coffee and nodded. "That's the truth. Speaking of, I've got fields that ain't tending themselves. How long until food is ready?"

"Biscuits will be done in fifteen minutes." Bethany eyed the gravy. "Momma will be impressed, Ainsley, that looks delicious."

"Thanks." I smiled at her. Turning around, I avoided Papa's eyes. "Gravy is almost ready," I said, wishing for the first time we hadn't gotten such a jump on breakfast. I needed Papa to go back outside and forget about Meg before he decided to tell me I couldn't be friends with her. If I could just get him out the door, I could slip over the hill to see her after we finished eating.

"Guess I better wash up, then." Papa turned to the sink.

Dang it.

Papa sang "Jailhouse Rock" under his breath as he scrubbed, using a brush to get under his nails because Momma didn't allow grubby hands at her table.

I tried to breathe normally, focusing on the gravy that was coming together nicely in the skillet. Yesterday had been such a good day.

Please, please don't ruin this for me. I couldn't say it out loud, but maybe if I thought it hard enough, it would get through to him somehow.

I scooted to one side so Bethany could slide her heavy trays of biscuits into the ovens, lowering the flame under the skillet while still stirring the gravy.

Bethany grabbed a frying pan and melted a glob of butter before she started cracking eggs into it.

"Can I have mine—" I began and she cut her eyes sideways.

"Scrambled with cheese," Bethany said. "I know. Do I ever forget?"

"I don't suppose you do," I said.

Papa shut off the water. "Ainsley."

"Yes, sir?" I shut my eyes, like that would somehow stop me from hearing what I knew he was about to say.

"I think it might be best if you stay on our side of the holler, and let the new people stay on theirs."

"*No.*"

Every bit of air vanished from the room.

Dear heavens, did I say that right out loud? I couldn't even clap a hand over my mouth on account that I was holding the skillet handle with an oven mitt in one hand and the whisk in the other.

At least two of my sisters gasped.

Papa chuckled, but there was no joy in the sound—it came out low and dangerous. "I'm afraid I didn't hear you, girl. You want to try that again?"

"I'm sorry, sir," I chirped before I sucked in a deep breath.

I was nineteen—an adult, according to the state—after all. Didn't that at least mean I could go see a friend if I wanted to?

Not if the look on Papa's face had anything to say about it.

"I just mean, well, we knew Mr. Lester since we were babies," I stammered.

"And how many times did he step foot in this house?" Papa asked. "You know company agitates your momma."

I shut the flame off under the gravy and turned, a tiny speck of hope floating in my heart. He didn't actually care about me seeing Meg. He just didn't want Momma upset.

I hadn't had a friend since Momma pulled me out of the county school in the ninth grade. I read that some important scientist once said necessity is the mother of invention, and right that second, I invented a way to keep my friendship with Meg from aggravating Momma. At least, from aggravating her in a way she could tell anyone about.

"What if I go over there?" I asked, clasping my hands in front of my skirts and meeting Papa's eyes. "I was going to take her a jug of fresh lemonade today, she really liked it, and she has a baby and a home to take care of." Words rushed out of my face as I held his gaze, a pleading note laced around them. Papa's brow scrunched. He was thinking.

Thinking wasn't a "no."

"I could ask about her husband," I said. "See if he likes fishing." Papa and Mr. Lester had sometimes fished together when I was little, before Mr. Lester's knees got too bad to walk to the pond.

The entire kitchen held its breath in the summer sunshine, Bethany's fingers curling around mine. The girls liked the baby, too. But not a one of us was brave enough to defy Papa—never mind Momma.

"Don't upset your momma," Papa finally said. "And don't neglect your chores, neither."

"Yes, sir." I grinned and kissed Papa's scruffy cheek. "Cross my heart."

He smiled back and ruffled my hair. "Get on with making your lemonade, then."

I got an old jug out from under the sink and went to the pantry to get the sugar, Bethany's bare feet whispering over the wood plank floor behind me.

"Can I come?" she murmured when we were in the pantry. "I'll keep the baby busy so you can visit."

"How do you know she doesn't have a sister of her own to do that?" I whispered back.

Bethany's eyes dropped to the floor. "I don't suppose I do know that, but I got the feeling she wasn't used to being around a lot of folks."

I nodded, because I had seen the same thing in my new friend—the kind of quiet that set in when a person spent too much time alone. You wouldn't think I knew much about being alone, growing up the oldest of six, but you'd be wrong.

I could be completely alone in a whole room full of people. Secrets had a way of building those kinds of walls, and lies filled in every crack until nothing could get through.

"Come with me next time," I said, grabbing the sugar bag.

"You know she might not let there be a next time."

"We'll make sure there is," I said with more confidence than I should've felt. But for some reason I'd never be able to put words to, I just knew it would work out, the twisting in my gut that had me disgusted by the thought of breakfast just minutes before fading into a kind of calm I hadn't felt since before my world turned upside down. Before I became the kind of person who could cover up a murder.

Bethany looked up at my face without blinking for five breaths and then nodded.

Meg had brought new hope to Firefly Grove.

My sister could feel it, too.

SIX

SarahBeth
March—Three Months Earlier

My sweet baby Francine demanded a third princess book just as the dryer buzzed and the timer rang from the kitchen that meant tomorrow's bread was done in the oven.

Some days, I looked around Firefly Grove and the family Burt Godfrey and I had raised here and couldn't imagine feeling more blessed or thankful for everything we'd been given and everything we'd built.

And some nights, like this one, I just knew in my bones that one more squall from a child or bleat from an appliance that required my attention would flat cause me to shatter into a thousand pieces on the polished oak floor.

Ainsley, my eldest, was a good girl with a kind heart, and so responsible in some ways, but it still took too much direction to get her to do simple things—especially at nearly twenty years old. I hadn't been much older than that when Burt's father died of a heart attack in this barn that had become our house, and Burt and I had gotten married and moved in with his momma in the old Victorian farmhouse we used as an office and sewing studio these days. Less than a year later, we had Ainsley.

I flat couldn't imagine any of my six children being on their own—not even Ainsley or Alexander, and they were grown, by their birthdates.

I tucked Francine's teddy bear under her ruffled pink quilt with a sigh and told her I'd be right back to read the other book, turning on the music box next to her bed and hoping to myself that by the time I got back up there, she'd be asleep.

Hurrying down to the kitchen, I pulled the bread from the oven and put it on the island to cool in the pans before I climbed the stairs for the twenty-third time since I got up that morning, ignoring the stabbing pain in my hips, and scurried down the hall to turn off the dryer before the buzzer blared again and woke a child or annoyed my husband.

Pulling warm, lemon-scented bedsheets from the dryer, I breathed deep as I shook out fabric and folded it, making a neat stack of the children's sheets on top of the dryer. When I had folded the last one, I opened the washing machine and peered inside, grabbing Alexander's boxer shorts and sweaters—his clothes were nearly impossible to distinguish from Burt's these days, but I kept track well enough. It was hard to believe my little boy was eighteen years old. I still looked around some days for the child who fit under my chin when he hugged me, and was always just a bit surprised to find a grown man who delighted in looking down at his momma instead. I shoved the sweaters and shorts into the dryer before I turned back to the washer to get his pants. I noticed the spot just before I dropped the gray ones into the dryer.

Dark.

The splotch was bigger than my fist, curved neatly on one side with a flatter edge on the other.

What had that boy gotten up to now?

I held it up to the light.

It wasn't black.

It was deep, deep burgundy red. The color blood gets when it dries.

I felt my breath quicken as I picked at it with my fingernail.

Nothing came off. Weird that he didn't say anything: somehow while I was busy running a household and caring for seven people, my boy had grown into a six foot three wall of muscle who looked intimidating, but could still hardly stand a paper cut.

Last time I could remember him bleeding would've been over a year ago, and he'd come running like he was seven and not seventeen, honest-to-God tears welling in his eyes when I dabbed the orange mercurochrome onto his hand after he'd cut it trying to change a plow blade.

This much blood should've made Alexander panic.

Unless it wasn't his.

I shook my head like I could take back the thought. Things had been better for so long now. Surely, he hadn't. Surely, he wouldn't.

Surely, I hadn't missed something. Again.

Pants in hand, I turned for the door to the laundry room, pausing before I stepped into the hallway. I was already on the girls' side of the house, after all.

I stopped two rooms down and knocked on Ainsley's door, waiting a beat before I walked into her room when she didn't answer.

Her easel was by the window and held a wide canvas with a painting of the hills outside, their just-greening slopes rolling gently toward the sky. I admired Ainsley's ability to find and capture beauty everywhere she looked. My daughter had seen more of the terrible things life can throw at you than I'd ever intended, but her sunny soul remained unshaken, at least as far as I could tell.

Outside the window, the night was black as a coal mine. On

the canvas, the reds, pinks, and oranges of a spring sunset in southern Kansas rolled near the horizon with the kind of life that shouldn't have been possible for anyone to create from paint and cloth. Ainsley had a God-given gift—the kind I wished we could give back. It just wasn't practical. Being a farmer's wife didn't require painting a sunset so real and beautiful it made me want to cry. It required knowing how to bake bread without turning the kitchen into a disaster zone and getting up to shut off the dryer buzzer. Knowing how to look at your husband and make him feel like the smartest man in the county. Knowing how to keep him happy on both sides of the bedroom door.

I'd been good at all that, once. Still was at most of it.

Ainsley still needed work. I shook my head at the painting. If she'd put the same effort into making bread and improving her sewing, she might be married already.

"Ainsley?" I turned a circle, taking in her lace-covered lavender quilt, a piece Burt's mother had sewn entirely by hand just before she died, the year Ainsley was seven, and her white ash dresser, its simple drawers crooked because it was Burt's first attempt at making a real piece of furniture. The room was tidy, everything in its place, her paint jars tightly closed.

Ainsley was a good girl. Maybe if I'd made different choices, she would've been closer to being a good woman by now.

"Momma?" Her voice came from the hallway and I whirled, still clutching Alexander's pants. "Did I do something?" Ainsley smiled, her eyebrows twitching up.

"No," I said, holding out the pants. "I was moving laundry and saw this spot on Alexander's trousers, and I just wondered if you knew if he'd hurt himself."

"Doesn't everyone know when Alexander hurts himself?" She laughed and closed her door, leaning over to look at the spot. "Barbecue sauce," she said. "We had chicken for dinner the other night, and I'm sure he didn't get through that meal without dropping some on himself." She raised one eyebrow. "Why did you think he'd hurt himself? He's always been like a scalded cat at the sight of his own blood."

Mostly because I was afraid it wasn't his. Not that I would ever say that.

I laughed, wadding the pants up and shrugging. "He really has," I said. "I guess I'm just overly worried today." I thought of dropping a kiss on her cheek because the days when I could reach the top of her head were long gone, but I didn't do it. Burt said I'd coddled her, and he might've even been right about that. I mostly found regret foolish—what good is worrying over things you can't change? But with Ainsley, there was just so much I could've done different. Should have done different. "I'll wash them again." I turned for the door.

"I read Francine two more books," Ainsley said. "I went in because I heard her fussing, but she's asleep now."

I stopped with my foot hanging in midair as I turned to my daughter, ashamed of my unkind, and apparently somewhat unfounded, thoughts about her immaturity. Maybe she wasn't ready yet, but she was learning.

Learning to be a fine wife and mother. Someday. When I could let her leave Firefly Grove.

Maybe I hadn't failed her after all.

"Thank you," was all I said.

"Love you, Momma," she said, turning the bedcovers back.

I slipped back into the hall and restarted the wash with just the barbecue-stained pants in the drum before I walked into the room I'd shared with Burt for the past nine years, since we moved to this house, and pulled a soft flannel nightgown from the top drawer in my own white ash dresser, much sturdier and straighter than Ainsley's, a gift for our fifth wedding anniversary.

He came out of our bathroom and walked past me to the

bed without a glance, peering through his glasses at the head-lines on the cover of the issue of *Modern Farming* in his hand.

Better than the *Playboy* I'd walked in on him reading last week, I suppose.

I scrubbed my face and teeth and retreated to the bed, easing myself onto the thick feather mattress and curling into a ball on my right side, Ainsley's words about reading to her baby sister rattling around my head and bringing a smile to my face as I drifted off.

I had a beautiful home. Gorgeous, capable children. A handsome husband who was just starting to age a little around the edges. Life had thrown big challenges our way, and we'd survived them. Maybe not whole and healthy, but we were still here. Burt might not be truly interested in me anymore, but he wasn't going anywhere, either. And he put on a good show for the kids so they didn't worry.

That really ought to be enough.

Exhausted, with pride in my daughter swelling my heart, I closed my eyes believing for the first time in a long time that enough could possibly be enough to soothe my battered soul.

SEVEN

Meg
June—Three Months Later

I slept better that night, after I met Ainsley, than I had in far longer than I could remember. We'd trekked back to our side of the hill just before supper time, and my little man had crashed right out in my arms on the way.

Skipping our own meal in favor of cuddling in the wide king-sized bed that was the only new furniture I'd ever owned, we dozed off around sunset, and when my eyes opened to light streaming through the windows and a warm, squishy little person stuck to me, grunting as he sucked his thumb, I took a deep breath and just let the peace settle around me.

I had made a friend. And she had a big, loud, kind family. Just like the ones I'd grown up watching on the TV.

"I'm going to give you every last thing I never had," I whispered, pressing my lips against the soft curls on top of my son's head. "You will never know a minute of fear or a second of shame. I swear."

His jaw stopped working the thumb as his blue eyes popped

open, staring into mine like he was looking straight into my soul and understood every word I'd said. It took my breath away sometimes, how wise this tiny person could look in certain moments.

It always vanished in a blink, and that morning was no different: spitting out the thumb, his face crept into a wide grin, showing off his four new teeth. He reached up and grabbed a handful of my hair, brittle from being bleached, squealing as he pulled.

"Ouch," I said softly, never able to be stern with him. I took his chubby hand and pried my hair free, pushing it behind my ear. "Not nice."

He prattled and cooed as I carried him in just the diaper toward the kitchen, his legs kicking and arms going out when he spotted his blue and white highchair.

"Yep, let's get your breakfast," I said, buckling him in and scattering a handful of plain Cheerios on his tray. While he picked at the cereal, I mixed and warmed a bottle and heated up some apple and sweet potato puree. The market in the closest town was a thirty-minute drive and it wasn't big, but they kept a healthy stock of our favorite baby foods—my little champ loved apples, sweet potato, bananas, green beans, and carrots.

I had abandoned the idea of bibs or any other sort of mealtime clothing as soon as the weather turned warm—every bite was a fight for control of the spoon, so my boy ended up wearing a good bit of his food. The bright side was that he also loved water, so spraying him down with the kitchen faucet after he ate was both easy and fun.

By the time I got to the table with his food and bottle, he'd picked all the cereal off the tray, banging his fists on the white plastic as he gummed at the last piece.

"Food is fun, isn't it, boo boo?" I smiled as I handed him the bottle and watched him tip it up and latch onto it, his jaw working furiously. He had it empty in two shakes, and hurled it at the brick-red tile floor.

"Fast hands, Momma," I said as I snatched it up mid-fall, putting it on the kitchen table out of his reach. Nothing sharpens your reflexes like becoming a mother: whether it was a dropped toy or pacifier or his general fascination with tossing his empty bottles to the floor, I had become an outright ninja at catching his things before they landed, though I kept these floors so clean, eating off them wouldn't hurt anybody.

I winked at him as I scooped up some baby food and he shrieked, his pearly little teeth gleaming in the sunshine when he opened his mouth.

Pulling the spoon back a little, I shook my head. "No screaming," I said.

The screech cut off immediately.

"Yes! Good job, buddy," I smiled and gave him the spoon. He grabbed it with both hands, flipped it over, and opened his mouth, his hands and neck moving in opposite directions as his breath came faster, his forehead bunching.

I counted to ten and then reached in with one finger, pushing the rubber-tipped spoon toward his mouth even though there was barely a coating of food left on it.

The way his wide eyes lit up when his lips found the edge of the spoon made my heart a kind of happy I wouldn't have said was possible a year ago.

He worked the spoon into his mouth as the food finished dripping down the handle and splattered on his pudgy little fist. This, of course, made him drop the spoon—it landed with the handle in the front of his diaper—and smash both fists into his lips, sucking the orange goop off while I retrieved the spoon.

And then we started over.

I didn't mind. I'd never known the kind of unhindered joy I'd found in motherhood—so far anyway. Every little thing he did was more adorable and entertaining than the thing before.

And it wasn't like anything more important needed my attention.

"Nothing is more important than you, buddy. Not to your momma."

"Ma. Mamamama." He grabbed for the spoon, but my hand had stopped just out of his reach. Time itself stood still as tears welled in my eyes that magic morning in our sunny kitchen when my son said his first word.

"Yes, that's right," I said, giving him the spoon when he banged on the tray, a tear escaping my lashes and skating down my cheek. "I'm your momma." I tapped my collarbone, though I didn't really figure that would help him understand any better what I meant.

But it didn't matter. He'd said it.

I left him to wrestle with the spoon while I ran to the calendar on the wall with a pen, jotting, *First word, Momma, 7:21 a.m. Breakfast apple sweet potato* in the little square for today.

By the time I returned, he'd dropped the spoon in his lap and was happily sucking on his fists. Unfortunately for him, the bite he was looking for was splashed across his belly.

I got two more "Momma"s before the food jar was empty. Carrying him at arm's length to the sink and removing his diaper before I began a game of "keep away" with the sprayer as I rinsed him clean, I thought about Ainsley and what mornings at her house might look like.

I'd picked this place—in its own picture-perfect little valley between two rolling hills—so that we'd be insulated from the rest of the world, but yesterday was the first time I'd wondered if I was doing my best for my son when I made that choice. Nothing made me happier than seeing him smile, and he'd smiled so brightly at the little girls on the next farm over you could light a room with it.

A big, loud, loving family like Ainsley's might not be on the cards for us, exactly, but watching him with the other kids was the first time I'd realized he might need someone besides me to be happy.

I bet they made breakfast together, after hearing the girls talk about supper the night before. I usually ate an apple or a banana with my coffee, but a family that made their own bread and butter probably had biscuits—the scratch kind, just like the lemonade, nothing from a cardboard tube in that kitchen— maybe gravy, and... oh. Bacon.

I hated cooking bacon. The grease popping my hands and arms reminded me too much of Daddy using lit cigarettes to punish me—the scars had faded such that I could almost fold that memory down small enough to make it disappear, but one pop of bacon grease brought it right back.

But I wasn't that scared little girl anymore. I had my own little family—and we had our very own home, a whole farm I'd bought all by myself. Didn't seem like it could've been nearly six whole months ago that I'd first met that prissy real estate lady here, thinking back.

———

"You could have maybe eight hogs and two or three cows out here." She wrinkled her nose as she stepped around a clump of what I was pretty sure was just dried mud in her high heels, flicking imaginary dust away from her white wool suit. "The barn is sturdy."

I walked to the wide doorway of the big barn—in jeans and boots like a sane person headed to a farm—nodding as I examined the outside walls like I knew what I was doing Me and my halfway-through-seventh-grade education, buying a farm complete with its own postcard-perfect big red barn. The paint had faded in the sun on the eastern side of the building, but it somehow only added to its charm, and the three stalls and equip-

ment room inside looked to be in good shape, the exposed wood showing no signs of water damage or weathering.

"There are even still some tools in here," I said, looking around the storage area. "A lot of tools, actually."

"Everything that was here when the previous owner, um, departed, would still be here, I imagine. There was no heir and the state wouldn't bother with an auction way out here. Who would come?" She laughed like she'd made a joke.

"The man who lived here died, right?" I didn't mind dead folks. In my experience they tended to cause less trouble than live ones. Most of the time, anyhow. "And there's no chance that a long-lost kid will show up and try to run me off this land?"

She shook her head. "Not a chance. The state has taken ownership of the property, you'd be purchasing from the government, all perfectly legal and rightly documented." She leaned closer, peering at my face. "You said you're paying cash?"

"I did."

She stared for a beat, but I didn't say anything else, so she just smiled.

"I hope you don't mind me saying you look amazing for just having had a baby," she said. "I looked like an absolute whale for nearly a year after mine was born."

I nodded, but didn't feel the need to comment, climbing the ladder to the hayloft. A few bales rested near the rafters, and I pulled a handful from each and didn't see or smell any mold. "I could bring this place back to life," I muttered, patting the baby's backside when he started to squirm in the genius little sling contraption that let me wear him around and still use my hands. I liked feeling his little body squished up over my heart, and I could still do things while he napped.

"Is the price negotiable at all?" I asked as I climbed back down the ladder.

"It's been sitting on the books a while, they're probably ready to deal." She leaned closer. "Plus, cash makes everything easier. Especially out here."

I nodded. "I'd like to pay fifteen percent less than the asking price." I ran the numbers in my head as I spoke, knowing I really only needed them to come down about ten percent.

I didn't have any explanation for it, but the certainty that had settled deep and sure in my bones from the minute I'd hopped out of my truck in front of the farmhouse an hour ago had only dug in for a stronger hold as we walked through the house and surveyed the rest of the property.

We were home.

But that didn't mean I didn't have a responsibility to my son and myself to spend our money wisely.

She pulled out a cell phone. "Let me see what I can do." She walked outside as the baby began to fuss. I pulled the edge of the sling back to see him making what I called his baby bird face, shaking his head and huffing as he hunted for food.

"I left your bottle in the truck, bit," I said softly, rubbing his tiny head and pulling a pacifier case from my pocket. "Here, get the binky for just a minute and then we'll set you straight."

Latching onto the rubber nipple, his little jaw worked as he settled, cuddling his head into my breast. I patted his bottom and swayed my hips as the realtor walked back in with her scarlet-lipsticked lips stretched into a grin. "You have yourself a farm, ma'am."

I felt my face melt into a grin that matched hers. I had a farm —and at a great deal, too. We had a home, far from people, and farther from cameras. Where no one would ever think to look for us. Who else even knew this place was here? I bet I could count the people on my fingers. If you tried to put a pin in "The Actual Middle of Nowhere" on a map of the United States, you couldn't do any better than this place.

I forced myself to pay attention as she prattled about how the county could close quickly on account of the all-cash sale.

"*Would next week be okay for you?*" *she asked.* "*Thursday morning?*"

Nine more days. Nine more days in the motel, and then we'd be here. Forever. I followed her outside nodding, looking at the hills that rose gently from the fields on either side of the property. Everything was still bare and quiet, spring just barely rousing the land from the winter, but I saw promise all around. Walking back past the house, I noticed the neon-green baby leaves of new tulips, just barely peeking out of the ground on either side of the porch. Tulips. New life. I rubbed my son's back and waved my other arm at the beautiful blue sky. "*How close are we to the next farm?*"

She turned and pointed to the west. "*That's a protected state park there, on the other side of that.*"

I frowned and she raised her eyebrows. "*Usually people like backing up to land that can't be developed. The guarantee that you won't wake up one day with neat rows of what my daddy used to call McMansions when we'd drive into the city to shop for school clothes or Christmas presents, right up in your backyard.*"

"*I do like that. I just don't want hikers back there either.*"

"*Folks would have to go pretty dang far off the trail to wind up here,*" *she said.* "*I wouldn't be worried about that.*"

Good for her. She wasn't me, though.

"*I suppose if it's a nuisance I can put up a fence,*" *I said.*

"*Fair enough.*"

I nodded to the other hill. "*What about over there?*"

"*Family farm, been in the same family since before the county started keeping records.*" *She smiled.* "*If you're looking to be left alone, you've come to the right place. Neighbors don't get any quieter unless they're six feet under.*"

I laughed with her and shook her hand, taking the card with the address and time for the property closing after she wrote it down.

As soon as I shut the door of the truck, the baby spit out the pacifier and screamed. It wasn't the first time his timing had been so spot on, and I wondered every time how their instincts worked when they were so tiny, and whether or not this was something special about him. His father's natural gift for reading a room, maybe.

Not that I liked thinking about his father.

I dug the bottle out of the little cooler pocket in the diaper bag and plopped it in the portable warmer plugged in under the dash in the truck before I extracted the baby from the sling.

He stopped crying, squinting at first at the sunshine streaming through the windshield.

"Hey, boo boo," I said, pressing on the front of his diaper. "You are wet."

I changed his diaper while the bottle warmed, then settled in to feed him, waving at the red-lipstick real estate lady when she finally put her phone down and drove off in her blue Ford Explorer.

Staring out the windshield at the house and the hills beyond, I smiled. There were stairs inside that house. All my life, houses with stairs inside had been rich-people houses, and I was about to have one of my very own.

"A home that's all ours, buddy. With quiet neighbors."

If there was such a thing as heaven, it couldn't be much better than that.

———

With the summer sun warm on my skin through the kitchen windows and my little one in a fresh diaper and one of them cute little blue bodysuits that snapped between his chunky thighs, I pulled on my boots and then settled him on my hip as I grabbed a milk pail and headed out the back door to the barn.

Past eight and Betty the cow would get annoyed with us for taking too long to get her milked.

I was pulling open the door to the barn when I heard Ainsley's voice. "Hey there, Meg." She sounded far away and when I turned, I saw her walking down the hill carrying a big white jug, her cheeks pink from the sun, and a wide smile on her face.

Betty mooed from inside with increasing volume. "I'm coming, girl," I said into the barn, waving for Ainsley to follow me before I put the baby in his big green and yellow playpen when he started wriggling to get to his toys.

"I hope it's okay that I just walked over," Ainsley said, stopping in the doorway and holding up the jug. "I made you some fresh lemonade."

I turned my head from my post on the tiny stool I used to milk the cow.

"You are so sweet, thank you!" I said. "I'll be done here in just a bit. Betty and I are still getting the hang of this."

She put the lemonade down inside the door and walked closer, clucking and murmuring soothing words to the animal while she bent to watch what I was doing.

"May I?" She raised her eyebrows.

"If you want, sure." I stood and backed away, and Ainsley settled on the stool.

"How many pails do you usually get from her a day?"

"Just most of that one," I said.

"And how old is her calf?" she asked.

"Calf?"

She laughed, putting her hand under Betty and doing something that made a whole lot more milk than I'd ever seen come out at once. "Cows are like people, they only make milk when they have a baby to feed."

I blinked. "Really?"

She kept going, filling the pail to brimming in just a couple of minutes and putting out her hand for another. "Really. Where'd you get her from?"

"There was an auction," I said. "Not long after we got here."

Ainsley sighed. "So either her baby died or was sold to someone else. We see it all the time, family farms that have been here forever folding and having to sell everything off. Or filing bankruptcies, even. It's so sad."

I stepped closer to the playpen almost by reflex. "They sold her away from her baby?"

I'd die first. Or kill whoever was trying to take him from me. Not that Ainsley needed to know that.

"Pretty terrible, isn't it?" She filled the second pail and stood, grabbing a handful of grass mash from the bucket on the wall to feed Betty. "There's a good girl."

Turning to me, she held out the pail. "You have to start squeezing at the top and then work the pressure down as you milk her—like a baby's latch would drain milk. Otherwise you both get frustrated and you give up before she's empty. That can make her uncomfortable and even give her an infection."

"I didn't hurt her, did I?" I closed my fingers around the handle of the pail so tightly the metal bit into them. "I wasn't even looking for a cow, really, but this man was bidding on her, and I didn't... I don't know." I couldn't say he'd reminded me so much of my daddy I'd thought for a minute I was looking at a ghost. "Something about him made me want to keep him from getting her."

"My papa calls that your gut. He says you should never ignore it."

"It doesn't usually steer me wrong," I agreed.

"I don't see any signs of permanent damage here." She pointed at Betty, who was munching hay. "I can come back out later and show you how to milk her properly. Nice of you to rescue her."

"Seemed after the fact like I was supposed to have a cow, since I have a farm," I said.

"I think she's found her home," Ainsley said, picking up the lemonade with her other hand. "Speaking of which, I would love to meet the rest of your family and see what you've done with the house."

I swallowed hard when a lump lodged in my throat, flashing a smile. "Sure thing."

I settled the baby on my hip and started back for the house with the second milk pail dangling from my free hand. Ainsley talked about how much she loved summer.

"You could come meet us at the pond and swim if you want," she said. "It's still a little cold, but not too bad."

My heart hammered hard against my ribcage as we got closer to the house, my head too full of panic to think about swimming.

I liked Ainsley. And at some point—probably pretty soon—I'd have to tell her it was just me and my little buddy here. She was too smart for me to sidestep that much longer without making her suspicious, and suspicion was the last thing I needed. She was also kind and trusting, so she'd believe my carefully rehearsed story. There was no reason for her not to. No reason for her to think that the baby and I weren't exactly who I said we were.

We'd been alone here for months, but I hadn't let that make me sloppy. I'd been careful to keep every bit of my old lives—my old selves—tucked far away where they couldn't hurt us.

There wasn't a single good reason to keep Ainsley out of my house. It'd be downright rude of me not to invite her inside.

EIGHT

Ainsley
June

"Momma won't let anyone in our house go swimming without me, on account of the plants that grow in the bottom of our pond." I could hear myself talking, and Meg nodded along, walking beside me toward the house holding the baby in one arm and a pail of milk in the other, but her face plainly said she wasn't interested. I wasn't even offended by that—I just couldn't make myself stop talking. "I've always loved the water. I used to think maybe I wanted to live near the ocean, even. But anyway, I'm the strongest swimmer and it's easier than you'd think for people to get tangled up in those water weeds."

Meg nodded at the right time, but I could tell by the pinched look her face had taken on that there was definitely something bothering her.

She'd looked so happy yesterday. What had I done wrong now? Should I not have come over this morning? Was I too pushy about showing her how to milk her cow?

Meg stopped at the back porch steps, kicking off her barn galoshes on the steps before she pulled a key from her pocket and unlocked the door. I laughed right out loud before I could help it.

"What?" Meg furrowed her forehead, confused, while the baby twisted himself around backwards, staring at me.

"Sorry." I grabbed the screen door to hold it for her. "I've just never seen anybody lock the door to their house. I didn't mean to be rude."

"Oh." Meg stared at the key for a few blinks before she laughed, too. "I don't suppose there's much reason to out here, is there? Force of habit."

"Did you live in the city? In Utah?" I asked, stepping inside as she opened the door and motioned for me to go ahead of her.

"It wasn't really what anyone would call a city, where we came from, it just wasn't as safe as it is here," she said, walking through the kitchen to slid the baby into the seat of his Exer-Saucer, inside a little fence that encircled most of the living room floor. A dozen toys competed for his attention, and he looked around for a minute before grinning at a rainbow-colored plastic piano and banging on the thick keys.

"Here, I can take that lemonade," Meg said, turning back.

"Oh, I've got it," I said, hurrying to the fridge. "I thought you and your husband might like to have some out on the porch later." I fidgeted, Papa's questions worrying around my head.

"That stuff is so good you could sell it," she said. "Really nice of you to bring some over." I waited for her to say something else, not missing the casual overlook of my mention of her husband.

She sipped her lemonade and shifted her gaze to the window behind me.

"It only takes a few minutes to make," I said finally, scuffing the toe of my flat summer moccasin over the red tile of her floor. "It's nothing, really."

"It's not nothing." She leaned against the front of the farm-house sink. "Even thinking to do something kind for someone else is something special, and taking the time to make something for someone else is a real gift."

"I'm glad you like it." I allowed myself a small smile.

Meg pulled a candy thermometer from a drawer and added water to the bottom of the double boiler sitting on her stove, turning a flame on under the pot before she grabbed a milk pail.

"I'm not sure I have enough pitchers for this much," she said. "I haven't used all of what I got yesterday, even." She glanced at me. "Do you need milk?"

I smiled. "I wouldn't turn it down, though we have our own cows. But just two counties over, there's a store where you could sell the extra. Or you could can it to use later."

"Can it?" Her eyes popped wide. "I used to help my granny make plum jelly, but I wouldn't know how to can milk."

"Not too different, really," I said. "I could show you some-time. If you want."

She smiled. "I'd like that."

I watched her heat the milk, one eye on the thermometer, and then count off twenty seconds at the 161-degree mark even though fifteen would do. She was careful.

People learn to be careful by having bad things happen to them. Maybe we had more in common than I'd thought at first.

She took a big metal mixing bowl down from a shelf over the sink and filled it with cold water, then moved the top pan from the double boiler to the cold-water bath.

"You've sure gotten the hang of pasteurizing the milk," I said.

"I asked a man at the feed store and his wife wrote down instructions for me," she said. "Didn't take too many days in a row of doing it before I'd learned." She grabbed the other pail and started over while the first batch cooled.

"Where are your bottles? I can put this first batch up." I clapped my hands together.

"They're in the cabinet next to the sink." She tipped her head toward the one she was talking about. "I only have four bottles, though, and one of them is still in the fridge from yesterday."

"Any pitcher will work, just use what's in there first." I pulled the bottles and a pretty yellow pitcher out of the cabinet. The cool milk filled two, and I screwed the lids down tight and put them in the fridge.

Silence settled easy and comfortable over the kitchen, broken only by the occasional bleep from one of the baby's toys. It was weird to me that it didn't feel weird, being there with Meg. I could count on one hand the number of days I'd ever in my life spent with people who weren't kin to me—but it had taken me about four minutes in this calm, sunny kitchen to feel right at home. Better than home, in some ways. It was so quiet here.

My house was almost never quiet. The feeling of peace was so charming that by the time we finished putting up the milk I felt like I didn't ever want to leave.

"Mamamamama," the baby chattered from the next room.

Meg's face softened as she closed her fridge. "His first word —he just said it for the first time this morning."

"It's so adorable when babies learn to talk," I said. "Though with a couple of my sisters, I kind of wish they'd skipped that now. Bethany will talk your ear right off about whatever she's reading, and Daisy makes up these crazy stories about her dolls and follows us around telling them."

Meg grinned. "Your house is fun. So loud and alive—we had a really nice time yesterday, thank you for inviting us over."

"I was just going to say the same thing about being here, though I reckon I kind of invited myself. It's so quiet here. I love it. You can hear yourself think inside this house."

"I guess we all want what we don't have," she said.

Wasn't that the truth? About so much more than the noise level in our homes.

"Where are my manners? Can I get you something to drink?" She turned back and pulled a blue pitcher from the fridge. "I have some tea if you want to repeat yesterday."

"That sounds great to me."

We took the drinks to the living room and settled on the marigold-yellow sofa centered on the longest wall. The baby waved a stuffed duck at us and turned back to a plastic activity table, slamming his chubby little hands down on buttons that caused all manner of lights and noise.

The way she'd smiled when he said "mama" earlier told me she was his momma and not his sister—I had wondered the day before. The number of people who had assumed Francine was mine when I was seventeen, two years back, was downright shocking, especially given that everybody we ever saw in three counties knew I wasn't married.

I wasn't sure how awkward it would make things if I tried any harder to find out if Meg was married. So I changed focus to the baby. Maybe I could get her talking about his father since she hadn't bit on my comment about her husband earlier.

"He's not big for eight months, but he's bright. And very good natured, it seems." I meant every word, but also figured it didn't hurt to compliment the little one. Any fool could tell he was the center of her whole world.

She smiled. "Thank you! I don't really know a lot about babies." Her voice dropped on the last like she was sharing a secret. This kind of secret was a good one, though—the kind that made me feel like I was being let into her circle. "We're learning together, my little buddy and me."

I waved one hand. "I know pretty much everything about babies—I've been helping Momma with my brother and sisters since I was barely big enough to walk. And I'd say you're learning pretty well—he is a dandy one. So don't worry your head about that."

"That's very kind of you," Meg said, her eyes shiny as she spoke. "I do worry, sometimes, that I can't be enough for him. So it's nice to hear I'm not messing this all up."

"Not a bit," I said. "If there's one thing I've learned about pretty much life in general growing up in Firefly Grove, it's..." I let the words trail, ducking my head.

She waited a few beats before she leaned forward. "Come on now, you can't leave me on the edge of my seat like that. What's your secret to life, Ainsley?"

I laughed right out loud—so loud I startled the little one and he wailed. Meg jumped to her feet and picked him up, looking at the wood-framed clock on the mantel over her small brick-faced fireplace. "I bet you need a new diaper, don't you?" She made a face when she pulled him close and winked at me. "We have a five-skunk emergency here, but I'm still waiting for you to finish that sentence. So don't think you're getting out of it."

She disappeared through a door I could only assume led to a bathroom, and I listened to her tease the baby, his giggles making me smile.

What would it be like to have a mother's undivided attention?

Well. As long as you had the kind of mother you wanted attention from, I guess.

Meg came back with a smiling baby, putting him down in his little play contraption before she went to the kitchen and came back with a box of Cheerios. She scattered some on his little piano keys and he swiped one up in his fist with the cutest little squeak of delight.

Meg returned to her seat and leaned toward me, resting both elbows on her knees. "Okay, go. Secret of life."

"I—it's silly." I felt heat creep into my cheeks. I had no business pretending to anyone that I was worth listening to.

Meg caught my gaze and stared at me like she could see into my soul, tipping her head to one side. I wasn't sure how long we sat there before she said, "I don't think it's silly. I didn't realize before I saw you yesterday how much I've wanted a friend, even... even though I didn't think I did when we came here. I loved being in your house because it was so loud and full of life, but I bet it's hard to not feel like you get lost in the crowd there, huh?"

Wow. Among other things I wouldn't talk about, but—yes.

I nodded. "I was just going to say, before, that I don't think anyone really feels like they know what they're doing. With kids. I think my momma has gotten used to routines and milestones, but for a long time I don't think she figured she knew what she was doing."

"And you're all still here." Meg's eyebrows went up.

I sucked in a sharp breath, then swallowed hard as I nodded. "Don't be too hard on yourself. Just give loving him the best you've got every day and it'll work out. I guess that's all I mean."

"I think that's a pretty smart secret of life. Thank you." She sat back. "So tell me about the people around here."

"There aren't many of them to tell about. That's one of the things about living here that makes or breaks folks, really. I've seen families move here talking about wide open spaces and country life, and they hightail it back to civilization two months later because they can't stand living in a place almost nobody else does, where nothing much ever happens."

"I guess I've passed the first test, then," Meg laughed. "We'll be here four months next week, and I don't figure we're leaving anytime soon."

"I'm sure you've figured out town is about a thirty-minute ride in the car," I said.

Meg nodded. "I've worried a little about getting anywhere if it snows. My truck has four-wheel drive, but it seems like it might get icy and muddy quick around here with all these dirt roads."

"We usually get a handful of storms a year, but Papa has a subscription to an agricultural weather service, so we'll know when they're coming. Sun usually gets the snow off the hills in a few days."

She leaned closer, lowering her voice even though we were the only people in the room. "Does anything bad ever happen around here?"

Not that I could talk about, so I played dumb. "Bad how?"

"Are there any people I should avoid?"

Yeah.

Me. Being friends with me meant being around my family, and we had a corner on the market of people Meg ought to avoid around here.

But I couldn't say that, so I smiled and shook my head. "Old Mr. Daniels at the feed store will pinch you if he's had a nip of whiskey in the winter and you bend over to get something, but he's harmless. Most folks here are the hard-working, God-fearing kind. If you're inclined to go to church on Sundays, Blaine County United Methodist is probably the best one."

Her face pinched up like she'd gotten a mouthful of bleach and she shook her head. "We're not church people." She closed her eyes and swallowed so hard I heard the ticking sound her throat made. "Anymore, anyway." I wasn't sure if she meant to say that out loud, but I found the whole thing interesting. Not that I could ask her why.

"We haven't been in years," I blurted, hoping she wouldn't ask me why, either. I just wanted to lose the awkwardness that bringing up church in the first place had tossed into our conversation.

No one had ever turned away from church as quick and clean as Momma had. She said often now that a person didn't need a preacher to have a relationship with God. I figured that was true, I just also figured God probably wasn't interested in a relationship with me.

Meg's eyes widened with surprise, but she didn't say anything.

Time to change the subject. "What do you miss most about Utah?" I asked.

"Knowing who everyone is and where everything is, I guess." Her face looked far away for a second. "It seems like I get used to a place and the people and then I have to move."

"I can't imagine just packing up and moving so far away from everyone," I looked past her head at the clock on the mantel. That was a lie, too—I had imagined it plenty of times. I even had a whole plan once. But then everything went sideways, and three years later, here I sat.

"My family wasn't like yours," Meg said, her forehead scrunching up briefly.

I pressed my fingers to my lips to keep from laughing as I nodded like I understood what she meant.

"He's lucky to have a momma who cares so much for him," I said. "I'm sure his papa does, too."

I held my breath until my lungs hurt after I blurted that out, the words tripping over one another. I didn't want to stick my nose in where it didn't go, especially today. But I knew my family—Papa in particular, but everyone to a certain degree—would be expecting me to come home with details about Meg and her life.

"His father died last winter." Meg's voice was flat, her face blank as the words dropped one by one.

I clapped one hand over my mouth. "I'm so sorry, I didn't mean to..."

She shook her head and smiled. "Of course you wouldn't." Her shoulders rose with a long, deep breath. "We're okay. We're happy and safe here."

Dangit. I'd put my foot in my mouth with questions plenty,

but I'd never wished quite so hard that I could stuff one back down my throat.

Meg took one more deep breath before she looked at me, her face scrunching instantly. "Please don't feel bad, Ainsley."

"But that must be so painful to think about, and we were having such a nice visit. I overstepped."

I knew a few things about getting sideswiped by painful memories. It could throw me off for days on end.

"I'm getting by," Meg said. "And we're still having a nice visit. I'm okay, I promise."

That right there was the last nosy question I would ask about Meg's past. Some folks at my own house would be irritated by that, but they could just get glad in the same britches they got mad in.

Sitting there in Meg's still, peaceful living room watching her absolutely adorable little boy giggle, I couldn't bring myself to care.

I did enough for the family. Carried enough, sacrificed enough of my soul for them. I could have this one thing for my own self.

The more I let that thought swirl in my head, the more I liked it. Something—a whole person—that was mine.

I'd never had so much as a doll that was just mine.

The eldest, the most responsible. The "little momma." I had always had to put my own wants, my own heart, aside for the good of the family.

Not this time. Not with Meg.

I had told Bethany I'd bring her over next time, and I wouldn't go back on my word to my sister. She'd been through enough disappointment without me adding to it, and besides, bringing her would keep her from talking Momma into forbidding me to come myself. Even if I only brought Bethany once, the vague hope of another visit should be enough to keep her from interfering. But once would be it. This magical, quiet house where the storm in my heart calmed for the first time in so long I could barely remember—this was mine.

Whatever I had to do to keep it that way.

NINE

Meg
July

As June's chilly mornings bled into long, hot July days, I realized I looked forward to Ainsley's sweet face appearing at my door, flushed from running down the hill and usually carrying a jug of lemonade or a pilfered loaf of fresh bread.

She'd brought her sister Bethany once, but otherwise, she always came alone. And I'd never been invited back to her house. I got the feeling she liked having a friend that was all hers, and I didn't really mind. Her family had been fun—not counting the Arctic freeze I'd gotten from her mother, anyhow —but they were a lot. A lot of noise, a lot of eyes, and a lot of people who might ask questions I didn't want to answer. Besides, I was getting better at accepting the things I couldn't change. If my friendship with Ainsley was just with Ainsley, well—that was more than I'd expected or wanted, wasn't it? Keeping mostly to myself was working for me here. Maybe I'd finally run far enough to escape the demons I'd battled for most of my life—even the one that lived inside me.

I was ten days from my eighteen-month chip, and though I hadn't been brave enough to ask anyone if there was a meeting around here where I could get it, I also hadn't so much as spared a thought for whiskey since our first night here. I'd been afraid at first, that being here alone with a baby to take care of would be too stressful—for weeks, I'd meant to drive the two hours to Kansas City and find a meeting to join, but our little slice of heaven out in the hills was so warm and safe, it was easy to keep putting it off. And as days blurred by and the cravings stayed quiet, it was almost easy to believe I had slayed that demon once and for all.

I was just getting the baby dressed on the kind of sweltering Wednesday morning that made me wonder why nobody had ever had air conditioning put into this house when she knocked.

The baby squealed and kicked his legs, putting his arms up. "Mamamama," he babbled, as he did all the time now. He was also getting quite good with "no" which was usually just funny to me.

"Mama take me to see Ainsley, is that what you mean?" I grinned as I lifted him high over my head. "Is Ainsley here?"

He squeaked and nodded, his little head still bobbing just this side of uncontrollably, like the silly little statue Granny got at a baseball game once.

"Come on in," I called, settling him on my hip and hurrying down the hallway. "I stopped locking it weeks ago." She was right, there was never anyone out here but us.

"The fireflies are finally back," she huffed, stopping in the entryway out of breath. "I have no idea why it took so long this year—Papa said something about the late cold snap in April— but I couldn't wait to tell you. You have to come up the hill tonight and see. It's the most beautiful thing in the world, and it never gets old."

"We'd love that, thank you." I smiled as she took the baby from me before he squirmed out of my arms reaching for her.

She'd told me she was almost twenty—so not much younger than me, but when she got excited it was easy to see the little girl still lurking beneath the surface. "Does anyone else come to see them?"

"Oh sure, people come for miles, lots of folks from town even—but they won't come until the weekend, after word gets out. Tonight it will just be us."

"What can I bring?" My granny taught me that you should never go to anyone's home empty-handed. That first day I'd kind of counted the blackberries, but if I was going back, even if I had only been invited to come sit outside and see fireflies, I wanted to take Ainsley's mother something.

"Do you have time today to make another one of those blackberry pies?" She flashed a hopeful smile. "It was one of the best I've ever had. You're a good cook, Meg."

"Thanks. The nicest thing anyone ever said to me was that this casserole I made was better than sex." I laughed. "I've never loved cooking the way some women do, but that comment will stay with me until my last breath."

"Such a funny thing to say!" She carried the baby to his ExerSaucer and plunked him in front of the piano, her cheeks blazing red as she turned to me and bit her lip. I knew that look. She was about to ask another one of her off-the-wall questions— the first few had shocked me, like when she'd asked about the baby's father the first time she came over here. But in the weeks since, I'd figured out they were just part of who she was.

"Do you miss having sex?" she blurted. "I mean, is it so much fun that if you do it some and then don't for a while, do you miss it?"

I tipped my head to the side, considering that.

"Is that not okay for me to ask?" Ainsley's eyes went wide.

"I mean, I wouldn't suggest you ask the grocery store checkout person or, like, a preacher, but I like to think we're friends now, aren't we? And friends talk to each other."

"It's just that, well, everything I know about that came from library books I've managed to sneak past Momma." She pointed to the baby. "Obviously, you have experience I don't."

I laughed. "I don't miss it, really. I think people are different, and some folks might miss it a whole lot. But I'm content with what I have. And a content heart has no room for missing or wanting." I smiled at the baby. "Or regret."

"That must be nice," she mumbled, dropping her eyes to the floor.

I stepped closer. "I don't guess I've ever really thought about your social life in the context of growing up out here," I said. "You're a virgin, then?"

Her cheeks got so red I thought they might actually produce flames as she nodded. "I let one of Alexander's friends kiss me once. It wasn't romantic, it was sloppy and weird. But books make sex sound like... life changing, and Momma and Papa are always touching each other. I'm nineteen already and I guess I usually feel like I'm missing out, but it's not like I can do much of anything about that. But then when you said someone told you food was better than sex, I wondered if maybe I don't need to be so worried about it."

Oh, my heart. I had never seen someone look both so earnestly curious and so absolutely embarrassed in the same second. But that's what we do to young women, isn't it? Teenage boys and grown men can blather about conquests and particulars and it's not only acceptable, it's expected in some places. But young women—maybe especially this one, raised in a house where it seemed more like 1956 than 2026—when they're not taught outright that sex is shameful, are often left to figure it out on some mythical wedding night, like a white dress and a gold ring impart carnal knowledge nobody has ever put words to.

Well. Not on my watch.

"I definitely don't think you need to be worried about it,

Ainsley," I said. "At the right time and with the right person, it can be downright magical. I suspect that's a lot of what you've seen between your parents. But that kind of ease and security will find us when it's time. At least that's what I believe. Worrying and missing and looking for it won't make it find you faster. When it's meant for you, it will happen."

I only had three years on her chronologically, but something about the way her face lit with relief and understanding as she stared at me made me feel like the little green guy from the *Star Wars* movies.

"Thank you." She squeezed my hand. "I have to go before Momma notices I'm missing, but y'all come right before the sun goes down—I'll meet you at the top of the hill. That's the best view."

TEN

SarahBeth
March—Three Months Earlier

"Did you know somebody moved in over at the old Lester place?" Burt's voice would've sounded perfectly normal to anyone who didn't know him like I did.

My ear, with nearly twenty years of practice catering to his every whim, learning every little nuance to his speech, caught the thread of accusation woven softly through the words even through a veil of half-sleep as I drifted off at the end of a long day.

Did you know, SarahBeth, and not tell me because it's a pretty young woman with a sweet little boy and no man anybody claims to have seen? That's what he really meant.

He just thought he was clever, only saying half of it out loud.

"Really?" I asked, turning over in the bed and facing him with my head on the pillow.

I raised my eyebrows; a practiced look of surprise etching features I knew weren't as striking as they'd once been. Twenty years ago when Burt Godfrey had asked me to be his partner for the Virginia Reel at a barn dance hosted by the Cottonwood County 4H Club, I could've had my pick of any boy in the county. Hell, I could've had my pick of any boy in five counties back then. But from the first minute his hand had touched mine, I'd never wanted any man but this one.

Decades of life and loss later, I stared at his face, smashed slightly into his peach-pink pillowcase, and wished he still wanted me.

"I ran into that woman from the real estate office over in Boone, and she said she sold the place lock, stock, and all, including his furniture. Folks got a baby, nearly brand new."

He held my gaze, steady and strong. I let the barest hint of a smile touch my lips before I put one hand up and reached out to run a fingertip over his stubble-roughened jawline. I wasn't giving anything away, and I wasn't worried about Burt guessing what I knew or didn't know, either. He only knew what I told him. He'd never paid enough attention to think any different.

Sparks skated from that fingertip up my arm and straight to my core, just like they always had when we touched.

Like they used to for my husband, too.

He grunted and tossed his head like an impatient stallion throwing off a fly. "Been a long week," he grumbled.

I pulled my hand back to my side of the king-sized bed we used to joke about. *We don't know why we got such a big bed,* we'd said. *We take our half out of the middle.*

Watching Burt turn his back on me after he'd asked about the new woman on the next farm over, it felt like a thousand years had passed since we used to sleep wrapped up in each other in the middle of this big old bed, no matter how hot or cold it was in the room.

Since a stupid mistake had upended the perfect life I'd put every ounce of me into building. I was just in a hurry that day. I was always in a hurry then, with five kids and a husband to look after in this place that vomited endless chores and problems. If only I had been more careful, I'd still be able to give Burt what he wanted. To give myself what this family so desperately needed.

If only. Hindsight always brings clarity, doesn't it? But seeing how stupid I'd been, how much one thoughtless little thing had the ability to roil and rattle our entire world—that was a bitter pill. One I was still trying to choke down years after the fact.

Yes, I knew she was there: her name was Meg, nobody had seen or heard tell of a husband, but she had a sweet baby boy who was still pretty new. No, I wasn't stupid enough to say anything to Burt about that.

Old Man Lester had been the perfect neighbor for nearly two decades. He was kind, helpful, and strong, and he kept to himself unless invited to do otherwise.

New people made me nervous. If it really turned out this Meg person was a young single mother... well. I couldn't even let myself think about that. I could only lay there and pray, hoping God wouldn't do that to me.

But if he did, I couldn't deny that I deserved it.

ELEVEN

Ainsley
July

Everyone pulls their weight.

That was the way Momma ran our house. There weren't many acceptable excuses for skipping out on chores—sickness, and even then only when you had a fever. I had already fed chickens, collected eggs, and milked cows. But I was a few minutes late getting breakfast started, even though I'd gotten up early to give myself time to go to Meg's after sunrise.

I went around to the mudroom door, hoping I could slip inside and get to work before anyone noticed. Bethany's bike wasn't in the yard, so chances were good my sisters weren't back from cleaning stalls in the barn yet. They rotated that chore with Alexander by the week, and it always put Bethany in a foul mood—she didn't like anything to do with cleaning up poop, whether it was in a horse stall or a diaper. She'd have to figure that out if she was going to have as many babies as she was always telling Momma she wanted. I'd accepted long ago that Momma loved Bethany best, but sometimes Bethany talked like she was still running a campaign to be Momma's favorite, anyway.

I walked smack into more chaos than I was ready for when I opened the mudroom door.

"Are you sure the girls didn't take her to the barn?" Momma wailed from somewhere upstairs.

"I didn't see her with them when I was coming up from the corn field." That was my brother's voice. "Where the hell is Ainsley?"

"Oh, maybe she's with Ainsley!" Momma's voice cracked, the sound making my heart speed up. My momma was a whole lot of things, but scared wasn't one of them, not that I had ever seen, anyway. And if anyone would've had cause to see Momma scared, it was me.

"Momma, what's wrong? Nobody is with me, but I'm right here, how do I help?"

"Francine has just up and disappeared," my brother said from the top of the staircase. "She isn't in her crib, she isn't anywhere."

In my heavy skirts and long sleeves in the July heat, I shivered. My baby sister, who hadn't yet seen her third birthday.

Who loved water more than all the other little ones put together.

No time right then to think about why I was the only person who knew that.

"The pond!" I barely got the words out before I was out the door. My skirts tangled around my legs, but there was no time to tie them up, so I pushed through. Sweat beaded on my skin as I ran, making me colder. Blood roared in my ears, muffling the shouts of my brother behind me and entirely drowning out the birds calling from the trees—I'd heard them on my way home from Meg's, but it was silent as a winter night now.

"Francine!" I screamed, the volume and violence of it hurting my throat. "No swimming without me!"

I had no idea when they'd even noticed she was gone, let alone how long she'd been missing.

My lungs hurt with desperation for air, but I pushed on. She was tiny. Her legs were short, and she fell down an awful lot.

Maybe I could still get there.

Jesus, why did we have so much land? My chest burned like I had run clear to Kentucky and I still couldn't even see the pond.

"Francine! Freeze, bitsy!" I was breathing too hard to yell very loud by then.

Finally, I passed the horse barn, the morning sun glaring off the pond and blinding me at first. I squeezed my eyes shut and kept running straight. "Francine!" I hollered, my voice raw. "Freeze tag!" She loved that game.

My steps were shorter now, my skirts sweaty and sticking to my legs as they strangled my stride.

I opened my eyes, the light now strewing the choppy surface of the water with diamonds, tiny rainbows of color hanging over the pond by the dozen. It was the kind of breathtaking miracle of nature you'd stop to commit to memory if you weren't worried that your two-year-old sister was dead under there somewhere, tangled in the blasted water weeds.

I scanned the shoreline and the water over and over, looking for any sign of her gold hair or her purple pajamas—Francine loved purple pajamas and wouldn't wear any other color—my hammering heart crawling right up into my throat.

Nothing.

"Francine!" I pulled up short at the water's edge, a single sob escaping into the summer air. "Please, God. No."

"Francine, come on now," my brother Alexander bellowed in a voice that had gotten deeper than Papa's over the past year. "Don't hide from us."

I staggered into the high grass that drew around the far side of the pond, snakes be damned. I'd rather tangle with ten copperheads than face the idea that my baby sister might be drowned because I selfishly took off to go see my friend this morning. If I had been in the kitchen where I belonged, surely I would've heard her. Seen her. Before it was too late.

A sob fought its way up my throat.

Wait.

There. I saw a flash of gold in the grass, down low. Heard the softest giggle somehow over my labored breathing.

Splashing.

I half ran two steps in my heavy skirts and then dove at an angle, grabbing her around her soft, warm middle.

"Gotcha!" I crowed, sitting down in the shallow water near the edge of the pond and pulling her into my lap.

"Ainsley!" She stared up at me with the biggest green eyes, her long lashes framing them with a natural curl most models would pay good money for. None of us Godfrey girls were homely, but Francine was already the prettiest by far, with Papa's gold hair and emerald eyes that Momma said came from a grandmother we'd never met.

"Were you hiding from me, bitsy girl?" I tickled her, tears of relief flooding my eyes and down my cheeks, landing on her tummy as I blew a raspberry on it, making her screech with laughter.

I raised my head and she poked one pudgy little finger, already tanning in the summer sun, at my cheek. "Why sad?" Her forehead puckered, and I sniffled and planted a kiss between her eyes.

I heard my brother yell, "Momma, Ainsley's got her!"

"I was scared when I couldn't find you," I said, standing and putting Francine on her feet.

She was wet up to her waist.

"Why did you come outside alone, sweet pea?" I tried to

sound stern, but I was just flat so glad she was okay, I couldn't really pull it off.

She shook her head, golden ringlets bouncing like a fairy tale princess.

"You did so," I waved my hands. "Here you are. Momma was scared, too."

"No," Francine said, pushing her bottom lip out. "I freezed."

I took her little hands in mine and swung our arms. "You did? When you heard me say 'freeze'?"

"I was going in the water. I freezed. I came back to wait for you."

"You waited here for me to find you?"

She popped her thumb in her mouth and nodded. I hadn't seen Francine suck her thumb in months.

"You were a very good girl to freeze." My voice broke on the last word as more tears spilled out of my eyes, my brain showing me what could've happened if I hadn't thought to shout that as I ran. I wasn't even really sure why I did—it just popped into my head and straight out of my mouth in the same second.

She smiled around the thumb, her eyes clouded with worry as she brushed tears off my cheek with her other hand.

"My baby!" Momma's voice came from behind me, and I barely managed to step aside before she would've trampled right over me to snatch Francine up in her arms, hugging her so tight for a minute I was afraid my sister couldn't breathe.

"Don't you ever run off outside alone again," Momma said, pulling back and Looking at Francine—that Look Momma had that felt like it need a capital L, the one that had always put the fear of God in everybody but my slow-witted brother, who didn't have the sense to fear the Devil himself. "You don't go out of the house unless a big person is with you, you hear me?"

She was shouting by the end, and her fingers sank so far into the soft, little-girl plumpness of my sister's arm I knew it had to hurt before Francine started to squirm.

"Momma." I put one hand on her arm. "She's okay. Well... mostly okay. I think you might be squeezing her arm a little tight."

She blinked, then looked at Francine's arm like her own fingers weren't under her control. Gasping, she put the baby down and whirled back to me.

I steeled myself for whatever might be coming.

"Ainsley." She grabbed my shoulders.

I tried not to flinch.

"Momma?"

"Thank you." She sobbed, pulling me into a breath-stealing hug, her tears soaking my shirt in just a few seconds. I spotted Bethany over her shoulder, standing about halfway between us and the barn and shading her narrowed eyes with one hand, watching for a minute before she turned back for the house.

"I. Well. Sure thing, Momma." I patted her back, not sure what to do. I couldn't remember the last time she'd hugged me, and right then she clung to me like I was the last door in the north Atlantic and the *Titanic* was sinking behind us, crying her heart out. "It's okay. It's all okay. Francine is fine."

"Because of you." She finally let go of me, wiping her face on her sleeve and catching her breath. "I can't think about what could've happened if you hadn't known right where she was. I should've thought of it, but I didn't." She pressed the heel of her hand to her forehead. "But you knew."

Her voice trailed off, a little too high, a whole storm gathering on her face as she stepped backward and stared at me.

"How did you know where she was? And where were you? You weren't in the house when we figured out she was gone."

Now I stepped backward, raising my hands.

"Momma, I was down at the barn. I forgot to put feed out

for the cows when I milked them," I lied, desperate to calm her down.

She used to tell us she could smell it when we lied to her. I was nearly fourteen before I figured out that itself was a bald-faced lie.

She paused. "The cows?"

"Yes, ma'am." I swallowed hard and stood up straight. Cowering made things worse in our house. "Francine loves swimming more than anyone I've ever met. She loves it more than all the other kids put together. I heard you, you sounded so scared, and then Alexander said she wasn't in the house and I just figured this was the most logical place. So I ran. And I got her. She's okay. Everything is okay."

The tension went out of her so fast she slumped forward for a moment before she turned and picked Francine up, just a slight limp noticeable as she started back toward the house.

I stood there in the breeze, the waving grass tickling my arms, forgotten.

Again.

TWELVE

Meg
July

Pure magic.

It was the only way I could think to describe the way stars fell on the little valley where Ainsley's family lived.

I wasn't sure what to expect when we got there, to tell the truth.

Night settled around us, the last of the daylight fading from the horizon just as Ainsley finished setting up the chairs she'd lugged up to us. The pie was mostly cooled, nestled in a kitchen towel in the bag at my feet. Cicadas whirred softly in the trees. In the distance, I spotted the first pinpoint glow.

"Here we go," Ainsley said, her voice muted, almost reverent. She leaned forward in her chair.

I tried to avoid blinking, and it wasn't hard, because right in front of my eyes, one pinpoint of light became fifty, a hundred, a thousand, a hundred thousand, until we were looking down on a canopy of light I'd bet you could read by. As far as I could see in every direction, thousands of fireflies hovered and darted, their little bodies pulsing with light that could've made me believe in fairies, once upon a time.

I'd seen fireflies all my life—we called them lightning bugs and caught them in mayonnaise jars to make lanterns when I was little. I'd even spotted a few here and there outside my own house in the past few days. But I'd never seen anything like this. Not many people have, if I had to guess.

"Ainsley, wow," I breathed. "This is some kind of miracle. They do this every night?"

"For two or three weeks, then it peters out. I've seen it dozens of times in my life, and it's never any less incredible."

"Do y'all know what causes it?"

She shrugged. "My grandmomma used to say we were blessed. That the land here was blessed, really. Our crops grow, our animals stay healthy, and this was her ultimate proof—weeks of magical nights every summer. Papaw said it was no different than a swarm of locusts, we just happen to get swarmed by pretty bugs that don't destroy everything we work for."

"So they don't eat up your garden?"

"They don't eat anything, at least a lot of them don't," she said. "I looked it up once at the library. They only live for a few weeks, so the ones that don't just eat nectar or pollen either eat other bugs or nothing at all."

The baby squeaked in my lap, reaching both hands out. I jumped in the seat and hugged him to me—I was so enthralled by the fireflies I'd nearly forgotten I was holding him altogether.

"You like them, little buddy?" Ainsley asked.

He bounced, not taking his eyes off the lights.

"I can't imagine anyone could possibly avoid liking them," I said.

I can't even say for sure how long we sat there, enjoying the balmy breeze after melting all day, quietly marveling at the beautiful miracle the evening offered, before the fireflies started moving, their flickering getting more pronounced, like they were agitated.

"Is the show over?" I was surprised by the genuine disappointment in my voice.

Ainsley, who'd sat up straight at the first sign of movement from the bugs, swiveled her head like she had ball bearings in her neck, standing and waving to her parents, who were sitting a little ways down the hillside in the grass. Her mother had little Francine snuggled in her lap, both arms tight around her youngest. Ainsley's sisters were higher up, like we were, but about twenty yards closer to the back barn. Her brother sat on the ground, plucking at the grass about halfway between us and their parents.

"Y'all, something isn't right," Ainsley called.

The words no sooner left her mouth than the breeze kicked up into a strong, gusty wind. Ainsley staggered sideways, grabbing the side of her chair. Lightning cracked the sky open overhead and sheets of rain ripped through the darkness, the fireflies vanishing into the wind or the water or both.

I jumped to my feet, turning my son around and hugging him to me, his skin prickling with goosebumps under my fingers as the temperature plummeted around us.

"I have to get him home," I shouted over the howling wind. "Thank you for—"

Blaring storm sirens cut off the rest of my sentence. The baby screamed, his little face screwing up and going red in another lightning flash.

Entirely too nearby, I heard a train. Except the closest tracks I'd seen were ten miles east of us.

Every drop of color drained out of Ainsley's face as another bolt of lightning ripped through the clouds, her eyes on something behind me.

"Tornado!" She grabbed my arm and started running down

the hill toward her house. "Leave everything, we have to get to the shelter!"

I locked my arms tight around the baby's little body, easier with him clinging to me like a frightened koala, and ran alongside her. Her family was a crowd when they were all together, and they were, running in front of us toward the big red barn behind the garden.

The screaming sound I'd thought was a train got louder, so loud I couldn't think. Tree branches and green leaves flew past and into us, gravel and dust and fat, driving rain pelting our soaked skin, stinging us as we ran.

A low whistling sound warned us half a second before something good-sized crashed to the ground in front of Ainsley. One step ahead of where we were, and it would've landed right on her—not that I had time to think about that or anything else but getting my son out of harm's way right then.

She screamed, stumbling backward and losing her grip on my wet arm. I kept running, and she scrambled around the dark shape sticking out of the ground and caught up, pointing. "Back there, the side of the hill behind that barn."

I saw her family in the next flash of lightning, her father holding open a squatty metal door as everyone filed through.

"Ainsley!" he bellowed. "Come on! It's here!"

Lungs screaming louder than my little one, legs burning with every stride, I pushed harder, sprinting with Ainsley to the door. We ducked through and her dad slammed it shut just as a crash from outside shook the earth all around us.

"What was that?" Bethany, the sister who'd come to my house with Ainsley once, flinched into the smooth wall of earth behind her, holding one of her younger sisters' hands.

"Probably my truck," her father said, his lips disappearing into a pale line. "Hopefully not part of our house."

"We're safe," their mother said quietly from a small wooden bench along the wall. "That's the most important thing." She hugged Francine close with one arm, putting a hand on the next smallest girl's shoulder. I was pretty sure Ainsley called that one Daisy.

I balanced the baby on my hip and reached for Ainsley's arm with the other. "Are you okay?"

She held up her left hand, blood dripping from a bright red gash on the back. "I must've put my hand out while I was running."

Bethany gasped. "Momma, Ainsley's hurt!"

"I'm fine. It's just a cut." Ainsley's voice wobbled.

Burt stepped forward, his face scrunching up as he examined her hand. "That's pretty deep. What did you do?"

"Something nearly fell right on her," I said. "When we were running. A big chunk of something fell in front of her." I heard the tremor in my voice as my hands started to shake, the adrenaline that had gotten us into the shelter fading as I looked around.

The room was wide and short, like the door, the ceiling barely more than six feet tall with a single bare lightbulb overhead and deep shelves loaded with mason jars of every kind of vegetable and fruit you could name running along both walls. The space itself was probably twenty by ten, and I noticed another metal door on the other end of the room, just behind Ainsley's brother. Bolts sticking out of the walls at six-foot intervals made me wonder if this had always been food storage. It was cool inside, and quiet, muffling all but the loudest of the thunder from outside.

"I think it was the mailbox," Ainsley said. "The thing that fell in front of me. I'm pretty sure it was our mailbox."

I clapped my free hand over my mouth. "I bet you're right. Post and all." I shivered, thinking about how close we must have been to the tornado if it had yanked the mailbox clean out of the ground just behind us.

Blood dripped from the end of her middle finger, splattering into a dark spot on the dirt floor. Her father pulled a bandana from his hip pocket and wrapped her hand.

"Burt, don't wrap that nasty thing around her open cut!" Ainsley's mother said.

"It's clean, I just got it out of the drawer this morning," he snapped, pulling a knot tight in the fabric. "I guess you think we should just let her bleed and see if she runs out before we get out of here?"

Every eye in the room got so big I could see white all around the irises. I looked around and tried to shrink myself and my son into the wall at my back as the storm raged outside, thunder booming for the fourth time since we'd shut the door.

Ainsley laid her free hand on top of her father's. "No need to be short with Momma," she said. Her voice was calm, but I'd gotten to know her well enough to hear tension threading through her words.

I watched the children, their wide eyes all fixed on their mother, who was watching me.

"We're all upset," she said finally, and I swear the whole room let out a breath. "Ainsley, hold pressure on that until the bleeding stops."

"Yes, ma'am." Ainsley looked relieved to have something to squeeze.

"We shouldn't have taken the beds out of here," the brother said from the other end of the room, shuffling his feet. "It'd be nice to have somewhere to sit."

"So we should let this space sit here for 360 days of the year so we can spread out more on the five days we might use it?" His mother rolled her eyes. "Very efficient of you, Alexander."

"It stays cool in here no matter how hot it gets outside," Ainsley murmured to me, leaning against the wall between me and the door. "It was a nuclear bomb shelter back when people worried about that, so there were beds—and a bathroom, too, but it doesn't work anymore. The plumbing rotted out before I was born. Momma replaced the beds with these shelves so we could store extra canned goods out here about five years ago. It's never too warm for them and it gets them out of the house. We can make more at once, too, so we've started selling some at the markets."

"And it's handy for tornadoes," I said. My voice was still shaking and she poked me gently with one elbow.

"I don't guess you got many tornadoes in Utah," she said.

I shook my head. "It just came out of nowhere." I looked around. "We're safe in here, though?"

"Completely," she said. "And just so you know, this is the first tornado we've had in a while."

"Four summers ago was the last one," Burt said, pressing his ear to the door. "Still pretty loud out there. I wish I'd had time to grab the radio."

"We'll just stay put until it calms down," Ainsley's mother said. "Y'all have a seat."

With most everyone packed into the narrow aisle between the shelves, there was a fair amount of grumbling about squished fingers and stepped on feet as Ainsley's family tried to get comfortable.

"Why can't we go in the back?" A waifish girl I was pretty sure Ainsley had called Claire asked, more than a touch of whining in the words. She looked about ten, and was sitting on the floor a few feet from us rubbing her eyes with clenched fists. "There's a bed in there."

I patted my son's back and swayed against the wall, relieved and proud that he was so quiet and content, despite his soaked diaper and wet clothes in the cool, crowded underground room. His little fist curled tight around the wet fabric of my T-shirt, his head resting on my shoulder.

"No!" Ainsley's voice was so sharp I jumped. So did Claire, a wounded look creasing her face as Ainsley glared at her. She opened her mouth to say something, but their brother spoke before she did.

"What is that smell?" Alexander's almost-offended voice boomed in the small space, drawing every eye to his post outside the door to the back room. Ainsley caught a deep breath beside me, her hand going to her forehead as she leaned against the wall.

"The plumbing back there," SarahBeth said quickly. "It rotted clear through to the old septic tank and we haven't figured out how to go about fixing that."

The sleepy little girl who'd complained about the lack of beds looked like she was winding up for a tantrum when Burt unlocked the door with a sharp clang. "The one good thing about tornadoes is they pass quickly. All clear, y'all. Beds and septic-free air this way." He winked and SarahBeth laughed softly.

"Yay, Papa, thank you!" The whiny one I was pretty sure was Claire sprang up and... curtsied. Yep. She sure did.

I glanced at Ainsley, who was tracing a series of light scratches on the dark earth of the wall.

"What's that?" I asked.

She smiled. "We played house in here when we were little, just to get out of the actual house in the winter. Alexander and Bethany and me. We used to count down days from Christmas to summer."

I surveyed the wall as everyone filed out of the shelter. "That's not nearly a hundred and fifty whatever days."

"We got bored easily." She winked.

"It's kind of a unique thing to have." I waved my free arm. "Do the little ones still play out here?"

"Never." Ainsley shook her head. "Momma forbids it."

I started to ask why, and Burt leaned back in the door.

"Y'all waiting for a fancy invitation?" he asked.

"Sorry, Papa." Ainsley ducked her head and hurried out the door.

"Thank you, Mr. Godfrey," I said, stepping to the door, glad that my boy was still sleeping.

"Mr. Godfrey is dead and gone," he said. "You're a landowner here, same as I am—call me Burt." His eyes twinkled a little too much.

They lingered on my boobs a lot too much.

Please God, no. Not this man who seemed so in love with his wife, who I really wanted to like—and wanted to like me.

"Thank you for letting us be here tonight," I said, the words stiff as starched sheets.

I'd picked up enough about SarahBeth and Burt to know their house ran under cover of what I would have said were old-fashioned roles for the men and women—I still didn't quite believe my own eyes that Ainsley's sister had curtsied in her long skirts before she trooped back outside. Maybe it was a dated way to think, but I had to admit I'd thought as I watched Ainsley's dad guard the door that it might be nice to have someone to take care of Little buddy and me. A strong shoulder to lean on when I was scared or tired.

Someone to guard the door in a storm.

Not that I could have that. Marriage requires honesty, trust, and fingerprints—none of which I was capable of giving anybody. But I couldn't help thinking, sliding past Ainsley's tall, muscular father after he stepped closer to the doorway than he'd stood while everyone else walked outside, that it might be nice.

THIRTEEN

SarahBeth
April—Three Months Earlier

Burt's questions about the new woman next door hadn't stopped for a month. Why hadn't I taken over some bread, didn't I want to get to know her? Seemed like she'd moved in out there with a little one and just kept to herself all the time, shouldn't we check on her?

Like I hadn't checked.

Some days it felt like keeping up with her was all I did.

And there was something there to keep up with. For starters, I had to go all the way to the courthouse and check the property deed to get her last name, because nobody in town knew it.

"Here it is," the county clerk said, bringing a copy of the deed for the farm next to ours to the counter. I had made up a question about water rights and the pond because I didn't really know what I was allowed to see and not see about someone else's property, but the clerk hadn't so much as blinked, she'd just dived into the maze of file cabinets and returned with the deed. "Sold for cash to Meg Whitney, sole owner, right? The deed was filed on March ninth." She flipped through pages. "It doesn't say anything about water rights."

"Great, thank you," I said, forcing a smile.

"Would you like a copy?" she asked.

"Could I get one?" I tried not to sound surprised. Either it worked, or she didn't care.

She licked her finger and flipped through pages. "These farm deeds are long ones. Seven pages will be three dollars and fifty cents."

I counted the money out of my hand-sewn calico purse and put it on the counter. She turned and went to an old gray copy machine, running the document through and then taking her copy back to the files.

"Thank you," I said as she put the pages in my hand.

"No problem. You have yourself a nice day."

I took the deed out to a bench and looked over it, but there was no prior address for Meg, no husband's name, no mention of whether Whitney was her married name. Just her name, and hers alone, which was more than I knew when I left my house.

Two first names, too. I wasn't sure what to think about that. Not that Whitney couldn't be a last name, I'm sure it was for plenty of folks. But something about Meg's story was off. And while I'd never been a nosy sort of neighbor, I needed to know now.

Too much was at stake for my family—I had to figure out just exactly who was living so close by.

FOURTEEN

Ainsley
July

My eyes went to the sky first, and after a minute I noticed everyone else was staring up, too. The vast blanket of night above us winked with stars, thin wisps of see-through clouds the only evidence of the storm that had just kept us locked up for nearly half an hour.

I couldn't stand the old bomb shelter. Just having the fresh air on my skin and being out of that room lifted a hundred pounds off my chest.

A gasp drew my eyes from the sky, and once they'd focused in the darkness one hand flew to my mouth.

"Oh, Ainsley," Meg said.

I swallowed tears. I couldn't tell if my heart was breaking more for me, or for Papa.

"Is God mad at us?" Daisy asked, her small voice thick with tears.

"No such thing." I wondered if anyone else heard Momma's voice shake. Or knew why it did. I shut my eyes, but it didn't matter—the destruction played on a loop on the backs of the lids like they were still open. Papa's pickup was crumpled like an empty beer can, nose first into the ground just a few feet to my right. One wheel dangled in the air, hanging off the back axle by a single screw, the bits of metal littering the ground around it shining in the silvery moonlight.

The big barn was missing probably more than half its roof, and at least one wall sagged badly. The other barns had fared about the same, with missing chunks of roof that had splintered and scattered in the storm. The old house, the one we used for Papa's office and Momma's sewing studio now, was just gone—a couple of pipes sticking out of the ground and rubble piled high in the place it had stood for more than a hundred years all that remained.

The mailbox was indeed the thing that cut my hand what felt right then like a lifetime ago as Meg and I ran for the shelter, its post crammed upside down into the ground so far my brother would have to dig it out.

"Burt, the house..." Momma's voice was strangled, up ahead of us around the side of the barn. A cold fist of dread closed around my guts as I stopped in my tracks. I couldn't go look. Papa was scared, too, I could tell by the way his shoulders hunched as he crept toward her, like a dog that knew he was about to get beaten.

Papa seemed to fold in on himself as he rounded the corner of the barn, the stress almost physically attacking him. I reached out one hand, but couldn't make my feet walk the way they were supposed to. Me and my big mouth, invoking Granny talking about us being blessed here—what if I'd jinxed us? What if this was all my fault? I couldn't make myself go look at the house Papa built out of an old barn with his own two hands and sweat and blood. Our home. Alexander and I were alone among us kids, the only ones who remembered clearly a time when we didn't live there.

Papa got to the corner of the barn right about when I started having trouble breathing. His hands went to his face, but I couldn't see why. I wondered if he was covering his eyes.

His shoulders straightened, his back shooting into a line.

"It's a miracle," he whooped, jumping in the air with one fist raised. "Thank you, Jesus. Maybe Mother was right when she said this land is blessed."

My feet suddenly feathers, I ran to his side. The house, our big goofy house, was untouched. It didn't look a lick different than it had that morning, not so much as a shingle missing that I could see.

Momma was halfway to the mudroom door already, Francine bouncing on her hip as she hurried, her limp barely noticeable.

She got the door open before we caught up to her.

"Power's out," she said.

"I'll check the generator in a minute." Papa walked through the mudroom and out into the living room, spinning in a slow circle, his head back to study the beams holding up the roof. "A miracle," he said again.

Everyone straggled in, Bethany herding the little ones, who were pinching and poking and growling with each other because they were tired.

"Thank you, Jesus," Alexander's deep voice, which had only been deep for about six months and was still startling, boomed when he stepped into the house. "I'm going to bed."

"You will wait to be told what you're doing." Momma's voice was clear, but lacked its usual edge, like the relief of standing in her home after a tornado was enough to soften her, for the moment.

"Yes, ma'am." My giant brother froze in the hallway.

"Burt?"

Papa shook his head, walking over to Momma and pulling

her and Francine close, resting his forehead on Francine's gold curls. "So much to be thankful for tonight."

Was it just this morning we'd been frantically searching for my baby sister? It felt like a month ago, standing there as the adrenaline wore off for the third time in one day, and realizing how utterly whooped I was. It was all I could do to keep from melting into a puddle and passing out right there on Momma's shiny wood floor.

"Alexander, girls, y'all go on to bed," Papa's voice was rough, his face now buried in Momma's hair.

I started to follow my sisters to the hallway that led to our rooms when I remembered Meg. Spinning on my heel, I ran back to the mudroom door. She hovered just outside, the baby's sweet head nestled into her shoulder as he slept.

"I'm so sorry," I said, opening the door. "I got caught up in... well, I felt bad about what I said before, bragging about our blessings, and then the house was okay and I just followed everyone in, not that that's an excuse." I had to stop to take a breath and Meg laughed softly, not disturbing the baby. "I'm babbling. Sorry."

"You don't owe me an apology," she said. "I'm going home. I'm just sort of scared to." Her eyes filled with tears so fast she couldn't keep them from spilling over. "I love my house. What if it isn't there anymore?" She sniffled, swiping at her face with her free hand.

I pressed two fingers to my lips, a lump lodging in my throat. "I'm sure it's there." The anguish and fear on her face was so plain it made my heart hurt, and I scrambled for anything that might help. Desperate for some kind of reassurance, I looked up at the wide, calm sky before I bowed my head, keeping my voice low. "Maybe we should say a prayer?"

Meg looked like I had asked her to eat manure for just a second, and then she shrugged with her unoccupied shoulder and closed her eyes, grasping both of my hands in her free one.

"Lord, thank you for watching over our home through the storm tonight and keeping us all safe," I said, my heart thudding in my ears as I spoke. "Please, Jesus, I ask that you have watched over Meg's home, as well, and let her little family return safely there and find their house standing and stable, and help our neighbors and friends to recover and rebuild quickly and safely. In Jesus's holy name, amen."

"Amen," Meg said, squeezing my hand and pursing her lips like the word tasted sour. My eyebrows went up and she flashed a small smile. "Just a little weird after so long."

Oh, that. I nodded. "Yeah, for sure."

A flashlight beam brightened Meg's middle from behind me and I turned to find Alexander, his hair much neater than normal, lurking behind me. Somehow a simple thing like combing his hair made him look all grown up to me—and he was, really, he'd turned nineteen this summer. I just didn't think of him that way.

"You shouldn't walk home alone, not knowing what you'll find," he said, staring calmly at Meg for a good five seconds before he ducked his head, clearing his throat before he looked up again. "I'll take you."

He said it with authority, like Papa would almost, and the flesh crawled right up both my arms in the balmy summer night air.

No.

I wanted to say it, but Meg was looking at him with the oddest expression I'd ever seen on her face, her lips pinched into a tight line, her eyes narrow.

I didn't think she wanted him to go with her. But maybe she didn't know how to tell him no.

Or maybe I was wrong.

Before I could force a single sound out of my face, she nodded and said, "It's nice of you to offer, thank you." And they were gone.

I watched from the window in the top of the mudroom door, pushed up on my tiptoes, until the flashlight's beam disappeared over the hill.

From far off, they looked like a family. Alexander was so tall he even towered over Meg, and the sweet baby finished off the picture.

"No." Sure, now I could say it. When it wouldn't help her.

"Ainsley? What in the world are you still doing down here?" Momma's voice came from behind me, soft with exhaustion.

"Alexander decided to walk Meg home," I said, turning to face her.

"Al—" Her face crumpled. "Why? Why would you let him do that?"

"He said he was going to, like it was fact or law, like when Papa talks." I dropped my chin to my chest, ashamed of myself.

"I'll speak to your father." Her teeth clacked together she shut her mouth so violently. "This cannot happen."

I looked up to find her shaking her head, her eyebrows pinched together over the top of her nose, disappointment dripping from her eyes. "Ainsley Anne. How could you?"

"I don't know. I'm sorry, Momma."

"Let's hope this is the only bit you have to be sorry for."

FIFTEEN

Meg
July

I couldn't see anything from the top of the hill. The moon had vanished behind a thick cloud, and there's no darkness like middle-of-the-night country darkness—it's thick, almost alive in its own right, pressing down, slithering around, and stealing your sight. It was only because Ainsley's brother had a flashlight that I could see my hand in front of my own face. But that was about the extent of its help—the darkness ate up the light maybe a foot and a half in front of us, keeping its secrets cloaked as we started down the hill. Squinting as if it would somehow help me make out anything past the relatively short reach of the beam, I blew out the breath I'd been holding when I realized I truly couldn't tell anything about anything from so far away.

"It will be okay," Alexander, who hadn't said a word since he invited himself to walk me home, said in a voice so deep it sounded almost comical.

Once, when I was a little girl, my granny had a dog— Granny had taken the poor thing from the meth heads in the next trailer when she nearly died from eating some of their product, and that dog had loved the tiny old woman who'd raised me so much I was sure she'd have eaten anyone who tried to cross Granny. We called her Sadie and Granny said she was a Rottweiler. I didn't really know the funny word was a breed of dog until the dog was long dead, but Sadie was a love—she would try to get any part of her that would fit into my lap whenever I sat down, she sat outside in place of a concerned grown-up and watched over me while I played—and she almost never barked. But when she did, everyone in our trailer (and probably the next few over, too) took notice.

Alexander reminded me of Sadie as we walked down the hill. Quiet most of the time, noteworthy when he decided he had something to say. Big. Strong.

Safe.

He walked carefully next to me, shortening his stride to match mine, and staying almost exactly three inches from my side the entire way. Honorable, I thought.

In another life, another me who hadn't been battered and damaged by men—men who weren't safe and didn't know the meaning of honor—might have liked him as more than my friend's stoic brother. Probably for the best that things were the way they were for a lot of reasons.

"How old are you?" I asked as we picked our way down the hill by the flashlight's beam.

He kept the light pointed in front of my feet. "Nineteen."

"I thought Ainsley was nineteen."

"She's nearly twenty. My grandma used to call us Irish twins because we were born ten months apart. My birthday was last month."

I liked listening to him talk. But I was a grown woman with a baby to take care of. I had less than no business taking up with a nineteen-year-old boy no matter how tall and pleasant he was.

The closer we got to the bottom of the hill, the harder my

heart pounded against my ribs. What if the house was gone? I'd seen the one Ainsley said her parents used as an office reduced to rubble.

So I expected to find a heap of wood and plaster when we got close enough. But I couldn't stop myself from clumsily begging God silently to spare us. After some of the things I'd seen, I wasn't too sure I trusted anybody—least of all church folks—but I did believe in God and Jesus, and right then, I wasn't sure I'd ever needed their help more.

I shut my eyes tight with a last quiet prayer, blinking hard into the darkness when my feet hit the gravel of the driveway. Alexander pointed the light up, and three steps later he let out a whoop so long and loud I bet it woke people clear over at his house.

I stopped, hugging my son and shaking my head at the tears streaming over my cheeks. "It's there. It's still there."

I felt Alexander's big, warm hand close over my shoulder. "Why are you crying?" He sounded genuinely perplexed.

"I wasn't expecting it to be," I said. "Things don't really go my way. Not big things."

He took a step back, his hand falling away, and pointed the flashlight at the baby. "Was he one of those things?"

Wow. I almost staggered backward from the weight of the question, except he couldn't have possibly known how loaded it was when he asked it.

"Of course not." My arms tightened protectively. "He's the only thing I've ever gotten really, completely right."

In the filtered light of the flashlight beam, Alexander's face stretched into a smile. I swallowed hard at the revulsion that made me want to back away, because I couldn't give an immediate reason for it. I only knew, in the kind of bone-deep way that had never failed me, that something in his smile made him far less kind. Far less safe.

It didn't reach his eyes, that was part of it. They looked

hollow and flat, like moss-covered rocks staring out of his face. But the eyes weren't the only thing telling me to run.

And we were alone in the dark. I didn't think it was wise to hurt his feelings—or to upset him. I swallowed hard, trying to think of something to say that would get him to stop looking at me like that.

"Ainsley spends a lot of time here," he said before I could come up with anything. When he talked, the smile vanished. And it didn't come back.

Thank heavens.

"She's been such a good friend to me—a true bonus, I didn't expect to find friends here."

"We don't really know people outside our family well." He tipped his head to one side, staring like that was his whole thought and he was waiting for me to say something.

"I'm very thankful Ainsley has been so kind to me," I said finally. "And that your family let us join you in the shelter tonight." I laughed. It was too high pitched, with a nervous edge. But maybe he wouldn't notice. "And to you for walking me back. Thank you, Alexander." I moved toward the front porch.

"It's what gentlemen are supposed to do." He sat down on the second step, folding his long legs up so that his knees were nearly touching his chin.

So he wasn't leaving. I wasn't sure what to do about that. I desperately wanted to take my child inside and put him down, I couldn't even feel my right arm anymore. I was the kind of tired you feel in every cell, even though you're too wound up to close your eyes.

And when Alexander patted the step next to him, the hair on the back of my neck stood straight up in the still summer night air. It took all the effort I knew how to muster to make my feet move to the other side of the steps and sit next to him.

And then he didn't say anything.

I didn't really figure "go home, you clueless creep" was going to help me here on any front, and the memory of that strange smile was enough to make the thought of using my son as an excuse to scurry inside give me chills—I didn't want Ainsley's brother irritated with him even more than I didn't want to see the smile again. So I stuffed the words back down my throat and let the silence stretch. A lot of folks don't like silence.

He didn't let it last long. "What are you and Ainsley doing together all the time?"

"I..." I blinked, trying to shake exhaustion from my brain. "We cook, we visit, we play with Little Bit here. She's teaching me how to can milk and grow a garden. Just... you know. Stuff you do with friends."

"Ainsley said your husband died last winter. She said she asked and that's what you told her."

I shut my eyes when he pointed the flashlight straight at my face. When I opened them, his lips were twisted to one side as he stared at me with his eyebrows pinched down into a V over top of his nose.

I figured the story I'd told Ainsley was the easiest one—and not entirely untrue. The baby's father was sure enough dead.

I bowed my head and sniffled for good measure. "It was tragic. It's still really hard for me to talk about."

He kept the light on my face for another thirty seconds or so, then pointed it back down at the dirt. "Momma says when people are sad about death you say, 'I'm sorry for your loss.'"

"Thank you."

"Maybe that's what you're supposed to say," he went on, like I hadn't spoken, his words halting, his hands curling into fists in his lap. "But maybe I'm not so sorry. I don't reckon you'd be here if he hadn't, right?"

I sensed the smile again before I turned my head and saw it. It was all I could do to keep my seat.

"My granny used to say everything happens for a reason," I

said. "Some of the things I've seen have made me wonder how she could've possibly been right, but she believed that with her whole heart. Maybe it's true."

"Everything happens for a reason." I felt my shoulders relax when his smile faded, which felt like the strangest sequence of events. He bobbed his head from side to side. "Everything happens for a reason."

I couldn't tell what he was thinking, but he stood, and his face stretched into the smile again. It was almost like his mouth was too wide—maybe that was what made it feel threatening instead of attractive? The corners of his lips stopped just below his eyes, like a jack-o'-lantern someone didn't quite carve right.

I shivered, despite the balmy July overnight weather.

"I think I'm glad you came here, Meg," he said. "I hope you stay glad, too."

I couldn't help but hear a threatening edge in those last words, though I couldn't swear I hadn't imagined it on account of his disturbing grin.

He turned and left.

I watched the flashlight beam disappear over the hill, trying to squash the urge to get in my truck and drive as far and fast as I could away from this place.

"That's enough," I muttered to myself, making the baby stir. "You are just wrung out, and you don't trust men. He's an awkward kid who was trying to be nice. Nothing more."

I felt the heave of air go into my son's chest before he let loose with a scream, and I jumped to my tired feet and hurried inside.

When he was diapered and fed and curled happily against me under the covers, I let the steady beat of his little heart against mine soothe me to sleep. But the last thing I thought of before I drifted off was Alexander and his creepy smile and obvious interest in me.

Had I managed to find trouble again?

All I knew for sure as I drifted off was that for the first time in weeks, I had locked all the doors before I went to bed.

SIXTEEN

Ainsley
August

The fireflies didn't come back to the grove after the tornado. Not like we were used to, anyway. Papa said this year's brood was probably mostly killed off that night, since the storm kicked up right in the middle of magic hour. I knew enough about science to guess that might mean we wouldn't have them next year, either—maybe never again.

When I worked myself into a sweat twisting up in the bedsheets at night because I couldn't sleep, I wondered if that was in any way my fault.

If this generation of our family wasn't as blessed as the ones who came before us, didn't it stand to reason we'd done something to deserve that?

We hadn't been to church since I was little, but I had dreams sometimes about a sermon I'd heard once, about God passing judgement and handing out punishment to the wicked. In my sleep, I heard the preacher as I watched the life drain from a pair of frightened green eyes before I'd closed them for the last time.

Maybe the law hadn't caught up to me. Maybe it never would.

But you can't hide from the Almighty.

All I could think to do was keep my head down and work hard for my family, and pray harder for forgiveness. I wouldn't risk my friendship with Meg by confessing my sins no matter how tempting it got, so I tried to be good enough to earn forgiveness. Maybe then God would let me keep her.

Papa found a pickup two counties over almost exactly like the one that had been smashed to bits and brought it home for a fair price, which meant the boys could clear the rubble we couldn't put in the burn pit out to the dump.

Alexander's back should've broken, lifting heavy sections of walls and beams in the pile of trash that was Papa's childhood home for hours in the sun every day. Every time he found a piece of paper, he brought it inside and added it to the pile Momma had started on the kitchen counter. So far we had their marriage license, the deed to Firefly Grove, a few photos, everyone's birth certificate except Papa's and Francine's, and some newspaper clippings—Grandmomma had apparently been diligent about cutting them out. They covered every major news event in the world for the past several decades, plus the annual 4H list of champions from the county's local newspaper. The stack of papers grew thicker as the pile of rubble outside shrank, and my brother never said a complaining word.

"You find anything interesting out there?" I asked one night when he came back in as I was finishing the dishes.

The kitchen was quiet, the rest of the house exhausted after weeks of extra work. Regular summer days are busy on a farm, and adding storm cleanup to the list had really wrung everyone clean out.

"Interesting how?" Alexander got himself a glass of

lemonade instead of asking me for it, and sat down at the end of the counter.

"I would've gotten that for you." I rinsed a dinner plate.

"Why? I don't get you stuff." He downed half the glass in one gulp.

"Momma says it's our job to take care of you and Papa. Always, really, but especially right now while you're working so hard. And I know you went back out to work more after dinner. I want to actually go outside and help you, but Momma won't stand for it."

He plunked the glass onto the counter. "First, I don't need you to get me stuff, I can do it myself." He frowned. "Second, it's nice of you to offer to help, but it's hot and gross and not really very safe. I wouldn't want you to get hurt."

"Then why is it okay if you do?" I asked.

"I won't." He blinked.

If anyone else had said that to me, I'd have laughed. But my brother wasn't being funny. Alexander wasn't the smartest of the Godfrey kids, but he was agile and athletic—and he had a weird sixth sense for where other players would move that had always made him a standout on the football field. Maybe he could read the pile of rubble like an opposing defensive lineman.

"Interesting how?" he repeated.

"Oh, I—I don't know. I was just wondering if Momma and Papa were hiding anything out there, like stuff they didn't want us to see."

Alexander shrugged. "I don't guess I'd know they didn't want me to see it if I saw it. But mostly it's Momma's broken dress forms and ruined cloth, smashed glass, and every once in a while, a paper that was in Papa's office."

"You come across the other birth certificates yet?"

He shook his head. "Momma said they must've blown away in the storm. But she can order more from the state."

He emptied the glass and stood up to go to bed.

"I'm beat. Night, Ainsley. If you paint tonight, make it something pretty. Don't paint the mess the storm left behind."

"I might be too tired to hold a brush, and how often does that happen?" I smiled. Alexander was the only person in this house who didn't act like my interest in art was annoying. "I'll paint something pretty. Would you like me to paint you something for your room? Anything you want."

"You don't need to waste a painting on me," he said. "Your paintings belong in smart people places like museums. I'm too dumb to appreciate it."

"You're smart enough just the way you are, and I can give you a present if I want."

He ducked his head, then smiled at me. "That'd be real nice."

I dried the last plate and hurried upstairs, excited to have something I could do to help him, even if Momma didn't think I belonged outside.

———

Alexander loved his painting of the pond, with the morning light dancing over the water and hawks circling in the sky above. He talked about it at every meal for the next two weeks, until Momma said she'd take it off his wall and burn it if he didn't stop.

I didn't speak to her for two days after that.

And then we had a visitor in the middle of a Thursday.

Bethany was cutting strawberries for lunch, I had a huge pot of plums cooking down for jelly on the stove, Daisy was wiping down baseboards, and Claire was entertaining Francine.

I had just started ladling the jelly into jars when there was a knock at the front door.

"Ainsley, I can't touch anything." Momma nodded to her hands, lifting a loaf-sized wad of dough and shaping it.

I put the ladle and the jar on the counter carefully and eyed the little ones. "That's hot, y'all, leave it alone."

"I'll watch them," Bethany said as she cut a strawberry into quarters. She could also get the door easier than I could, but I knew it was a waste of breath to say so.

I hiked my skirts enough that I wouldn't trip and hurried to the front door, pulling it open just as the county sheriff was turning to go back down the steps.

Cam Blankenship was a local sports hero who'd won election in a landslide after the old sheriff died three years ago.

He was also the one guy who'd featured prominently in my dreams since I was old enough to have improper dreams about boys.

"Hey there," he said, flashing his easy grin as he turned back when he heard the door open.

A brick took up residence in my stomach. "Afternoon, sheriff. What can we do for you?"

"Well, Miss SarahBeth, I actually came by to—" He tipped the brim of his hat back and squinted. "Goodness, you're not SarahBeth, are you? Ainsley?" His voice faded with the kind of wonder that said he knew he was right.

"Yessir." I bowed my head and spotted my bare toes peeking out from under my skirt, dropping it hastily.

"My, time flies." He let out a low whistle. "You are all grown up."

I looked up when he didn't say anything else for a few beats. "Yes, sir."

In all the times I'd dreamed of Cam showing up here and speaking to me, he'd not once been wearing his uniform. My mouth felt like I had chewed a spoonful of sand, and I couldn't summon words to save my life.

What did the sheriff want with us?

He studied my face until he couldn't help but blink, then shook his head like he needed it cleared.

"I came by to see if y'all need anything, after the storm."

Oh. Was that all? I smiled.

"Very kind of you," I said, dropping my knee in a small curtsy that made him bark out a laugh.

"Your momma ought to be right proud of your manners, Ainsley." He cleared his throat. "I know y'all keep mostly to yourselves nowadays, it's just we're trying to make sure everyone out here has what they need to avoid losing time to the storm during the growing season. As much as we can, anyway. And today it occurred to me that I hadn't sent anybody by here. It's not hard to forget y'all are here. No disrespect intended."

"We're getting by," I said. "But thank you."

He nodded. "I couldn't help but notice the garden is right tore up in places. I know your momma prides herself on that garden, and I also know that taking care of a small army of hungry folks and a house is a whole lot. I got four deputies headed this way who can get the plantings right as rain before dark."

I opened my mouth to thank him, my eye drawn to the side of the hill near Meg's house, which she was walking down with the baby on her hip. Before I could get any words out, Momma appeared behind me, drying her hands on her worn grey apron.

"That won't be necessary, Cameron," she said. "As you said, I love my garden. As such, nobody touches it but me—and occasionally some of my children. I'll get to it, it's on my list."

"It's really no trouble," Cam began, and Momma cut him off.

"Appreciate it, truly. But we have matters here under control. Y'all go help somebody who can't help themselves." Her eyes went to Meg, who was nearly at the bottom of the hill. "Like that single mother who moved into the old Lester place." She said *single mother* like it was the name of a disease.

"Somebody's living there?" Cam's eyebrows disappeared under his hat. "I hadn't realized. Must be doing a real good job keeping to herself." He turned back to us. "Y'all giving lessons in self-reliance or something?"

"I don't have time for lessons in the summer. Or socializing. If you'll excuse me, I have bread to finish." Momma turned and disappeared in a rustle of skirts.

Cam laughed and shook his head. "Real good to see her feeling like herself again."

I nodded as I turned toward the hill, watching Meg start across the yard toward the house. In the distance, I heard the baby squeal, and Cam's head turned toward the sound.

"Speak of the devil," he said. "Is this the new neighbor? What's her story?"

"She moved here from Utah in the spring," I said, sticking my hand out to count off facts on my fingers as I recited them. "Her husband died last winter. The baby is almost ten months old. And... she's my best friend."

Cam nodded, his eyes still on Meg.

It was funny that Meg and I had grown so close so quickly that it was hard for me to remember a time when I didn't know her, even though we'd only met a couple of months ago. But standing there talking to Cam, I realized I didn't know terribly much about her, as close as I thought we were. Was that normal? It wasn't like I'd had many friends.

I might offend her with too many questions. People always told me I asked too many questions, didn't they?

Or maybe I just didn't want her asking questions about me. Because if she did, if I couldn't hide the truth about who I was from her, maybe I wouldn't have a friend anymore.

Cam walked out a few paces to meet Meg and the baby, putting one hand to the brim of his hat.

She was nearly to the side of the house, a bag slung over her shoulders with baby things and a pie plate in her free hand.

I raised my hand to wave and she smiled before her eyes skipped from me to Cam.

The pie plate plummeted to the gravel drive and smashed into a thousand pieces, blackberries and thick purple syrup oozing around the glass and rocks, filling in the gaps between the two.

Meg froze, her wide eyes going from the sheriff to the mess to me to her son.

Cam hurried toward her. "Step back carefully and let's make sure you don't get cut. I'll get this cleaned right up." He glanced back at me. "I reckon there's work for us here whether your momma wants anybody in her garden or not, now isn't there, Ainsley?"

I smiled and nodded politely because I'd been raised to, my eyes on Meg. She'd shaken it quick once he started talking, but I knew the look I'd seen on her face before and after she dropped that pie. It wasn't shock, it was fear.

Same as me when I saw the sheriff at our door, I'm sure. I was just lucky Cam was turned away so he didn't see it.

The thing was, I knew why I was scared of him.

But why was Meg afraid of the law?

SEVENTEEN

Meg
August

Adding the local sheriff to the merry-go-round of folks who popped into my nightmares to snatch my son away from me knocked me straight back to the kind of sleep deprivation I'd only had to endure for a few weeks right after he was born.

And the baby wasn't any happier about it than I was: it was almost like he could feel my anxiety. The more I tossed in the sheets those hot August nights, the fussier he got, even when I tried to scoot away from him so I wouldn't bother him.

I had only wanted to help when I'd headed to Ainsley's house that afternoon with a not-quite fully cooled blackberry pie in my hands, hoping I'd get it there early enough to keep Ainsley and her sisters from having to make dessert. I knew they'd been working hard since the storm, with Burt and Alexander doing what they could to get the farm back to full production. The women and girls had taken on extra duties in the barns and the garden to make time for that. I'd barely seen

Ainsley. She'd been busy with chores from sunup to bedtime every day, including Sundays.

It had been two weeks since the tornado then, and I was still so thankful with every breath, practically, that our home hadn't lost more than a couple of shingles, not to mention that the Godfreys had offered us a safe place to wait out the storm. I never wanted to bother anyone—that was a central principle of my life—but I was eager for a way to help out and thank my neighbors again at the same time. Since Ainsley had asked for the pie before the storm, I figured it might be a welcome addition to their supper.

And then I saw the sheriff standing in the yard staring at me and the baby, and completely took leave of my senses.

I'd played the scene in my head so many times in the days since. I hadn't ruined anything—by the time the sheriff and Ainsley got to us, I had hitched the baby up on my hip and blamed it all on him, poor little guy. "He saw you and tried to wiggle loose, and I was afraid it was him or the pie," I'd said to Ainsley.

The sheriff had chuckled. "Normally I'd say you have your priorities straight, but this looks like quite a pie nobody's going to get to eat." He'd insisted on cleaning up the mess, and Ainsley had taken the baby and waved me inside the house, watching me with a curious look that said she was trying to figure something out, but all she said out loud was that she was glad I'd dropped the pie, all things considered. "This little guy is far too sweet to go getting skinned up by that gravel." She'd lifted him high in the air as she spoke, and he'd squealed and kicked his feet, which brought Bethany running from the kitchen.

Nobody said another word about it until I ran into the sheriff a couple of weeks later at the Sack and Save.

And when I say ran into him, I mean I rammed his backside with my cart on account of the baby reaching for a bright pink fly swatter dangling from a hook and me paying so much attention to keeping him from grabbing it and dragging the whole display down that I didn't see the sheriff bent over looking for canned milk on the bottom shelf until it was too late.

The impact rattled my teeth and sent the sheriff sprawling, his cart careening into a Campbell's soup display at the end of the aisle, his wide-brimmed cowboy hat flying off and exposing a helmet of dark hair slicked down to his scalp with sweat. He grunted out a couple of choice words I hadn't heard since my daddy died.

I put one hand on my son at first, though he didn't look a bit bothered, kicking his legs and squealing, both fists curled tight around the cart's handle like he was riding a roller coaster.

The second I realized just who I'd clobbered, both hands flew to my mouth. So much for keeping to myself and staying off the local radar.

"I'm so sorry!" It took effort to make my feet move, but I hurried over just as a short, angular man in a button-up shirt and bow tie that screamed "manager" rounded the end of our aisle.

"What in the world?" The store manager broke into a run. "Sheriff, you okay?"

I knelt next to the sheriff's head. "I am so sorry, I didn't see you there," I said. "Can I help you up?"

"I believe I'll live." He pushed himself up with the agility of a man who was once an athlete, snatching up his hat and settling it back in place as the manager skidded to a stop in front of us, his black plastic-framed glasses askew.

"Nothing to see here, Matt. Just a bruised ego, I'm afraid. This pretty lady and her sweet boy are far more interesting than I am today."

The sheriff sent me a wink as the manager nodded, straightened his tie, and hurried past us when a voice on the store's crackly PA system called for assistance in produce. "We'll get that soup display right, don't y'all worry," he called over his shoulder.

"I really am so sorry," I felt my cheeks flush as the words tumbled out, probably at least as much from the way the sheriff was looking at me as from embarrassment and fear. "The baby was trying to pull on a flyswatter back there, and I wasn't looking, just for a minute." My eyes dropped to the beige-flecked orange linoleum, following a jagged crack in one section that ran at an angle down the aisle a few feet to the edge of the shelf. That was twice in a month I'd tattled on my son to the local law, though at least this time I was telling the truth.

"Miss... Meg, wasn't it?" He paused until I looked up at him. With the hat back on, he looked even more handsome than he did without it, his dark eyes warm and kind, crinkling at the corners when he smiled, flashing white teeth with the slightest crook to the front two. "Are you of the mind that I'm angry with you? Because I do not believe you make a habit of mowing people down with your grocery cart, if that's what you're worried about."

I felt the corners of my lips turn up. He was tall—taller than I'd realized in my panic at Ainsley's house. And charming.

I'd been flirted with enough in my life to know it when I saw it. Not that the sheriff flirting with me could get out of the starting gate—can you imagine? Me and a policeman. It was all I could do to keep from laughing in his face.

I couldn't hurt his feelings or make him mad, which was how I found myself walking a tightrope of sorts in the canned goods aisle at the Sack and Save on the third Tuesday in August.

I met his eyes for two beats, then lowered mine, keeping the smile in place.

"Aren't detectives supposed to avoid drawing quick conclusions? I could be a serial hit-and-run bandit, and you'd miss it entirely." The words just fell straight out of my lips like someone else thought them.

I caught myself before I pressed my fingers to my mouth because he laughed, tipping his head back and letting loose with a guffaw that shook his torso and warmed me from the inside out in a way that screamed *danger*.

I'd bedded exactly one man in my twenty-two years on this planet, and the sheriff of Cottonwood County, Kansas absolutely could not be number two.

I was making a life here, and if ever there was a situation worthy of the term "playing with fire," here I was standing smack in the middle of the flame.

The sheriff smiled, and heat streaked from my middle out to my fingers and toes with the kind of pleasant tingle I had absolutely no business feeling.

He was older. How much, exactly, I couldn't tell, but it didn't matter anyway because he was a cop. I just had to keep reminding myself of that.

I stepped backward as he glanced at my cart. "Making any more pies this week?"

"I've tried to take one to Ainsley's family twice, and both times it ended in disaster. I think I might try cookies instead," I said, taking a wide step back and putting the cart between us.

"Disaster?" He quirked one eyebrow up and I felt myself leaning toward him before I could stop it.

"I, um, the first one I baked the day of the storm," I stammered, glancing at the baby and willing him to fuss so I could get out of there. Normally he hated sitting in the grocery cart if it wasn't moving. He just tugged on the sheriff's fingers and gurgled. Little traitor.

"What was so disastrous about the day we met?" Hoo, boy. I made the mistake of meeting his eyes and looked away quickly.

You are trouble. I didn't say the words out loud, but I thought them so hard he might've heard them anyhow.

"I broke the pie plate," I blurted. "So see, I can't make another one even if I wanted to."

"You know, I didn't even know you'd moved in out there?" he said, tapping the end of my son's nose with his free index finger and making the baby chortle. "This sweet little guy and a woman all alone—I hate the thought that y'all were there for months and we didn't even know it. What if you had needed help?"

"I do have a phone in the house," I said. "I imagine if I'd called you'd have sent somebody whether it was news to you that I bought the place or not."

He nodded. "Fair point. But I didn't get the chance to welcome you to the county or anything."

"Is that normally the sheriff's job around here?" I asked.

"Did anyone else do it?"

I smiled back at him in spite of myself. "Nope."

"See, then I should've."

Before I could get myself in real trouble looking into his dark eyes and thinking about how many years it had been since I'd so much as kissed a man, Little Bit came through, looking around and deciding he'd had enough sitting still, which he let me know with a shriek as he dropped the sheriff's hand.

"He usually doesn't tolerate sitting still near this long," I said with an apologetic smile, taking the cart's handle and pushing slowly as the sheriff stepped backward.

"I'm very charming. Or so people tell me." The sheriff grinned.

God, save me, I prayed silently, as my lips moved with more words I didn't exactly approve of them saying. "By people you mean women."

He chuckled. "Mostly, maybe. Would you be included in the ones who say that?"

"I haven't had time to decide." I meant it to be flip, dismissive, but the way his eyes lit up said he heard it as a challenge.

It was all I could do to swallow a groan. It seemed I didn't have the ability to avoid getting myself in trouble around this guy.

I pushed the cart a few steps, pretending to be very interested in potted meat and Spam I wasn't actually going to buy. He kept pace alongside. "Could you decide over dinner? The little guy is welcome to join us, and I can do a lot better than Spam."

My brain all but short-circuited. I had come to the store on a Tuesday for the first time since we moved here, and instead of getting groceries I'd found about six foot three inches of disastrous temptation.

"I have plans tonight," I said.

I didn't, but I couldn't go to dinner with the sheriff, and I also couldn't hurt his feelings. I'd have been perfectly happy going all my life not meeting the local law, but now that I was on his radar, I couldn't afford to make an enemy of him.

"Anyone I know?"

"Ainsley..." I paused, chewing on the inside of my lip so hard I tasted blood. "And her brother."

The sheriff's brows shot down into a deep V, his face falling as I turned the cart toward the dairy case at the end of the aisle. I had learned to make butter, but cheese was a different story.

"You be careful, Miss Meg." He tipped his hat. "The Godfreys keep to themselves, and most of the folks around here are glad to let them."

I put a hand on my son. "Is there something I need to know?" I wouldn't believe anything bad about Ainsley, but Alexander? I could give myself chills standing in the August sun thinking about that smile.

"Just don't get too close. Nothing wrong with being friendly with the neighbors, especially out where you are with that little one." His face softened and he tweaked the baby's toe. "But there's such a thing as getting too close. I would advise you to avoid that. And the offer for dinner stands. Just call the station next time you have a free evening."

I watched him walk away before I picked up two blocks of cheese and some full fat yogurt for the baby. Pushing the cart to the checkout, I couldn't shake the image of Alexander's smile out of my head.

Exchanging pleasantries with the cashier on autopilot, I loaded my son and the grocery order into my truck and pulled out onto the road home.

We'd come here to get away from danger. I'd found us a quiet, remote place where life and people were supposed to be simple.

But what if danger had found us here? And if that turned out to be true, was Ainsley safe in her own house?

EIGHTEEN

SarahBeth
April—Four Months Earlier

I couldn't remember the last time I'd managed to sneak into the gray metal trailer at the end of main street that served as our public library without a quiet storm of children in my wake.

I had read to every one of my children nightly since before Ainsley could talk, and whether it was because of that or my strict rules about television time, or simply the luck of the draw, they all adored books. Trips to the library were currency in our house—a reward for a quiet week or someone doing extra chores.

They were never a solo expedition for Mom until I started snooping around about our new neighbor.

I couldn't risk having one of the girls see or hear something and go blab it to Burt.

"SarahBeth Godfrey, as I live and breathe!" The little gray-haired woman who had looked ancient, with her poufy white hair and wrinkles, since I was a girl, looked up from the open book on her desk. "No Godfrey family with you today?"

"I snuck over after a doctor's appointment." I laid one finger across my lips with a wink.

"Our secret. It's so good to see you! How are you feeling?"

The thing people don't know about small towns unless they've lived in one is that in some ways, time stands still. It had been five years since the accident, and it was still the first thing everyone asked about when they spoke to me.

"I'm good, thank you! How about you?"

Her brow furrowed. "My rheumatism acts up from time to time. But you... are you and Burt doing okay?"

I rolled my lips between my teeth, nodding as I gave her a tight smile. "Why wouldn't we be?"

She stared for a second, then fiddled with her book as her cheeks flushed. "I just heard. Well, you know how folks talk."

That's the other thing about small towns. Everyone knows everyone else's business, like every day is one big old gossip-fueled family reunion.

"We're as happy as we've ever been." Or we would be again. One way or another.

"Are you looking for anything in particular today?" She flashed the brittle smile of a small-town gossip who'd been called on her ways and was eager to change the subject—and to get me out of her sight.

"I came in to look at something on the computer, actually."

Her eyebrows shot up. "Nobody over thirty pays that thing any mind."

"I think it might be the fastest way to find what I'm looking for. Do you know how to search for information on the web?"

"Sure, let me just show you." She rose on shaky legs and reached for a cane she hadn't had last time I was in here, moving slowly.

I followed her to the computer, swallowing the questions I wanted to ask about why she was walking slowly. She'd said she had a cough, but the hobbling, hunched posture was the real change in her. But it wasn't my business, and folks around here would do well to remember to mind their own business more often.

"See here, you just click in this box and type in whatever you want it to look for, and then in a minute, it'll tell you what it found, and you can click on the blue type to go to more information about anything it turns up."

"Thank you," I said, sitting down in front of the machine. We'd gotten one for the business class at the county school the year before I graduated, but I was already all set to be Mrs. Burt Godfrey by then, and I had no interest in learning to operate something I'd never need.

I tried typing in Meg Whitney, but the results were all about some actress named Whitney or links to articles with a Whitney someone and someone else named Meg. Apparently, the track team at the high school two towns over had a Whitney and a Meg.

I went through three pages of results, each one taking about three or four minutes to show up on the screen, and found nothing. I glanced at the clock on the wall. Twenty-five minutes I'd been here, and I had nothing to show for it. I sighed.

"Are you sure you're spelling it right, SarahBeth?" I couldn't tell if the town's lone librarian was being nosy or helpful.

"I'm sure." I mean, I was spelling it the way it was on the deed in the front seat of Burt's farm pickup.

"Try putting quotation marks around it. That makes it look for the whole phrase together."

"Thanks."

I did as she said, and all that happened was that I got fewer results.

I twisted around in the chair, wincing when it pulled in my middle. "If there's a birth certificate for a person, will this thing find it?"

"Oh no, not like that," she said. "Do you need a copy of one of the children's or something? You have to go to the county vital records page and search there."

I didn't really understand all of that, but I got enough.

"So you'd have to do that for any county if you wanted a record from there?"

She nodded.

"What about newspapers? Newspapers show up, don't they?"

"Sure they do. Aren't news stories showing up for you?"

They were. I'd seen the coverage of the track meets featuring Meg and Whitney. What I hadn't seen, from anywhere at all, was any sort of news clipping about the woman next door.

Not a news clipping, wedding announcement, high school sports story. Not even one of the picture pages kids all liked so much these days.

And there was no way to look for her little boy's birth certificate, it seemed.

But that gave me an idea.

A wonderful, terrible idea. I jumped out of the chair so fast it flipped over backward, the clatter echoing in the metal trailer.

"Find what you needed, dear?"

"Yes, ma'am, I think I did. It was nice to see you." The door was closing behind me before she finished saying "you too."

Maybe I was crazy.

Or maybe instead of finding the information I'd gone in hunting for, I'd come out of the library with the key to saving my family.

Only time would tell.

NINETEEN

Meg
August

"Do you need help with that?" Alexander's voice so close behind me made me jump and sent the rusted old shovel I'd found in the barn flying. It bounced off the edge of the hole I was digging and flipped right back up, the wood handle whacking me in the arm.

"Sorry." He was staring at the ground a few feet away when I turned to him, kicking a weed with the toe of one boot.

"It's okay," I said, trying to smile but not wanting him to return the favor. "I just didn't know anyone was there, that's all." I tried to keep Cam Blankenship's words about being careful around the Godfreys out of my head. "How are things going? I haven't seen y'all much lately."

"Papa and I have the farm back up and running, all the major repairs made," he said. "Feels funny to be glad that things are back to just our regular work days when summer is always so hard on a farm." He gestured to the shovel. "What're you digging?"

"I heard coyotes or wolves or something the other night, and I wanted to put up a small fence for the chickens. For the daytime. I'm learning that putting in fenceposts is harder than I thought."

"Your hole is way too wide," he said, holding one hand out. "You're not using concrete?"

"Concrete?" I blinked.

He stared at my blank face for a second and laughed. "Okay, so, if you're not setting the post in concrete and you want it sturdy, your hole needs to be about twice that deep. But only about half that wide."

"But how do you get it deeper without it being wide enough for you to reach to dig?" I asked.

"Like this." He picked up the shovel and pointed. "You want the post here?"

I nodded. He dug down another foot in less than five minutes.

I took the shovel back when he paused to mop sweat off his forehead with a bandana he pulled from his back pocket. "Thanks. I can do it," I said.

"Digging is men's work," he said.

I stared for three blinks without saying a word. On the one hand, I wanted to point out that I might have been less efficient, but I'd done fine before he came over. On the other, the look on his face said he didn't know what he'd said might be considered an insult because that was the way they did things at their house. To him, he was telling me the dirt was brown and the sky was blue. He didn't deserve to be snapped at or talked down to for not knowing something.

"I've learned to do a lot for myself since we came here," I said. "And I don't mind hard work. It means I can eat as much of your momma's bread as I want without feeling guilty."

He opened his mouth like he wanted to argue, but looked at my face and thought better of it.

"Okay," he said. "Can I do something else for you?"

"You just said how tired and busy you've been." I laughed. "Why are you over here looking for more work?" I scooped a shovel full of dirt up onto the pile.

"I was looking for you." He scrunched his forehead, like that should've been obvious. "You're still working, and if I help you, you'll be done sooner."

Oh boy. The list of reasons I was not getting involved with Alexander was taller than I was. I couldn't deny that I'd wondered, here and there in the weeks since the storm—there were so many things that would be so much easier, and probably less dangerous, with a big, strong guy who knew so much about farm life around. But men were dangerous—at least, every last one I'd ever known had been, and my gut and maybe even the sheriff said this one was no different. Deeper even than that, though: I was not my mother. She had cared more about men than about me my whole life, and my son would never know for one minute how that felt.

"I have a lot left to do tonight," I said, frowning. "I have to get the baby from his nap in a little bit, then make dinner, and he needs a bath."

"Oh." His face fell. "I guess that's probably true. I didn't think about that."

I felt terrible, staring into the disappointment plain on his face. There were ten thousand reasons why I should have let him shuffle back over the hill, but my heart couldn't take the idea of disappointing my friend's brother when he was being so nice.

"You know what? I don't have another shovel, but the post is heavy if you want to get it and bring it over."

He nodded so fast his thick, sweaty hair flopped around, and he pointed when he spotted the fenceposts over by the barn. He walked over to get one just as my shovel ran into something that wasn't soft earth.

I moved dirt and leaned over, squatting to peer into the hole.

The sun glinted off something creamy white, with a web of cracks skating out from a central point marked by soil and a spot of the same rust that colored the spade of the old shovel I'd found in my barn.

My heart stopped for a few seconds, hand to God.

Alexander was steps away, carrying a post upright. "You want me to set this in there?" he asked.

I shook my head, stepping to the side and knocking some dirt back into the hole with my shoe. "If you could just lay it there, I want to fuss with this more later, but I hear the baby."

He stood still, laying the post on the dirt pile and cocking his head to one side. "I don't."

"Well-trained ear, I guess." I dropped the shovel and took a deep breath. "Would you like to come up to the house for some lemonade? Ainsley made it."

He nodded and waved one hand in a "ladies first" gesture. I didn't hear a word he said on the way back to the house—I couldn't honestly tell you if he spoke at all. Every cell in my body was focused on how to politely get him to go home so I could go back outside alone.

I didn't want to believe what I thought I had seen, but I wouldn't sleep if I didn't go back and find out for sure what I'd just hit with that shovel.

———

Four hours later, we'd had dinner, we'd talked ourselves right out of topics to discuss, and just when I thought I was actually going to have to say "go home, Alexander," my little rock star saved the day.

Smashing his fists onto his toy piano as we sipped iced tea and watched him play, my son yawned so big and long I was afraid for about two seconds that his little head would crack at the jawline, and then he rubbed his eyes as he screwed up his face and howled.

"He's tired." Alexander stood. "I shouldn't have stayed so long, I'm sorry." He spoke to the floor, sticking his hands in his pockets.

"No apology necessary," I said, walking to the door. "Thank you for your help this afternoon."

"You didn't let me do anything."

"Moving that post was a big help."

He grunted. "It was nothing. Thank you for dinner. You're a good cook."

"I manage." I had to fight back the urge to smile so he wouldn't follow suit.

"It was nice talking with you," he said.

"Same here." I kept my face angled down just enough that I hoped he'd take the hint and wouldn't try to kiss me—there was a limit to my idea of "polite," and that was past it.

I shut the door behind him and took the baby to the bedroom. Thirty minutes later he was fed, changed, and curled against me in the bed. When his breathing had been regular for a while, I slid out from under him and turned my pillow sideways to keep him still.

Creeping out the door with ninja steps, I collected a small flashlight and a pair of rubber gloves from my kitchen and hurried back outside.

I didn't need a shovel this time. Laying on my belly at the edge of the hole with the end of the flashlight between my teeth, I reached one gloved hand down and brushed the dirt away. Using both hands, I pushed my fingers into the soft, dark soil until I found the other side, pulling gently. Something gave way when I tugged, and hope surged in my heart for a second.

It died entirely when I sat up and turned the buried object over in my hands.

One eye socket had crumbled, and there was a missing chunk of jawbone. But that was for sure and certain a human skull.

You wouldn't think that would freak me out, if you knew all the things I'd seen and done before I came here.

But you'd be wrong.

I dropped it and scooted backward, swallowing a scream.

A skull. Buried in my yard.

I had been good at taking care of myself since before I had boobs, but right that second, for the first time in my life, I wanted a man next to me. Someone who'd let me hide my face in his chest and hug me and then do something to take care of this.

Sheriff Cam's handsome face and kind eyes floated through my thoughts.

"Absolutely not," I said right out loud to the empty eye sockets. I might not have known the exact right thing to do, but I knew in my own bones I was not calling the sheriff to tell him I'd found a freaking skull on my property.

For all I knew the thing wasn't real, anyway. I mean... it looked plenty real: full grown-up sized with teeth that gleamed almost too white in the moonlight, but how would it have gotten here? Ainsley said Mr. Lester was a nice man who kept to himself.

Like that Jeffrey Dahmer fella I saw the TV program about last year?

I full on shivered in the barest chill of late summer.

"So what?" I didn't normally talk to myself. But nothing about this felt any kind of normal. I pointed the words at the grin beneath the empty eyes. "I didn't put you there. I don't know where you came from. But I do know my son needs a mother and that means I cannot pull the law into this. Who knows what kind of questions Sheriff Cam might ask?"

I stood on shaky legs. I shouldn't have to answer those questions because I hadn't done anything wrong. Not here, anyway. Walking around behind the skull, I picked it up and put it right back where I found it.

I didn't need a chicken fence this badly.

I grabbed the shovel and filled the hole such that nobody would know the ground had been disturbed at all, then hefted the post Alexander had moved for me and lugged it back to the barn.

I stuffed the gloves into the trash on the way back inside the house, washed my face, changed into a nightgown, and curled up next to my sleeping baby with his sweet, perfect little head nestled close to my heart.

In another life, another me would have drowned the memories in a fifth of whiskey, but not here. Not Meg. Not this precious child's mother.

Maybe something besides whiskey could make my brain forget. "It never happened. Forget it," I whispered. "Please, Lord."

I prayed for absolution, and as the days and weeks went on, that whole night faded until it seemed more like a bad dream than real life.

But in my nightmares, the skull was always waiting.

TWENTY

Ainsley
August

My twentieth birthday was the best worst day of my life.

It started off so nice: Momma made the girls do my chores, Meg and I had coffee and a nice long chat in the morning, then went out to lunch in town. I loved pizza, but Momma didn't allow junk food so it was a rare treat. I must've told Meg that, or maybe she'd guessed, but either way, there we were at a table at Angelica's, a huge pepperoni complete with orange grease pools between us, when the sheriff stopped at our table.

I was pretty sure I'd first fallen in love with Cam Blankenship when I was four and he was twelve. His momma got sick that year, and mine just had Alexander and me to look after. Back when we went to church—before more babies and massive loss had stolen her energy and hardened her heart—my momma was always helping someone with something. So when the pastor said one Sunday that Mrs. Blankenship needed help getting her son to and from his baseball practices, Momma loaded Alexander and me into the truck and made sure Cam got where he needed to be, usually taking his mother bread or eggs, too.

I spent months of long sunny afternoons hanging on the fence behind the backstop, watching him smash ball after ball over the fences, waiting for him to turn and smile at me like he did whenever I cheered one of those hits.

Momma stopped taking him to practice when Bethany was born the next year, but that was okay because I had started school that year, and I'd begged to stay after every day that spring to watch Cam and his friends at their baseball practices and games. He'd always flashed me that same smile, and sometimes he even ruffled my hair on his way off the field. He'd starred in every lovesick, romance-novel-inspired dream I'd had since I was fourteen, too.

Given all that, you'd think him stopping to say hello would be a great little birthday bonus. But instead it was the moment my day started to slide from lovely to horrible.

"Ainsley." His dark eyes barely flicked over me for half a breath. "Miss Meg." His face lit up with the million-dollar smile as soon as he looked at her.

How many nights had I lain awake, that smile rattling around my thoughts? How many books had I smuggled into the house, with love stories that told the parts Momma said were indecent? I hid them in my closet and read by flashlight in the small hours after the house was quiet and Momma was asleep, thinking about Cameron Blankenship and that smile.

The same smile he was now beaming at Meg.

I snatched my napkin up off the table and covered most of my face, pretending to wipe away pizza sauce and pepperoni grease so I could hide. If I could've gotten away with crawling under our table, I would've at least considered it.

Meg was my very best friend in the world. And just sitting there with her long, sun-streaked hair and her big eyes and shy smile, she was breaking my heart. The worst part of the whole thing was that I couldn't let her see that. Couldn't let either of them see that. I'd always known I would straight melt into the floor if Cam figured out I had a crush on him. In my dreams, he always confessed to carrying a torch for me—I couldn't even imagine it the other way around.

Wait. They were talking, and I was so lost in my anguish, seeing him look at Meg like I desperately wanted him to look at me, that I was missing it.

"... birthday," Meg said, waving a hand at me.

The smile turned on me. "Is that right? Happy birthday, Ainsley! How old are you now? Sixteen?"

"I'm twenty." Hoo, boy, the edge in those words could've shredded bone, and I wasn't the only one who heard it.

Meg sucked in a breath so sharp she dissolved into a coughing fit, turning Cam's attention back to her. As he pounded her back, the baby started to fuss.

I reached a hand toward the highchair, my cheeks burning with the fire of ten thousand suns. Sure. Happy birthday to me. I had lost my dream guy to my best friend and made a fool of myself in front of them both.

Not that I deserved any better. But I couldn't help hoping anyway.

The baby grabbed my finger and yanked, screeching. By then, folks at the other tables around us were looking, a couple of them whispering.

Wishing I could just fall into a hole, I handed my little buddy my napkin. He was forever reaching for anything we were using on the table, and that did the trick. He let out a happy gurgle and flapped the napkin like it was his favorite toy.

Meg stopped coughing and raised her teary eyes to mine, her right eyebrow creeping up the slightest bit. I was too busy trying not to cry myself, watching Cam's hand rub her back as he leaned closer than he needed to and asked if she was all right.

"All good," she choked out, lurching awkwardly to the left in her chair to get away from his hand. "Sorry about that. I'm such a klutz shouldn't even be trusted to drink water, apparently."

Cam moved back to the end of the table and ruffled the baby's hair. "Glad to be of service. Happy birthday, Ainsley, y'all have a nice lunch." He turned back to Meg. "I'm still waiting for that call about dinner."

I watched him walk to the counter and pay, Meg's eyes boring a hole into my face that I could feel without looking at her.

I decided maybe I should just never look at her again, and then we wouldn't have to talk about this.

That was a good idea, until her pointy-toed boot collided with my shin under the table.

"Ouch!" My eyes snapped right to meet hers as I reached down and rubbed at my bruise.

"What in the world was all that?" she hissed across the table as the door closed behind Cam. "Do you have a history with him?"

"Momma was sort of his babysitter when I was little," I said. "Just for a while, before Bethany was born. He played baseball and we used to take him to his games and practices because his momma was sick." I realized how ridiculous I sounded as I blurted out every fact that came to mind about Cam except the ones I knew she was asking about.

"That's not the kind of history I meant," Meg said, stabbing her fork into her pizza slice.

"He likes you." I didn't want to talk to her about any of this. But I'd rather put the focus on his obvious interest in her than on me and my silly farm girl daydreams. He'd always been too old for me, I knew that, but I hadn't been able to help but hope, the past few months as my twentieth birthday loomed and he was still single and I was still here, that once I was twenty and he was twenty-eight, he'd just realize we were both adults and nobody's age would matter. It wasn't like the county dating scene was a big one. But while I was busy hoping I'd finally grown up enough to catch Cam's eye, he'd fallen for the new girl in town.

Of course.

I would be a good wife. It wasn't what I had ever wanted, really, but it was the thing I'd spent my whole life training for. Sure, I might not know my way around a man's body in a dark bedroom for real, but I'd read enough that I was sure I could figure it out. And Momma had taught me well how to be respectful and submissive, how to raise babies and run a house and work myself bone tired without ever complaining. So what if I couldn't make bread? Was that really a deal-breaker? Cam bought his bread at the Sack and Save now, we could just use the store-bought kind.

"I'm…" Meg stopped, twisting her mouth to one side. "I'm aware that he likes me."

I didn't want to be jealous of Meg. But the tone in her voice said she wasn't grateful for Cam's attention—maybe even that she didn't want it. And for some reason that didn't make a lick of sense at all, that made me angry.

Shouldn't I be happy that she didn't seem interested in him? I should, for sure. But somehow the anger pinching my chest and making it hard to breathe didn't understand that. Just the thought of him being hurt if she rejected him made me see red. Actual, literal red—until right then I'd thought that was just a saying, but the color crept into my vision from both sides until it was like I was looking at the room through a scarlet veil.

She wasn't that much older than I was. Just a handful of years at most. She couldn't possibly be more than twenty-five, though I realized then that we'd seen each other nearly every day for months, shared stories and secrets, and I didn't know how old she was.

How had I managed to miss that?

The answer floated up from the deep well of things I didn't like to think about: because really, I had shared secrets and stories and dreams. I'd told her about Francine running to the pond that awful day, and about how I'd always wanted to live in a city with museums and neon signs and traffic, and about how much I missed school. Meg listened and commented and sometimes offered an anecdote that I pretended not to notice was so sterile and generic it could've been about anyone—except when she was talking about the baby, or the storm, or a racy comment from the old man who ran the feed store. Things that had happened here had names and details that made them feel real when we talked, but Meg didn't say anything real about her life before she came here, or what had happened to her husband. All I really knew was that she said he died last winter and then she showed up here with a baby and enough cash to buy a farm.

I tried to take another bite of my pizza and a wave of nausea washed through me with the kind of force that made me spit it out, my skin going clammy and the fire draining from my cheeks as I tried to hold my lunch down.

"Are you okay, Ainsley?" Meg leaned across the table toward me, but her voice sounded far away. "Just so you know, I am not getting myself into any sort of social situation with the sheriff. I'm not sure how to tell him that without hurting his feelings, and he seems nice. But that's the truth. And I would never date someone you're interested in."

I felt my head nodding because it was the polite thing to do, but I wasn't sure I could believe her. I had come here thinking she was my very best friend, but the truth was I barely knew her at all.

Who, exactly, had I invited into my heart and into my home because I wanted a friend more some days than I wanted my next breath?

TWENTY-ONE

Meg
September

I really wasn't going to go to dinner or anywhere else with Sheriff Cam Blankenship.

I swear.

The flower deliveries started the day after Ainsley's birthday and kept up until the only places I had to put another vase were on the floor or in the barn. So I called him.

"Sherriff Blankenship." Jesus, how did just his deep voice on the phone make my insides go all gooey?

I should've hung up.

But I didn't.

"I'm out of places to put flowers," I said instead.

"Then my work there is done for now," he said, not seeming to care that I hadn't so much as said thank you for the very kind, over-the-top gesture.

"How did you know I like daisies?" I looked around, twirling the phone's coiled cord around my right index finger and smiling at the bouquets in every shade and type, from small and white to huge, gorgeous pink and orange gerberas.

"I'm a detective, remember?" He laughed.

I let the silence stretch, and he chuckled, the low sound setting off pleasant sparks in my nerve endings.

"One of my dispatchers saw you buying some to plant in your yard at the Feed and Seed. I figured that made them a safe bet," he said. "I'm glad you like them."

"You can stop now," I said. "The house is so full it smells like a garden indoors."

"Have dinner with me," he said. "Just as friends, if that's what you want."

"Well, see, I might have, but now I'm in a relationship with the flower delivery guy." I couldn't stop the giggle that followed that.

"Dang, should've thought of that when I hatched this brilliant plan," he said. "He's still the ladies' man at eighty-two."

"You are too much."

"Back at you. How much am I going to have to beg here?"

"Friends." I said the word with the kind of firmness you usually attribute to a slamming door. I already had friends here, after all. And if he was this serious about a date, I was more afraid of making him mad than I was of dinner. Cam Blankenship was the kind of man who paid attention. Maybe I was better off at this point being able to direct that attention where I thought was safest. "I can get dinner with you as friends."

He let out a whoop that made me hold the phone away from my ear. "Tomorrow?" I could hear that megawatt grin of his over the phone, hand to God.

"Friends. I'm not kidding."

"Yes, ma'am," he said. "I promise to abide by any and all rules of the friend zone."

"Tomorrow is good. You don't mind the baby?"

"He's too cute for anybody to mind. I'll pick y'all up at seven."

"You pick up dates. You meet friends," I said. "I have his car seat in my truck, we'll meet you at Angelica's at seven."

"See you tomorrow. Friend," he said.

"Tomorrow," I echoed before I hung up the phone, thinking of Ainsley's face the last time I'd been at the little Italian restaurant and genuinely unsure whether I should fear her misunderstanding this more than I did making an enemy of the sheriff.

———

I tried on five different outfits the next afternoon—which meant about half of my wardrobe—before I settled back on the first thing I'd pulled out, a gray skirt with a lilac top that had a modest neckline and long sleeves. I grabbed a gray cardigan for good measure, though it was still warm outside. I wanted everything about this evening, from my clothes to the table at the restaurant, to scream "friend zone."

I was just putting on a dab of light-pink lip gloss when the baby's fussing from the bedroom got loud enough for me to hear.

"Be right there, sweet boy!" I called, patting my hair down and shooting myself a warning look in the mirror. "Friends. This is not the kind of fire you play with, it's the kind that could burn your whole life down."

I was two steps into the hallway when I heard the thud.

"No!" I felt the word rip out of my throat more than I heard it, sprinting for the bedroom in my bare feet. I rounded the doorway just as my son caught his breath and started to scream.

And when I say scream... I mean, *scream.* The kind of blood-curdling, ear-piercing shriek that could've put some horror movie actresses right out of work. His face was the color of a July tomato, his little body lumped onto the floor next to the bed. He ran out of air, sucked in more ratcheting breaths, and let loose again while I stood frozen in the doorway.

Oh my God. He fell.

He'd been napping in our bed for months and nothing like this had happened. I usually just turned the pillows longways on the bed and put them back away from where I'd laid him down. He'd taken to scooting himself along on his belly using his feet to push, and the pillow on the side closest to me was cockeyed. He'd pushed past it.

"No, no, no," I whispered, my face crumpling. I wanted—no, needed, in that crawling-out-of-my-skin way—to pick him up. But should I? What if I hurt him? Tears welled in my own eyes as I realized for about the thousandth time since he was born just how much I didn't know about babies.

Ainsley.

Ainsley knew everything about babies.

"I'm getting help," I said, my voice clear over the baby's cries.

I ran to the kitchen and snatched the phone off the wall with such force that the base came loose from one screw, hanging by the other one as I leaned over to dial.

"Godfrey residence."

"Bethany!" I sobbed. "Bethany, it's Meg. I need Ainsley."

"What's wrong?" Her voice went up an octave.

"The baby." The tears spilled over, running hot down my terror-chilled cheeks. "He fell. I don't know what to do."

"Fell how?" Her tone was urgent, but unruffled, and if I'd had the presence of mind in the moment, I would've been impressed.

"He was asleep on the bed," I said. "He's screaming, but I don't want to hurt him if I pick him up."

"Is he moving?"

Any other day I would've asked her to get me a grown-up,

but even at fourteen, she sounded so calm and sure of herself I didn't think to do anything but trust and listen to her.

"I... I don't think he did. I can go look."

"I'll wait."

I put the phone on the table and ran to the bedroom. Little Buddy had rolled onto his back. He was still screaming, his face more purple than red now, arms and legs flailing like he was beating the living hell out of the air.

I ran back to the phone. "He's moving. He rolled onto his back and he's kicking his feet and waving his arms around. Still crying, though."

"I can hear that. Maybe without the phone. But if he's moving everything okay, he's probably fine. Pick him up and try to calm him down. Don't give him food, but a little table sugar on a binky or your thumb might help, and check him over good. Lumps on his head are fine, swelling out is good. Dents are bad, you'd need to go over to the hospital in Kempsville. The black in the middle of his eyes should be the same size in each one, and make sure there's no blood or fluid coming from his ears."

"Are you... I..." I took a deep breath and held it for a couple of seconds. "How do you know all that?"

"We all know it," Bethany said. "All us kids, I mean. Babies, grown folks... the things you look for after a fall are the same for everyone. Papa taught us all on account of Momma. In case she fell again when he wasn't here."

I didn't have clue what she meant but I was too scared to even wonder.

"Thank you so much, Bethany, I have to go."

"Sure thing, hug him for me. And then when he's calm, maybe get yourself a shot of whiskey."

That definitely wouldn't be happening. I was counting down weeks to my twenty-four-month chip already, even if my chips these days were just little pieces of paper I colored and wrote myself notes on.

I hung up and ran back to the bedroom, sweating through my lilac blouse now.

My son turned his head toward me, caught a snotty breath, and screwed up his face like he'd bitten a lemon before he howled again, flexing every bit of his tiny body out in a tight stretch.

"Okay, okay," I said, swooping him off the floor and hugging him gently close, rocking my hips side to side. "You're okay, buddy. We're okay. Mommy is so very sorry." I kissed his head gently. It was impossible to miss the lump that had sprouted behind his right ear, but Bethany had said swelling out was okay. I bounced him as I walked to the window, inspecting his whole little skull for dents.

His cries softened in force and volume as he balled his little fists around my shirt, dropping his head on my shoulder.

"Sugar," I said, turning back for the door.

I was halfway to the kitchen when Ainsley burst through the front door, immediately bending at the waist, one hand on her side, her breath coming in sharp gasps.

"Hey," I said. "I think he's okay, but it means everything to me that you came." My eyes welled right back up, tears spilling over my lashes before I could blink them back.

"Oh thank you, Jesus," she said. "I was cut in the garden when you called, Bethany came outside to tell me after you hung up and I ran so fast I dropped tonight's tomatoes everywhere. What happened?"

I waved for her to follow me to the kitchen, where I grabbed a clean pacifier from the dish rack and ran it under water before I dipped it in the sugar bowl and popped it into the baby's mouth. He sucked it furiously. His eyes, the same violet blue as an old friend of mine from another life, popped wider than I'd ever seen them.

Ainsley leaned in to peer at his face and laughed, her breath more regular. "Baby's first sugar?"

I nodded, putting one hand gently on the back of his head and holding him close.

"I think he's a fan," she said.

I fought for a ragged breath, the adrenaline leaving my system like someone pulled the stopper out of a tub—and I felt about like a wet, wadded-up washrag that got left behind all of a sudden.

Ainsley grabbed a chair and whipped it around behind me in a blink. "Have a seat before you fall over." She eyed my shaking hands. "Do you need me to take him?"

I handed her the baby carefully and he curled himself around her curves and put his head on her shoulder, his jaw working the binky and his little eyelids heavy.

"Isn't he supposed to stay awake?" I asked, sitting up straighter.

"It's okay for him to sleep," Ainsley said. "I can feel him breathing, and he just has a little bump on the head. This isn't serious."

Something about hearing her say that made me dissolve into the kind of stomach-turning, soul-wrenching sobs I hadn't given into since the night my granny died.

"It's really okay, Meg." Ainsley reached across the table with one hand, her other arm wrapped securely around my son. "I know why it scared you, but I've seen way worse."

I sniffled, more sobs wrenching out of my chest.

"You're okay, too," she said.

I closed my eyes for a few seconds. "I didn't know."

"Know what?"

"He always naps in the middle of the bed between the pillows in the afternoon, and I was right there, in the bathroom. I didn't know he could get hurt." I fit the words around the kind of hitching breaths that mean you've cried too long and hard for your own good. "Then when I saw what happened, I didn't know how to help him, either. I totally froze. I was so scared I couldn't breathe, I couldn't move. What kind of mother does that?"

"Mine," Ainsley said calmly.

I felt my eyebrows jump toward the ceiling. SarahBeth Godfrey was a professional wife and mother if ever there was such a thing. "Your mother knows everything."

Ainsley barked a short laugh that made the baby flinch, rubbing his back as she shook her head at me.

"I assure you, everything she knows she learned just like this. The hard way. And I bet plenty of other moms do, too. Nobody knows all about taking care of babies when they become a mother, Meg. You learn as you go. And if you're lucky —and you are—the lessons come with little bumps and bruises, and not..." A cloud so dark it sucked light out of the room, hand to God, crossed her face for the quickest second. "Not things that are worse."

I took a calmer deep breath, watching the baby's back rise and fall in rhythm. He'd plum worn himself out.

"Bethany said something," I said slowly. "About your mother. That Burt made all of you learn what to look for after a fall because of her. What was she talking about? Is that why your mother limps sometimes?"

"When the pressure in the air is high." Ainsley nodded. "You'll see it a lot more in the winter, too. She was in the loft in the barn one day moving things around. She said she was in a hurry, she had a lot to do that day, and she was carrying a big heavy starter motor for the old tractor toward the ladder, walking backwards."

My hand went to my mouth because I knew what she was going to say next.

Or so I thought.

"She misjudged the distance and she fell backwards. The motor fell on her, and then the ladder fell too because her skirts caught on it as she went over the edge."

"She's lucky to be alive," I breathed through my fingers.

"Crushed her pelvis." Ainsley swallowed hard. "And... well, she was hurt really bad."

I shuddered. "I guess that would make Burt teach y'all about falls. I'm so sorry that happened to her."

"Me too," Ainsley said softly, running her fingers lightly over the baby's feathery curls. "The day she fell was the last day of my childhood."

She stared at something on the wall behind me, or maybe something past the wall behind me, for a few beats before she blinked and waved one hand at me. "What are you dressed up for?"

I swallowed hard.

"We were going to go to dinner," I said, trying to keep my tone easy and casual. "He likes the applesauce at Angelica's and I thought I was too tired to cook. Now I just might be too wrung out to drive."

She watched my face carefully, the slightest pinch to hers—so slight someone less observant wouldn't have caught it, and even I could convince myself with a bit of effort I'd imagined it. "You're going, just you and the baby?"

"We just went out a couple of weeks ago for your birthday," I said. "I didn't think SarahBeth would let you go."

Ainsley nodded, her eyes wandering the room. "Where did all the flowers come from?"

I kept my face flat. I had burned every single card from the florist so she wouldn't pop over and see one. I didn't want her to get her feelings hurt. "It seems I have a secret admirer." I didn't want to lie to her, but sometimes a lie is just kinder than the truth. Of course, this one was also easier for me, and I didn't discount that.

"Secret?" Ainsley's left eyebrow quirked up. "Is that what Cam's calling himself these days?"

"They don't say they're from him," I said. Anymore, but I wasn't saying that part out loud.

"And you're taking the baby to dinner?" She didn't blink.

"I am." I didn't want to sound defensive, but I might have, anyway.

"You can leave him here with me, I'll sit with him."

"Then I'll just be eating alone." Okay, fine, that was a bald-faced lie. But I was already in too deep.

She stared straight into my eyes for what felt like hours before she smiled. "I think he might sleep the whole drive into town, but I hope y'all have fun."

"Thanks."

I walked her out and transferred the sleeping baby expertly to his car seat—there was something I could say I did professionally as a mother—climbing carefully behind the wheel and trying to make sure I didn't stink of fear and sweat as I settled my foot on the brake.

I still smelled like lilac shampoo and drugstore perfume. Good enough for dinner with a friend.

I turned the truck around in the wide clearing next to the house.

I'm still not sure why I looked up at the hill toward the Godfrey place on my way down the driveway.

Or why it gave me chills that Ainsley was standing at the top, watching us drive away.

TWENTY-TWO

SarahBeth
May—Four Months Earlier

I hadn't done so much sneaking around since Burt and I used to meet in the hayloft in the big barn at Firefly Grove to make out.

Before sunup, I slipped out of bed and then out of the house and over the hill under cover of darkness, moving like a cat thanks to years of practice sliding out from under sleeping children and creeping out of their rooms.

Miss Meg, with only one child, one cow, and a couple of chickens to care for, lazed around in the bed until after the sun came up. She had the baby in a big king-sized bed with her, and the two of them made a sweet picture that I didn't have the luxury of appreciating, all curled up asleep. I only poked my head up over the sill high enough for my eyes to peek in the window, and every time she so much as twitched, I ducked.

Once she was up, I watched from the windows as she went about her morning. She changed the baby before she went to the bathroom herself, then carried him to the kitchen and put him in the highchair, giving him Cheerios to pick at while she made him a bottle and opened a jar of baby food—usually fruit, which I'd never done with my babies. Kids these days have enough of a sweet tooth without starting them off eating bananas every morning.

We'd have to remedy that.

When she put the baby on one hip and grabbed a milk pail to head to the barn, I darted around the side of the house where she couldn't see me, flattening my back against the clapboard siding and willing my heart to stop pounding. She wouldn't bring a milk pail this way, I was perfectly safe. I just had to be still for a few minutes.

I gave her a good head start before I peeked around the side of the house. She walked slowly, swinging the pail and singing to the baby, who had his head leaned back watching a hawk circle high above them.

He was curious. And mighty cute. And still, nobody at my house had seen either of them yet.

They disappeared into the barn, and I checked the time and hurried toward the hill that led home.

I hadn't learned everything, but it was a good first day. I could make this plan work—just like I had before.

I closed the door to our mudroom silently just as the hall bathroom door closed upstairs. The girls were up. I should check on Alexander. He needed to feed the hogs before breakfast, and it was already a little late.

"Hey, buddy." I peeked around his door frame, his big body with its long, hairy limbs overhanging the edges of his childhood bed in every direction. "You awake?"

My son grunted at me in teenager.

I was pretty sure that one meant "no."

"Come on, bud," I said, stepping fully into his room, looking across the hall at another one just like it where Burt kept his guitars. It wasn't supposed to be a music room. Burt built these wings onto the barn like dormitories when we decided we needed more space than the house. We should've had more boys to fill the rooms by now.

Maybe would've, if I was smarter. Or maybe God meant for us to have another son a different way. A son who wasn't like Alexander.

Maybe it wasn't too late just yet.

"Momma. Early," Alexander grumbled.

"The sun is up, sleepyhead," I said, tugging on his foot. "Hogs need feeding this morning."

"Why'd we have so many girls anyways? They never have to feed hogs."

"Feeding hogs is not women's work. We have the babies, you slop the hogs. You get the better end of that deal, believe me." I put one hand on my belly and he sat up, frowning.

"I'm sorry, Momma."

"No need to be." I winked and tweaked his nose. "Get up and let me make this bed while you get dressed. Five daughters, and my only son is the only person in the house with his own bathroom. Your sisters are all so jealous."

"I'll trade them the bathroom for slopping the hogs." He tried to pull the covers over his head and I leaned down and snatched them clean off the bed.

"Ainsley would do it, Momma. You know she would, to not have to share the other one. You go tell her for me. She can have my bathroom if she'll feed them right now."

"And where are you going to bathe?"

"The pond." He put his pillow over his face.

I laughed and took that from him too.

"Fine." He rolled to his feet, towering over me with a glare that would've been scary if I didn't find it so funny. I poked at his ribs and he dissolved into giggles that reminded me of a much smaller boy, his curls tickling my chin when he ran to me for a hug and I could rest my chin on top of his head.

My son. He was different. I avoided looking at the shelf over his dresser when I was in this room so I didn't have to be reminded of just how different. But I loved him with my whole heart.

"Shake a leg. The girls are ahead of you, Bethany's already cooking the eggs."

He shuffled to the bathroom with his dark denim overalls in one hand, rubbing his eyes with the other.

I hurried back to the stairs, pausing when I caught a glimpse of Meg's house out the window at the end of the hallway.

I had spent two months being sorry that girl had moved here.

It was her turn to be sorry for that.

TWENTY-THREE

Meg
September

Cam stood up when I walked into Angelica's ten minutes late. He had chosen the cozy booth in the back corner of the dining room, where I'd originally planned to get there early and get the table for four right in the middle of the floor.

Walking to the table with my little buddy, happy and babbling as usual, on my hip, I was too relieved that he seemed okay to much care about the seating arrangement for dinner.

"I was beginning to think you weren't coming." Cam flashed a grin that really could melt the iciest resolve—it was even thawing mine a bit and I had more good reasons for staying away from him and his dreamy dark eyes and movie star smile than a barn cat has lives. He'd chosen a deep, burgundy red polo shirt that showed off his tan—and his biceps—and a pair of khakis for dinner. Nice, but not necessarily date night nice.

"Sorry I was late, we had a bit of a catastrophe," I said, patting the baby's back.

"Everything okay?" Cam's brows drew down as his eyes met mine.

"He fell off the bed." I angled the baby's legs through the openings in the wooden highchair Cam had gotten for him, not missing the attention to detail from a man who didn't have children. Maybe agreeing to this was a mistake after all—I already liked the guy way more than I should—but it wasn't like there was anything to be done for it now. "Bopped his little noggin, and scared the life out of me. But Ainsley came running, and I bet she's seen more than her share of kids with injuries. She says he's fine, and he seems to be."

"It's really good of you to be so kind to her." Cam resumed his seat as soon as I was settled in mine. I pulled a plastic bag of Cheerios out of the diaper bag and scattered some on the table for the baby before I sipped my water. Cam watched with a small smile. "You're a nice person, and Ainsley really needed a friend, I think."

"She's easy to be friends with, I've never met another person as helpful and unselfish as Ainsley," I said, watching his face as he nodded. Did he know about her crush on him and just choose to seem oblivious?

"She's a sweet girl who has caught some tough breaks. She really lit up when she saw you walking up to their house the day I met you, and I'm glad for her. For both of you, really. I'm sure it can be a little scary out there all alone sometimes."

"What kind of tough breaks?" I'd barely heard anything he said after that.

His eyebrows went up. "She hasn't told you about Sarah-Beth's accident?"

Oh, that. Just barely. I smiled. "I just wondered if you were talking about something besides that. You said 'breaks,' plural, with an s."

"I just meant that SarahBeth's accident kind of upended Ainsley's life. Don't you think? I mean, she never went back to school after that summer, she kind of became a shut-in, really. Lost all her old friends. SarahBeth didn't allow visitors at Firefly Grove for... gosh, I guess it was nearly two years. Francine was walking the first time I saw her in town. And none of the kids ever went back to the county school."

My jaw would've been hanging near my lap by the time he stopped talking, except I was too busy grinding my teeth to let that happen.

Cam sipped a frothy beer from a mug and started to say something, but the waitress interrupted by stopping at the end of our table. "Can I get you a drink?" Her tone was a little short, but I was too busy trying to sort out everything Cam had just told me about the Godfreys to pay her much mind. "Iced tea, please," I said.

She walked off without a word.

"Sorry about that." Cam's smile had an edge of nerves that time. "We went out a few times last year. She's never very happy to see me."

"Why is that?" I managed to ask. I didn't want to let him see how much he'd rattled me with his comments about Ainsley's family, but I was trying to fit what I thought I'd known five minutes ago together with what he'd said, and an icy ball of dread had settled in my gut.

"I guess because we don't anymore," he said.

"But is she mad at you for breaking things off, or did you do something to her?"

"I suppose telling her I wasn't interested anymore was enough." He leaned forward and caught my eye. "I'm not the kind of guy who enjoys breaking hearts or hurting women. My momma, God rest her soul, taught me to treat every lady the way I'd want someone to treat Momma, and it's a principle I try to live every day by."

I nodded, stuffing half a breadstick into my mouth to try to fight the unease in my stomach. Nothing he'd said about

Ainsley was terrible. What bothered me was that I'd spent so much time with Ainsley, and she'd confided in me about a fair amount of stuff, but never said a word about any of this until I asked because of what Bethany said earlier.

It made me feel like there was a reason she hadn't told me this, and odds were heavy on the side of it being a bad reason. Before I could try to decipher any more of that, the surly waitress dropped my tea glass on the table so hard the liquid sloshed onto the red tablecloth.

"Thanks," I said.

"What are y'all eating?" she asked.

"I'd like the chicken Alfredo and a house salad, please," I said, catching Cam's approving nod.

"I'll take the same," he said, handing her both menus with a smile that said he didn't care enough to let her attitude bother him.

"Thank you for ordering more than just a salad," he said when she was a few steps away. "It makes me crazy when girls just pick at rabbit food when I ask them out to dinner."

"I like food," I said. "That tends to happen when you spend most of your life going without it." I wasn't sure why I said that out loud, I'd never really told anyone here any truths about my past.

He was easy to talk to. I'd need to watch that.

Not that there would be a next time. Cam Blankenship was proving entirely too distracting to have around.

Cam glanced at the baby, who had finished the Cheerios and was straining forward trying to reach the beer mug. "I'm afraid you're underage," he said, lifting the mug and moving it to the other side of his bread plate. Little Bit squawked and banged his pudgy fist on the table.

I leaned over and poked my nose an inch from his. "No temper fits," I said. He grabbed a handful of my hair, and I peeled his fingers free one by one. "No, buddy. Ouch!" He tipped his head and stared at me for two blinks, then laughed.

"That's a good boy," I said, reaching into the bag for his plastic key ring and handing it over. He grinned, turning to shake it at Cam.

"You got a prize for good manners." Cam smiled, and my son followed suit.

Cam turned his smile on me. "So. What brought you two to our little slice of middle America?"

"It's pretty here," I said, my hands fiddling with the napkin in my lap.

I let the silence stretch until he nodded. "That it is." He took a bite of a breadstick. "You don't have any family in the area?"

I caught myself just before I said I didn't have any family left at all.

"Just my little buddy here."

Cam nodded as he chewed. "How'd you even know we were here, then?" He tipped his head when I laughed. "That's not rhetorical, I'm genuinely curious. I hear people in movies and songs talk about map dots and towns with one stoplight. We don't really have a dot and we definitely don't have a stoplight—this isn't the sort of place anybody moves to. Until now."

"Would you like me to leave?" I blinked, unsure what he was getting at.

He laughed. "Am I making it seem that way? Because no, I would not. I just mean, I can't figure out how I got so lucky as for you to wind up here, of all the places you could've found a house."

His eyes softened as he said the words and I realized two things: one, though I couldn't give a reason for sure, my gut said a big part of his fascination was with the new girl in town, like a kid who wanted the shiniest new toy; two, I absolutely shouldn't look at his face when it went all soft and dreamy like that. Not if

I didn't want to have my panties catch fire in the corner booth at Angelina's, or maybe to do something really stupid after we finished dinner.

I shrugged and shifted my gaze to the wall behind him, talking to a sconce light shaped like a drippy candle. "We were driving, and I got a real peaceful feeling, driving through here. All this open land, and the sunsets—good Lord, they're spectacular. I never saw so many colors before, and it was practically still winter. And then right in my line of sight I noticed a 'for sale' sign. I took it as... well." I laughed. "As a sign. The other kind, you know."

"I suppose if country life is what you're after, Main Street was impressive." He sat back in his chair and watched my face.

"It was when we got there, sure. Where else can you find a five and dime store that still sells penny candy and has a soda fountain?" I smiled.

He nodded, reaching for another breadstick. "They take a loss on the candy because the old folks who have owned the place since the sixties love kids. I myself love the root beer barrels. And the floats, too." His eyes jumped from me to the baby and back again. "My granddad used to tell me everything happens for a reason. Maybe the reason you felt peaceful here is because I'm here."

My eyes popped wide and I snorted when I laughed. It would've mortified me any other day, but right then all I could think was maybe it would be good if he thought I was gross and liked me less.

The waitress walked up with our plates and plopped them down without a word, walking away before I could get the "thank you" out of my mouth.

"You're forgetting the friend zone rules." I turned back to Cam. "And you seem to think you're awful important to the universe's grand plan."

"Are you saying I'm not?" He folded his arms over his chest

and stuck out his full lower lip, and hand to God, I have never wanted to nibble on anything so badly in all my life. I crossed and uncrossed my legs under the table.

Say something funny. Anything he'll have to laugh at.

Not a thought in my head was anything but indecent.

Just when I was nearing true danger territory, the baby chucked his plastic key ring at Cam and hit him straight in the side of the face. The pouty lip retreated into a shocked expression for a split second before he busted up laughing. Holding up the toy, he leaned toward my son. "That is some arm there, slugger. And a southpaw, too." He arched an eyebrow at me. "Maybe the real reason you stopped here is so I could be his baseball coach."

"He hasn't even had a birthday yet." I let out a long breath, never more thankful for the little boy who had given my life purpose for the better part of the past year.

"When is his birthday?" Cam sounded casual, I thought, but I didn't know him well enough to trust that.

"Halloween." It was a three-month lie, but went along with what I'd been telling Ainsley, and ought to keep us safe. I didn't think he could find a record of the birth anywhere anyway, but just in case.

"Just a couple more growth spurts and he'll be ready for tee-ball." He handed the keys back to the baby as I ripped up some pieces of bread for him to nibble on. He loved picking up his own food and went after it immediately, scrunching his little face into the most adorable grin when he plucked up a chunk on the first try.

"'Look at me, Mom.' Can't you just hear him thinking it?" Cam asked.

"I can. I wasn't aware anyone else could."

"Half of being a good cop is being a good observer."

I nodded and stuffed a bite of chicken Alfredo in my mouth.

I didn't need Sheriff Good Observer getting any further under my skin. Or my anything else, either.

Keep telling yourself that, girl.

I shoveled the rest of my food in my face so fast it was a wonder I didn't look like I'd bathed in the Alfredo sauce before I was finished. By the time I looked up, Cam had put his fork down and leaned back in his chair to watch me, horror and fascination, with maybe a smidge of boyish admiration, plain on his face.

I retrieved the napkin from my lap and wiped my face and chin. When I opened my mouth to tell him I'd beaten him, a fraternity party champion belch came out instead of the words.

Clapping both hands over my mouth, I felt my face flush with heat just as the baby started to cry.

"I think you scared him." Cam laughed, reaching over to rub my son's back.

The ten fingers between my lips and the air were the only thing that kept me from blurting out "I was hoping it scared you," because at least if it had, I could've been relieved instead of humiliated.

The waitress dropped the check folio on the table and smirked at me. "Classy."

Cam actually stuck his tongue out at her back as she walked away.

I shook my head and dropped my hands to the table, turning to my son so I didn't have to look at Cam. "It's just not Mommy's day, is it, boo boo?"

He blinked at me and stuffed a bit of bread into his mouth.

"And here I thought I was doing okay." Cam put both hands over his heart and leaned back in his chair.

I laughed. "Letting out a burp that escaped from an old eighties frat movie is even humiliating in front of a friend, I'm afraid."

He sat up straight. "Two things about me: I find burps

funny because that part of being twelve has never grown out of me, and I would really like to be more than just your friend."

I shot him a look and he nodded. "That's okay. I can wait."

He pulled out his wallet and reached for the little black folder, and I shook my head. "I'll pay for mine."

He paused with his hand in midair. "I really would like to buy you dinner. As a friend. No strings. But I won't argue if it really matters to you to pay for your own."

Jesus, what are you doing to me? It's a wonder I didn't say that right out loud, too.

It was a punishment, that's what it was. Straight from God. The first time in my life I'd ever wanted a man like this, and it had to be the freaking sheriff, who my best friend had a raging crush on.

Served me right on a lot of levels when I really thought about it. Which was exactly why I didn't want to.

I locked eyes with him for as long as I could stand it, and read nothing but earnest kindness in his.

I nodded. "That's very kind of you. Thank you." *Maybe I'll get it next time.* I did not say that.

He winked. "You can get it next time if you really want to."

Completely unfair. I stood and picked up the baby and his bag, pressing a finger into the front of his diaper. I could tell he was wet by the squish, and it was getting late—no way he'd make it home without falling asleep with all the excitement today.

"I have to change him," I said, smiling at Cam. "I don't want to leave you standing around with your best friend over there at work tonight. But this was fun. Thank you for inviting us, and thank you for dinner."

"I'll wait." He stuck his hands in his pockets and pointed to the front doors. "It's nice out tonight, but I wouldn't feel right not walking y'all to your car. Dangerous neighborhood here."

"What neighborhood? It's one street, and an angry kitten is about the most dangerous thing on it."

"What can I say? Momma raised a gentleman. Can't go letting her down now."

I rolled my eyes and turned for the ladies' room. "Suit yourself."

I changed the baby like an expert and then balanced him on my hip and used my free hand to splash some water on my face.

"Punishment. Not temptation," I told my reflection, willing my cheeks to stop flushing and wishing I had foregone makeup altogether.

We stepped outside into the kind of crisp air that meant October was coming on quick, and Cam pushed himself away from the brown brick wall of the building and took the diaper bag from my shoulder. "Let me help, at least."

We walked a half block in silence before I stopped next to my truck. "This is us, officer."

"And where do you ride, partner?" he asked the baby.

"In a proper seat in the back, according to the law." I couldn't help smiling.

"You're a good mom."

Something about the way he said it made my whole heart swell. I whirled quickly for the truck and opened the door, settling the baby in the bucket seat he was just about to outgrow and buckling him in, centering the top clip over his chest and checking to make sure the straps weren't too tight.

"Thanks," I said to Cam. "I try."

I shut the door and turned back and he caught my hand in midair, brushing his lips across my knuckles.

Electricity rocketed up my arm with a force that nearly made my knees buckle.

It took every brain cell's full power just to stay upright and still and pull my hand back slowly.

All that nonsense I'd told Ainsley about sex was just that:

nonsense. In real life, my actual, past life, I'd done it willingly a whole one time with a boy who lived in my granny's trailer park when I was sixteen, and it was sweaty and messy and over in about ninety seconds. And I didn't get what the big deal was at all.

Standing there with Cam Blankenship's lips burned into the back of my hand, trying not to let him see my arm tremble, I figured it out.

"That wasn't flattery," he said, taking a step back that allowed me to breathe again. "You're really good with him. He's a lucky little guy." His brow furrowed. "I... did I not ever ask you his name?"

I swallowed hard. He had not. Nobody but Ainsley had, actually, though she didn't ever say it—I assumed because I didn't. And I couldn't even say why, really. It wasn't like it would give us away anyway, so why didn't I ever want to say it?

"Cory. His name is Cory." My voice was so soft a light breeze would've carried the words right away across the prairie.

Cam's mouth slid to one side. "After his father?"

The more time I spent around him, the more I didn't want to lie to him. So I just dropped my gaze to my shoes and stayed quiet.

"I'm sorry," he said. "I didn't mean to pry. I heard through the local grapevine that he passed on. That must be so hard."

"It wasn't easy." There, that wasn't a lie.

He rocked up onto the balls of his feet as I stowed the diaper bag in the seat. "Thank you," I said. "I had a really good time tonight."

"Don't sound so surprised, it's bad for my ego."

"I don't think there's much that's bad for your ego."

"You might be." His eyes locked on mine and the stark-naked longing in them straight stole my breath. "We'll see. Y'all drive safely."

I'm not sure my heart stopped pounding before we turned

into the long driveway at the farm. The baby had been asleep before we turned off Main Street toward home, and I had driven the entire way thinking about Cam's... everything, really. And wishing for the first time since we came here that my life had gone differently. Had brought me here with the kind of past that wouldn't make me afraid of what I felt.

"But it didn't, and we deal with what is, not what we wish," I said firmly to the empty passenger seat as I parked and shut off the engine. "And right now what is, is that I forgot the porch light and the baby is asleep. Thank goodness for a full moon."

Bucket seat in one hand and diaper bag in the other, I didn't see the possum until it nearly hit me in the face.

Stumbling back down the steps, I managed to avoid dropping the baby seat and stay on my feet. I could not stop myself from screaming, but it was short and Cory was so exhausted he didn't so much as twitch an eyelid. Moving slowly to the other side of the steps in a wide arc, I kept my eyes on the critter swinging from the porch ceiling by its own entrails, its mouth frozen in a snarl, its glassy eyes wide and staring. I peered into the darkness, walking up the far edge of the steps and shoving the front door open.

I should've turned the light on before I stepped into the house.

My flimsy summer flat was no match for the dagger-shaped chunk of broken vase waiting just inside.

TWENTY-FOUR

Meg
September

I didn't scream.

I couldn't tell you how for love or money, only that I didn't. A whimper fought its way past my lips as my shoe filled with wet, sticky warmth when the glass stabbed through it, but that was the only noise. The baby's breathing was louder than my reaction.

I flipped the light on, setting his car seat carefully in a relatively bare spot and pulling the sunshade up to keep the light dim around him. Perching on the stool inside the door, I crossed my bleeding foot over the opposite knee and grabbed the thick piece of glass that had sliced through my shoe and into the pad of my foot. I closed my teeth around the soft part of my other hand, under my thumb.

"One. Two." I pulled, biting blood out of my other hand. "That. Hurt." I huffed when my jaw had relaxed enough to whisper.

Taking short breaths, I hobbled on my heel across the wet

floor, picking my way around the glass as best I could—some of the vases had smashed into my hardwood with such force the pellets left were little more than sand—and retrieving the first aid kit from under the kitchen sink.

I slid the shoe off and put it directly into the garbage, propping my calf on the edge of the sink to run water over the cut. My breath hissed in through my teeth when the cold water connected with my injured foot, and I felt a little lightheaded and a lot nauseated.

"Grow up, it's just water," I muttered, leaning forward so I could see it. Not that I really wanted to look, but I needed to.

Five seconds later, I wished I hadn't. The gash was an angry shade of purple-red, blood streaming out of it about as freely as water poured from the faucet. Lucky for me, I'd long since lost my squeamish stomach where blood was concerned, thanks in part to having to clean so much of it up. Being more worried about leaving a stray drop that could send you to prison than you are about feeling sick will cure that quick, it turns out.

"Stop the bleeding." That was the first thing I had to do, before enough ran out that I actually did pass out. I couldn't allow that, I had a baby to take care of.

I twisted one arm behind me, groping for the dishtowel that hung on a drawer pull next to the sink. It wasn't exactly clean, but I'd rather risk germs than bleeding to death on my glass-strewn kitchen floor.

My hand found the towel and I held it up like a trophy for a second before I realized I had no idea how to go about this. I knew pressure was the goal, because last time I had to stop someone from bleeding to death I'd had to apply pressure, and that's what they always did on TV shows, too. But I couldn't really put a lot of pressure on my foot with just my fingers. I didn't want to put my foot on the floor, either, though—I figured whatever good the pressure did might be canceled out by gravity.

I shut off the water and hobbled to a chair, perching on the edge and propping my injured foot on the opposite knee, choosing leverage over brute strength, which had never been among my gifts. I folded the towel into thirds, then centered the band across the wound, pulling the ends around my foot and pinching them together under my toes, yanking tight with my left hand and using my right palm to press from the bottom.

The towel soaked through in seconds, but over the next two minutes, the spot spread slower and slower. I felt my breathing and heart rate slow as I realized it was working.

"I didn't live through a sad, scary childhood in a trailer park and kill two people to be killed in my own house by a bouquet," I said. "I mean, maybe it would serve me right, but it's not happening tonight. Not when I finally have people to live for."

I meant my son, really, but the thought of Ainsley followed right behind that, grabbing my heart and squeezing until I couldn't breathe and tears ran down my cheeks faster than they could drip from my chin, my eyes surveying the damage.

"How could she do this?" I whispered.

Every time I blinked, I saw the cold, flat look she'd worn as she watched me drive away a few hours ago. If the Pope himself had tried to tell me yesterday that Ainsley was even capable of making a face like that, I'd have called him crazy.

But I had seen it.

I thought I knew better, but that look sure said she hated my guts.

I cried harder than I had since my sister died—and it wasn't until then that I realized what I'd been doing, all these weeks I'd spent with Ainsley. She was older than my sister had been. Than my sister would ever be. But not enough to matter. She was sunny and kind, and smart and capable.

I was happy here because of the house and the farm and my son. All of that was true. But it was equally true that in the months since I'd met Ainsley, the hole losing my little sister had left in my heart had started, for the first time, to scab over. The girl next door had filled a void I thought nothing ever would.

I loved her with my whole heart, and feeling it shatter like one of these broken vases as I looked around at the mess and thought about that poor animal outside—well. That hurt a damn sight worse than the hole in my foot did.

How in the world had I gotten myself into this mess? Letting my chin slump into my collarbone, I sobbed quietly, ever mindful of disturbing the baby.

"I never meant for any of this to happen," I said. I didn't even want to go to stupid dinner with the sheriff who was too charming for his own good—well, for my own good, at any rate. But I was afraid making him mad would cause trouble for us.

Seemed like trouble came barging right in no matter how hard I tried to keep it out.

Like she was sitting across the table, I heard my Granny's voice clearer than I had since the day she died. "I used to think you were born with your daddy's gift for finding trouble. Now I know it finds you, even when you don't go looking for it. Thank the good Lord you also got a knack for digging yourself out of even the deepest holes. You're everything to that baby boy your momma should've been to you, and I have never been prouder. Chin up. You got a mess to put right."

I snapped my head up and looked around, but I was alone in my kitchen.

I guess I just knew her so well that I knew what she'd say if she was there, because that was exactly it.

And she was right, as usual. I did have a mess to clean up.

I peeled the bloody towel back and peeked under it, letting out a slow breath when I saw the blood had slowed to a trickle. I fumbled with the first aid kit and came up with some antibiotic ointment and a roll of gauze, and went to work making a thick pad to go directly over the cut and then wrapping my foot and taping it good. It took the whole roll, but I was pretty sure I'd done a good enough job. I wasn't at all sure I didn't need stitches, but I wasn't going to the hospital to find out, either.

Standing, I surveyed the floor. The area near the sink was one of the only ones not nearly obscured by a layer of shattered glass. The other was the baby's playpen.

That was how I knew for sure, in my bones, that Ainsley did this. Because no matter how mad she was at me, she wouldn't ever do anything to hurt him.

I stood, spinning on my good heel with my injured foot bent up behind me like a flamingo, then resting my knee on the seat of the chair I'd just vacated. When I had my balance good, I picked up the chair and hopped forward, putting it down and resting my knee on it.

Not the ideal way to clean a house with a sleeping infant.

"How about this then?" I lifted the chair and scooted it forward a bit, then led with the injured leg, resting my knee on the seat and taking a step with my good foot.

Slow, but much more comfortable. Also quieter and less tiring.

I felt a small smile creep across my lips. Granny might have been right about trouble hunting me for sport, but she was also right about me finding a way to get myself out of it. Or at least past it, even if sometimes that was by the very thin skin of my nose.

I used the chair to hobble over to the corner where the broom and dustpan lived, since I couldn't vacuum a single shard before I'd mopped up all the water that had been soaking into my hardwood floors for hours, probably. And to mop, first I had to sweep.

From the corner of the kitchen by the back door, I surveyed the house. And very nearly fell out bawling all over again.

I'd be up all night trying to clean this up, hobbling around on my little makeshift walker, but I only had the one shoe, and my injured foot was throbbing without any weight on it.

"Story of my life." I braced my knee on the chair and got to it, pulling the nearby glass into a pile and thanking my lucky stars I'd splurged the extra seven dollars for the dustpan with the long handle. That was, if ridiculous, at least a tiny bright spot in all this. I might just take the baby and go back to the truck and head west if I'd had to bend down to pick up the glass piles.

I wondered if anyone else ever thought about abandoning their entire life over what kind of dustpan they had in their kitchen. The thought was so absurd it made me giggle, and once I started, I couldn't stop. It was worse than the tears.

I pinched my lips between my teeth to keep the noise level down, but the fit went on until that hurt and I had to relax them.

Here it was: a date I didn't even want to go on, a dead animal hanging from the porch, and a ransacked house, and I had finally lost my mind.

I always figured it would happen sooner or later. There's only so much one person can take.

The giggles proved useful for one thing: distraction. I noticed when they finally faded that the kitchen floor was clean. Still wet, but I had gotten most of the glass and flowers up, dragging the garbage can behind me so I could empty the dustpan when needed.

And somehow, that made the rest of it look more possible.

I moved the chair slowly, checking on my sleeping little one. He looked like a baby angel, the very best bits of the people who made him shining from his adorable face and his sweet little heart.

I had gotten us out of worse messes than this.

And while my heart was hurt that Ainsley had done this, I knew her well enough to know hers must've practically been bleeding when she came back in here.

Even if I didn't understand how she could be so upset over a crush, that didn't mean she wasn't. I knew Ainsley. Her heart was kind and good.

Wasn't it?

The more glass I swept up, the more I started to wonder if I really knew as much as I thought I did. By the time I traded the broom for the mop, I wasn't at all sure things in Cottonwood County were what I thought they were.

Ainsley had talked to me a lot the past few months, but she'd never mentioned Cam Blankenship until we ran into him on her birthday.

If he mattered this much to her... why not?

She hadn't mentioned SarahBeth's accident, either, and Cam said it had really turned her life upside down.

What else hadn't she told me? Did I know my friend as well as I liked to think?

Or had I simply wanted a new sister so badly that I made her fit that mold?

I pulled out the photo of my sister that I'd stashed in a drawer the day I met Ainsley, tracing her smile with one finger and staring into her wide, kind eyes. She flat wouldn't have been capable of so much as ripping the head off a single daisy.

How much of the love I felt for Ainsley was about Emma, and how much was about Ainsley?

A loaded question if there ever was one. But it seemed like something I ought to figure out before our lives got any more intertwined with the Godfreys.

I mean, I knew better than anyone how good some folks can be at keeping secrets. Had I assumed too quickly that the family next door didn't have any skeletons in their closets? I tucked the photo frame back in the drawer, next to one of me with another girl I'd thought not long ago might help dull the pain of watching a bullet meant for me leave a neat round hole in Emma's smooth porcelain-skinned forehead.

Maybe everyone would be better off if I left Ainsley

Godfrey alone—when I thought about it, people I loved like sisters tended to end up dead. Or worse.

The first faint light of dawn peeked through my curtains as I closed the drawer, lifted Cory's seat, and put my injured foot on the clean floor, limping gingerly toward my bedroom.

After I locked all the doors.

TWENTY-FIVE

Ainsley
September

I saw Cam Blankenship's truck turn into our driveway from the door of the barn not long after the sun came up.

I'd never make it to the house before he did, lugging four full pails of milk, so I set them on a workbench just inside the barn door. "Bethany, y'all bring this milk up with you, I'm going to start breakfast," I called.

"Why can't you take it?" I heard her question fade out as I ran for the house, so if she complained any more I missed it.

No, no, no, no, no. It reverberated in my head with every footfall as I pushed my legs to go faster than they'd ever gone. I had to get to Cam before he got to Momma. It was as simple as that.

I rounded the corner of the porch and pulled up short as he shut the door to the truck. He was carrying something white. Was that a sweater?

"Hey there, Ainsley," he called. "Just who I was looking for. I figured y'all would be up and after chores already."

Why did his smile make my knees go right to water? I struggled to stay upright and catch my breath. Did he say he was looking for me? My skin went clammy from hairline to feet.

"Morning, Cam." My voice shook, but hopefully he wouldn't notice that. "Why in the world are you looking for me?"

"Wondering if you've seen Meg this morning." His dark eyebrows drew into a concerned V over the top of his nose. He was even handsome when he looked worried.

Not that I had any business noticing that. I wasn't stupid. The ridiculous number of bouquets in Meg's house was definitely the reason she had come here every day this week before I'd finished my chores. Secret admirer, my hind end—they were from Cam and I knew it.

She had won. And the really sad part of that was that I still believed her when she'd said she wasn't even competing. She didn't really want him, but he wanted her. And I'd seen this enough times to know he'd break her eventually. There had never been a woman in this part of the state who managed to resist Cam for long. What I had fantasized about Cam wasn't probably ever going to be, anyway. With time to think, I'd realized after my birthday that he wouldn't ever see me as anything but the little girl hanging on the fence at his baseball games, no matter if I was twenty or fifty. And if he wanted Meg—well, I knew he had a good heart, and she'd lost her husband.

Maybe God sent Cam to her. And who was I to resent that? I certainly hadn't earned any favors from on high.

"I haven't." I gestured to the sunrise, glowing orange behind the front barn. "But it's early yet. I've seen her most days this week before seven." I bit my lip, sizing him up. Did I really want to know? "I guess she might sleep in today if you had her out late last night."

I blurted it out before I could rethink it.

He chuckled, but the worried slouch to his forehead didn't relax. "She left Main Street at a decent hour, Scout's honor."

"We don't have Scouts here." The hair on my arms stood straight up, though I didn't fully understand why. Why did he look so concerned? "What's wrong?"

"Nothing." He said it too fast. "I went by there this morning to drop off her sweater, she left it at the table last night and the manager brought it out to me after she left."

"You're not telling the whole truth," I said, too worried about Meg and the baby to concern myself with things like Momma's coaching on being demure with men, not ever confronting them about little things. She'd done that with Papa and look where it got her.

"I don't really know." Cam sighed. "That's why I'm here, I was hoping you might be able to help me. She loves you, and I got the feeling y'all spend a fair amount of time together."

"We do. I love her too." Sour panic rose in my throat. "You could've left the sweater on her porch, you don't need my help with that. Tell me why you look worried."

"The truck is there, but she didn't come to the door and there was..." he trailed off.

"There was what?" The look on his face had my heart rate picking up.

"It's disturbing and you live right by her. Maybe I shouldn't have come here." He took a step backward.

"Cam, tell me, or I'm going over there. And then you'll land me in hot water with Momma when breakfast isn't ready."

"There was a possum, hanging from the roof of the porch. By its uh... insides." He swallowed hard and looked at the ground. "I was wondering if you had seen her, or if you might know why she'd have that there."

"She did not have that there," I said, my own insides turning to ice as the sun blazed up over the barn. "I... Meg didn't do that. Did you check inside the house when she didn't come to the door?"

"It was locked," he said. "I don't have a warrant or anything..."

I didn't hear the rest of what he said as I spun and ran for the hill that separated my home from Meg's.

I'd almost lied right to Cam's face and said I had no idea how such a horrifying thing could have happened, but I couldn't make the words come out. Not to him.

If anything had happened to my friend or her baby, it would be all my fault. And I wasn't sure how I could live with that.

TWENTY-SIX

Meg
September

I was trapped in a nightmare.

I knew it was a nightmare, somehow, but it felt so real I woke up with tears pouring down my cheeks. And... was that Ainsley's face pressed up against the bedroom window? She rapped on the glass, and I could hear my name faintly, in a strangled, desperate voice.

What in the world? I wiped my face on the sheet and tried to push the sleep away long enough to understand what was happening.

Dear God, my head swam like I was coming out of a three-day bender. I wasn't sure for several blinks what was going on, but I did know it wasn't that. Somewhere in the day-to-day of learning to run the farm and caring for my son, it seemed I had learned to have some faith in myself. Who would've thought?

Speaking of my baby... I patted the sheets frantically for a few seconds, the screams from yesterday afternoon rushing back, the dream crowding in at the edges until I leapt from the bed like I'd seen a snake, just as he started fussing.

Two things happened at the same time: my injured foot hit the floor way harder than I would've let it if I had remembered hurting it before I got up, and I spotted the baby in his bucket seat and remembered how he got there.

Last night. This morning, whatever. The glass. The flowers. Ainsley.

"Hey, baby boy," I said through gritted teeth as the rest of last night flooded back quickly. See? I hadn't lost it to booze. Just to good old-fashioned exhaustion.

I turned back to the window, but Ainsley wasn't there. Maybe that had still been part of my bad dream?

My son picked the moment I was standing in my bedroom—in my spotted puppy pajamas staring at the place I could've sworn I'd seen Ainsley's face—to kick both feet and rattle the window glass with a scream.

I hurried to him, unbuckling his belts and lifting him out of the seat. His little back and head were damp with sweat, and his diaper was bloated and squishy.

I grabbed a diaper from the dresser and laid him on the bed since there hadn't been any glass in the bedroom and my feet were bare. I'd just changed him when the front door rattled in its frame, someone pounding like they wanted to knock it down.

The baby's eyes widened, his face scrunching up to cry again before I picked him up. "Momma's got you, buddy."

"Meg!" Cam's voice boomed from the other side of the front door. "Meg, can you come open this door?"

I hadn't been asleep but a couple of hours, but damned if I could figure out what was going on here this morning.

I gave the window where I thought I'd seen Ainsley one last glance as I jammed my feet into slippers and tried to hurry out of the bedroom.

"Hold on," I called, limping to the door on one foot and one heel.

"Is everything okay?" Cam looked taller than he had just last night, his frame filling the entire doorway such that sunlight barely fought its way past his broad shoulders.

"I was up all night, so I was still asleep." I wiped at my face, thinking for the first time what I must look like, and then thinking that was just as well. I wouldn't carry anything on with him that could hurt Ainsley, and some flowers and one dinner had very obviously upset her.

Should she have wrecked my house and left the floor strewn with broken glass? Absolutely not. Would I forgive her after we'd had a chance to talk? I hoped I could.

Which meant I had to find a way around Cam. No matter how many shocks and shivers I got when he looked at me or brushed my hand with his lips. No matter what. If I upset him... well, baby Cory and I had government quality papers, and I hadn't broken a law in Kansas. Maybe I had been too worried about what he might be able to figure out. Hopefully.

"Up all night?" Cam echoed, looking over my shoulder and scanning the room before his eyes landed on my son. "You have a rough time with that head bump, little man?" He tweaked the baby's bare toe and I turned so that Cory was on the hip further away from the sheriff.

"He's okay. I hurt my foot and had trouble falling asleep, that's all," I said.

"What did you do?" Cam's face softened, the worry filling his eyes so inviting I had an absurd urge to step toward him. I knew in my gut in a way I couldn't explain that he'd open his arms and I could rest my head on his chest and put down so much of what I'd been carrying in my heart for so long.

If only I'd come here for other reasons. From other places.

If only it wouldn't break Ainsley's heart.

If only the baby yanking cheerfully on a handful of my hair was really mine.

Cam Blankenship couldn't be my safe harbor, and I needed to stop trying to reason my way past that fact.

"I dropped a glass," I said. "Cut myself. No big deal. What can I do for you so early, sheriff?"

His face flinched when I hit the last word too hard, like he heard in those two syllables he'd been relegated back to his official role.

He held out my white cardigan. "You left this at the table last night," he said. "I wanted to return it before it got coffee spilled on it in my truck."

"That's nice of you to come all the way out here. So early." I felt my eyebrow go up. There was something he wasn't saying. But right then I just wanted him off my porch and mostly out of my life before he noticed...

"You got tired of the daisies?"

Too late.

I squeezed my eyes shut. "Not tired," I said. "I just... Little Bit is moving around easier these days, and it occurred to me that it was a lot of glass, all over the house." I flashed a smile. "After I cut my foot, you see. I just got worried about him getting hurt and... well. They really were beautiful."

He held my gaze for I don't know how long, but he didn't say another word. When he finally nodded, I almost reached for his arm.

I hated this. No matter what I did here I was going to hurt someone who didn't deserve it.

"Cam, I got everything out here," Ainsley's voice came from behind him and I squeezed the baby tighter, images from that godawful nightmare crowding my thoughts.

It wasn't real.

I almost said that right out loud.

When Cam seemed to shrink with the sigh he let out I realized he'd been standing on his tiptoes and holding his shoulders out wide the entire time we talked.

"Ainsley?" I peered around him, panicking when I remembered the possum from last night.

She smiled at me like yesterday never happened.

My eyes scanned the porch.

The possum wasn't there.

"Have a good day, ladies. Stay out of trouble, little man." Cam tipped his hat before he climbed back into his truck. No one said a word about a mutilated animal dangling from my front porch. Maybe I really was losing my mind.

Ainsley jogged up the steps, holding her skirts up above her ankles, and swept past us into the house.

"I'm sorry we woke you," she said. "Cam came to our place looking for you and I was trying to help him. I wanted to make sure you were okay."

I followed her to the kitchen, where she grabbed my milk pails and headed out the back door.

"Ainsley, where are you going?" I called, trying and failing to catch up.

"You can't run a farm with a hole in your foot," she called over her shoulder. "The cow still has to be milked."

"You have chores at your own house."

She stopped and turned back, the look on her face the kind of serious I hadn't seen from her before. It didn't resemble the flat, dark hatred I'd seen just twelve hours ago either, though.

She looked... sad. Or regretful, maybe.

"They'll figure it out," she said, swinging the pails at her side. "I won't have you getting hurt worse."

"It's just a cut," I said, my throat tight. I had been so sure, sitting alone and bleeding in the dark, that she'd smashed the flowers all over the house. Standing there looking at her in the sunshine, I couldn't tell. Had I assumed something entirely unfair? "I can't ask you to come work here until it's better, Ains-ley, it's a deep cut. That's not fair."

She shook her head. "You didn't ask, I offered. And I don't believe a word of that story you told Cam. I'm sorry about what you came home to last night, Meg. But I promise it won't ever happen again."

The words hung thick in the air until she disappeared into the barn.

TWENTY-SEVEN

Ainsley
September

I had wanted to punch my brother right in the throat plenty of times—we were so close in age I literally couldn't remember a time when Alexander wasn't irritating me on a regular basis.

But I'd never wanted to stab him in the eye or strangle the life out of him until the night before Bethany's fifteenth birthday.

It started the minute Meg knocked on the door.

Bethany's face lit up. "The baby is here!" She ran for the door. Alexander jumped to his feet and beat her there, his long legs eating up the floor as he smoothed his hair. I stared, swallowing hard.

"Good to see you, Meg," Alexander's voice boomed a little too loud from the front door.

"It's *my* birthday," Bethany grumbled quietly. She was too much like Momma to question a man's actions, especially in front of a guest.

"I the baby," Francine protested from her spot on the rug, stacking colored rings on a stick.

Claire patted her leg. "We can have more than one baby, Frannie."

"She's right, sweet girl." And if I was right about the reason Momma had been so exhausted and irritable lately, we might well have one of our own in the spring. "You're still just as special."

Francine nodded and dumped her stack off, starting over.

I clicked on the television for distraction when I heard Meg's voice from the front of the house—it would take the awkwardness out of Meg and me not talking. Momma wouldn't know I was breaking the rules, she'd gone up to lay down before dinner for the first time since before Francine was born. A news show was on, which we usually weren't supposed to watch because Momma said they were too sad, but I couldn't really focus anyway. I set the volume to a tolerable background level and straightened the sofa pillows.

I was kind of glad Bethany was more excited to see little Cory than she was to see Meg. Things had been different between Meg and me these past two weeks, and I didn't need the added worry that my little sister was going to take my place. Bethany, with her straight, shampoo-commercial glossy dark hair, her petite figure, and her pert nose, already had everything I was supposed to want: she was always right up under Momma, showing off that she was the best at sewing and bread-making. If I had a nickel for every time I'd heard Momma say Bethany would make a fine wife, I could buy myself a train ticket out of here. I flat refused to lose Meg to Bethany, too. And I was losing Meg. Maybe even had already lost her and just couldn't admit it. I had climbed out of my tangled sheets in the middle of the night for two weeks now to keep up with my own chores plus milking her cow, picking the last of summer's cucumbers and tomatoes from her little garden, and cleaning her floors. I still worried about glass shards after daily sweeping and mopping, though Meg said every day she hadn't seen or felt a single one. But that was about all she said, other than being over the top grateful for my help.

We didn't talk—not about the baby or Cam or the daisies. Especially not about the secrets that were slowly eating me from the inside out. I had thought, not long ago, that Meg might understand. That I had finally found someone I could trust to see my heart above my sins. That I was right about the impossible position I'd been in. I'd had daydreams of telling her and getting a hug instead of horrified silence or banishment.

And then she went to dinner with Cam and everything else went to hell.

My heart ached with the loss of not just a friend, but a sister, and I had no one to talk to about it... again. Maybe this was my particular curse. How many losses and secrets could a soul accumulate before it flat couldn't take anymore? And what happened then? Those questions had kept me up enough nights that I had purple smudges under my eyes that wouldn't go away. Would I explode? Stop caring about anything? Just fade away? I wasn't even sure any of that was worse than the purgatory I'd lived in for the past three years.

"Meg and the baby are here," Bethany announced from the doorway with all the enthusiasm of a teenager who was almost never allowed to have guests. "I have strawberries and cheese in the kitchen, and dinner should be ready in just a little bit."

"Let me take your jacket." Alexander's voice came from behind me, his words slow and deliberate—and free of his usual accent. "Your dress looks nice."

"Thank you." A perfect stranger would've recognized the guarded tone in Meg's reply. "Bethany said she wanted everyone to dress up. I don't think I've ever seen you in anything but overalls or jeans."

"I only have this one pair of slacks," Alexander said,

sounding more relaxed. "I was glad they still fit, I haven't worn them in almost a year. Since Old Man Lester's funeral."

They moved awkwardly through the living room doorway, with Meg stopping and then Alexander, towering over her, gesturing for her to go first.

Meg didn't so much as look at me.

But she also wasn't looking at him, which was probably to his benefit, since he was obviously infatuated with her. I'd always found his smile creepy. It was too wide, especially when he was nervous. Momma said he got it from her father, though we had no way to know that because not even Papa had ever met the man, he'd been dead for years by the time they took up with each other.

"That's nice that y'all went." Meg picked up a glass of iced tea from the tray Bethany had put on the coffee table. I'd tried to tell her that she wasn't supposed to do all the work for her own birthday party, but she insisted that all she wanted for her birthday was to be able to throw a party, even if we were only allowed one guest who could eat the food. "I heard Old Man Lester didn't really have anyone. Did you know him well?"

Her voice was just a little too high, with the smallest tremble. Why was she nervous about asking that? I tipped my head to the side and met Alexander's eyes over her head, twitching my eyebrows up.

"I reckon I knew him better than most folks," he said. "I used to help out over there a lot. He didn't have any family or farm hands, and he was pretty useless for farm life there at the end."

"What kind of st—"

Meg's words cut off and her glass hit the floor and shattered with the tinkling of a thousand bells, shards shooting off in every direction.

I jumped to my feet and put one hand on Francine's head, her hair as soft as goose down under my fingers. My own was prickly and thick, with just enough curl to be frizzy, but not so much as to be pretty unless I slept in poky curlers. I'd been jealous of Bethany and Francine's hair their entire lives. Did that make me a terrible person?

"Bethany, we need a broom," I called, my eyes on Meg's face.

She hadn't moved, except to press her fingers to her lips, her eyes on the TV.

It almost looked like she might cry. What in the world?

I turned, paying attention to the screen for the first time since I'd clicked it on.

A policeman with shaggy dark hair Momma would definitely call "too long" was standing on the steps of a big white building—maybe a courthouse or capitol building—and the bottom of the screen read "Arkansas State Police bust human trafficking ring" and underneath "Most arrests in US history, hundreds of victims rescued."

"Lieutenant, is it true that you started this investigation in sort of rogue-mode, without an assignment?" a reporter asked.

The policeman, who had a dark goatee and eyes so green they practically glowed on the screen, laughed. "I've never done well with doing as I'm told. But I'm so proud today to say we've arrested forty-eight offenders involved with this Dixie Mafia syndicate and returned hundreds of people to their families throughout the region."

"What about the ones who didn't have families?" I couldn't swear that Meg actually whispered that, it was too low for me to be sure. But that's what I thought I heard.

"We've made safe house foster care placements for some of the victims as well, and want to thank the department of children and families here in Little Rock for their assistance there. This is the kind of day that made me want to be a cop, folks. We helped a lot of people and made our state safer today, thanks to one very lucky break and your tax dollars. That's all for now, appreciate you coming out."

"No harm no foul," Bethany said behind me, the glass tinkling as she swept it into the dustpan, and stood. Her lips pinched into a thin line like they always did when she lied. Annoyance at a blemish—however small—on her perfect evening settled over her face like a dime store Halloween mask.

I shook my head and blinked, my eyes still on Meg, who was nodding to herself, her lips pressed to the baby's head and her eyes closed. Alexander had disappeared in search of a towel for the tea that had splashed onto his slacks, and Claire was busy keeping Francine's attention on the toy while Bethany cleaned. Daisy was in the kitchen watching the soup Bethany wanted to serve before dinner.

So I was the only person watching Meg.

She opened her eyes and they met mine, and I nearly fell over from the relief and guilt I read in hers. Maybe because I knew her better than I'd feared these past few weeks. Maybe because something in me recognized a fellow traveler since I knew those feelings all too well.

I tipped my lips up into a small smile and nodded. "I'll get the mop."

I hurried to the pantry, puzzle pieces fitting themselves together in my head as I walked. Could you know someone, really, when they had a monstrous secret? I had struggled with that for months now, thinking I was good as lying to Meg by hiding the things I'd done.

Picking up the mop and the bottle of Pine-Sol, I took a deep breath.

A young woman alone, with a good deal of money, a new baby, and a "dead husband."

I'd actually assumed that husband bit. She'd told me the baby's father was dead. I remembered specifically because I thought the phrasing was odd; I had asked about her husband and she'd said "his father."

Had Meg been a victim of whatever in blazes a "human trafficking ring" was? I didn't quite know for sure what that meant—like I said, Momma doesn't like us watching the news—but I could guess well enough, I reckoned.

And if she'd been a victim of something so terrible, how had she escaped? Had she maybe even killed someone, too? What were the chances?

Maybe we were on more equal footing than I would've ever guessed.

By the time I got back to the living room with the mop, Francine was showing baby Cory how her toy worked, Bethany was serving fruit and cheese from a platter we usually used for Thanksgiving, and Alexander had returned. Someone had turned off the TV, too.

"His bump is all healed," Bethany said, kneeling next to Meg's baby on the rug. She kissed his soft brown curls and glanced at Meg. "I bet you haven't left him on the bed for a second, have you?"

Meg laughed. "Am I that obvious? I've been making him sleep strapped in his car seat, which he does not like a bit."

Bethany frowned. "They taught us in Home Ec that it isn't safe for babies to sleep in those car seats. The incline can make their little heads fall forward and block their airway."

Meg's hand flew back to her lips, her eyes going to her little boy. "I didn't know—"

I pasted a smile on and stepped toward Meg, patting her arm. "That's news to me, too, Meg. I think our little buddy here holds his head up plenty well enough to escape suffocating in his seat."

"But—" Bethany began.

"I remember you sleeping in the baby swing for months when you were little." I stared at her, forcing the words through a tight smile. "Momma said it helped your reflux. And you're fine, aren't you? Meg is only trying to keep him safe."

Alexander scratched his head. "What?"

"The baby fell off her bed and bopped his head," I explained. "She doesn't want him to do it again."

His eyes lit up, an eager smile spreading too far on his face. It truly was like the Joker from the old *Batman* show Papa liked, but without the cuts or makeup. "You need a crib, then, right? That's where babies are supposed to sleep anyhow."

"I do, but I haven't seen a furniture store around here," Meg said.

"Don't need one, we got a crib you can have." Alexander grinned and the skin on my arms prickled as Meg averted her eyes. So I wasn't the only one who didn't like it when my brother smiled.

"I'm pretty sure Francine is still using ours." I said to Alexander. "Sorry, Meg."

Alexander shook his head. "No, not that one. The one out in the storm shelter. You know, in the back room? There's one in there."

Until right then I didn't know it was possible to want to punch someone in the throat to shut them up while needing to vomit all at the same time.

Bethany stood up, eyeing our brother. "I'm pretty sure Frannie's crib is the only one we have," she said. "There's nothing but old camp beds in there."

"No, there ain't," Alexander frowned. "I've seen the crib with my own two eyes. It's just sitting out there and Meg could use it. What's the matter with y'all?"

"Let's go sit down for dinner." Bethany pretended he hadn't spoken.

"Alexander," I said, a pleading note in my voice I hoped only he would notice.

Meg turned to me. "Are you okay?"

I flashed a quick smile. "Fine. Just wondering if we're going to need to move the table." I poked my brother. "Come help me."

"Bethany can help you." He scowled, turning for the mudroom. "I'm going to go get that crib. We'll clean it up good as new for you, Meg."

Damn his stupid stubborn streak.

"It'd be so nice for him to have a bed of his own. I can help you move it, and I'll get it cleaned up myself, too," Meg said, glancing at Claire. "Can you keep an eye on the baby? I imagine they'll just play until we get back."

I stood there with my jaw loose and not a single good thing in my head that I could say to stop them.

Maybe it was all for the best. I'd carried these secrets for so long I didn't remember what my heart felt like without the extra weight. Come what may, at least I'd be relieved of that.

I was trying to hold off panic by convincing myself that was true when my parents walked in, holding hands, Papa's head bent close to Momma's ear.

She giggled, her eyes bright after the nap, and swiped at his arm. "You are still too much, Burt Godfrey."

"That's why you stick around, sugar."

Momma spotted baby Cory and patted Francine's head, looking around for Meg.

"Where's your brother, girls?" Her eyebrows went up.

"He left with Meg," Claire said. "She trusted me to watch the baby."

Papa tipped his head to one side. "Alexander? Really? Good for him."

Momma frowned. "Where'd they go? Bethany has been planning this birthday party for weeks, I don't want her to be disappointed."

"To the storm shelter," Claire chirped, peering through the hole in the smallest ring at the babies.

"For what?" I felt Momma's gaze hot on my face before I met her eyes.

"To get the crib out of the back room," I said slowly. "Alexander saw it there, and Meg said she needed one, and I... I'm sorry, Momma, I couldn't stop them."

"Why would you not want your friend to have something if we're not using it?" Papa asked. "Meg is so... well, she's your friend and we should help her."

Momma shot him a look that could've lanced right through him if he'd been paying her any mind.

"Burt honey, I think we all understand how you feel about Ainsley's friend." She turned back to me. "It's *fine*, Ainsley. Things work out the way they're supposed to."

Easy for her to say. This particular thing wouldn't work out by sending her to prison if it came down to it.

"Momma—"

"I said, enough, Ainsley. There is a perfectly good crib sitting there not doing anyone any good. Meg can have it." She took a deep breath and smiled at Bethany. "Now then, your soup smells amazing, honeybug."

Heaven forbid anything upset Bethany.

Everyone, including Momma, had lost their mind. I couldn't go outside, but I was afraid to stay in here.

Unless...

I caught Momma's elbow as Bethany led Papa into the kitchen and handed him a plate of strawberries and cheese.

"What have you done?"

She jerked her arm away. "What had to be done. Just like I always do." She set her lips into a hard line and narrowed her eyes. "Bethany is waiting."

I watched her go with a brick of ice where my stomach was supposed to be.

We'd built a web of lies as gossamer fine and fragile as a barn spider's home, Momma and me. And it was about to come fluttering down in the middle of my sister's birthday cele-bration.

190	LYNDEE WALKER

fluttering down in the middle of my sister's birthday cele-bration.

TWENTY-EIGHT

Meg
September

The first thing I noticed when we got close to the back room of the storm shelter was the smell.

It wasn't overpowering, but it was noticeable: sickly sweet, but with an almost unbearable sour note and a tinge of copper. Alexander pried the door open and flashed a smaller, less creepy smile at me as that smell leaked out into the air around us. I read somewhere that smell is the most powerful trigger of memory, and it sure was for me right then: in a split second, I wasn't a grown woman with a home and a baby who needed his own crib. I was seven years old, holding the edge of the bathroom sink in Granny's trailer with my pants around my ankles, screaming every time Daddy's leather cowboy belt lashed my bare skin. I could practically feel the tears on my face fifteen years on and a thousand miles from home.

"It kind of stinks in here," Alexander said, sounding far away. "Sorry about that. Momma says the plumbing lines must've rotted out all the way to the septic tank. We'll just be a second if you can grab one side of this."

I heard him, but I didn't want to step into the small, metal-lined underground room with him. The memory had ahold of me and didn't seem inclined to let go.

My nose knew that the back room of the Godfreys' storm shelter wasn't plagued by an antique septic tank. It stank like rotting meat, the scent clinging to the walls though it didn't seem strong enough for anything to be decomposing in there presently.

I wouldn't forget that smell as long as I lived. My baby sister Emma really was a baby then, smaller than little Francine, and she'd pulled a steak Daddy bought for his dinner out of the fridge when she was hunting for her juice cup while I was at school, because we didn't have grown-ups who helped us with things when Granny was at work.

My sister found the cup and closed the fridge the way she'd been taught. But she left the steak on the floor, and it must have been right after she got up—they often left her there with the TV playing babysitter and no air conditioning running. The metal-sided trailer was like a hot box with the AC off, and by the time I got home that day, close to this same smell smacked me in the face when I opened the door.

I had panicked, of course. Daddy would be mad, and Emma was so small. He might actually kill her. I'd dropped my books just inside the door, picked up the package, gagging, and run it outside to the trash, then sprayed the kitchen with Granny's drugstore perfume. Not that it helped anything really. The trailer just smelled like church lady and rotten meat. To this day, Coty Emeraude makes me feel sick instead of nostalgic.

Daddy came slamming in drunk just before five o'clock and went straight to the fridge to get his steak, slurring orders at me about cooking it because Granny wasn't home.

His face went from drunken red to furious purple in a

heartbeat when he realized it was gone, the string of swear-laden threats spewing out of his mouth so vile I hadn't even fully understood some of the words then.

My sister ran for Granny's bedroom and hid. I stood in front of the TV and told Daddy I cooked and ate the steak. I knew he'd hurt me, but I would survive.

And I had. I'd made it out of that dingy little trailer park and into a home and a family that little girl couldn't have even dreamed of. Emma didn't make it out, and I would carry that regret in my heart for the rest of my days.

"Meg?" Alexander's forehead scrunched up as he leaned toward me. "You okay?"

I shook my head and smiled. "I'm sorry. Don't know where my mind went." I pointed to a small lamp on the floor in a back corner. "Should we turn that off?"

"Momma must have it on for a reason, she's the only person allowed in here as far as I know."

Good enough. I reached for the end of the crib.

"Can you lift that?" he asked.

I laughed. "Are you kidding? You know how heavy a hay bale is, right?" I picked up one end of the brown wooden crib with one hand.

"A farm wife needs to be strong," he said. "That's what Papa always says."

"I'm sure your momma is plenty strong. I know Ainsley is."

"Watch your step," he said, guiding the crib backward through the door and into the main room where SarahBeth stored food. We had let the smell escape and it seemed to cling to everything in here now, too. I hoped it would fade after we left, but the doors were designed to seal out radiation—maybe all these years later, they sealed in stench.

I stepped backward, my eyes falling on the rusted back of the door as I reached to pull it shut.

Tiny dents. Dozens of them, maybe even a hundred, pockmarking the lower half of the metal. Like it had been left out in a hail storm.

Or maybe like someone small, who could only reach so high, had been trapped behind it, banging away with whatever they could find in this cluttered space anyone could rightly call a junk room.

About two thirds of the way down the door, I spotted the scratches. They were faint, far less noticeable than the dents. Two sets of four, roughly the same height off the floor.

And the one on the left was spattered with dark, brownish-red mist. It might not have been blood—but that was the first thing that came to mind.

My eyes swung to the main door, and the wall next to it where I'd seen scratches on the wall that Ainsley said they'd used to count off days one winter until they bored of it.

This didn't look like counting.

This looked like desperation.

Let me out, the marks on the door called. *Help me.*

I slammed it shut, my skin crawling right up my arms.

Had Ainsley's parents locked their children in this room as a punishment?

TWENTY-NINE

SarahBeth
July—Two months earlier. The day after the tornado

Septic tanks contain bacteria that consumes their contents over time—so even if years of neglect had rotted this one clean through the pipes, it wasn't stinking up the place.

I was slightly disappointed that my own children believed such a lame excuse for the stench that had finally worked its way through the earth in the old bomb shelter, but I couldn't risk the possibility that Ainsley's new friend Meg was smarter than my crowd. She'd been in here for too long last night during the tornado, and Alexander had even complained right in front of her. That boy slopped hogs and mucked out stalls daily, but apparently being in here offended his delicate nasal passages.

The one thing I hadn't been able to hide or avoid was the dang smell. It was the only remaining sliver of the secret I'd kept for too long, letting it eat away at my guts until I felt as hollow as I was inside.

Rotten septic tank. For the love of God.

But I suppose at least it worked. Ainsley was always the

most likely to ask questions, but guilt—and a healthy dollop of self-preservation laced with fear—had kept her mouth sealed for too long for her to go blabbing now.

Well. She might, if she knew what I was up to here, but we'd reached a breaking point—we weren't isolated anymore, and I couldn't sacrifice my family on the altar of appeasing my stubborn eldest child.

"Ainsley brought this on herself," I said, covering my face with a handkerchief as I pulled the door open. My eyes watered anyway, the trapped, stale air still putrid with rotted flesh. "Bringing that damned girl and her baby over here."

I wasn't sure I would ever get over it. I'd had a plan for the new people—for the baby in particular—and it wasn't a bad one. Until Ainsley had to go wreck everything because she wanted blackberries and then came home dragging Meg and the baby in to meet our whole family.

But it was too late for any of that now. The girl next door and her baby were part of our lives. Bethany had a fit over the little one at first sight—he was truly an extraordinarily beautiful child, more like a doll than an actual human, with eyes so blue they almost looked purple, creamy peach-pink skin, and soft chestnut curls that were already getting thick, though he was barely bigger than most newborns that first day we met him.

His small size told me he must have been born early, which would've helped. I'd seen that from the window when I watched Meg cuddling him close in her bed.

He would've been perfect.

But it was too late now. Ainsley had ruined everything, just as spectacularly as she always managed to ruin the bread.

I love all of my children all the time, but I had a hard time liking Ainsley lately. More often than I liked to admit.

The lamp in the corner that Ainsley had insisted I keep on around the clock for years now gave me just enough light to see what I had come for. Swiping at the tears pouring from my eyes,

I moved the pile of old farm equipment parts, broken tools, and discarded furniture that we had so carefully constructed in one corner. It was built to look haphazard, while actually being structurally sound. A tomb built of unwanted things, for an unwanted thing.

There was something fitting, if not exactly poetic, about that.

And it helped, to think of it that way while I dismantled the crypt we'd built one broken piece at a time.

I was careful these days not to lift too much, or move too suddenly. One stupid mistake that had very nearly cost me everything had taught me I wasn't invincible. I used to believe I was almost superhuman, running this place while raising polite and respectful children, taking care of my husband and also keeping him interested and satisfied in every possible way. On the days I got tired or something ached, I pushed through by picturing myself telling my own mother to jump off a cliff with her insults and assumptions about what kind of life I would have. What kind of wife I would be.

Maybe she hadn't been able to keep a man, but that would never happen to me. I had decided that when I was younger than Bethany, and literally broken myself making good on it.

A bitter laugh ripped out of my throat in the thickening air, the smell worse the closer I got to the center of the pile.

I was so sure I had it all figured out. I knew how to keep my husband's eyes and attention and everything else right here where it belonged.

Until I miscalculated a half a step in that damned hayloft. One stupid mistake, and everything I thought was rock solid about my life and my marriage crumbled and blew away like sand in a summer storm.

And the most galling bit of it all was that I knew better. A farm is one of the most dangerous places there is to live and work. The land doesn't give you life and livelihood willingly—

you have to wrestle it away with sweat and tears, and sometimes a little blood and a lot of luck. Snakes, rats, possums, massive pieces of equipment boasting giant blades, storms, wildfires... as a mother, I knew every danger and how to best keep my babies safe. Until a hayloft and an old tractor motor Burt wanted moved to the workshop killed our baby Elizabeth before she even got to take her first breath.

The accident didn't kill me, exactly, but it killed the best part of me. The part that made me a mother.

The part that made Burt want me.

The very worst thing wasn't that, though. It wasn't even that I had miscarried the baby girl I'd been expecting when I fell.

It was that it had turned me into my mother.

In the years since my fall, I'd counted hours until Burt would come home or call every time he went out, which was suddenly more often than it used to be. He'd joined the local Lions Club, which in Cottonwood County was just a men's club where they drank Budweiser and grumbled about politics while they played cards mostly. Twice a year they collected used eyeglasses to help folks who couldn't afford them, and sometimes they wore bright yellow vests and marched in the July Fourth parade—when we had one, which wasn't every year.

Every time he left the house for a "meeting," I fretted. And worried. And wondered. Was he lying to me? And what was her name this time?

I refused to live that way. I'd fought my entire life to not end up like my mother, and I didn't like to lose. So when I saw a way around that sad, empty existence, I took it. And the price it carried, too.

Every sour thing in our lives had grown out of my stupid accident. Everything that had gone wrong, from my miscarriage to Burt's deceptions to Ainsley's meddling, had happened because I fell that day.

Nearly three years ago, it had even led to the worst, most desperate choice I'd ever made, when the fear that I was becoming my mother had wriggled its way so far under my skin that it felt too small for my bones, like I was losing my mind, and I had to do something.

I had to give Burt another child. Somehow. To replace the baby I'd so carelessly lost.

And that had ended in tragedy I'd never intended. Never saw coming.

Tragedy I'd entombed here, when Ainsley refused to let me bury it.

As I moved the last broken spade from the center of the pile, the blade that had so perfectly covered the little girl's skull, I told myself the bones beneath were just more broken pieces of another thing that had been left here to rot. It wasn't untrue, just heartless. But that was okay. Maybe my heart had died that day, too, staring up at the roof of the barn and trying to get enough air to scream for someone to help me.

I lifted the bones out and wrapped them in a sheet, putting the pile of junk back, though not as carefully as before.

"Momma, she hated the dark." I had to turn my head to make sure Ainsley wasn't standing behind me, I heard her voice so clearly.

"Nobody likes the dark," I said out loud. Laying one hand on the spare crib I would never use again now on my way out, I kept my breathing shallow because of the stench that would fade now, with the last of the rotting flesh clinging to the bones in the sheet I had gathered in my arms.

"I would've liked one more son. For Burt. And for me. One I knew couldn't be odd in the same ways Alexander is."

I shut the door on the bad memories and picked up a shovel from the barn on my way to the garden, the light of the full moon plenty to work by. I picked a spot near the back barn, in the opposite corner of my garden from the tomato patch. The earth was damp and easy to turn. I dug until my arms felt like they'd fall off, then dug some more. When I had a hole deep enough for Alexander to stand in, I dropped the bundled sheet in. It took an hour to shovel half of the dirt back in, the sun peeking over the horizon by the time I stabbed the shovel into the pile and went to the barn hunting a possum.

I found two behind the ladder—the barn cats kill them by the dozens in the summer, and everyone was forever complaining about them stinking up the barn when they were in hidden spots and blind corners.

Maybe this secret could quit stinking up our lives now.

I carried the dead possums outside. One of them was already stiff as a board, the other floppy.

When I dropped them into the hole, the floppy one scrambled to its feet.

"Oh no you don't." I scooped shovels full of dirt in faster than my spent arms should've allowed.

Nothing in that hole was coming back to haunt me.

I'd only done what I had to.

Five years ago in that barn, steps from where I'd found the possums, I'd lost my ability to create life.

And then fate—God, the universe, luck, whatever you want to call it—stepped in. Sent me a gift.

The miracle of life coming back to our house had carried a steep price. I had to hide what I wouldn't be able to explain.

The bastard child my husband had fathered in the immediate aftermath of my accident.

Like he was just waiting for an excuse, all those years I'd told myself I had him wrapped around my pinky finger.

I hadn't really meant for her to die, but I couldn't say I wasn't relieved when she did.

"And now nobody will ever find her." I tamped the dirt down over the grave and walked on it. "Nothing is going to take any part of this family from me."

Tomorrow, I would plant some blackberries right here, since Ainsley looking for blackberries next door had dredged all this up again in the first place.

Anything to make sure this terrible secret stayed buried. For me, and for Ainsley.

PART TWO

The Wages of Sin
Three years before Meg's first summer in Kansas

THIRTY

Ainsley
August

"If Momma finds out you're painting she's going to have your hide." Bethany's chirpy almost-twelve-year-old voice came from my doorway. The part she didn't say was that the only way Momma might find out anything right now was if Bethany told her. But I knew my sister well enough to know nothing I said would change her mind, so I sighed, but didn't put down my brush or take my eyes off my canvas.

The skyline landscape of New York City at night thrummed with the energy of the city, and the light in the windows was so hard to capture correctly with a paintbrush. I barely touched the gold tip to the canvas, not disturbing the windowsill I had painted with a magnifying glass and a flashlight the day before when I was supposed to be studying.

"Momma has barely been out of bed since her fall," I said. "For nearly two years now, I've done most everything she usually does, plus I'm trying to stay caught up so I can go back to school. This is the only fun thing I have in my life. Leave me alone."

"You're not doing everything around here," Bethany grumbled. "I make bread every other day, and Alexander is taking care of all the men's work while Papa is gone."

Her tone said she knew I was right. And that meant she wouldn't run and tattle to Momma.

Which also meant there was a reason she was still hovering in my doorway.

"What's on your mind?" I still didn't look at her, but I hoped the question sounded sincere.

"Do you think you're coming back to school with us?" Bethany's voice sounded thick with emotion that was not normal for her. My next younger sister was five years behind me, but our school was small, with everyone from kindergarten through twelfth grade in one two-story red brick building.

I hadn't stepped foot inside it in two years and three months. When Momma fell out of the hayloft and miscarried our last baby sister two summers ago, it broke her in every way you can imagine. Physically, sure: the doctors, when Papa finally carried her to the truck and drove her carefully to the hospital over her howling objections—said her pelvis was crushed, her hips shattered. She wouldn't be able to walk for months, maybe never again. But the part Momma hadn't wanted to hear—the part that made her refuse to go to the hospital in the first place—was that she hadn't just lost the baby she and Papa were calling Elizabeth already. She had lost her ability to have more children.

She barely got out of bed at all for six months, and she needed help with everything from remembering her medicines to using the toilet. Papa had a farm to run and it wasn't a man's job to play nursemaid, he said. Which made it my job.

I understood better than anyone what family loyalty and responsibility meant. I never spoke a word of complaint, I just laid my dreams aside for a while and stepped into Momma's shoes the best I could, though we did go without bread for a month before Bethany mastered making it. If I closed my eyes I could still hear Momma, her mouth full of bread and butter, saying, "Bethany, you're going to make some lucky man a fine wife someday." That was the highest praise Momma knew how to give any of us girls. Not that she ever once said it to me in the months I'd kept the house and the farm running at least nearly as well as she always had.

But Momma was better now. Maybe not in her heart and her mind, but her body was as healed as it would ever be, Papa said, and she'd been up and around every day doing chores since before Christmas.

It was time. I could paint again, after so many months of not having the time or the energy or the hope to pick up a brush. My life was about to be out of this holding pattern, my dreams my own again.

"Of course I am," I said, almost more to God than to my sister. School was going to be my ticket out of Firefly Grove. Out of Kansas, away from a mother and a life that had groomed me to be a submissive wife and dedicated mother despite the fact that I wasn't interested in or particularly good at either thing.

I was good at painting. The hours I spent in front of a canvas with a brush in my hand melted into nothing, the world around me fading until time and space didn't exist—it was just me and the crisp white of the canvas and sharp smell of the paint on an old plastic baby's dinner plate I'd turned into a palette after Momma told us the doctor said four-year-old Daisy would be her last baby.

I would never admit it to another soul, but I wasn't sorry about that part of this whole mess.

I remembered finding her in the barn that day, her leg crumpled at an unnatural angle and a pool of blood spreading too fast from under her skirts, a motor resting in a crater in her middle that had been swollen with a baby that morning. It had taken me a few minutes to make sense of it, and I'd run screaming for Papa, my heart frozen solid with terror that Momma would die and my life would be ruined.

I didn't want a farm or a husband or babies, and I had no interest in spending my days baking fresh bread, cleaning up after people who just left more messes right behind me, or tending a garden and canning what came from it. That was Momma's life and it was fine for her, but everyone expected me to want the same things she did and I had never been able to find the guts to tell anybody I didn't.

I wanted noise and lights and messy, interesting people and a tiny apartment with space for a bed and an easel and plenty of paint. I wanted art and pizza right outside the door and something to do no matter what time it was. I wanted to see my canvases hanging in museums and galleries.

There was a God, I knew because he heard me that day and Momma didn't die. She was still here, a light mist compared to the tornado she'd been before she fell, but she was here. So I'd dropped out of school to help out until she was back on her feet.

Which was supposed to be right about now, with Labor Day and the start of the new school year looming.

"I'm going back with y'all next month, Bethany." I put my brush down, fighting to keep my breathing even as I turned slowly in my ladder-backed wooden chair.

She was staring at her shoes so intently I could only see the top of her head.

The hair standing straight up on my arms and the ice in my insides said she knew something I didn't. Bethany always knew everything. Even though I was the oldest, I was the one who quit school and gave up my life to help out and take care of Momma, Bethany would always be her favorite. Because they wanted the same things.

"Okay," she said finally.

"What?" I couldn't keep the edge out of the word. It came out too sharp, and twice too loud.

"I just was thinking, that if Momma needed more help, then you might ought to stay here with her a while longer. You're keeping up." She narrowed her eyes until I couldn't tell what color they were. "When you try."

"Momma is fine," I said, keeping careful control of my voice and fighting my temper. "She might not be her old self, but she may never be her old self again. I can help her before and after school, that will be good enough. It's been nearly two years."

I couldn't help that my voice sounded like I was begging before I finished talking.

I was.

I needed out of this house more than I needed air. It got a little worse every day, the fear that I would get stuck here and be forced to become my mother. I had to get back into the world, even our tiny corner of it, around other people, where I had more room to breathe and felt more like myself, before it was too late.

"I guess we'll see what Momma and Papa think."

So they hadn't told her I had to stay home. But that didn't mean she couldn't fix it so that I did. It didn't matter that I was the eldest, or that I was the one the most ready to help. Bethany was Momma's mini-me, the one—at least so far, Claire and Daisy were still practically babies—who wanted Momma's life, wanted to be everything Momma expected. Momma would listen to her. And Papa, when he got back from Kansas City and the livestock expo, would listen to Momma.

"Bethany, please," I said. "What can I do for you?" I wasn't above bribing her to get what I wanted.

"Why do you want to go back so bad?" She raised her head, her eyes brimming with tears. "So you can leave us in a couple of years when you're done with school?"

Ah ha. I sighed. My sister was observant for someone so self-absorbed.

"Why do you care?" I asked.

"Are you kidding?" she asked. "I don't want to be you. If you go, I'm the oldest."

"Alexander would be the oldest."

Bethany rolled her eyes. "He's also the only boy. Nobody's making him do extra work because you decided to take off to be a painter in the city."

Wow. I had never told a soul that, and I'd sooner write a secret on a highway billboard than tell it to Bethany. I looked at the canvas on my easel. Maybe it wasn't as hard to figure out as I wanted it to be.

I slumped in the chair, hanging my head for a second as I realized I was going to lose. Definitely this battle with my sister. Maybe everything I had ever wanted from life, and before I'd even had a chance to really live. I had never kissed a boy, never ridden in a train car or shopped in a big department store. And it sure sounded like Bethany was about to see to it that I wouldn't anytime soon, at the very least.

I wouldn't talk her out of doing what she wanted if it served her own interests.

"I was really excited about school starting," I said, the words aimed at my lap.

"I wish things were different." Bethany left before I could say she was the one of us who had the power to make them different, by simply keeping her mouth shut and not damning me to another year trapped in this house.

I stared at the canvas until it was so blurred out by tears I couldn't even see the outlines of the buildings, then stood and put my foot through the center of it, kicking the easel to the floor.

I sat back down, unable to look at the ruined painting, tears streaking hot down my sweaty cheeks.

Momma would listen to Bethany, and there would be some reason I couldn't go to school with everyone else next month, even though she'd been up and around more and more this summer.

Voices drifted up from the front porch, too muffled by the walls and windows for me to make out words. Two women, so Bethany had already found Momma. I walked to the window and cracked it. Maybe if I knew what angle they were coming at this from, I could nip their argument in the bud.

"You have thirty seconds to get yourself off this land, and don't you ever come back," Momma's voice sounded so steely and cold I had to lean out and look to make sure that was really her.

Oh. A salesperson.

Momma didn't like people who knocked on the door selling things. Not that we got many of them out here, but every once in a blue moon, someone would swing in wanting a word about new farm equipment, or some kind of miracle seed or fertilizer. I still felt bad for the fertilizer guy from two summers ago. Momma had laid into him about spraying chemicals on the food she fed her babies until I thought he might cry.

But I'd never seen a lady salesman. I craned my neck, trying to look around the corner of the porch roof.

A skinny blonde in a short skirt and a blue T-shirt stumbled backward down the front steps. "Please—" she began, before Momma charged down the steps and slapped her.

I leaned so far forward I nearly lost my balance and crashed right out onto the porch roof, both hands clamping down on the windowsill as my heart hammered in my chest.

I had seen Momma mad plenty of times—I had been the cause of it more times than I could count, even. But I had never seen her hit anyone. She didn't believe in spankings, and she'd never so much as tapped one of us on the rear as far as I knew.

But the way her hand cracked against the blonde's face, you'd think she knocked people around on the regular.

The other woman's head snapped so far to the side I was afraid—for a split second—it would just spin all the way around like a top. She staggered backward, groping for the handle on the door of a small blue car.

"Don't ever come back." Momma spit each word like a nail into a coffin.

I couldn't imagine what the girl was selling, but I felt a little bad for her.

The car sped away, throwing up dust that refracted the pink and orange light of the sunset so it looked like diamonds hung in the air over the front yard. Distracted, I looked at my palette and wondered if I could get that kind of glitter on a canvas with acrylic paint. It looked like the air was shimmering.

Grabbing the sketchbook I kept in my nightstand, I got the scene down on paper in minutes so I wouldn't lose details. I set my easel back up and grabbed a fresh canvas from the pile I kept hidden in the closet. We Godfrey kids didn't get money often, but I saved every dime to spend on canvases and paint, and rationed them to last me until next time I could get Papa to take me two counties over to the craft store and drop me off there while he ran errands.

Putting the canvas on the easel, I grabbed the palette and went to work, capturing the sunset out the window and the shimmering dust from my memory. The brush flew across the canvas and I lost myself in the rhythm and scratch of the strokes, sitting back when I had the hill in the distance, the rail fence in all its weathered detail, the mailbox, and most importantly, the light.

I'd learned from the destroyed city skyline. This one was better, the light and shadows playing off each other and balancing, the dust kicked up by the horse I'd replaced the car with shimmering in the fading sunshine.

I'm not sure how long it took me to paint it, but the sun wasn't all the way down yet when I looked back out the window. And Momma was still standing in the same spot in the front yard.

I blinked, standing and moving to the window with the brush still in my hand.

She was alone, her back to me, her shoulders heaving such that I was afraid she might be sick.

Anyone else, I'd think they were crying, but SarahBeth Godfrey didn't cry.

Suddenly cold in my stuffy little bedroom, I stepped back. It was just my mother, standing in the front yard of the only home I'd ever known, but somehow I felt like I was intruding on a private moment no one was supposed to see.

I put my brush in a cloudy gray cup of water and picked up the pieces of the city canvas, breaking the frame over my knee and folding it up for the trash. I could take it out back now without Momma seeing me.

I paused in the doorway, looking back at the new painting before I turned off the light.

It was better than the skyline. Maybe better than anything I'd ever done. I didn't know who that girl was or why Momma got so mad at her, but I was glad she'd stopped by.

THIRTY-ONE

SarahBeth
August

Burt put on the usual show for the children when he came in from the livestock expo on Friday night, sauntering up behind me and wrapping his arms tight around my waist as he rested his chin on top of my head after he'd dropped a loud kiss there.

"How's my best girl?"

I swallowed hard. "Today was a good day," I said. "I picked two baskets of corn for dinners this week and made it through three loads of laundry. Even changed the sheets on our bed."

It was paltry compared to what I used to get done in a day. I knew that better than anyone, a bitter taste rising in my throat as I rested my hands over his, still clasped around my flat belly, and wished for the millionth time that everything was different.

Everything. I had broken everything. Like the nursery rhyme where all the king's horses and all the king's men can't put Humpty Dumpty together again. I'd been trying for two years now, and I could finally move, but I was slow. I looked older.

I felt ancient.

And any attempt at making love with my husband, something we had always enjoyed, something that kept us feeling connected on days when the farm and the children and life were too busy for much of anything else, was excruciating.

"Sex might be uncomfortable." That's what the doctor had said after the fourth surgery had finally put my hips back where they went in relation to my pelvis, which had been crushed in the fall.

Uncomfortable, I could handle.

Moving hay bales in the July sun with blisters on my hands was uncomfortable.

Letting a baby with yet another case of thrush—it was Daisy, our youngest, on her third bout of gentian violet—latch onto my chapped, infected nipple, which felt like having my most sensitive skin raked through a maw of shattered glass—that was uncomfortable. But I did it four or five times a day for six months because damned if any of my babies was getting weaned early. I had always been blessed with plenty of milk, and I wasn't about to deprive my child of it because of a stupid skin infection. So I washed bras daily and hung them in the sun and applied the violet until everything we owned was purple, and I fed my daughter. Uncomfortable or not.

Standing at the counter at midnight kneading bread when I'd been on my feet for eighteen hours with hips that had given life to five humans. That was uncomfortable.

Two years after I came home from the first hospital stay and seven months after the last surgery, any attempt at relations with my husband was not simply uncomfortable. It felt like he was literally going to break me in half.

I tried anyway, but he almost always stopped because no matter what I thought about or how determined I was, the tears always came.

The last time, on his birthday two months ago, we'd made it

all the way through to the finish line for him because I'd told him I wanted to blindfold him as his birthday gift.

He fell for it—or maybe he just let me do it because it would absolve him of guilt, I couldn't be sure. But just as he finished, I whimpered and he pulled the blindfold off and shoved himself backward so hard he nearly vaulted off the bed.

"You said you were feeling better." His tone was almost accusatory.

"I wanted to do this for you. It's your birthday."

"SarahBeth, I can't stand this. What this has become."

He hadn't touched me since, unless there was a child watching he felt like he needed to perform for. We'd always been the parents who made our kids groan and giggle, the high school sweethearts who never fell out of love. We held hands. We cuddled on the couch. We danced in the kitchen and stole kisses in the pantry and on the porch.

And we still did all of that when there was an audience. But as soon as our bedroom door closed, Burt became a different person. Cold. Distant.

I wondered some of the time if he resented the fact that he built this massive house out of his parents' barn because we'd planned to fill it with babies, and now I couldn't give him that. I wondered a lot of the time if he was disgusted by the scars. Or maybe just by me.

I couldn't really do anything to hide the scars except to keep my clothes on. So I had looked on the computer at the library, my cheeks burning the entire time, and ordered myself something called "split crotch panties" and a frothy black lace nightgown that was so short and slutty I hoped my husband would be too shocked to think when he saw me in it.

I was a master at putting his needs above my own, it was the hallmark of being a good wife. And I knew how to be uncomfortable. I could even take the pain, somehow.

The only thing I couldn't stand was the idea of becoming my mother.

The fear of winding up a sad, bitter, alcoholic shell of a person thanks to a string of men I never could find a way to please... that was the only nightmare worse than the one I was living in.

I had always excelled at two things: pushing myself to the limit, and keeping Burt happy.

As God is my witness, I would find a way to do that again in the bedroom. I wasn't letting that stupid accident ruin my life the way it had ruined my body.

THIRTY-TWO

Ainsley
August

It was nine days until Labor Day before Momma said anything about school.

"Ainsley, come in here when you're done with the floors," she called from the kitchen.

My jaw flexed so hard I was afraid for a second I'd cracked a tooth. I had lived on pins and needles since Bethany walked out of my room the night I painted the shimmering dust over the yard. I'd hidden that one in the stack of paintings I thought might be good enough to sell if I could ever get to a place where people appreciated art. Here—not just in Firefly Grove but here in Cottonwood County—being able to make water move and light glow on a canvas took several back seats to baking a perfect loaf of white sandwich bread, growing juicy strawberries, and having a baby about every other year. Only the art teacher at school really cared. Everyone else we knew was much more interested in who all the girls my age were dating than what we could paint or sculpt—even in my art class, the other girls talked about boys more than anything else. But at least we had good supplies there, and they all left me alone to sit in the back and do as I pleased, with just the teacher popping over to exclaim about my talent now and again. I missed having that time to myself every day.

Taken with the view out my window because I was pleased with the way the dust painting turned out, I was working to recreate our summer twilight miracle, the thing that gave this place its name. Fireflies are hard to capture accurately and harder still to paint by the hundreds, because they're small, but advanced. The subtle green in the glow, the way they light each other and the night closing in around them. But I was getting it, I thought. One little bright spot at a time.

It had helped me focus on something other than waiting for the "you can't go back to school" shoe to drop. I knew Bethany, she wouldn't let it go. Once she got an idea in her head, she was like a dog with a bone, Papa always said.

And the bone was now my problem.

I worked up a sweat pushing the mop, getting the wood floors extra shiny clean before I wiped my face and strolled into the kitchen, putting the mop away before I joined Momma at the counter. She was sitting on a stool kneading tomorrow's bread for the final time.

"We could eat breakfast off those floors," I said cheerfully, getting myself a glass of water before I sat next to her. "Can I help?"

She slid her eyes sideways at me. "I don't need another mess to clean up, thank you," she said. "I want to—"

"I can't wait for the start of the school term," I interrupted. "New notebooks and fresh pens, and so many things to learn. I only have this year and next before I'm done with school. I'm really going to try to be mindful to enjoy small things. Like you used to tell us when I was little, you would say we shouldn't wish time away because we're only little once. Well, I only get to do the eleventh grade once, too, right?" I finally had to stop for a breath, all those words flooding out as Momma stopped kneading the bread and turned her head toward me, her eyes big and sad.

"I understand why you're excited, but—"

I gulped a lungful of air and switched gears to something she actually cared about.

"It's also just about the only way there is around here to meet boys." I forced myself to maintain eye contact. "I know how important that is for my future." How I managed to get the words out without choking on them, I'll never know.

"I met your father at a barn dance." Momma's voice was firm, the hard line set to her lips proof that she knew what I was up to and was calling my bluff.

I slumped on the stool, spinning my water glass. "We don't have many of those these days."

"But we still have some. And anyway, I thought you set your cap for Cam Blankenship a long time ago."

I sucked in a sharp breath so hard I fell into a coughing fit. "How did... I mean... He's a lot older than me."

"Not in any ways that will matter in a few more years." Momma went back to beating up the bread dough. "Cam is a fine match for you. He's sharp—smart enough you won't get bored of him, I think. And handsome enough that my grand babies will be beautiful." She slid a smile my way with the compliment. "And that's why it doesn't really matter that you can't go back to school this year."

"Momma, please—" I began, careful to be respectful.

"It's not open for discussion, Ainsley. I just need too much help here, I still can't risk not having anybody here when your papa has to be away during the day. What if something happened again and there was nobody here?"

Her voice trembled on the last word.

So the truth, at least, was finally on the table. Or, the big stone island in our kitchen. It wasn't that she couldn't handle the house for the day, not really. It was that she was afraid. My momma had whisked her way through every day of my life until the fall like a force of nature: she was unstoppable. Invincible. And then she got hurt and now, after all the pain she'd been through to get better, she realized she was just as human as everyone else. She was scared.

And I was paying for it.

"I'm sorry," I said quietly. "I want to go to school with my friends. With Alexander and Bethany. But I don't want you to be scared."

"Thank you. That's all I ask, is just not to be here and be scared." She looked around, her lower lip quivering. Was she going to cry? "This is my home. The only place I've ever really wanted to be. I hate being afraid." Her voice got raspy at the end, but she didn't let a tear fall.

"Can't Alexander stay this year?" I asked. "He's stronger than I am anyway."

"Boys have to be in school," she said, patting the bread into a well-practiced loaf-pan shape and setting it into a pan before she pulled another blob of dough off and reached for another pan. "Your brother needs to learn math and agricultural science, and he needs to be in a place full of girls he's not related to." She paused, looking up at me. "And he needs sports. Football is a good outlet for him."

I nodded. I knew what she was saying. Smashing into other boys on the field helped with Alexander's temper, and that benefitted everyone.

"What about Bethany? Why can't she have a turn? Or I could just stay home on the days when Papa is gone. It's not like there are that many." Running a family farm required Papa to go to regular meetings with grocery distributors and to market to deliver product, but it was only a few days out of every month at the most, and less during the winter.

Momma slammed both fists into the dough on the counter. "There are enough. Enough that the county might ask questions. I don't need everyone knowing my business. Knowing I'm too afraid to be in my own home, to run this farm, by myself."

"What do you think they're going to think about me just not being there again this year?"

"You're young. People won't judge you as harshly." She flipped the dough, slapping it down harder than necessary.

"And you won't keep Bethany instead?"

"I love you all the same, but different." Momma shook her head, a mischievous smile touching her lips. "Bethany can be insufferable."

I laughed in spite of my disappointment. Momma never had anything bad to say about Bethany. She was the obvious favorite child to anyone who spent ten minutes in this house. I mean, besides my brother, of course. None of us girls could ever measure up to Momma's only son.

She wasn't going to change her mind. I was stuck, another year wasted, another chip away from my dream of getting out of here. I might as well find some joy in it.

"Momma! I didn't know you knew that." I smiled back.

"I know more than most people give me credit for," she said. "She's a lovely and accomplished girl, and she will make someone a fine wife someday, but she tries too hard to impress everyone all the time. I can't have her underfoot, just me and her, all day every day. You understand, don't you?"

I did. I was shocked that Momma did. For the first time in about as long as I could remember, it felt like Momma and me had a secret.

"You're a smart girl, Ainsley. Sometimes I think too smart for your own good. You don't need more schooling, you'll make Cam a fine wife someday. And he's going to be a good sheriff."

"He's just a deputy," I said. "And don't you think you're getting ahead of yourself? He barely knows I exist."

"He'll know, all right. When he needs to." She finished that loaf and put it in the pan to rise. "You're excused. I'm okay down here for now."

I slid off the stool. "I wish—" I began.

Momma raised one hand. "I know. Me too."

I went up to my room and picked up the composition books and pens I'd picked out at the general store, laying them on the floor outside Bethany's room. *You won.* I wanted to write that on the cover of the purple book, but I didn't.

I would keep Momma from being afraid, and help her get strong again. Maybe I would be allowed to go next year.

You've had enough schooling, she'd said.

Or maybe not. But either way, I knew my own mind, and this would be so much easier if I convinced myself it was what I wanted.

Maybe Momma was right and big cities were dangerous and full of murderers and filth. And maybe painting was a really hard thing to make money at.

Maybe my dreams were just too big.

I had been raised to make myself small, to defer to the happiness of Papa, Alexander, and someday my own husband.

That was it. I nodded. I just needed smaller dreams.

I went to my closet and pulled out a box, then retrieved a paperback book from the pile behind it, studying the cover. Did boys really bend you over backward like that to kiss you? I'd never seen Papa do that once, and I loved that he was always so kind and affectionate with Momma—I complained about it, of course, because it seemed like they found that funny, but really I hoped it would never stop. The best thing about our family was the two of them—we had never wanted the same things for my life on almost any level, except that I did hope I found that kind of forever, head-spinning, soul mates sort of love that

Momma and Papa had. I had just always wished I'd find it far away from here.

But I could adjust.

Maybe Cam Blankenship just might be a big enough dream for me.

THIRTY-THREE

SarahBeth
August

The biggest difference between my own momma and me wasn't looks or brains—it was determination. She flopped right down and let life walk on her, where I did whatever I had to do to take care of my family.

Even things that were unpleasant.

I took a deep breath as I finished shelling the last of the summer peas from the garden, keeping an eye on the canning jars. I had two dozen jars of peas put up already, but we had so much more room with the new shelves Burt had built me for Mother's Day in his grandfather's old bomb shelter that we barely set foot in unless a real wallop of a storm came this way.

I had taught all my girls to can and how to make their own jams and jellies, and with all that gorgeous shelf space and a good crop from my garden this year we'd eat well all winter long.

Ainsley was the best at this, though. She wasn't as good as Bethany was at most domestic things, but if I wanted something canned right and I didn't want to worry about it exploding or spoiling, I needed Ainsley.

She was still mad at me for telling her she couldn't go back to school, but there was nothing for that. I would never understand that child. If someone had told teenage me that I could skip the last two years of school to focus on catching the husband I wanted and learning how to be a proper wife so I could keep him... I'd have jumped at the chance.

Having to spend days alone with my momma wouldn't have appealed to me, but Ainsley wasn't with my momma. She was with me. I could help her. Guide her. Give her the life I was supposed to have.

The life I needed to make sure right this minute I was going to get to keep—at least, the sad semblance of what I'd once had that was our current reality.

School hadn't started yet, so everyone was home and I knew that meant my hard-headed eldest was in her room in the middle of a rainy afternoon, reading books she thought I didn't know she had or painting a canvas. I hoped Cam Blankenship liked paintings, because she was going to want to fill his house with them.

Funny, how shocked Ainsley had looked when I'd mentioned Cam in the kitchen that night. I paid attention to everything to do with my family. And I had a plan for Cam, too, when the time came.

I went to the foot of the stairs because going up them still hurt my hips and I tried not to if I could help it. "Ainsley!" I hollered.

Footsteps. A door opened. "Momma?"

Claire. My little caretaker. She was probably up there playing dolls with Daisy. My God, I wished I could give them a real baby to watch over and shower with love. Little girls their ages were such good helpers. Ainsley always had been.

"Hey, Cuddlebug, could you get Ainsley for me?"

"Sure thing." I heard her little footfalls on the floor and a knock. "Momma needs you."

"What else is new?" Ainsley retorted.

I took a deep breath and pretended I didn't hear that. It stung, but it wasn't untrue, and I didn't have time to fight with her, especially not when I could see why she was upset.

Her door opened and closed, and she stopped short at the top of the stairs. "Momma."

"I forgot I have an appointment this afternoon, and I have to get going," I said, my voice bright. "Can you finish canning the peas?"

She smiled, relieved, and nodded so hard her hair came loose from its bun. Putting it back up, she talked around the pin she held between her teeth. "Sure. You don't need Alexander to drive you?"

"No, I can do it now." It would hurt my leg, but I had to go alone. There was no other option.

I went to the pantry and swallowed two aspirin before I got the keys to Burt's truck. He was over at Old Man Lester's place next door helping re-shingle the barn roof that had been half lost to baseball-sized hail in our last big thunderstorm. Nobody in the county had gotten out of it unscathed, and now that most folks had taken care of their own property, the men were pitching in to help those who were too old or poor to handle their own repairs. Grabbing my gardening gloves from the mudroom, I went to the truck and pulled Burt's hunting knife from the glove box, dropping it into the deep pocket in the folds of my skirt. I could feel the weight there, pulling the band of the dress into my right hip bone. Powerful.

Hopefully unnecessary.

I started the truck and turned right out of the drive. I hadn't wanted to believe the blonde when she rang our doorbell. And maybe she was lying. But there was only one way to find out:

some research had told me she was living at a boarding house in Emery, a little under an hour away.

With time to think, I had a whole list of questions for her. I wondered how I'd feel if her answers proved her right.

Most of all I wondered what it would take to get rid of her. And how far I would actually be able to go to ensure that if it came down to it.

THIRTY-FOUR

Ainsley
September

"What? Momma, no. We talked about this, Ainsley can just help you like she has all this time." Bethany's voice took on a whining edge by the time she finished talking, and I rolled my eyes before I could help it.

Not another one of us would dare to talk to Momma that way. Papa wouldn't stand for it. Momma didn't believe in spankings, but Papa had no trouble taking a belt to a disrespectful child when she wasn't looking—or wouldn't admit she knew.

But Papa was still helping out at the Lester place, and Bethany was a world champion whiner when she wanted something. Or in this case, when she didn't. And she really didn't want the fate she'd so eagerly chosen for me. I was sad for Alexander and Claire and Daisy, but I had to admit the slightest twinge of satisfaction watching Bethany try to work her way free of Momma's edict that nobody was going back to school.

"Why is it we have to all stay here?" Alexander asked, his

forehead scrunching up the way it did when he was trying to puzzle something out.

"Because there's no better education for your future than what you can learn doing the everyday work of running the farm," Momma said, like she had practiced it.

I blinked, watching her look everywhere in the room except at me. It was exactly the opposite of what she'd said to me just eight days ago. Not that anyone else knew that.

She moved around the end of the island to get out the cutting board and set about chopping potatoes for dinner. Papa had gotten a fresh side of beef from two farms over and Momma had a brisket in the oven, so she was making potato salad. Everyone thought it was a last summer supper until she'd called us all in here a few minutes ago.

Watching her more carefully than I usually did, I realized she was limping.

"Are you okay?" I asked.

"I'm fine," she snapped. Pinching her lips into a thin white line, she shook her head. "I'm good, yes." Her voice softened. "Thank you for asking."

"I was supposed to get to go to the sixth grade this year," Bethany said. "That's in the second floor with the older boys."

"Bethany Lynn, do you think I can't teach you everything you need to know? Exactly what is it that you think I don't do as well as you want to be able to do it for your own family?"

Oooh. Point—Momma. Bethany hung her head. She might be defiant when she wanted something, but even Bethany had her limits. She wouldn't dare criticize Momma in her own kitchen. Momma had said that to shut her up.

Every eye in the room bounced between them like a little rubber ball.

It worked. Bethany muttered, "No, ma'am" into the counter and didn't say another word.

"Alexander, since you don't have to get up early, why don't

you walk over to the Lester place and see if your papa can use any help? I'd like y'all back for dinner in about an hour and a half. Bethany, you may fold the laundry I washed for you girls this morning. Claire, watch your little sister." She turned solemn eyes I had trouble reading to me. "Ainsley, you help me with supper."

Bethany opened her mouth to protest, no doubt because she thought herself a superior cook. But then she looked at Momma's face and thought better of it, recruiting Claire and Daisy to play upstairs so she wouldn't have to be up there alone.

I waited until the kitchen was empty and Momma was in a rhythm chopping the potatoes before I spoke.

"Why did you lie? And why are you limping?"

My tone was quiet, no edge of accusation in my words.

I knew there was nothing I could do about whatever she was going to say. I had long ago learned to recognize when Momma had made up her mind about something, and not a single Godfrey child would go to school this year.

But since that was such an about-face from the path she had clearly already chosen just a week ago, I was curious about what caused it.

"What is it you think I lied about?" She put the knife down and peeled another potato.

"You told me just the other day that Alexander needed to be at school. Now suddenly none of them do. You're not usually one to change your mind without good reason."

"I read an article on the value of technical education," she said without skipping a beat, the knife moving expertly through the potato. Momma might be slower these days, but she still had the wiry upper-body strength of a woman who had routinely lifted hay bales for hours several days a week over decades. "Do you know there are children your age training to be welders? Boys, of course, but in the cities they're finding good jobs right out of public school, no fancy colleges needed. It said it was a new movement in big city schools to teach career and technical skills." She glanced up and smiled. "You'll all have gray hair by the time something like that trickles all the way down to our school. But then I realized that I could do that here. Odds are you'll all end up on a farm somewhere." She cut her eyes to me. "I think."

"Momma." I put one hand across the counter and laid it over hers.

She sighed, but stopped chopping. She kept her eyes on her hands, though.

"Please look at me," I said.

She raised her eyes slowly, a smile starting at the edges of her lips and then stretching her whole face crossways by the time her gaze met mine.

It was the first time I'd ever seen shades of Alexander's weird grin in anyone else.

I didn't care for it, but I couldn't let on.

"What in the world is going on?" I asked.

"You have to keep it a secret for now." She lowered her voice, but the higher register that said she was excited came through loud and clear.

It had been so long since we'd had truly good news in this house. I felt the corners of my mouth turning up at the light dancing in her eyes that had been missing for far too long. I didn't want to grow up to be Momma. But I loved her, and seeing her happy made my heart swell. It wasn't until right then that I realized that for months now, I had just accepted the fact that Momma had lost hope, and with that, joy had been very hard to come by in our house.

That was what I saw in her eyes, standing in the kitchen that day in early September.

Hope.

"I'm good at keeping secrets."

She tipped her head to one side and studied me like she was trying to decide if I was telling the truth.

She put the knife down after a few seconds and took both my hands in hers.

"You're going to be a big sister again, Ainsley," she said. "The Good Lord answers prayers. And we're going to have a baby."

My jaw fell open like someone had pulled the hinge pin, tears filling my eyes.

"But the doctors... your miscarriage..."

"The doctors were wrong," Momma said. "So, you see, I'm going to be even slower here in just a matter of months. And I don't know how long it will take me to get back on my feet after the baby comes." She rested her hands on her belly.

"We'll take good care of you both." I ran around the end of the island and threw my arms around her. "I know this is what you wanted most in the world," I said, my words muffled by her shoulder. "I'm so happy for you. And I hope it's a boy."

She pulled back, and a frown flickered across her face. "But even if it's not, that will be okay. Right?"

"Of course!" I laughed. "It's not like we don't know what to do with girls around here."

She smiled and touched the end of my nose. "My kind, smart girl. Our secret until I say so, right? And you'll help me take care of the baby?"

I hugged her again.

"You can trust me, Momma."

I forced the words out because she shouldn't trust me, but I couldn't let her know that.

THIRTY-FIVE

SarahBeth
September

I took extra care with my hair that night, pulling the pins and piling them on the counter in the bathroom, then letting the weight of it spill down my back, waves making it glow in the light after being twisted up all day. I brushed it until it was soft and shiny, and pulled thick sections forward over my shoulders before I opened the door and walked out into our bedroom.

Burt sat on the edge of the bed, taking off his socks. His whole body went rigid when he saw me. "You left your hair down."

I usually braided it before bed so it wouldn't get tangled. "You like my hair down."

"SarahBeth, I..." He shook his head. "I can't. I don't want to hurt you."

"Sometimes there is purpose in pain, my love." I perched on the edge of the bed next to him, taking his hand.

"No." He sighed, his shoulders going up and down before

his head dropped backward, his eyes on the ceiling. "Can I ask you something?"

"Of course."

He didn't move, his Adam's apple bobbing with a hard swallow before he started talking.

"I know that you think you need to do things for me. No matter how inconvenient or uncomfortable it is for you."

"That's part of being a good wife."

"Let me finish." His voice was harsh, and I flinched. I dedicated my whole life to making sure Burt was never mad at me. If he got mad, I had failed.

He squeezed my hand without looking at me. "I'm sorry. I just... I need to get this out or I'll lose my nerve. And it has to be said."

"Okay." Everything in me felt simultaneously numb and like I was sitting on a live wire. This was it. He was leaving me. I was too late, and my mother's fate would be mine, too, no matter how hard I had tried or how much I had sacrificed.

When Burt started talking, his voice sounded far away. "Not everyone thinks the way you do. That being a good wife means doing more than your share of the work, making sure I'm never so much as inconvenienced, raising as many babies as I want to have no matter what. Maybe most people used to think that way, but I don't think it's true anymore." He swallowed hard again, raising his head but focusing on the wall. "I know things move slow here, and folks here put family above everything else. But the rest of the world has moved on, and I've spent twenty-some years letting you do for me because that's the way my momma and daddy were. But I was thinking last week when I was gone. There were a lot of women at the expo this year. Some with their husbands and some running their own places. And I thought about Ainsley and Alexander and which one of them would really be the most capable of running this place, and about you and what you'd have to say if I said it was Ainsley. And then I thought about how you'd be just fine running everything if I wasn't here. And you wouldn't have the worry of whether or not I was satisfied. In here, in bed."

He turned to look at me and the tears in his eyes punched me right in the gut. "I love you, SarahBeth. And it's true that men have needs, but I can't stand the thought of hurting you."

"I feel the same way," I said, hearing the tears in my voice before I felt them in my eyes. "I like making you happy. I like knowing I can make you happy the way no one else can."

"And you're sure that matters to you more than the pain that makes you cry when I try to make love to you?" Something in his voice told me what was happening here.

He didn't want to leave.

He just didn't want to feel guilty.

"You're asking me if I could be okay with you... having relations... with other women." My voice was dull.

"I don't know what I'm asking." He buried both hands in his hair. "It was easy to think I had figured it all out in the motel last week."

My head snapped around. "Were you alone?"

He shrank away from me like I'd slapped him. I remembered how my hand had stung when I'd hit the trashy blonde girl. I'd never slapped anyone before in my life, and that fire in my palm had felt good. Powerful, as she staggered backward down the steps of my house. Away from my family, where she belonged.

But I would never—could never—raise a hand against my husband.

"Of course I was alone."

I nodded, though I wasn't sure I could believe him. The one thing I was sure of was that I didn't want this conversation to go on any longer. And I knew I could stop it cold with two words.

I had told Ainsley, sure, but I still wasn't sure I could pull this off.

I guess we were going to find out. At least if everything fell apart, I would know in my heart that I had done everything I could to keep my family together.

Everything.

"I'm pregnant," I said.

He fell off the bed.

Actually—his legs went to water and he hit the floor with a thud that shook the boards.

Looking up at me, his face said he might as well have been looking at the Virgin Mary herself, tears flowing freely over his tan cheeks and into the stubble that always lined his jaw at the end of the day.

I knew everything about this man, from how he liked his eggs to every freckle, birthmark, and scar on his body. And I wasn't giving up any part of that without a fight.

He scrambled to his knees after a minute of stunned silence. I rested my hands over my belly, and he grabbed them both. "I don't understand."

I shrugged. "The power of prayer." I wasn't entirely sure it was fair to apply that to this situation, but I had prayed for a baby, and it had been answered, and technically that was all that mattered, wasn't it?

I didn't have time to think any more about it right then. Burt framed my face softly with his big hands, pushing my hair aside like feathers as he stood slowly, tipping my face back and kissing me—gently at first, and then with growing heat as he laid me back slowly on the bed and settled over me. I lost myself in the smell of hard work and Old Spice aftershave and the gentle pressure of his hands on my cheekbones, the feel of his tongue sweeping over my lower lip. This.

This was what I had missed.

Being close to him. Feeling cherished and special and protected. Was that so much to want for all the work I'd done, all the sacrifices I'd made for this family?

I didn't think it was. Why did it always have to be sex or nothing at all? I never understood why he was so all or nothing. And finally, maybe I'd found the key.

"I love you so much," he breathed, resting his forehead against mine.

"I love you." I blinked tears back. "I have always loved you, Burt. And I always will."

"How?" He traced the lines in my forehead when I scrunched it. "How did I get so lucky as to have you love me?"

"God smiles on good hearts," I said. "And even with all that has happened, we are so very lucky."

He kissed me again, his hands moving down my body and under my nightgown, his lips demanding more until I forgot my own name.

All or nothing.

I turned my head, fighting to catch my breath and slow my heart rate. I couldn't afford to lose control. Everything had to go just the right way.

"We shouldn't," I said, reaching down and catching his hand. "The baby."

"Sure," he said, rolling to one side and propping his head on his hand, staring at me with wonder on his face. "You are incredible. Leave it my girl to show them fancy city doctors they don't know their own ass from a hole in the ground.' He flopped onto his back, laughing. "A new baby. Maybe another son."

"Maybe," I echoed softly, reaching for his hand. "But just so you know, what you said before, about Ainsley. She is smart and strong and I know why you think the way you do. But she doesn't want this life. She doesn't want to be me." Not any more than I wanted to be my mother. It hurt, but it was true. "If you don't think Alexander can handle it, I'm taking them out of school. Teach him. He won't have another path besides inheriting the farm. Sometimes I think that's why God only gave us the one son. So we wouldn't have a choice."

This baby was going to save my marriage. Keep Burt where he belonged. Save my family. Keep Ainsley here with her family. Save me from my mother's fate. I would never be alone.

And if I had to trade a piece of my soul for that? Well. It wasn't the hardest choice I'd ever made.

THIRTY-SIX

Ainsley
October

"Pa—" Alexander stopped in the doorway, leaving the door standing open, the chill breeze of the fall's first true cold front whistling in around him. "What're you doing in here?"

"Helping Papa," I said like it was obvious.

"With what? Where is he?"

Why did he always have so many questions?

"He left right after dinner. Didn't say where he was going." I left out the part where I didn't ask, because my brother was right to look for Papa here this time of the year—when the sun started to set earlier as October stretched on, he usually spent any evening there wasn't football on the TV working in his study in our old house. Momma's sewing room took up half of the first floor now, and they stored holiday decorations and other random things that most people kept in garages in the kitchen and the upstairs bedrooms. I had asked two summers ago if I could clean out one of those rooms and have it for a painting studio, and Papa had smiled and started to nod before Momma cut him off with a sharp and final "no."

I kept my hands in my lap, under Papa's big desk. Out of Alexander's sight.

"I needed to ask him about something." Alexander looked around and realized the cold air was coming from behind him, stepping inside and closing the door. "I was wondering if I might be able to talk to coach about playing football still, even if I don't go to school there."

"The season is half over, isn't it?"

"I know." His hands disappeared halfway to his elbows in the huge pockets on his dark blue denim overalls. "It's probably dumb. I just saw Jimmy at the feed store the other day and he said our QB is getting clobbered without me, and... well. You do your painting in your room still. I can always smell the paint from the hallway." Momma used to joke that Alexander was part bloodhound. She said it was the only explanation for his superhuman nose, his occasionally surprisingly soft heart, and his killer instinct when needed.

"And it didn't come from my side of the family," she would always say, one eyebrow raised at Papa.

"But you can't play football from home," I finished for him.

"Yeah. So I was just gonna see if I could take the truck and go to practice and stuff, in the afternoons. He wouldn't miss me, he barely has much he lets me do anyway." He stared at the blue carpet. "It's probably a stupid idea."

"I don't think it's stupid at all," I said softly. "Why shouldn't you have something that you love that's just yours?"

He looked up at me, his eyes brighter. "You think?"

"I really do."

He grinned, and I dropped my eyes to Papa's dark-brown leather desk blotter, which had belonged to his father and grandfather before him and came with the house and the farm when he inherited it. I loved my brother, but his smile was... different. I didn't like the way it made me feel afraid of him.

"I don't think you're stupid, Alexander. And nobody has good ideas all the time. Don't be so hard on yourself." I looked up. "Do you ever wonder about Papa, you know, before he was Papa?"

The smile disappeared as his forehead scrunched. "Huh?"

"I was just looking at this desk and thinking how it belonged to Grandad and Great-Grandad, and Papa inherited it, just like you will someday, I expect. Do you think there's a chance that there was time when Papa wasn't sure he wanted this? To run the farm the way they had? To have the lives they had, for the most part?" I paused, meeting his eyes in the dim light thrown off by Papa's ancient desk lamp. "Do you ever think you want something else?"

Alexander stared at me for several beats without blinking, then barked a short laugh that sounded far too bitter for a boy of sixteen—I'd turned seventeen in August, right after he turned sixteen in June. So I was back to being the older sister now. "What else would I possibly want? I'm not as smart or as talented as you are, Ainsley. I don't even think Papa thinks I'm smart enough to run this place, but Momma will make him give it to me anyhow, I expect."

I was stuck a few words back, thinking at the same time that I couldn't remember that last time Alexander and I had really talked and wondering just why that was. We'd done everything together and shared every secret, once upon a time. Sitting there I realized it had been so long since the last time we'd really talked, I didn't know what he wanted.

"You have options," he said. "I don't. I've made my peace with that. But I'd sure like to play out the rest of the season. I think it would help me with... I just want them to say yes."

"Don't ask Momma first," I said. "I think you were right to

look for Papa. Get him on your side and then you both go to her. She won't say no to both of you."

"You think she's being weird too, don't you?" he asked.

"I think she is really afraid of being alone. Maybe she's afraid of what might happen if she falls again? I don't know. But what started with her wanting me here all the time seems to have spread to y'all."

"I don't think fear was the only reason she didn't want you to go back to school." Alexander scuffed the toe of his work boot on the carpet. Maybe he wasn't as slow as everyone thought.

"I don't guess I do either, but I love Momma and I don't want to be mad at her, so I try not to think about it."

"Is that the trick?" He stepped closer to the desk, his hand out like I was going to give him something.

"Trick?"

"To not being mad. Not letting it get away from you. Not... doing stuff you shouldn't."

I stood, tucking the folded bills I'd taken from the cashbox in Papa's drawer into my skirt pocket before Alexander could see them.

"What kind of stuff?" My heart rate picked up, the blonde girl I'd seen Momma hit before the end of summer flashing through my thoughts. I hadn't recognized her, but I had been busy with my own plans for months now. Maybe someone had moved to the county while I wasn't looking. Was she looking for Alexander, the blonde? Back in August, my brother had been going to two a day practices, thinking he was headed back to school and football. He hadn't been here to see her.

And I hadn't seen or heard anything about her since.

Was Alexander capable of hurting a person the way he sometimes hurt animals?

I took a deep breath. "If you need to talk—"

"Nothing." He shook his head. "Forget it."

"Alexander—"

He was gone before I got another word out, his boots heavy on the steps of the old porch as he ran down them.

I closed the check ledger I'd been reading when Alexander came in, wondering why it said Papa had spent four hundred dollars last month on violets when winter was coming and we didn't usually grow violets. Seed, maybe? Was he aiming to branch out into farming flowers in the spring?

Whatever he was doing, I wouldn't be around to see it. I shut the light off and patted my pocket to make sure the money was still there.

Alexander and whatever he had done without football—which Momma said herself was good for him—that was Momma's problem. She had decided to keep them out of school.

And I had my own things to worry about. My own plans to make.

THIRTY-SEVEN

SarahBeth
October

"Momma, why is your belly so big?" Claire reached one hand up to pat at Momma's skirts and Bethany laughed.

"Claire Bear, that's not polite," Bethany said.

"She's okay," I said, pressing a pie crust into the bottom of a blue glass pan and passing it to Bethany to fill with bubbling chicken pot pie filling from the pot on the stove. "There's a baby growing in there, Claire."

"Like Daisy?"

"Not as big as Daisy," I laughed. "But yes."

"When will I get to see?"

"Just a few more months," I said, pulling another pie plate from the cabinet and rolling out more crust. "It takes a while to grow a baby. Remember?"

"Like when we got Daisy." She nodded solemnly, her seven-year-old eyes wide.

"Yes, sort of like that."

Claire scampered off to play and Bethany laid the top crust on the first pie for dinner and slid it into the oven. "You feeling okay, Momma?"

"I am. Why?"

"I just remember you being really sick with Daisy and I thought you said that was a sign of a healthy pregnancy."

"You're too young to know, of course, but I wasn't sick with Alexander." I passed her the second pie plate. "Every one of my pregnancies has been different."

"Your belly is getting bigger," she said.

"This is number seven. I'm surprised my belly didn't pop the day after we conceived." I winked and Bethany snorted, then laughed so hard she doubled over.

I loved hearing my children's joy better than anything in the world. I wasn't a bad person. I was a great mother.

And all the rest of this was just about making sure everything in my children's lives stayed the way it was.

The way I had always wanted it to be.

If people besides me had to sacrifice some for that, so be it.

"Momma," Alexander called from the mudroom door. "Papa told me to ask you when I got home which room you want the crib in. He said you might want it in your room for now, but he told me to get it for you after practice."

"Come and get something to eat," I called, glancing at Bethany to see if she noticed the shrill note in my voice. "We can talk. That coach works you boys too hard."

"Supper smells good," he said, ambling into the kitchen in his sweaty socks, leaving damp marks on my clean floors with every step. "I can wait to eat. I don't want Papa to get mad at me."

"Nonsense." I pointed to a stool at the bar and grabbed an apple from the bowl on the counter and a sweet potato from the bin under the island. I poked holes in the potato and stuck it in the microwave with a small bowl of water, then washed the apple and handed it over. "You need your strength for the game tomorrow night. And I'm not ready to bring the crib inside yet."

He bit the apple, but his eyes went wide when I said the last part.

"I'll talk to your father," I said. "I appreciate you wanting to do as you were asked. You're a good boy, Alexander, and you'll make a fine man." I patted his free hand, resting on the counter. "With just a little more help."

He swallowed. "I don't mind, Momma."

"I know. I mind. I don't want to... jinx anything."

He got another bite and shrugged. "Suit yourself," he said around a mouthful of apple. "As long as Papa isn't mad at me."

"He won't be."

The microwave beeped and Bethany fixed the potato with butter and brown sugar and cinnamon, sliding it across the counter.

Alexander watched the steam come out of it as he stirred it, and I put the discarded carrot tops and celery leaves from dinner into the compost bin. Bethany opened the fridge and turned for the back door.

"Where are you going, Bit?" I asked.

"Out to the canning shelves to get more peas. I didn't put them in the filling because Daisy won't eat them, but I want some for mine, and I know you do, too."

"No, you finish cleaning this up and I'll get that," I said, pushing the cutting board toward her.

"Momma, it's almost dark. I don't mind."

"I can go." Alexander put his fork down and stood. "You sure you don't want the crib?"

"No!" My voice echoed off the rafters, both children flinching and looking at each other. Deep breath. "That was louder than I meant it to be. Really, Alexander, your muscles need the potassium in that yam, eat your snack. Bethany, clean up those dishes and check on your little sisters. I'll be right back. I could use the fresh air."

"Be careful," Bethany said, the worry in her eyes making my heart lurch.

"I always am now. I promise."

I crossed the yard without noticing the cool fall wind blowing through the little valley where Burt and I had raised our family. The one thing I had always been glad Firefly Grove didn't have was a family burial ground. They were common in the county, but way back when, Burt's great-great-something-grandfather—or maybe grandmother, I didn't really know—had believed very strongly that graveyards belonged near churches, and fire cleansed the human soul. Every generation of Godfreys since had been cremated and buried near the Lutheran Church.

Now I wished that ancestor had made a different choice.

I stepped into the long-defunct bomb shelter, wondering for the millionth time if this thing would've actually worked for what it was built for. It was fine for summer storms in this part of the country, but keeping radiation out? I didn't think Burt's grandaddy was qualified to decide that.

The door to the bathroom he'd designed so poorly in the back was notorious for sticking shut. I'd made Burt put a lock on it when Ainsley was a baby, high up where she couldn't reach, just in case. I had nightmares for years about her getting stuck in there.

Plucking a jar of peas from the shelf, I inspected the door to the back room. Nobody had noticed the padlock I'd put there weeks ago for the first time in years, and I didn't expect anyone would, either. We didn't ever set foot in here during the winter except to get food, and it would be easy enough to make sure I was the only person who did that for a while.

I turned back to the shelves and loaded my arms with more peas, plus green beans, carrots, and three kinds of jelly.

"There," I said. Now nobody had any cause to come out here poking around for a good while.

Except me.

I had a secret to hide.

THIRTY-EIGHT

Ainsley
November

Thanksgiving was a true production in the Godfrey house.

Momma was big on tradition, and as such most of us kids were, too. Three years ago Papa had suggested putting up the Christmas lights before Thanksgiving so that decorating the house wasn't quite as much work after the big dinner Momma cooked, and Bethany and Alexander almost rioted. I remembered it because it was one of the only times in my life I'd seen Papa back down. He'd raised both hands in surrender and taken a seat on the sofa to watch football, saying he knew when he was beaten.

Momma always got up practically in the middle of the night on Thanksgiving to start cooking. The turkey, a fresh one Papa got from a neighbor a few days earlier, was resting in a butter and spice rub in the fridge and had to go in the oven no later than four in the morning. And then there were a thousand other chores to do while it cooked, from pressing the linens and setting the table to chopping and sautéing and baking the side dishes. The cornbread and biscuits for my favorite holiday specialty, Granny Godfrey's special cornbread dressing, were on the countertop getting stale and had been for days.

I was awake at 3:45, staring at the painting I'd finished a few hours before. New York City, again, but this time in the rising sun.

"Someday," I whispered to the ceiling. "Maybe someday soon."

I listened to the sounds of the big house shifting in the wind. Winter's bite had come to the valley this week, and yesterday there had been frost on the ground when I went to milk the cows.

The creaks and moans of shifting and settling timbers could have lulled me right back to sleep on any other winter day—the nice thing about living on a farm in the off season is that all the hard work of the spring, summer, and early fall gives way to long days with far less to do.

For most of my life I hadn't really noticed because I'd been in school this time of the year, but since Momma's accident, I was starting to love the colder months in a whole new way. I'd done that entire painting yesterday, and the longer I looked at it, the more I thought it might be the best thing I'd ever painted.

The clock ticked closer to four, and I still only heard the wind. No footsteps.

I threw my quilt back and stood, shivering in the chill and reaching for my long skirts, pulling them on under my night-gown. Legs covered, I found socks and pulled them up to my knees before shrugging into a thick sweater and twisting my hair up into a messy bun I'd have to fix before dinner. But that was okay, because I would have to change and get dressed for dinner anyway.

For now, I would get that turkey in the oven so Momma wouldn't be upset. She'd been so tired lately. Papa said he thought it was because she hadn't been at full strength when she got pregnant this time, and he blamed himself for that. He'd been spending more of his evenings at the Lions Club than I could remember him ever doing before, and Momma's usual excitement as the holidays approached was nearly completely missing.

I couldn't make whatever was bothering them better, but I could make sure the holiday season was just as special for my little sisters as it had always been for Alexander and me. And that started with Thanksgiving dinner being on time, cocoa being ready when they woke up this morning, and the parade from New York on the TV as soon as we finished our cinnamon rolls at eight.

All that and milking the cows was a fair amount to do between now and sunup. But I wanted the holidays to be special this year for a lot of reasons, and I wanted Momma to have a good Thanksgiving, which wouldn't happen if she woke up to find she'd overslept and nothing was done.

I crept past their room and down the stairs silently, turning on only the small light over the stove to work by in the kitchen and tying an apron on. Pulling the turkey pan from the fridge, I removed the towel Momma had wrapped him in and put it in the laundry bucket by the garbage can, washing the skin with buttermilk before I added salt and slid the pan into the oven when it was heated to the right roasting temperature.

"Happy Thanksgiving, y'all," I said, turning to wash my hands with a proud smile. I'd never been in charge of the turkey —Momma only trusted herself with that job—but I'd watched her enough that I thought I had pulled that off pretty perfectly. In just a few hours, the whole house would smell like juicy roasting meat, the spices of the dressing and the sides melting in until it smelled perfectly like the holidays. One of my favorite smells in the world.

Hands clean, I grabbed the milk pails from the mudroom and slipped out the back door, pausing to look up at the full moon, glistening off the frost covering the yard with a silvery glow that made me excited to see snow soon.

Would snow in New York City be as magical as snow in Firefly Grove?

"It'll be in New York City, where there are people and music and art galleries and the kind of life you want," I muttered, shaking my head. Nobody was going to bring my dreams to me. I would have to go chase them.

I just hoped I was brave enough.

I was almost to the new barn, the big elm tree between me and the house, when I heard the shriek of metal scraping metal. Pausing, I looked around the tree trunk toward the old bomb shelter on the other side of the garden. The doors on that thing were temperamental on a nice day. In the cold they got downright fussy.

The clearing was still. I stepped toward the barn just as the door to the shelter opened, falling into the side of the hill where it had been dug. Momma stepped out into the moonlight, looking around before she shut the door and hurried to the house.

I watched the door even after she went inside, not quite sure I should believe my eyes.

I hadn't heard her move upstairs because she was outside, not asleep.

But why? She hadn't come out carrying anything I could see. Maybe she had jars in her coat pockets, though.

I remembered Alexander arguing with her about the crib and wondered if she'd gone out to look at it and thought better of moving it. But something in my gut stopped me from asking if she needed my help.

Most people didn't slip in and out of dark rooms in the middle of the night for any good reason. My momma was a good person, but something was weighing on her. I'd told myself

Papa was right, it was just her weakened body and this pregnancy. But I wasn't sure I believed that.

I also wasn't sure I wanted to know what she was doing outside at this hour, especially on this day.

I had secrets of my own to worry about, I didn't need to carry Momma's, too. Did I?

THIRTY-NINE

SarahBeth
February

My boots crunched through the stiff layer of frost covering yesterday's snow, the night still, the small sliver of moon behind the clouds providing cover of darkness so thick I couldn't see my hand in front of my face.

But I'd walked this stretch in the dead of night for months. It was ninety-one steps from door to door, and there wasn't so much as a stray rock in between. I couldn't risk a flashlight—if anyone in my house woke up and happened past a window, everything would be ruined.

I put my hands out at eighty-nine steps and found the door latch two steps later, right where I knew it would be.

Wincing at the squeal of the old metal door, I stepped into the shelter and shut it behind me before I turned on the light. I hurried to the other door and pulled the key from my pocket, unlocking the padlock and yanking the door open enough to peek around.

It was quiet.

Perfect.

I scooped a soft bundle up and straightened a blanket on the crib, ducking out and cutting the lights, waiting for my eyes to adjust before I went back outside.

Ninety-one steps later, I stepped into the kitchen.

"Welcome home," I whispered, kicking my boots off and hurrying up the back stairs. "Shhhhh."

I slipped through our bedroom, where Burt was snoring in the bed after coming home late from another Lions Club meeting. For a group that was supposed to focus on charitable work, our local chapter did a lot of socializing—and drinking.

After a dreamy early fall that rivaled the early days of our marriage, nights of kissing and touching until it was late and we fell asleep in each other's arms, he'd begged one night, just before Halloween, and I'd given in, telling him I wanted to keep my skirts on so he couldn't see my scars. I'd clawed at the edge of the mattress so hard I lost three fingernails on my left hand, and it hadn't mattered. I lasted four strokes before a sob escaped. He'd muttered a swear word I'd never heard him say in nearly twenty years together and left before I could suggest trying something else I'd never been willing to do.

That was the turning point. He'd been out most nights since, and I'd tried to ignore it. I hadn't done all this for no reason. I just had to hold it together until the baby got here, that was all. He'd fall in love with us both, and I would get my life back.

"My saving grace," I said.

I laid my bundle in the bathtub and retrieved a canning jar from under the sink, smearing the drain area and the lower walls of the tub with thick, sticky red. I stood and surveyed the bathroom, wiping more on the floor, then coating both my hands and leaving handprints on the gleaming white sides of the tub, and wiping my hands on a towel I wadded up and dropped next to the tub. Stripping off my clothes, I stuffed the padding I pulled from my skirts under the sink for now. I could burn the fake belly later, coming back inside without it would've been too risky.

Lifting the bundle gently, I pulled back layers of blankets and marveled for a second before I stuck my finger in a jar of thick white skin cream and wiped spots in several places on her face and hands before I wrapped her back up.

She watched, quiet, wrinkling her nose when I wiped the cream on it.

"Such a good girl," I murmured. "My good baby girl."

Sitting back, I tried to look critically at the scene. I knew nobody here had reason to doubt me, but I didn't want to miss anything obvious, either.

Her hair.

It was so much longer than any of my other babies' had been, hanging in little golden ringlets nearly to her shoulders already.

I hated to cut it. But I didn't see a way around it.

Pulling scissors from the drawer, I pulled up sections and chopped them off, getting as close to her scalp as I dared, and then taking the hair and flushing it down the toilet.

"That doesn't count," I whispered. "You'll have a real first haircut, and that's the one we'll save."

Now then. I took a damp washcloth to her hair and frizzed it up, then put her hat back on before I looked her up and down again.

Pajamas. Dang. "Where in the world would I get footed pajamas?" I shook my head and stripped her naked, adding the pajamas and the diaper to the pile under the sink. She scrunched up her face twice at all the activity, but never so much as whimpered.

Okay. Third time was supposed to be the charm, right?

She wasn't much bigger than Alexander had been when he was born—twelve pounds, seven ounces—and some newborns already had a tooth. I wasn't stretching the bounds of belief too far.

"Perfect." I kissed her little head, splashed some water on my face, pulled my nightgown on and smeared it with my sticky red hands, then sat down in the tub and rewrapped the infant, pinching her toe as I did.

Her face went bright red and she screamed a high, raspy scream that stabbed straight through my eardrums into my brain and made me glad she was such a quiet baby. I straightened her blankets and sat back in the tub, lowering my voice and quickening my breathing.

"Burt!" I called. "Burt, help! I need your help!"

Footsteps. Good.

At least I knew he hadn't been drinking while he was out, because that always made him sleep so soundly he wouldn't hear a tornado if it plowed through the wall.

"SarahBeth?" He slammed the door back into the tile wall. "Are you okay? Did you fall?" He wiped at his eyes, blinking in the bright overhead light. "Is that blood? SarahBeth!"

I leaned my head back, curling my neck over the edge of the tub and smiling, raising one red-smeared hand.

"I am better than okay. Come and meet your daughter."

I got that out without letting the betrayal and hurt seep into the words, and figured it would get easier from there.

"My... oh, my God, did you?"

I waved him toward us. She had settled her little face against the pillow of my breast and dozed off.

"She... she's just as beautiful as you are."

There was nothing he could've said in that moment that would've cut deeper. Or given me more hope.

Most of my plan hinged on his reaction in this moment. If Burt was with me, I was set.

Tears dripped from his face and landed on top of my head.

"Oh SarahBeth. I'll never not be sorry I hurt you that night, but she is perfect. Thank you so much."

"She's not a boy." I hung my head, hiding a smile.

"She's healthy and strong, and she's here. And she's you. I don't need anything else." He touched her face and she sighed, like she knew she was home and safe. I smiled. "Welcome to the world, sweet... What do you want to name her?"

"Francine," I said softly. "After your great-grandmother."

"Our F baby," he said. "It's perfect. Just like her."

He rested his cheek on my hair and wrapped us both in his arms, and my heart stuttered in my chest. This was more perfect than I'd even dared to imagine. Francine was mine as much as any of our other babies. I'd fought for her. Killed for her. Her mother had no money, no family, and nowhere to go—nobody had so much as looked for her from what I could tell. And even if I was wrong about that, where would they look? They'd find nothing here, and Burt Godfrey was the definition of an upstanding family man, you could ask anyone in five counties.

I may not have given her life, but I'd given her a home and a family. Her father's name. She was mine. Just as much as she was his.

This baby girl was going to save us. In more ways than this one.

PART THREE

The Secrets We Bury
Present Day

FORTY

Meg
August

I wasn't even sure how long I stayed there in the Godfreys' driveway with the gravel eating slowly into my kneecaps after Ainsley stopped breathing. It might have been fifteen minutes or three hours.

The sun was higher in the sky by the time I got up.

And Ainsley was gone.

"Where did you take her?" I asked Alexander, spinning to face him and almost falling on my cramped legs that didn't want to work. He put one hand out to steady me and I shrank away before I could help myself. I didn't want him to touch me. Didn't want anyone to touch me, not right then. The grief had me wound so tight I was afraid breathing too hard would make me shatter into a million pieces.

But I couldn't think about that right now.

"Just trying to help," Alexander said, looking me straight in the eye even though that was usually hard for him. He kicked a rock. "I know you loved her as much as we did, and I'm thankful Ainsley had you for a friend. I'm sorry if anything I did ever messed that up for her, even for a little while. Momma has been on me about my temper ever since I can remember, and I'm doing better now."

My forehead puckered as I stared at him with my head tipped to one side. "I don't think you messed anything up. And just so you know, Ainsley loved you, too."

"Oh, I know that." His voice went soft, his eyes moving from mine to focus on the sky behind me. "She was a good big sister. She took care of everyone, and kept everyone's secrets. I hope she knew I loved her."

"I'm sure she did." I looked around. "Where is she?"

"In the back barn."

"How long before the coroner gets here?" I asked.

"Coroner?" His forehead scrunched.

"You know, they have to take her body to a funeral home. The funeral home." There was only one in the county.

"I don't think they do." Alexander shook his head.

"Ainsley told me once that everyone in your family is always cremated."

"I think that used to be true," he said slowly. "But I don't see Momma letting anybody burn Ainsley up. No matter what someone Papa was related to said once about fire and cleansing." He held his hands up when I shot him a glare. "All I know is that Momma said take Ainsley to the barn, so that's what I did."

I turned to run that way and didn't get two steps before the front door flew open and my little man came charging out of the house.

"Momma!" he hollered, bounding across the lawn with wide blue-violet eyes, his chestnut hair a little too long and blowing in the wind. "Bethany said I can cut the biscuits!"

He leapt at me like he nearly always did these days, wrapping arms and legs around me when I gathered him up and buried my face in his hair. One of these days he'd be strong enough to just flat tackle me. But not today.

Pulling his little face back as quickly as he had run out, he touched my cheek with one finger and tipped his head to one side. "Mommy sad?"

I sniffled. "Yeah, buddy," I said.

"How come?"

"Oh, because Ainsley—" Alexander stopped talking when I landed a kick to his shin that made my toe throb.

"Where's Auntie Ainsley?" Cory looked around. "Want to tell her I'm cooking."

"She's not here, buddy."

His face fell for a second, then he smiled. "I'll cook again for her."

I nodded as he started wriggling to get down, kissing his head again and putting him on his feet.

"He's a happy little guy," Alexander said.

I nodded. "This will be hard for him." I balled one hand into a fist and pressed my knuckles to my lips. "He loved her so much," I choked out.

"I should check on Momma," Alexander said. "I've never seen her look like she did when she told me to take Ainsley to the barn. Not even after her accident, when she lost the baby."

SarahBeth's face had been completely blank as she stood over Ainsley's body. I'd never really understood that expression before—how could a person just not have any kind of look on their face at all? But I knew what it meant now because I'd seen it. I wasn't sure if she was in shock, or if maybe she just couldn't or wouldn't believe what was happening right in front of her.

I wondered if maybe she felt guilty—the doctor had said that something left over from the measles Ainsley had when she was a toddler had caused a brain infection all these years later that killed her. Cory'd had shots as a baby that would stop him from getting the measles. But I'd heard SarahBeth say last night that Ainsley didn't have a shot. After Ainsley and Alexander got sick, she'd said, then her other children got shots as babies like Cory did.

"You're the oldest now," I said, watching Alexander and wondering if he might get sick like Ainsley had, too, if he'd also had the measles like his mother had said.

"I never wanted to be." His eyes were sad as he turned for the house.

As soon as the front door closed behind him, I darted around the side of the house and made a beeline for the back barn. I needed to see my friend one more time. I wasn't exactly sure what to do with her last words—was she talking about whoever belonged to the skull I'd found in my backyard that awful summer night I'd tried so hard to forget? But the skull hadn't been in my garden, and the way Ainsley kept saying "little girl," made me think it wasn't—and made me regret not asking her when I had the chance. At the very least I had to look at her face and say goodbye.

I slipped into the barn, shutting the door behind me.

They had put her bed in the middle of the floor, and the horses weren't excited about it. I stopped to rub their soft noses. "It's okay, girls," I said. "It's all going to be okay. Somehow."

I turned to the bed, leaning over to plant a soft kiss on Ainsley's cool forehead. "I'll miss you so much, my best true friend. My sister of the heart. Fly high. And don't worry about anything here anymore. I will take care of everything."

I patted the horses again on my way out, shutting the door and heading for the house, my eyes roving over every square foot of the garden on the walk.

Could there really be someone buried there?

What little girl? Why?

How did Ainsley know, and why didn't she tell anyone before today, as she was dying?

I just had to figure out what she was talking about, and why it had mattered so much to her that she told me today.

She's in the dark—that's what she'd said. And Ainsley had been perfectly lucid as far as I could tell.

I was no detective, but I owed Ainsley everything—she had given us a family, she had forgiven me for breaking her heart, and she had proven to my jaded mind that there were good people in the world. I couldn't let her soul carry a burden of guilt into the next life.

Under the surface of that conviction floated the image of the grinning skull I'd found in my own yard. For something I'd tried so hard to believe I'd forgotten, it was right there at the ready. The size of it, and the teeth I'd seen that night, meant it belonged to an adult. And it was nowhere near my small garden, which I'd built on Mr. Lester's old garden.

Things would be easier if I could assume that's what she was talking about and maybe move those bones to a place where they'd be found. But in that odd, inexplicable way that Ainsley and I had sometimes been able to talk without talking, I just knew she was talking about this garden. Her garden. Sarah-Beth's prized garden.

I couldn't just walk over there and start digging.

Ainsley had babbled about the little girl in the garden for hours last night. I just didn't know why until there was no time left to ask her to explain.

But her words had colored all my memories of her and her family in a split second. Was this why they were so old fashioned and tight knit? Was the entire Godfrey family hiding a terrible secret? Or had this been Ainsley's burden—why she didn't go to school, or hardly anywhere else, ever? What could've happened, and to who?

An accident? A sister? A murder?

So many questions.

And the most logical place to look for answers was in that huge, rambling house.

I should check on Francine and Daisy anyway. And my son, who had no idea one of his favorite people was never coming back, and was helping Bethany cook biscuits and eggs.

FORTY-ONE

SarahBeth
August

A part of my heart shriveled and faded away when Burt closed Ainsley's eyes for the last time.

I watched him and nodded, but I didn't cry.

I couldn't. If I started, I'd never stop.

My beautiful, kind, capable oldest child. The little girl who made my biggest dream come true when she made me a mother, back when I hadn't seen much more of life than she'd gotten in all her days.

She would never see another sunrise, another firefly summer, another canvas she had created something wonderful and moving on.

And it was all my fault.

We grew into a family together, me and Ainsley and Burt. She was always supposed to grow up and have her own home and her own life, of course. I'd always been ready for that, I thought. But when it came down to it, her dreams were so much bigger than mine. I didn't like the path she chose for herself. A path that would take her away from her home and her family. I pushed. I schemed. I took away her options one by one until she didn't have any left but to stay here.

I thought I had paid for that in my own blood years ago.

But it wasn't enough, and now she was dead. Mothers aren't supposed to have to bury their children.

Bury. Oh, God. Burt would want to cremate her. To take her away to the cemetery. I couldn't have that. Wouldn't be able to stand the thought of her being there in the dark alone.

I turned and caught Alexander's sleeve. "Take the bed to the back barn."

"By myself?" His eyebrows went up.

"Figure it out," I said. "Get the truck, there's a furniture trolley around here somewhere. I won't ask Papa to carry her. Not now."

"Yes, ma'am." He turned and then paused. "Momma, what happened to Ainsley—is it going to happen to me, too? I mean, we were both sick when we were little. I don't remember it good, but I remember the fever."

I shook my head. "The doctor said what Ainsley had is very rare."

"But how would I know?"

"The headaches," I said. "She's been getting headaches for months now, every one worse than the last. I thought she was reading after bedtime, or getting too much sun, or... I don't know. A hundred things." I pulled in a shaky breath. "Do you have headaches?"

"Sometimes. I used to get them after football practice a lot."

"That's not the same thing."

Alexander nodded and turned away, and I looked back at the house. I had to go inside. There were things to do. But I didn't want to go into our house, not when Ainsley wasn't there. Would never be there again. I made my feet take two steps and noticed Meg, her body slumped over her folded knees as she sobbed, a few feet from Ainsley in the yard. She'd sat up with my daughter all night, that girl, and then moved when the time came for her to leave this earth so we could stand with her.

Another regret for me to bear. I had misjudged Meg at every turn, starting with assuming she was a threat to my marriage. I never gave her a fair chance, so intent on getting her out of our lives at any cost. I closed my eyes, shame flooding my heart when I remembered the first time I saw her sweet little boy. The ridiculous plan I'd hatched at the library one gray spring day to make him my own, giving Burt the son he wanted —the son my Alexander could never be. I'd convinced myself that would keep Burt's attention on me, where it belonged, and that taking the baby would be easy. I'd done it with Francine. Surely I could manage it again. Meg had been a regular hermit since she moved in, who would miss her?

I had let such horrible envy into my heart. I'd sabotaged my daughter's only true friendship six ways from Sunday, caring more about what I wanted—or didn't want—than I did about something my daughter so clearly needed. No matter how big they get, they're always babies to their momma. I should've been more worried about Ainsley than I was about myself. Or about my marriage.

The hardest thing to admit to myself, standing there in the glare of the August sun, was that Meg hadn't deserved a bit of it. She'd been such a good friend to Ainsley.

And now she was alone with her little boy.

A better person would go to her and comfort her. See if they could find words that would help her feel better.

I wished I could be better, but that didn't make it so.

I spotted Francine, her four-year-old face pressed against the window, nose upturned, eyes big and sad. She didn't really understand what "dead" meant, but she knew her sisters were sad, so she was sad, too.

My sunshine baby. Our miracle child. She made my heart

happy every day. I started for the porch and stopped halfway there, watching Francine and wondering, my knees going weak, if God had taken Ainsley from me to punish me.

For taking Francine and raising her as my own. For the secrets I hid. The lies I told. The bodies I buried.

FORTY-TWO

Meg
August

The Godfrey house was a maze that had taken me at least a year to solve, but by the day Ainsley died, I knew it nearly as well as my own house.

The old barn was the main living area, with the giant great room, the kitchen, and the mudroom. The eastern wing had the girls' bedrooms, Burt and SarahBeth's room, and the laundry room. And the west wing was mostly Alexander's. Ainsley told me once her dad built it for the sons they wanted, so God just kept giving them girls. But she told me something else I remembered as I watched my son pucker his little forehead and arrange biscuit dough on a baking sheet: after the tornado that first summer I lived here destroyed the old farmhouse that held Burt's study, he'd bought a new desk and set up his new office in one of those empty bedrooms.

"I did it!" The baby held up both hands like he'd won a race.

"Good job, bud." I smiled, looking around. Burt and

Alexander had gone to town to talk to the doctor and whoever else they were supposed to notify about Ainsley.

"He's precious," SarahBeth said, washing potatoes for hash browns. "You're doing a good job with him."

It took me a few seconds of silence to realize she must be talking to me.

"I—um, thank you."

SarahBeth nodded. "I've earned that, I suppose. That's okay. But I want to thank you for being such a good friend to Ainsley. I know she was younger and more inexperienced than you in a lot of ways, but you were the first real friend she'd had in a long time, and you meant a lot to her."

It was maybe more words than she'd said to me in total in the two years I'd known her.

Seemed like I should respond, but I wasn't sure how.

"I'm really so sorry for your loss." I pointed to my son, who was working on placing a third biscuit like he was taking a test. "I cannot imagine."

"It hasn't fully hit me yet. I can only really pray it never will." SarahBeth turned off the faucet and peeled the potatoes in a blink, then retrieved a cheese grater from a high cabinet and started shredding them into a big mixing bowl.

"I will never be as good at working fast in the kitchen as you and Ainsley," I said, smiling.

SarahBeth froze, the half-potato in her hand dropping into the bowl as she pulled in a slow, ratcheting breath. Shaking her head, she stepped back and wiped at her eyes, sniffling.

"I'm so sorry, I was just trying to be nice," I said, handing her a towel. "I didn't mean—"

She held up one hand. "Trust me when I say you don't owe me any apologies." She caught her breath, then washed her hands and picked the potato up. "Ainsley was very good in the kitchen. Because I pushed her to be. I made her do things that I thought worthwhile instead of what she wanted to do with her life." She looked at my son, then at me. "If you learn nothing else from your time here, learn that. Let him chase his dreams, no matter how big or far away they might be."

"Yes, ma'am." I dropped my eyes to the counter, afraid to say anything else.

Bethany put the last biscuit on the tray and carried it to the oven. "Momma, I've got a few minutes," she said. "Let me finish the hash browns for you."

"I'm perfectly capable of making breakfast," SarahBeth snapped, yanking the bowl toward her chest.

"I didn't say you weren't." Bethany sighed, her shoulders drooping. "I'm sorry."

"For what?" SarahBeth asked, her face still pinched.

"Right this minute? That I'm not Ainsley, I guess." Bethany's hand clapped over her mouth, her eyes going wide like she hadn't meant to let those words out. SarahBeth went back to grating potatoes without acknowledging them.

I jumped to my feet, laying one hand on my stomach. "I don't feel so good. I'll be right back," I said, pressing my fingers to my lips and ducking my head.

"Understandable," SarahBeth said, nodding to my son, who was watching her with big, curious eyes. "Cory's just fine here with me."

I met her eyes, still red, for a second before I nodded, going out to the foyer.

Out of sight of the kitchen, I took the long hallway to the west wing and went up the stairs silently.

The hallway was lined by eight doors, and I had no idea which one might lead to Burt's study, but the study seemed like as good a place as I could think of to look for evidence of a missing or dead child—the more I thought about Ainsley's last words, the more I wondered if something more sinister than

SarahBeth's accident had been behind the Godfreys' sudden withdrawal from school, and from the rest of the county at large. But if a child had died here, how did it happen? And why didn't people in town talk about it?

Cottonwood County was the kind of place where a couple of inches of rain or the antics of the local drunk counted as news, because nothing interesting ever happened here. The death of a child is a tragedy. The suspicious disappearance or death of a child is a scandal. Tragedy and scandal have long shelf lives in places where the birth of a new calf makes headlines. Which might make a family want to keep it quiet. Say, by burying that child in their garden and dropping completely off the community's radar? That would explain Ainsley's confession, as well as why I hadn't heard so much as a whisper about this in two years here.

So I started with the first door on the right.

The rumpled bed was visible even in the dim light from the drawn shades, and I started to shut the door—this had to be Alexander's room, and it felt creepy to go prowling around in there.

But with the door halfway pulled, my eyes lit on a small shelf over the dresser, carved from a tree branch, about a foot and a half long and half that deep.

I swallowed hard, taking two steps into the room.

One, two, three, four... thirteen.

Thirteen skulls, no two from the same kind of animal, snarled from the little shelf on the wall.

I blinked and shook my head, backing out of the room suddenly paranoid that he'd be able to tell I'd been in there somehow.

Closing the door, I tried the one across the hall, blood roaring in my ears as the animal bones danced through my head.

I tried to reason it out. Burt had hunting trophies on the

walls right inside the front door. They had a real bearskin rug on the living room floor.

Country people feel differently about animals.

Except I was "country people," raised in an Appalachian trailer park, and I wouldn't have a skull in my house no matter where it came from.

Another memory from that first summer here floated up, this one of a possum that had been mutilated.

And there was Sheriff Cam, looking at me that day in the supermarket like he wanted to be so much more than my friend, and telling me to watch myself. Not to get too close.

I felt like today was proof I had failed at that. But I didn't see any way out except through.

The door across from Alexander's was locked. So was the next one down. Beside Alexander's room, I found a bathroom that was the kind of gleaming clean that told me SarahBeth kept up with it, not her son, especially given the state of Alexander's bedroom.

The next door on that side of the hallway led to a room stuffed with boxes, tinsel peeking out of one and colorful Christmas lights out of another.

I turned for the locked one across the hall and heard voices at the bottom of the steps.

"I'll just be a minute." Alexander's voice carried clearly. "Y'all set the table. Is Meg still here?"

Someone answered him, but I couldn't make out what they said or who it was.

What I did know was that he was nearly to the top of the steps.

I stepped into the box room, my heart hammering as I crouched behind a stack of boxes taller than I was.

I didn't know what exactly I'd thought I was looking for up there—a diary with a confession and a story about burying a little girl in the garden would've been great—but animal skulls and locked doors weren't even on the list of possibilities when I snuck upstairs.

I had spent two years carefully hiding part of myself from everyone here, even—maybe especially—Ainsley.

Why hadn't it ever occurred to me that I might not be the only one with something to hide?

FORTY-THREE

SarahBeth
August

Ainsley didn't cry when she was born.

Twenty-two years later almost to the day, listening to my husband rant about family traditions, that was the thing I remembered best about the day I became a mother.

She was smart, right from the get-go. I'd pushed for an hour and fifty-three minutes, and was sure I was just going to split right in half from the pressure in my hoo-ha, when the midwife said "one more push and the head will be out."

I squeezed my eyes shut and gave it all I had, hoping I'd just have one more after that to deliver her shoulders. And then somehow the pressure was gone, and someone said "it's a girl," but there was no cry.

I opened my eyes and met my daughter's for the first time, big and curious, just looking around at the world we'd made for her. Her head was so big the rest of her slid right out.

"That's some brain this little one must have," the midwife said as she stretched a cap over it and laid her in my arms.

And she really had. But I hadn't wanted that for her—had stopped her from chasing the dreams that brain had given her. And now it was too late to take it back.

"Generations of Godfreys have been cremated and laid to rest outside the church," Burt said, dropping onto the edge of the bed like a wet rag, his voice fading. "I want Ainsley with her family. If she can't be with us." His voice broke, and he sobbed into one hand.

"I can't put her into a fire, Burt," I said.

"I'm not asking you to do anything but let me follow the tradition. It's not like I want to build a sacrificial altar out back and have you light a match." His words hitched around the sobs.

"She was afraid of it," I said, my words falling with the kind of fatigue that comes with a shattered heart. "She made me promise her once that I wouldn't ever let anyone burn her. Remember, when she learned about the Salem Witch Trials in school? She checked out every book in the library and read about it for months. It was all she talked about."

"She won't know, SarahBeth," he said.

"I will know."

I would also know the darker part of that story, the part I'd never say out loud to another soul, especially not Burt. The part where Ainsley chattered so incessantly about witches being burned at the stake that fall and how awful it must have been, and then I'd smelled smoke and heard the most God-awful scream from the edge of the pond. I'd dropped a basket of the broccoli I'd been picking and run, my lungs starved for air and burning right out of my chest.

I had known something was wrong—deeply, intrinsically wrong —with my only son, even before I'd actually seen what he was capable of. Somehow. A mother always knows.

"Alexander, stop!" I'd tried to scream as I ran, but it just came out as a wheeze.

He was six and Ainsley was seven that year, and he had gotten the notion to bring an illustration from one of her library books to life, and built himself a small sacrificial stake by the pond.

I rounded the back barn and stumbled, crashing to the dirt when I tripped over my skirt, or maybe just falling on my face from the horror of seeing my son sitting so still, watching the rodent he'd tied to the stake as it burned.

Ainsley screamed louder than the rat, thrashing and kicking the best she could, but even then he'd been so much bigger than she was. He held her in place. As I got closer, I could tell he was talking, but I couldn't make out his words over her screams.

I had jerked him backward, sending them both tumbling to the ground, before I snatched up the branch he'd tied the rat to and dunked it in the pond.

By the time I had stomped out the fire and untied the animal, Ainsley had run off.

Alexander just sat there in the dirt, watching me. "I just wanted to show her how long it would take something to burn like that. Those people couldn't have really burned women like that. She shouldn't be scared."

I had sighed and dropped to the ground next to him.

Alexander was different. Different from me and Burt. Different from Ainsley and baby Bethany.

And I didn't know what to do to help him understand that.

"You know, that hurt the rat, Alexander."

He shrugged. "The barn cats kill them anyway."

"It—" I sighed. I didn't really know why he thought about things without emotion, but I wasn't sure I could find the words to explain this to him because of that.

"It's different when you do it," I said. "You're not a cat. People don't torture animals for fun."

"It wasn't fun. I wanted to see what would happen. I wanted Ainsley to see too." He frowned. "She didn't want to see."

"Why didn't you let her go when she got upset?"

"I was trying to tell her—" He threw up his hands. "She's been talking about this so much."

I could see the storm on his little face. He didn't understand, and I had seen this enough to know what was coming.

I stood, putting my hand out. "Come on."

"Where are we going?" he asked.

"You're mad."

He nodded.

I took him to the hayloft and pointed at a bale. "Go on. Kick it. Hard as you can."

I stood back and watched my little boy beat on that hay bale until his boots were scuffed and his hands bled. When he sat down and looked up at me with a smile, I squatted. "You can't hurt other people or animals when you're mad, buddy. But you can come out here, we'll stuff a leather bag with hay and you can hit it until you feel better."

———

Was that the right thing to do? I still didn't know, fifteen years later arguing with Burt about what to do with our little girl's body. I just didn't want Alexander taking out his temper on living things, so I gave him a safe, not-living one.

"Why would you promise Ainsley that?" Burt asked me now.

"I was supposed to die first," I said. "Didn't figure I'd be the one who had to make good on it."

"What would you have us do?"

I turned to him, grabbing his hands in mine. For the first time in ages, he didn't jerk away. "I want her with her family, too, Burt. Here. With us."

"She's not a deer, SarahBeth." His face looked a mix of confused and horrified.

I rolled my eyes before I could stop myself. Did he think I was a monster? "I'm aware. I mean, let's bury her with Elizabeth." After my fall, we'd decided to bury the tiny remains of the baby I'd lost here in Firefly Grove. My heart lifted the tiniest bit at the idea that we could keep Ainsley here, too.

"Behind the pond?" He tipped his head to one side. "I... this is different. Ainsley was a grown woman. I understood, before. You were so upset after your accident, and it wasn't like anybody would expect a funeral or anything for a miscarriage. Tradition didn't really cross my mind then. But now... I don't know. Can we do that?"

"It's our land, isn't it? Who's going to stop us?"

"This time people will expect a funeral. You know how things like this go around here. Kids who haven't talked to her in years will show up at church and cry."

"So we'll get an urn, we'll have a service. Fill it with things that mattered to her." I held his gaze until tears filled my eyes. "I can't let anyone take her from here, Burt. Not when I wouldn't let her leave when she wanted to."

He squeezed my hands. "You're a good mother, SarahBeth. Please don't doubt that. If this is what you want, then okay."

"Tomorrow?" I asked.

He nodded and stood. "I'll get up early and dig."

I put on my nightgown and slid into bed. His back was already to me, and I didn't reach for him anymore. I closed my eyes and thought about my son. Our only son. How many animals had I found cut to ribbons because he wanted to see what their insides looked like? I had made my peace with having girls after Daisy was born, figuring maybe God just knew better than we did, and all our prayers for another son went unanswered because another boy would be like Alexander.

And then I'd lost Elizabeth. It was all so stupid—I knew well that a farm was a dangerous place. I'd been sixteen weeks pregnant for the sixth time the day Burt asked for someone to bring that blasted tractor motor down. I should've known better than to try to do it myself, fifteen years after I'd had Ainsley—I had no business trying to carry something so heavy down a rickety wooden ladder. Now, I knew in my bones that one stupid, stubborn decision put me—and this family—on the path that had led us to this terrible day. I'd miscarried a miniature, yet already perfect, little girl on the floor of the barn, nearly bleeding to death, and we'd buried her out by the pond when I got out of the hospital. Then I had parlayed that loss—and my injuries—into a scheme to squash my eldest daughter's dreams and keep her here, where I thought she belonged.

Baby Elizabeth's burial wasn't what you'd call a ceremony, just the family gathered around a small grave with Burt praying over the freshly turned dirt. The children had spotted a rainbow just as he'd said "Amen." Children had a way of seeing the truth in big things that I had always found wonderful and amusing.

That night, just the idea of my children seeing the truth about the things I'd done terrified me in a bone deep way that had me shivering until the whole bed shook and I thought I'd never be warm again. Burt didn't move, and I just laid there shaking and wondered if any of my children would see the truth of the role I'd played in their big sister's death. If they'd hate me if they understood what had started with one stupid decision and a catastrophic fall.

FORTY-FOUR

Meg
August

"I didn't even know this many people lived in Cottonwood County," I muttered to myself as I shuffled, part of a large and growing crowd, into a church for the first time in more than two years. Ainsley's funeral might well be the only occasion that could've made me do that willingly.

"Tragedy has a way of bringing folks out of the woodwork." The familiar voice behind me sent a shiver so pleasant it made me ashamed of myself from my ears to my toes.

I gripped my son's little hand so tight he squeaked and smoothed my black skirt down with my other hand. "It's good of you to come, sheriff." My voice sounded fake, the words so stiff and brittle I thought for just a second they might shatter in the air, vanishing before they were heard.

Maybe that was more of a wish than a fear.

"I knew Ainsley most of her life," Cam said, stepping around to walk through the church lobby on Cory's other side. "I wouldn't be anywhere else on Earth today for love or money."

I froze with one foot in midair. "What did you say?"

Cam slid his eyes sideways as I started walking again when the woman behind me bumped into me and enveloped us both in a cloud of bergamot perfume. "Just something my Momma used to say. I've been thinking about her a lot this week. The Godfreys came into my life when she first got sick, you know?"

"My granny used to say that, too," I said, sliding into a row of pews when he pointed and pulling my unusually subdued toddler onto my lap. "I've never heard anyone else say it."

Cam smiled. "Small world."

We watched people file in until the pews were full, and an elderly woman with a walker paused next to Cam at the end of our row, looking around at the full sanctuary, her rheumy green eyes filling with tears when they landed on a photo of Ainsley, her hair blowing in a prairie breeze, next to the polished brass urn on the table near the pulpit. "Ainsley Godfrey." She shook her head. "What a shame."

Cam shot to his feet. "Mrs. Owens, please take my seat."

I looked up at him, all broad shoulders and earnest smile, and wished for the thousandth time that things had gone differently. Looking around at the rest of the room, I wished desperately that so much was different.

"Cameron, how kind of you. You always were a kind young man," Mrs. Owens' voice was the kind of high and thready that often came with advancing age, her hands shaking as she leaned on the end of the pew and folded the walker. "I don't need you to stand. I'm not as big as a minute these days, if you could see your way to scooching over, I believe we'll all fit."

I scooted closer to a blonde with a curvy figure and big blue eyes whose handbag was on the seat on her other side. She glanced at me, then at Cam and the elderly lady, but she didn't speak or move, her black sundress showing off a little more of her tan than I'd have been comfortable with in church myself.

"Plenty of room," I said, smiling at the woman Cam called

Mrs. Owens and keeping my voice low as the pastor walked in with Burt and SarahBeth, escorting them to the front pew where their children were already seated.

The blonde on my other side snorted and I landed a sharp elbow to her ribs as I situated Cory on my lap. She pulled in a sharp, hissing breath and moved her purse into her lap, sliding over a few inches.

It made just enough room for Cam to squish in next to me and give Mrs. Owens a comfortable space at the end of the pew.

"Sorry." He whispered as he stretched his arm along the back of the pew behind me for a bit more space.

"Don't be," I whispered back, trying to think of anything except the sparks popping from every last inch of his left thigh, wedged against my right one. "That was kind of you."

"Mrs. Owens was the art teacher at our school for," he shook his head, "probably fifty years? She loved Ainsley like her own daughter and spent hours encouraging her, and more hours telling anybody who would listen how talented Ainsley was."

I turned my head toward him. "Art?"

"Sure. Her paintings, you know. For a while she even talked about moving to New York City and trying to sell them. Or at least, Mrs. Owens talked about Ainsley doing that—I was getting ready to graduate when Ainsley was in the sixth grade, and Mrs. O showed Ainsley's paintings to the seniors as examples of what we should be working toward, told us someday we'd all be able to say we knew the famous painter Ainsley Godfrey."

My breath sped as a brick settled in my stomach. How did I not know this? A God-given gift, a child buried in the garden... what else had my best friend kept hidden from me? Realizing where I was sitting, I arranged my face in what I hoped was a casual expression and nodded. "Of course." When I slid a glance at Cam, his face said he didn't buy it.

The art teacher let a raspy sob out into a yellowing lace-trimmed handkerchief, and Cam turned, patting her hand. "I know how much you loved her," he murmured.

"She was so gifted." The elderly woman fixed the back of SarahBeth's head with a glare I was half surprised didn't cause her hair to catch fire. "Such a shame."

My heart climbed right up into my throat, my eyes filling for what I was sure wouldn't be the last time today. "Thank you for making room for her," I whispered to Cam.

He nodded as the pastor patted SarahBeth's shoulder and walked past the table with the urn and stepped to the pulpit.

"It is a testament to the impact Ainsley Godfrey had on this community in her short life, and to the kind hearts of this community, that so many of you are here today," he said. "Burt and SarahBeth have asked me to make sure y'all know how much they appreciate you."

He talked about the promise of the kingdom of Heaven, read John 3:16, and praised Burt and SarahBeth for having Ainsley baptized as a child. "I will never forget how much that girl loved the water. She told me the fishing pond at Firefly Grove was her favorite place in the world, and she worked extra hard to get her chores done early in the summer so she could swim for as long as possible." The pastor smiled. "She was so disappointed that our baptism wasn't by immersion I thought for a minute she was rethinking her faith and we might find her over at Timber Creek Baptist before long."

That got a laugh from most of the room, but I heard the sobs from the front pew.

"At this time, I'd like to invite anyone who wants to share a memory of Ainsley to come forward and do so. Her spirit was so bright, I know she touched many of you, and her family will find comfort in that today."

A small line formed, and the pastor stepped aside for a woman who said she was Ainsley's teacher in elementary school. "I have so many memories of Ainsley's kind heart and motherly instinct, which was as strong as you'd expect from SarahBeth Godfrey's eldest daughter," she said, dabbing at her eyes. "But the one that stands out to me happened on Bethany's first day of kindergarten. Ainsley was just a year away from moving upstairs with the higher grades, but she still had lunch with the little ones and she was sitting with her friends chatting about whatever little girls that age get excited about when Bethany wailed from across the room."

My eyes went to Bethany, who was sitting up straighter, her shoulders square as she watched the teacher. "Now mind you, Ainsley was across the room and her back was to her sister," the teacher said. "But the very same second that cry split the air, our sweet little Ainsley was on her feet, her face set in a scowl. An avenging angel if there ever was one, I swear it. She shot across the room to Bethany's side, and I stood up, half afraid for whatever small one had upset Ainsley's sister."

I leaned slightly forward in my seat, my arms tightening around my son. The teacher smiled. "Thankfully, it turned out that Bethany didn't like peanut butter, and she had gotten Alexander's sandwich by accident that day. Ainsley made quick work of finding her brother and making the trade, but I still wonder if her protective reaction in that moment didn't make a few children think twice about messing with Bethany Godfrey."

Heads nodded and people chuckled as she stepped aside for the next woman in line, whose husband owned the Feed and Seed. We listened to four more stories before Cam leaned over as the line dwindled. "You don't want to go up? I can sit with Cory."

I pulled in a deep breath. On the one hand, I wanted to stay in my quiet, unknown little cocoon. I had come to like not knowing many people in the past couple of years. On the other, everyone so far, including the pastor, had talked about Ainsley as a little girl. I wondered if I might be the only person here not related to her by blood who really knew her—or knew her a little, as the case may be—as an adult. Didn't I owe it to my friend to say something?

Letting the air out of my lungs, I nodded and whispered in Cory's ear that Cam was nice and he could sit with him while I went to say something about Auntie Ainsley.

"I want to say something." My son widened his blue eyes and stuck out his lower lip.

"Sure, buddy. You just come with me."

I stood and took his hand, scooting past Cam and the art teacher and joining the back of the line.

We listened to the grocery store manager talk about how Ainsley was always respectful when she came in to sell the extra vegetables from the Godfreys' massive garden, and to a childhood friend who couldn't stop her hiccupping sobs long enough to finish her story about the fireflies at Ainsley's house, and then we stepped up to the pulpit.

It felt weird to stand in front of a church and look out at the congregation, so I kept my eyes on the back of the urn on the table.

"I don't know many of y'all, but I'm Meg, and Ainsley was my closest friend for the past two years." My voice faltered at first, but gained strength by the time I said her name out loud. "I have loved listening to the memories everyone has shared about my friend today, but I wanted to come up and talk a little about the woman the Ainsley Godfrey from your stories grew into. The friend I knew." Or thought I knew, anyway, but I couldn't say that.

"Ainsley was always looking out for others," I said, my voice ringing back off the rafters as I raised my eyes to the crowd for the first time. Heads bobbed as some folks murmured to those around them. "The very first time I met her, she saved me and my little one from a copperhead, and she just kept right on saving us in a thousand little ways from that day on. She gave us a family here, of sorts," I glanced at SarahBeth, who had been nicer to me since Ainsley died than she had ever been before, and she smiled and nodded her head, just once. "She gave me the sister I had wanted for so long. She helped teach me to be a good mother and to have faith in myself. Even with her very last words, she was concerned for someone else." My eyes slid back to SarahBeth's before I could help it. Her forehead bunched the tiniest bit before I looked away. "I wish I'd had more days with her, but she will be part of my heart forever because of her kindness."

More nods and murmurs. Cory tugged on my hand and I picked him up. He leaned toward the microphone. "I'm glad my Auntie Ainsley isn't sad anymore," he said. "I wish I could see her. I just wanted to say how much I love her and I'm happy she's happy now." He turned to the pastor. "Like you said before."

The pastor smiled and I put Cory down and moved aside so he could step back to the microphone. "From the mouths of babes, folks. We are all so glad and blessed to know that Ainsley is happy." He glanced toward the teacher who'd told the story about Bethany. "Even if it is such a shame she never got to be a mother herself."

SarahBeth slumped into Burt's shoulder. I saw Bethany's eyes go to her mother. What I couldn't quite make sense of was the mix of fear and anger on her face.

Until Mrs. Owens, the elderly art teacher, started talking.

"Don't you dare sit up there and pretend grief in front of these good people in the house of the Lord, SarahBeth Godfrey!" There was nothing weak about the old woman's voice as every head in the church swiveled her way.

That sanctuary went so quiet you could've heard a gnat sneeze.

Mrs. Owens grabbed the back of the pew in front of her and stood. Cam hopped to his feet, putting a hand on her arm that she shook off, her eyes boring lasers into the back of SarahBeth's head for the second time in an hour.

"Ainsley was a smart girl with an extraordinary gift." Mrs. Owens paused to catch her breath, and Bethany and Alexander stood, turning around. Burt strained to turn his head backward, his eyes wide as he patted SarahBeth's shoulder with one hand while he gestured to the pastor with the other.

"Some folks here might not believe you put Ainsley in that jar there, depending on what they think about vaccinations, I guess, " Mrs. Owens said, taking one lurching step into the aisle without her walker. "But you killed her spirit with your jealousy and scheming as sure as I'm standing here, and I hope God judges you as he should."

Burt wriggled out from under his wife as Bethany started toward the teacher. I felt Cory grab two handfuls of my skirt and hide his face, the entire room transfixed by one tiny old woman and Ainsley's large, grieving family. SarahBeth had flopped into the arm of the pew such that I couldn't even tell if she was still conscious.

"You just—" Bethany snarled, stepping into the center aisle before she was cut short when Alexander's hand closed around her upper arm.

"Don't." His deep voice seemed to fill every bit of vacant space in the sanctuary all the way up to the dark wood rafters. "Ainsley loved Mrs. Owens, and she has a right to speak her piece. She loved Ainsley, too."

Like it had been choreographed, every pair of eyes went back to the old woman.

She looked from Bethany to Alexander and opened her mouth before her whole face kind of went slack.

Cam lunged for her, his arms going around her just in time to keep her from hitting the floor when she collapsed.

FORTY-FIVE

SarahBeth
August

"Mrs. Owens has been old since God was a boy." Burt parked the truck outside our house and turned in the seat to face me. "She was old when we were in school, she was even old when my momma and daddy were in school. She probably didn't even realize what she was saying."

I nodded, my eyes only even half seeing my husband sitting there, my arms tight around Francine, who had cuddled right up in my lap and gone to sleep on the drive home.

Burt was right, the art teacher had to be a hundred by now. But that didn't mean the old bat was wrong. Age gives people both the wisdom to cut through nonsense and the courage to tell the truth, even when others are afraid to speak it—or sometimes, even to see it.

Which was why I couldn't tell my husband what was going through my head right then. But I couldn't quiet it, either, so I did the only thing I knew how—sucked in a deep breath and pushed it as far aside as I could. I had a family to take care of. Who was to blame for Ainsley's death didn't change that.

We trooped back into the house after the children hopped one by one out of the bed of the truck.

No one had the energy to speak, which was just as well. I felt like I'd come out of my skin if I heard one word out of anyone in my house. It turned out the anger portion of grieving was the one I was best at.

Back in my kitchen, I got a load of bread from the box and started cutting slices for sandwiches. Alexander washed an apple and sat down on a stool across from me.

"Momma?"

I looked up, not trusting myself to mind my manners if I spoke. I'd heard him defend Mrs. Owens in the church, and whether she was right or not, it had stung to have my only son say anything kind about her in that moment.

"I'm sorry to pester you, I know you're... well. I just have to ask because it's coming on September soon. Um, see, I went to town yesterday to pick up a part from the machine shop for Papa, and I ran into coach. You know, from the high school?"

I nodded, my eyebrows going up.

"So he told me that Kip moved to Kansas City for a new job, something with computers, and they need an assistant coach this season. And he asked me." He flashed a small smile, and I could see pride in his eyes that I wasn't sure I ever had before. "They want me. To coach the team this year. But two a days have already started, and I gotta tell him something by tomorrow. Otherwise I wouldn't ask you right now. So. That's it. I wanted to see what you thought. And I'm sorry."

I nodded, pulling in a deep breath before I started slicing a tomato for sandwiches.

"I think that's a big responsibility," I said. "But it sounds like you'd like to do it."

He started nodding before I stopped talking. "I promise I'll get up early and stay out late and it won't interfere with my work here. But I really would like to try. I miss football, these past couple of years. You know?"

I did. And with Mrs. Owens' words still ringing fresh in my ears, I was through stopping my children from going after what they wanted from life.

"I think it's a great fit for you, son. And I'm proud of you. You were a great player, and you'll make a great coach."

He jumped to his feet so fast he knocked the stool right over. Burt came running when he heard it hit the floor, pausing in the doorway when he saw what had made the sound.

"Y'all okay?"

"Alexander here is the new assistant football coach over at the school," I said.

"No kidding?" Burt stepped into the room and shook Alexander's hand, making our son's face stretch into that grin that I used to think must be a curse of some sort. Right then was the first time I was ever able to see joy in it. "You're the right man for the job."

"Thanks, Papa." Alexander ducked his head. "Appreciate that."

Burt clapped him on the shoulder. "Why don't you go on and see if you can still make it to practice, tell coach you're in? The keys to my truck are on the table in the front hall."

"Thank you." Alexander looked back at me, holding my gaze for several beats. "Thank you both."

"Drive safe," I said.

"Yes, ma'am."

The door slammed behind him and Burt turned to me. "You're okay with this?"

"I can't make them do what I want them to do. They're not mine anymore. I shouldn't have ever tried." I sniffled as I finished making the sandwiches. "I just wanted to be a good wife and mother. To give you the life you wanted to have. That's all I've ever tried to do."

He rounded the end of the island and put one hand on my back. "Losing Ainsley doesn't make you a bad mother, Sarah-Beth. It certainly doesn't make you a bad wife."

It took every bit of strength I could muster not to tell him Ainsley's death was his fault.

If I was honest, I was mad at everything and everyone, but I was maddest at Burt.

"What if Alexander gets," I waved my hand, "whatever this was? He had the measles when they were babies, too. Are you at all concerned that we might lose him now?"

"The doc said that wasn't likely," Burt said carefully, his voice flat. "But I suppose that doesn't mean it's impossible."

"I won't survive it, Burt," I said, my head bending until my chin rested on my collarbone. "I should've gotten them their shots."

The words slipped out on a whisper in front of a sob, and his hand dropped away from my back.

"Are you blaming my momma for Ainsley?"

"Nope." I turned to face him, heat flushing my cheeks. I couldn't see my eyes, but in my thoughts, they blazed with a fire hot enough to burn away my grief and regrets. Hot enough to consume us both.

Maybe I was right—he stumbled backward, grabbing the edge of the counter to stay upright. "SarahBeth, you know I would never do anything to hurt one of my children. My momma said getting them vaccinated would weaken their immune systems. That we should let them get sick if they were meant to get sick. People say they put chemicals in those shots. I did what I thought was best for them."

And I did what he said, because I wanted to be a good wife.

I couldn't look at him. I turned away, biting my lips between my teeth so hard I tasted blood, and put the mayonnaise back in the fridge. I couldn't speak again right then—I knew if I did, my next words would bring our entire world crashing down around us.

Standing in my kitchen on the day we buried my daughter, I learned two things: I could let my children choose their own paths in life, and still watch them grow and thrive, even if it wasn't as I had always imagined—and I didn't have to be a good wife to be a good mother.

For the first time in nearly a quarter of a century, I didn't care what Burt Godfrey thought of me. Putting sandwiches on plates for everyone, I realized that I could refuse to care what he thought, that I could direct all that anger at him and save the best of whatever was left of me for my children. And I felt freer than I had in so many years.

FORTY-SIX

Meg
September

I went to Ainsley's house every day for the next five weeks. I couldn't stop thinking of it as Ainsley's house no matter how hard I tried, so somewhere around week three, I gave up.

Knocking on the front door on a Friday afternoon the last week of September, I smiled when Bethany opened the door. "I thought y'all might like some of the last of the blackberries I put up this summer."

"Bethany!" Cory pointed. "We cook?"

She smiled at him and took the jar from me. "I'm afraid I'm not cooking tonight, bud." She picked him up. "Jimmy is coming to take me to a movie over in Elgin, and Alexander talked everyone else into going to the football game."

"Football." Cory scrunched up his face and growled. "Grrr."

"How's Alexander liking the coaching job?" I asked Bethany.

"It is all he talks about. Seriously." She tipped her lips up and nodded. "He always said Ainsley had a gift, you know, with her painting, and he was her dumb little brother, but they haven't lost a game yet. Newspaper says they have a shot at a deep playoff run this year. I caught myself thinking maybe she helped him find his gift. Coach offered him the job because Jimmy told him how down Alexander was about Ainsley, and he thought it might help. Turns out this is what he was meant to do, I think. I'm so glad Jimmy talked to the coach about hiring him."

"Me too."

"I worried about Alexander for a long time." She flashed a tight smile, pinching her lips together and gesturing behind her. "I gotta get ready."

"Oh sure," I said. "Need any help with your hair?"

She gave me a once over. "That would be... really nice of you... actually."

We followed her inside and upstairs, where she perched on a stool in a big, bright hall bathroom. "I've seen it on TV, where the front is in a French braid and the rest is down?" Bethany said, holding up the front sections of her hair. "But maybe we can put the rest in curls?"

"I can do that." I took the comb she held out and pulled the front section of the left side up, dividing it in three near her hairline in the front and starting to braid, my fingers flying.

She watched in the mirror. "You're really good at this. You should have a little girl someday."

"I think my little buddy might be a one and only," I said. "But I'm happy to help you."

"Where did you learn?"

"School." It was a lie. My sister had been obsessed with French braiding her hair and I did it for her every morning for years. But I still couldn't talk about her without crying.

Bethany started to nod and then laughed. "I guess that's not the best idea."

"I can adapt." I caught her eyes in the mirror. "Why weren't you and Ainsley close?"

She shrugged. "I was jealous. She was the oldest, she was the smartest, and her paintings. I used to look at art books when Momma would take us to the library. Ainsley was really and truly better than some people who are famous painters. It wasn't fair."

"Why did she stop?" I asked. I had spent an ungodly number of hours the past few weeks wondering why Ainsley never mentioned painting to me in the years we'd been such close friends before I realized I'd spent a chunk of her last night on earth in her bedroom and seen not so much as a paintbrush. Maybe it wasn't that she didn't want to tell me. Maybe it hurt her to talk about it because she missed it.

"She never said. It was after she met you, you know. If I had to guess, I'd say it had something to do with that. Maybe she spent her painting time with you? Or maybe she gave up on the idea of leaving home because she had a friend here? I don't know. I just remember going in her room one day while she was over at your place, and all her art stuff was put up in her closet."

"She wanted to leave home?" I raised one eyebrow, trying to keep my voice steady. The Ainsley I knew loved Firefly Grove almost like I loved my son. I couldn't fathom her leaving.

"That was the other part of it—no matter how hard I worked at being like Momma, she loved Ainsley best. She couldn't stand the thought of Ainsley going away to New York City like she always talked about. Ainsley didn't want to be here, even, and I tried so hard, and Momma never noticed."

I stared at her reflection in the mirror. "You're not serious. Ainsley said you were your mother's favorite. That SarahBeth listened to you because you were more like her."

Bethany blinked a dozen times before she spoke, like the words had to sink in one at a time. "Momma doesn't listen to anyone but Papa, not really. She took my suggestions because I suggested things she wanted to do anyway."

"Seems like you two were wrong about each other." I didn't understand that kind of jealousy. My sister and I had never done the sibling rivalry thing. We were too busy surviving and taking care of each other, I guess.

"By the time I wasn't jealous of her anymore, it was too late. I had done too much." Bethany brushed at the corner of her eye. "I wish I could tell her I'm sorry."

"I'm sure she knows." I patted her shoulder and reached for the curling iron as I finished the last braid. "You okay over there, bubba?"

"Color," Cory said, holding up the bath crayons he was using to draw on the tile wall over the tub.

"You're sure those come off?"

"Momma can clean anything. When Frannie was born, she got up and cleaned all the blood out of the bathroom right the next morning. He's fine."

"That's pretty serious cleaning."

My thoughts wandered as I curled her hair, the conversation running out of steam. I didn't like Bethany because she hadn't been very nice to Ainsley, but I had needed her to let me in the house. I'd seen the dust from the truck when everyone else left for the game and wanted a few hours to snoop by myself. Cory was fascinated with their huge TV and would watch a cartoon while I looked around in places I wouldn't normally have reason to go. Like that locked office across from Alexander's room.

I'd been there when the house was full every day for weeks and found nothing. I didn't want to give up when I'd promised my friend, but it wasn't like I had a good reason to look in the kind of places people might hide something about a body in their garden, and with so many people always in the house, the constant risk of getting caught wasn't worth it.

I finished the last curl as a car horn sounded outside.

"Jimmy's here!" Bethany jumped to her feet, running down the hall and snatching a jacket from her closet. "Let yourself out, thanks for your help!"

"Have fun!" I called, listening for the door.

When I heard his truck drive away, I pulled a list from my back pocket and beckoned Cory to follow me to the hallway.

I stared at the door to Ainsley's room for a good thirty seconds before I opened it. Ainsley hadn't once invited me up to her room—the only time I'd been in it was that last night, when she was sick. I never gave that a second thought, really. We weren't children, playing in each other's bedrooms, after all. But now I wondered if her painting was all she'd forgotten to mention to me.

SarahBeth hadn't let anyone touch a thing. The bed was missing—SarahBeth had made Burt burn it after Ainsley died —but otherwise, every single thing was just as Ainsley had left it.

I went straight to the closet, where Bethany had said Ainsley put her painting supplies.

Her skirts and blouses were crushed into one corner to make room for a folded easel and two chest-high stacks of canvases. The top one on the left wasn't finished. I picked it up by the edges.

"Pretty," Cory chirped from behind me.

"Very pretty," I said of the lake landscape. Hand to God, it looked like the water was moving if I stared at the canvas long enough. I put it down and flipped through several more—the hills outside, the house, the pond. The one of New York City at sunrise stole my breath.

"Momma, look. I see Cory." My son waved a silver-plated hand mirror he'd found on the dresser.

"Cory is such a handsome boy." I barely glanced at the mirror or at my son as I closed Ainsley's closet and went to her nightstand, hoping I was at least a little right about how well I'd known my friend.

"Bingo," I said, pulling out a sketchbook. Seeing that Ainsley was indeed as gifted as everyone said, I figured she couldn't just stop creating cold turkey. And it looked like maybe I was right.

Cory clapped his hands. "B-I-N-G-O, and Bingo was his name-o." He danced as he sang and I grinned and ruffled his hair.

"Good job, bud."

I pulled in a deep breath and whispered, "Come on, Ainsley" as I opened the sketchbook.

Flipping pages, I was so taken with her extraordinary talent I almost forgot the mission. The word "gifted" didn't even do this justice, and these were just sketches. Some were dated years ago, some had notes written over them, some were detailed enough to pop right off the page, others were rougher.

I paused on a landscape of the yard, looking out and down from... I got up and went to the window. This room.

A woman with SarahBeth's signature bun stood near the driveway, her shoulders hunched up, arms wrapped around each other, watching a small car drive away in a cloud of dust. I shouldn't have been able to get from a pencil sketch that Sarah-Beth was upset or that the car was speeding, and yet... I knew it as sure as the sky was blue. That was the depth of Ainsley's talent.

That was why she never belonged in this place. Was Bethany right? Did she stay here—did she give up something that had to have been part of her soul—because of something to do with me?

I couldn't think so.

I put a finger on that sketch and kept turning.

The pond, a tractor in the field, Alexander in his football helmet. Burt standing behind SarahBeth, his arms around her waist, a soft smile on her lips. I could almost see them breathing. But on the canvases in the closet, I hadn't seen a single person. I wanted to ask Ainsley why she sketched people instead of painting them.

But I couldn't ask Ainsley anything anymore.

I ran out of pages, and started to close the book when my finger traced a pair of deep etchings inside the back cover. Inspecting them, I spotted a small scrap of paper where a page had been torn from the spiral wire binding. Turned out there were a whole lot of lines in the back cover. Deep lines.

"She was mad when she drew this, buddy," I said to Cory, who was using an oil pastel he'd pulled from a box in the open nightstand drawer to color his left arm purple. "How about we get you some paper?"

"Paper," he repeated.

I handed him a piece, then took one myself and pulled a pencil from a Cottonwood Secondary School 4H cup on Ainsley's desk and laid it on its side, running it back and forth over the paper, over the imprint on the sketchbook's back cover. I'd seen people do this on TV shows and it always magically revealed something important at just the right moment. Maybe it would work for me, too.

I got to the bottom and held the paper up to the light coming in the window.

Strike ninety-four: it was just a sketch of Francine, standing in a doorway with a crib behind her. I didn't have enough detail for anything beyond that, but it wasn't a magic key to whatever Ainsley had been talking about the day she died.

"No treasure maps here, bubba." I took the pastel from Cory, tucked the etching in my back pocket, and grabbed his hand. "Let's clean your arm."

"Treasure map," he said, toddling behind me to the bathroom. He was a little parrot these days, soaking up new words like a thick sponge, and I loved everything about it. We could even have simple conversations. I had loved his baby stage, but I was just as excited to have a little friend I could talk to as I had been to have a giggly baby.

I almost had him cleaned off when I heard a sharp rap at the front door, followed shortly by the knob turning.

"Burt? SarahBeth?"

Was that Cam?

I froze for a second, debating just staying quiet. They weren't here, he'd go on in a minute.

He wasn't looking for me.

"Hello?" he called.

Cory splashed the water at me and squealed. "Hello!" he shouted.

I shook my head at him. "Thanks," I whispered.

"Welcome," he chirped. Good to know the manners were sticking.

I pulled the plug from the sink drain and went to the door just as Cam came around the corner from the stairs. "Meg." He stopped, sticking his hands in his pockets. "I didn't know it was you."

"I was helping Bethany with her hair. She had a date," I said. "Everyone else went to the game."

He nodded. "Alexander seems to have found his calling. Glad to see it. I worried about him for a long time."

"Ainsley worried too."

"Football has been good for him, for all the grief it gets," he said. "Some folks don't handle pent-up aggression well. Alexander is one of them."

"What do you mean?" The hair standing up on my arms meant I wasn't sure I wanted him to answer that.

"I... it was a long time ago."

"Cam."

"Ainsley told me—do you remember the day after our one

and only date, I showed up at your house, and you had cut your foot?"

I nodded. Wasn't the kind of day people forget. Not that he needed to know that.

"There was a possum hanging from your porch when I got there." Cam's face flashed a disgusted look at the memory. "It had been... I mean, there's not another word for it but mutilated."

"I know. I saw it, it was there when I got home the night before."

"Why didn't you tell me that?"

"Tell me!" Cory said.

"Hey, buddy." Cam held his hand out and the baby slapped him five.

"Why didn't you tell me?" I countered.

"Because Ainsley said it was her brother. She said sometimes he'd seen him doing things like that to animals he'd trapped. She swore to me he'd never hurt a person, and she cut the thing down and got rid of it. You live next to them, I didn't want you to be afraid."

My heart stuttered in my chest. I had doubts, true, but I'd thought horrible things about Ainsley. Had been angry with her and pushed her away for weeks. Maybe months. And it wasn't even her. Not that she ever told me. She protected Alexander even at the risk to our friendship.

I wasn't sure how to feel about that. I also wasn't capable of being mad at Ainsley when I missed her so much. So I snapped at Cam.

"What if he had decided to, I don't know, gut me like a fish and hang me from a tree?"

"She said he didn't like you going out with me," Cam said. "Well, you made it clear that you didn't want to anymore anyway, so I didn't argue. I stopped calling. And nothing like that ever happened again. Right?"

True. I just nodded.

"Sorry," I mumbled. "I miss her."

"Of course you do," he said. "I've been worried about you since the funeral. By the time I got Mrs. Owens sorted at the hospital, everyone was home asleep. And I've gotten good at resisting the urge to call you."

"We're getting along." I left out the part where I was possibly trying to solve the mystery of a dead child.

Cam nodded. "You said they're at the game?"

"Yeah."

"I'll come back out tomorrow." He turned for the stairs and paused. "Meg—lock your doors."

I waited for him to say something else, but he just stood there, scuffing the toe of his boot along the edge of the carpet.

"Cam?" I prompted.

"I need to talk to Burt and SarahBeth, but I can't not warn you, either. Doc Mulligan called me this afternoon. He took blood samples from Ainsley the night she died, before he knew she was really going to die. Then his nurse sent them on to the lab in Kansas City before she knew there was no need. The lab sent the results back yesterday and Doc went up there today to make sure they weren't wrong."

I tightened my grip on my son. "What?" I bit out as Cory squirmed.

"Ainsley didn't have encephalitis from a case of the measles twenty years ago. She died of something called lactic acidosis, but the lab says it was caused by poisoning. Cyanide poisoning. That's why it took them so long to send the results back—the tests for that are apparently pretty complicated, and they ran it three times to be sure."

"Did you just say cyanide? Like, capsules for people in old movies to kill themselves, Nazi gas canister, cyanide?" My stomach flipped slowly over thinking about all the times I'd eaten in this house in the past two years.

"That's what the doc said. I'm not saying it was on purpose, I don't really know much of anything yet." He waved a paper. "I have a warrant to search the house, but I'd rather have them here and tell them to their faces what I'm doing."

"That's nice of you."

"I can do it tomorrow morning, I don't think they're a flight risk," he said. "Can I take y'all home?"

I held his gaze until I had to blink because my eyes hurt. I was raised to think of the police as the enemy. But every time I looked Cam Blankenship in the eyes, all I wanted was to be his friend. More than his friend, if I was being honest. Two years of keeping him at arm's length hadn't changed that a bit.

"I'd like that."

Cyanide. What in the actual blue hell?

Should I tell him why I was here and what I was looking for?

Probably. But what if Ainsley had been hallucinating, like the doctor said? SarahBeth and Burt had been kind to me and my son. I wanted to know more about whether there was anything here to worry about before I went involving the law in it.

I mean, there was something horrible buried in my own yard and I hadn't gone running to the sheriff about it. I knew that decision was a selfish one, but I couldn't fight the urge to apply the same logic here.

Whatever Ainsley had been on about, if there was someone buried on their property, too, it was a long time ago. Ainsley said "years." I wasn't in any immediate danger.

"Me too." He reached for my hand. I let him take it, closing my eyes when the sparks skated up my arm and right into my heart.

"Me too!" Cory kicked his feet. "Buddy."

I followed Cam downstairs and outside, realizing as I

climbed into his truck that I still hadn't made it inside the locked upstairs room in the west wing.

FORTY-SEVEN

SarahBeth
September

Cam Blankenship walked into my house with a search warrant on the last Saturday in September.

"I'm sorry to bother y'all," he said, stepping inside without waiting to be invited when Claire opened the door. "But I need everyone in the house to come to the living room and sit there while we conduct a search of the premises."

"While you what?" I walked into the foyer with a broom in my hand. Sweeping used to be Daisy's chore, but since Ainsley... staying busy was far better than not.

"Hi there, ma'am." The little boy I used to babysit was a full-grown man, staring straight back at me without blinking. "We have a warrant from the county judge to search the house this morning."

"For what?"

"Mrs. Godfrey, I'm not real sure how to say this except to just come out and say it like they taught me. Ainsley did not die from an infection related to a childhood case of the measles."

I sagged into the wall. Claire gasped, clapping one hand over her mouth as tears sprang to her eyes. "Papa!" she screamed after a few seconds.

Cam stepped toward me. "Are you okay?"

"I saw Ainsley with my own two eyes," I said. "She was sick."

"Yes, but not from the measles—or from encephalitis caused by them, either. We need to get more information to determine what happened here. Anything you can do to help with that will be appreciated, and may help protect the rest of you, too."

"Sheriff, can I help you?" Burt came through the hall with his eyebrows up. "What's going on?"

"Mr. Godfrey, I have a warrant to search your property, sir."

"For what?"

"Evidence relating to the death of your daughter Ainsley, sir."

Burt's face flushed. "Have you lost your ever-loving mind, Cameron Blankenship?" He crossed the floor to gather me in his arms, and I hid my face in his chest. "Ainsley had the measles when she was two. Doc said she got a brain infection. What in the hell do you think you're doing here except upsetting my wife and stirring up grief?"

"I find no joy in this, Mr. Godfrey."

"Ainsley was sick," Burt repeated. "Ask Doc Mulligan. He'll tell you."

"He's the one who told me she was poisoned," Cam said. "He got lab results on some blood back yesterday and called me because he was worried about the other children."

"Poisoned?" My voice sounded faint. "You can't be serious."

Cam nodded to the deputies in the doorway. "Y'all know what you're looking for. Start in the kitchen." He turned back to me.

"I'm running out of patience with you, Cameron."

"Ma'am, I am doing nothing but trying to figure out what

happened to your daughter and whether or not any of the rest of you might be in danger."

Danger.

My babies. I swallowed hard. "What exactly is it that Doc Mulligan says happened to Ainsley?"

"Cyanide poisoning. It has most of the same symptoms of the brain thing you can get from measles." He checked his notes. "Sclerosing pan encephalitis, Doc said. He said he just assumed that she had that because he treated her for the measles when she was two, and the symptoms matched up."

I blinked.

"That's... that's just plain crazy," Burt said. "People don't die from cyanide except in black and white movies."

"I was up late reading about this and I was shocked by what I found," Cam said. "It's more common than you'd think." He looked from me to Burt. "Do any of you shop online?"

"We don't even have the internet," Burt said. "No computers in this house."

Cam pulled a piece of paper out of his pocket and unfolded it.

"Seen anything that looks like this?" There was a picture of a small black case with two jars of powder and some capsules.

"No," Burt barely glanced at it.

I studied it. "No."

Cam tucked it into his notebook. "Was anyone here unhappy with Ainsley?"

"I'm not sure I like where you might be going with that," I said, realizing I couldn't feel my face. The numbness spread from head to toes until I couldn't even feel if I was still breathing. Cam Blankenship, a boy I once babysat and then briefly thought might be my son-in-law someday, thought there was a murderer in our house.

Besides me, I mean. But of course he didn't know that.

I looked at Burt.

He didn't have any reason to want Ainsley dead.

Did he?

I stopped breathing for so long my lungs hurt. Punishment. Not from God. God had more important things to concern himself with than a cheap tramp my husband found in a motel, after all. But rather from Burt.

"Are you okay?" Cam touched my shoulder. I jerked away.

"Would you be okay if I walked into your house accusing someone you love of murdering your child, Cam?"

"I suppose not."

I pointed to the paper. "So is that what you're looking for?"

"Maybe. It's a kit available online."

"A cyanide kit?" Burt shook his head. "I told you no good would come of the internet."

"The kids do call it a suicide kit," Cam said. "Are you sure Ainsley didn't have access to the internet?"

"Su—" My voice faded out and I waved my hands in front of my face.

"Come on, SarahBeth," Burt said, putting his hand out and leading me to the living room.

"I'll be in Ainsley's room," Cam said.

"My daughter did not kill herself," I said, my voice breaking on the last word. I fell into Burt's arms and sobbed, every tear I hadn't cried in the past five weeks flooding out of me.

Because what if she did? What if I made her so miserable and guilty keeping her here with a secret that wasn't even hers— with a lie that was entirely mine—and she got dragged down so far she didn't see any better options? How would I live with myself if my scheming, and not a virus she'd had years ago, had actually killed my daughter?

FORTY-EIGHT

Meg
October

Cam didn't find anything conclusive at the Godfreys' house, but somehow his presence there broke SarahBeth.

Ten days after he served his warrant, she still wouldn't get out of bed. Burt threw up his hands on day three and kept on with the harvest.

I checked on them every day.

"She'll get better, Meg," Bethany said, kneading dough at the kitchen island. "She never cried. About Ainsley. Not until the other day. She's just grieving now." She nodded like she was telling herself that more than she was telling me.

"Did you hear what Cam was talking to her about?" I asked, handing Cory a wooden puzzle to play with and sitting him on the floor.

Bethany pinched her lips and shook her head.

She was lying. She always pinched her lips together when she lied.

"She said Ainsley didn't um... kill herself," Claire said softly from the table, where she was reading. She had grown into a quiet girl of twelve who preferred books to people most of the time. "That was the last thing Momma said before she started crying."

"Of course she didn't," I said, hurrying across the floor and squeezing Claire tight. "Ainsley wouldn't do that."

"Then what happened?" she asked. "The police were here for hours. They even searched in my room. They said they didn't find anything. But if there was poison in her blood it got there somehow, didn't it?"

Bethany dumped the bread into its pan to rise and covered it with a towel.

"Claire," she said. "Go check on Francine for me."

I watched Claire go, and then watched Bethany move around the kitchen. She had gotten comfortable being in charge right quick.

"You hanging in there?" I asked.

"Why wouldn't I be?" She pulled a chicken from the fridge and started prepping it for dinner.

"Just making sure you're not overwhelmed. I have one child and a small farm to take care of, and it still feels like I'm drowning some days."

"I'm set. Momma taught me well." Her voice was tight.

"I'm right next door if you need help," I said.

"We're good at taking care of our own here." Her voice took on a chill. "I don't mean to be rude, but you were Ainsley's friend, and Ainsley is gone now. Why have you been here every day?"

"Bethany Lynn!" SarahBeth's voice came from the doorway, and Bethany dropped the chicken, muttering a swearword and squatting to clean up the mess.

"Forgive my failure to teach my daughter manners," Sarah-Beth said. "I'm always glad to see you, Meg."

That was news to me. But I smiled anyway. "Thank you.

I'm glad to see you up and around. Your girls have been worried."

"I miss my Ainsley," she said quietly. "Having you here makes that a little less. She loved you."

"I loved her." I held SarahBeth's gaze. "She was one of the only people I've ever met that I would do just about anything for."

"Ignore Bethany. You're always welcome here," SarahBeth said.

"I appreciate that very much. I like being here, I think. Where Ainsley was."

SarahBeth nodded, and Cory brought me his puzzle.

"Good job, buddy!"

He beamed, his tiny teeth gleaming. SarahBeth smiled. "Blink and he'll be as big as you are."

"I can believe it." I picked him up and planted a kiss on his cheek. "Speaking of growing, we have grocery shopping to do. Thank you for your kindness, as always."

"Anytime." She touched the baby's hand as we passed her on the way out. I didn't bother to say goodbye to Bethany.

I was stuck for any way to figure out what the heck Ainsley had been talking about, a little girl in the garden. I'd looked everywhere I could think to look in their house without a search warrant of my own, and Cam had actually searched the whole house, and I still didn't know any more than I had the day she died. I couldn't very well just get my rusty shovel and go start digging.

Could I? I mean, I had picked the exact wrong spot to dig on my own property once. Maybe I could do it again.

I wondered if Bethany wasn't kind of right: if I was using this whole idea of playing detective to feel closer to the friend I had lost. I didn't want to give her up, so I was doing something for her, something big enough to consume every minute of every day that I wasn't taking care of my little boy. Losing people we love makes us all go a little crazy. Staring at my ceiling fan in the small hours of the night while Cory slept in his crib, I even questioned whether Ainsley had ever said there was a little girl under the garden in the first place. It sounded insane. That was part of the reason I didn't want to repeat it to Cam. I knew it was crazy to think she said it and crazier still to be sneaking around weeks later trying to uncover a mystery that might not even exist when I was about as far from a cop as a person can be.

Turning on my side, I stared at the baby's crib in the glow of his night light. SarahBeth was right. It wouldn't be long before he outgrew this, too. A gift from the Godfreys that had kept him safe for two years now.

The ripples on the rails cast funny shadows on the wall.

Ripples. I furrowed my brow.

Ripples.

I sat up and groped for my nightstand drawer. Pulling it open, I found a flashlight and the etching I'd made from Ainsley's sketchbook cover.

Francine in her bedroom doorway.

Except that wasn't Francine's crib, it was this crib. The one Alexander and I had retrieved from the stinky storage room in the back of the old bomb shelter on the night before Bethany turned fifteen. When Francine was still sleeping in her crib.

The one that made Ainsley look like she saw a ghost when Alexander offered it to me.

I leaned closer.

The little girl looked like Francine... now.

But that book had sketches of all the other kids too, and they were all from years ago.

I looked closer. It was harder to make out here than it would've been if I had the real sketch, but all of a sudden I didn't see Francine at all.

The nose here was wrong. Francine had the cutest upturned nose.

The eyes were set a little too far apart, their corners a little too narrow.

Anyone else, I would say it was close enough.

But Ainsley wasn't just anyone. She had a gift.

What if this little girl in the drawing wasn't Francine?

That question opened a floodgate of dozens more.

Did the Godfreys have another child before I met them? Did Ainsley lose a sister, too? Was that the thing we'd had in common?

Could it be a secret someone would kill to keep?

FORTY-NINE

SarahBeth
October

Ainsley's friend knew something.

I wasn't sure exactly what, but she'd been poking around too much, asking questions that sounded innocent enough, but then listening too hard while they were answered.

For better than two years, the bones had rested in the garden. The blackberries I'd planted over them were thick now.

What if Cam came back and dug up the blackberries? Just because I didn't see a reason for that didn't mean he couldn't find one. Had anyone so much as mentioned them when he was here before?

I couldn't remember.

But I knew something had to be done about Meg. I had fought through too much to keep this family together to have it splinter to the four winds now.

I tried not to care about Burt, but I couldn't make myself stop. *For better or worse.* That's what we had said to the preacher in front of God and everybody so many years ago.

Well, we'd had a lot of better for a long time, and this... this was going on our fifth year of worse.

I prided myself on my stubbornness—it was what allowed me to keep pushing and get things done. And for five long years, I had banished the memories that I knew would drag me under. Beat me, eat at me until I might go looking for a suicide kit on the library's computer.

Until now, that had worked out for me.

Francine was mine. Burt was still here.

And Ainsley had stayed in Cottonwood County and kept our secrets.

But in the dark, I wondered: when I made my secret hers, when I let her blame herself for the other child dying, had I broken my daughter in a way that made her not want to live anymore?

I bit my lip and let the tears flow again, the memories washing in faster than I could fight them.

———

Sweating through those long ago August nights praying for the peace of sleep, I couldn't stop thinking about the blonde who'd knocked on my front door with a story about my husband and a motel, and a little girl staring at me through a car window with Burt's nose and my mother-in-law's eyes.

I never wanted to know her name.

But finding his mistress's name was the only way to discover where she lived. And my husband, arrogant as he was, hadn't even really bothered to hide it well. A week after the tramp sped off our land while my hand still stung from slapping her face, I spent fourteen minutes digging through Burt's desk and came up with twenty-seven canceled checks made out to Lila Fuller with the memo line "Violet." Four hundred dollars a month in what I had to assume was child support.

Another twenty-six were made out to a Joshua Roberts, and the consistent amount of seven hundred dollars made a pretty sure bet that they were to pay rent. I snuck off to the library eight days after this woman turned my world upside down and found an address for Joshua Roberts two counties over, and a bird's-eye photo of his property showed a detached garage with a staircase running up the side.

The questions were eating me from the inside out by then, and I was half convinced what I imagined had to be worse than the truth. So I went looking for her.

I'd driven all the way there with the hunting knife heavy in my pocket, hoping it wouldn't come down to using it. She was small and slight, and hadn't even tried to hit me back that day in the yard. But I would not live with this kind of threat to my family, waiting every minute of every day for her to show up again, never breathing or sleeping easily. I had to make sure she was scared enough to stay far away from us.

I knocked on the door to an apartment above a sagging garage sided with green shingles coated in peeling white paint. I stood close to the frame instead of stepping back like I'd always taught my children. Good manners weren't necessary when calling on the woman who'd been sleeping with your husband.

She opened the door just as a child shrieked, pulling her attention away from me. "Violet, leave your sister alone." She spit the words between her teeth, turning back with a small smile that faded as she stepped backward when she saw me. She swung the door like she meant to slam it, and I shot one hand out to hold it open. I wasn't big, but working a farm for decades had made me strong. Stronger than Burt's whore was, anyway.

"I just want to talk to you," I lied. "I'm sorry I was rude before."

She turned her head and I couldn't stop a gasp when I saw her jaw. Purple and puffed up like a balloon, it looked hideous. And painful.

I could sort of see the outline of my thumb and forefinger in the bruise.

I glanced from her face to my hand, still wedged against the flimsy plywood door.

What in the world? Had my hand flown at her face with the power of Zeus?

"It looks worse than it is," she said, not moving anything but her lips.

"I don't suppose it could be any worse than it looks, at any rate," I said.

"Why are you here?" Her words were slow, but I could understand them because of that, so I wasn't complaining.

"I don't know." It was the truth. The knife was heavy in my pocket, the metal cool against my leg through my skirts, but I was kidding myself. I couldn't kill anyone. "I couldn't stop thinking about you. I thought I had questions. Now I don't know if I really want the answers."

She stared at me for three heartbeats and opened the door, waving me inside.

I looked around, breathing stale air that smelled of soiled diapers and strong coffee. The little blonde girl I'd seen in her car the day she came to our house had lost interest in her sister, transfixed by a woman in overalls singing on a small television. A squeak behind me made me turn, my heart falling to my knees when I spotted a tiny girl in a pink onesie, lounging in a bouncy seat.

Two of them. Were they both Burt's? Violet was the only name I'd seen on the checks.

"I don't have anything to offer you," their mother said. "We're getting kicked out of here next week."

"Why?" I furrowed my brow, my eyes still on the baby. She was gorgeous, so tiny and perfect. She didn't belong here.

"Burt told me last winter that he couldn't leave you." She had the decency to look at the floor when my head snapped

around toward her. "We fought. I told him I wouldn't have my daughter being raised like she was a secret. That he made promises to me. He said he promised you first and he never meant to let this go so far. A week later I found out I was pregnant again." She barked a grim laugh through her broken jaw and pointed to the bouncy seat. "I didn't tell him about the new baby because he stopped paying my rent after we fought that night. I had a little money stashed that I had saved up from what he gave me for groceries, but I ran out last month. So we have nowhere to go. Why do you think I came to you? I'll take care of myself, but I reckon my girls have just as much right to that big house as yours do. They don't deserve to suffer for what Burt and I did."

I wanted to hate her, pitiful purple face and all, but she was barely more than a kid herself, in this tiny apartment alone with two little ones. I wouldn't give her more than four or five years on Ainsley. And this girl hadn't done anything to me. She didn't stand in front of a church and promise to be faithful to me forever. Burt did.

"When did he take up with you?" I asked, the words so strangled they were raspy.

"We met nearly three years ago when he was in Kansas City at some kind of expo." She shrugged. "I don't remember what it was for. I was waiting tables in the bar at the Double Deuce Motel, and this guy Burt was with had too much whiskey and stuck his hand up my skirt. Burt laid him right out, quick as a blink. The bouncers tossed him for throwing a punch and I went to his room with some ice. He asked me in. And... well." She turned to the toddler. "We made Violet. I found his name in the room register at the motel after I found out I was pregnant, and he took care of us. Until I pushed him about you, anyway." She leaned forward, and I took a small step back. That's all.

Just one small step backward.

Just like that day in the barn.

This time, my hip tried to fold under me and I lost my balance. Flailing, I grabbed at the air, nothing stable in reach in the sparse little apartment.

The girl's eyes went wide and she reached a hand toward me. I grabbed it, panicking at the thought of falling even though the floor was just right under my feet, not fifteen feet below them.

She wasn't nearly strong enough to help, though. I fell backward and sideways, yanking her forward. I hit the floor, and she crashed into the coffee table, a sickening crack thundering over even the thudding of my own panicked heart as the corner of the wooden table disappeared into her bony side like a stick poking into a marshmallow.

Her face went slack. She opened her mouth and blood gushed out, warm and thick where it sprayed my face.

I rocked slightly from side to side, my hands finding the edge of the coffee table and using it to push me to my feet. I watched with eyes that refused to even blink as my husband's mistress slid to the floor like a cheap sweater.

Blood trickled out of her mouth, her eyes wide and glassy, staring at nothing.

The blonde toddler with Burt's nose and my mother-in-law's eyes screamed, both hands going to her face.

That got me moving. I squatted to talk to the child. She shrank away from me, terrified eyes wide.

"It's going to be okay. You're going to be okay." Saying the words in the tiny, hot apartment, I had no idea how they could be true. Maybe I was talking more to myself than the little girl.

She had a bandage wrapped around one arm, her blue dress dotted with food stains.

"Mommy!" she screamed.

"It's all okay," I said.

That was a lie. Nothing here was okay.

"Don't look at your momma right now, okay?" I pointed to the singing woman on the television, and the child scrubbed tears

from her eyes and nodded, turning back to the screen as I turned toward the horror show on the floor.

This girl had given my husband two children, had come to my home where I had apparently broken her face—nobody would ever believe me if I said I'd simply slapped her, and she and I were the only two people in the front yard that night. And now I had come here looking for her with a hunting knife in my pocket, and she was dead before I had even had the chance to warn her to stay away from my family. All from falling three feet into a garage sale coffee table.

It made no sense. But that didn't make it any less true.

I couldn't go to prison. I wouldn't leave my children.

I stood, pacing the room slowly and putting my hands in my hair. Think. What was I going to do with these children? I couldn't just leave them here alone.

I paused beside the bouncy seat, the newborn's sweet face peaceful with sleep even with all the screaming around her.

She wriggled in her sleep, a noise entirely too big for a baby so tiny escaping her backside, her eyelids lifting as her face scrunched and she howled.

I laughed. "Is that so?"

Finally, something I knew how to fix.

I found diapers that looked like they were made for Daisy's dolls they were so tiny, and lifted the baby from the seat, changing her on the table in the corner. My breath caught when I picked her up again and she nestled her head on my shoulder like my babies used to, her tiny hand resting over my heart. She didn't weigh as much as a sack of flour, her whole little body about the size of my breast.

Burt had taken care of this... waitress... Lila, and by extension carried on an affair with her, because of the older child. I was certain of that the minute I heard her story.

"He wanted the baby, not the mother. Probably worse after I

couldn't give him any more babies," I murmured into the little one's downy hair. "And he doesn't even know about you."

She sighed. I melted. And in that moment, I had a fleeting thought that would change my world forever.

Could I?

"It's insane," I said, pacing the tiny apartment.

But she was so tiny and perfect, and her mother, who'd been so desperate less than a week ago that she'd come to me, of all people, was very definitely dead.

I couldn't let Burt's own flesh and blood go to foster care. Not this perfect little girl. I wouldn't.

By the time I had walked the apartment fifty times, I knew what I was going to do.

"We're going to save each other, me and you," I murmured, planting a kiss on her perfect little head.

I put her back into her little chair and rolled up my sleeves, hunting around the makeshift kitchen until I found bleach and a sponge for me and a handful of crackers at the bottom of the only box left in the bare cupboards for the TV-obsessed toddler. The older child was so silent and fixated on the screen I wondered if she was in shock, but when I put the crackers in front of her, she ate them. I rolled Burt's girlfriend up in the raggedy carpet I pulled from under the coffee table and scrubbed up every drop of blood before I packed two grocery bags of things for the girls and backed the pickup to the base of the steps, loading the body in the back and the children into the front.

By the time I got halfway home, I had the details straight.

"Please help me, Lord, to make this right," I whispered.

The baby would be ours. I could sew padding for my skirts and fake a pregnancy—I'd been pregnant six times, for heaven's sake. I knew how it went. A baby was the only thing that could save my marriage, and this one now needed us as much as we needed her.

The old bomb shelter stayed about fifty degrees all year long, *and we stored the cribs in the back room. I could put the girls in there and put the lock back on the door as long as I had the only key, and when the time came, I would "deliver" my baby in the bathroom, in the middle of the night.*

The spare child, the toddler, was a problem, though.

I couldn't keep a child in a crib forever.

I thought for a second I could say we were adopting her, but Burt would know. He knew this one, the mother had said. And I couldn't risk making him suspect anything about the baby.

So I'd have to find a way to leave her somewhere. Somewhere safe.

She had a bandage on her arm. I would take her to the hospital. After I'd had my new baby. Since the infant would have to stay out in the shelter until I could reasonably convince my family I'd been through a whole pregnancy, I'd keep her sister with her to help keep her happy, like a living security blanket. With no windows in the room, it'd be easy enough to get them both on a reverse day and night schedule. Burt barely noticed when I was in our bed, anyway—I'd wait for him to fall asleep and go outside to take care of my baby at night, then let her sleep while everyone was awake during the day. I was a mother five times over—sleep deprivation and I were old friends.

Crazy? You bet. But I could do it. I would do it. To save my family.

My hospital plan got me thinking about school, where they'd want a birth certificate to enroll the little one someday all too soon. Maybe we could get one, but if I didn't want to risk it, I could homeschool her.

My fingers tightened on the steering wheel.

"I can homeschool all of them," I said out loud. Ainsley had already been out of school for two years, and I'd just told her she wasn't going back this year. "They can all just stay home." I nodded to myself.

A second chance. That's what I had here.

And I was going to make the best of it.

———

Nearly five years later, lying next to my sleeping husband, I knew that pushing his dead girlfriend over the hill in our rickety red wheelbarrow and burying her on Old Man Lester's farm, along with doing everything else I'd had to do, had saved our family. And though my heart ached every second with guilt and sadness about Ainsley, I couldn't fully regret a bit of it because I still had everyone else.

I didn't know what Cam was up to or what Meg knew, but I did know this: I had done too many unforgivable things to keep my family together to stop now.

If one or even two more sacrifices needed to go on that altar, so be it.

Once upon a time, I had entertained the thought of taking little Cory the way I took Francine. Before Ainsley met Meg and everyone in my house saw her baby.

Maybe Burt would get that second son he'd always wanted after all.

Taking lives was hard. Forging a document for a young woman nobody knew, giving custody of her toddler to the only friends she had in the world? That would be easy.

All I needed was a good plan.

They should be together, but without the baby. It couldn't be poison, and their bodies would have to be found. So it had to look like an accident. Not in the dark, where there would be room for questions. In broad daylight. With a witness.

Fire? Too much risk to our property.

Car crash? Not reliable enough to know they'd both die.

Drowning... I nodded. The pond.

And thanks to Francine, I knew exactly how to get them both there.

FIFTY

Meg
October

The sun trickled in the windows on Saturday morning, and I arched my back and stretched before I even opened my eyes.

I turned over, my face already stretching into a smile before I opened my eyes. "Good morning, sleepyhead."

We did this every morning now. Cory would giggle and either say "good morning" or "sleepyhead" whichever he felt like parroting, but never both.

The silence in the room that day was the loudest thing I'd ever heard.

My eyes snapped open, my heart already racing. "Cory?"

Empty crib.

I vaulted off the bed and hit the floor with my feet already running.

"Hey, buddy," I shrieked, because trying to keep the panic out of my voice was like trying to hold water in my fingers. "Where'd you go? Hugs for Mommy!"

None of my tricks worked.

I ran through the living room and into the kitchen, and my heart fell right through my feet and shattered on the floor.

He could climb out of the crib.

He could also apparently open a door.

This was one hell of a way to learn both of those things.

I ran to the phone and dialed Cam.

"Meg?" He picked up on the first ring. God bless him.

"Cam, it's Cory." I couldn't talk without sobbing. "Help, please. I can't find him. I woke up and he's not in the crib, the door is open." I sank to my knees on the floor as the door to his truck slammed in the background.

"I'm ten minutes away. Make that five." The words were tight over the engine gunning. "Meg. Meg! Pull it together. You can panic later, right now your son needs you to think. If he left on his own, where would he go? What does he like, that he could walk to?"

"There are so many dangerous... I don't know." My brain vomited images of snakes and possums and the hayloft, the tractor... "He's obsessed with climbing."

"So what does he like to climb the most? Kids will go to their favorite thing, unless something else catches their eye on the way."

"The tractor." I dropped the phone and sprinted out the back door barefoot, not even feeling the gravel under my feet. I ran until I thought my lungs would burst, my eyes scanning for Cory, my voice ragged with screaming.

I was coming out of the barn when I heard Cam's truck round the corner of the house. He squealed to a stop, jumping out and running to me. "Nothing?"

"I can't find him."

"Meg, what's wrong?" Bethany called from the top of the hill.

"We can't find Cory." My voice broke. "He got out of his crib and out of the house while I was asleep."

"We'll help," she said, disappearing. I heard her hollering, and doors slamming and shouts.

"The pond," Alexander bellowed. "Remember when Francine disappeared?"

I looked up at Cam, my eyes filling again. "Oh my God, he's right. He loved going there with Ainsley last summer. He's been after me about going back."

Cam and I started running at the same time, no spare air for words. We were further back, and cutting across the fields on both sides of the hill, we beat all the Godfreys to the water. Cam dove in fully clothed when we didn't see Cory anywhere, and I followed. Behind me, I heard Alexander yell again.

"Wait, no," he roared, the sound traveling through the water. "The plants."

What plants? I didn't care anything about plants. I was looking for my son.

It was about the last thought I had before my foot got tangled in something. Looking around panicked when I realized I was stuck, I spotted Cam slashing at chutes of something green with a pocket knife. He got one foot free, and the other got stuck.

My lungs burned. I stopped kicking, watching Cam fight his way free of one tangle just to get snared by another.

I'm sorry.

I couldn't say it.

The last thing I remember thinking was that at least I didn't see my baby. There were so many people in Ainsley's family who loved him.

Surely someone would find him.

FIFTY-ONE

SarahBeth
October

Alexander always had the worst timing, from checking on sick people when they're sleeping to walking in on Burt and me making love.

It even extended to playing the hero, apparently.

Standing halfway between the barn and the pond, I watched Meg and Sheriff Cam disappear beneath the surface of the pond. I counted. Thirty seconds. Forty. Their lungs would be getting tired. Too tired.

And then my son dove into the freezing water clothes and all, his pocket knife in his hand.

I sighed.

Alexander was strong. He'd grown up here—he knew the key was to avoid the hydrilla growing out of the floor of the pond himself by keeping his whole body inverted or flat. The stuff was always there, but between the heat and the fish, it was short enough in the summer for the water to be pretty safe. This time of year though, it grew long, tangling chutes that were crazy strong like the weed it was, and it was easy to get stuck in if you didn't know to stay away from it.

We all knew that. I had counted—correctly—on the fact that Meg and Sheriff Cam did not.

But Alexander was about to throw a wrench into this plan, too.

I couldn't let anyone see my irritation, though. Picking up my skirts, I hurried a few steps toward the pond, yelling for Burt.

Alexander surfaced with Meg in one arm and Cam in the other, yelling for help.

Claire ran to the edge of the water like her tiny, weak person could be at all useful. Bethany pushed her back and took Meg from Alexander.

"She's not breathing." Bethany didn't sound that bothered.

"He's not either. I learned CPR for my coaching job, move," Alexander ordered.

I watched until he had the sheriff breathing again.

Damn. I turned slowly. My hips had gotten worse over this past winter, so I had to be careful with any kind of pivoting. I crossed behind the big barn.

Through two steel doors built to keep radiation out, I found Cory exactly where I'd left him after I took him from his crib in Meg's bedroom that morning—in our shelter, in Francine's old crib.

"Hey, buddy," I whispered. Old habits die hard.

I lifted him out and turned back to the door, noticing the pockmarks and the scratches for the first time in a long time. It's funny how the brain only lets us see what we want to see.

I wondered what would be different today if I hadn't gone looking for the blonde, Lila. If I hadn't had to know the details of what Burt had done with her behind my back. Not that I would trade my little Francine—but would some of the other sorrow we'd been through in the years since be absent from my life and my heart?

Burt was waiting in the doorway by the canning shelves, watching me with hooded eyes and the strangest, coldest blank look.

"The kids said he was lost," he said.

"And you think he wasn't?" I raised one eyebrow and stepped through the doorway, pausing to close the door.

"I don't think he opened that door and climbed into a crib." His voice was quiet. "But I've spent the last few years wondering, off and on. About a lot of things. And watching you lift him out of that crib... I got the most horrifying, sickening thought... SarahBeth, what did you do? Did you take him?"

"Why would I do that, Burt?"

He shook his head. "I don't guess I've ever really understood you, as much as I liked to think I did. I can't imagine what would drive you to do that. But I also can't think of any other reason for what I just saw with my own two eyes."

He turned for the door.

"Where do you think you're going?" I asked, my voice so low I gave myself goosebumps.

Burt turned slowly. "To tell Meg her son is okay. And try to make up a reason for him being here that doesn't involve kidnapping."

"Kidnapping?" I barked a dark laugh. "Are you listening to yourself?"

"What else would you call taking a child from his bed while his mother is asleep?" He shook his head, his face quivering, shaking off the shock until he just looked revolted.

Disgusted. By me.

Something inside me snapped, looking at my husband's face, my mother's voice whispering in my ear that I was going to end up just as alone as she'd been. It was almost like I felt the break, and before I knew which end was up, words gushed out of my mouth as fast as I could think them.

"How dare you?" I hissed. "I gave you every part of myself, carrying six babies for you. I nearly died helping you run this farm, and the thanks I got was a tramp ringing my doorbell telling me her children had just as much right to this land as mine?"

"Children?"

Oops. That wasn't even what she'd said, that first day. I had only seen Violet then. It just slipped right out into stale shelter air before I could swallow it.

His eyes went from mine to baby Cory to the crib. They lingered there for a long time, then jumped back to me full of understanding. And horror.

"Dear God. Francine? You stole her? What did you do to her mother? Her sister?"

"Jesus, Burt." I rolled my eyes. "I didn't shoot your whore in the back, as much as I might argue she deserved it. It was an accident. She fell on her coffee table in that stifling little apartment. I think there had to be something wrong with her."

"Brittle bone disease," he said, his eyes filling with tears. "She was so careful. When I told her about your fall from the hayloft it terrified her."

"*She* was terrified?" I didn't recognize my own voice. Rage poured out of my throat, hot and bitter, giving my words a thick, panicked, shrill quality that made them seem like they weren't mine. "You had children—not just one mistake, Burt, children, plural. A whole other family. With someone else. You told me you loved me. What else could I have given you? Given this family?"

I stepped toward him and he backed up.

I laughed. "Are you afraid of me, Burt Godfrey?"

"Everyone who draws breath in this house is afraid of you," he said. "Isn't that the way you've always run things here?"

"You should tread carefully," I said. "You were the one who didn't want to get Ainsley vaccinated when she was a baby. You said it would be good for them to get sick, it was good enough for your mom and dad and you. You killed my daughter."

"The doctor and the sheriff both say she was poisoned," he shot back. "Who else would've done that but you?" He pointed to Cory. "Clearly your moral compass is completely busted."

"Why would I poison my own daughter?"

"Because she wanted to leave this place? Because you were jealous?" His eyes went from my face to the door behind me. "Because she knew." He put one hand over his mouth, shaking his head. "She knew about Francine, didn't she? Is that how you kept her here? Why she was so protective of her baby sister? Was she protecting her from you? What did you do to my Violet?"

The look on his face would've broken me once upon a time. But right then all I could feel was righteous anger. None of this was my fault. All I had done was try to save my family.

"Your Violet," I spit the words so violently I half expected them to cut him. "Got sick. I guess she didn't get the good old Godfrey immune system your mother insisted would protect our babies from the plague itself. Ainsley—" Tears welled and spilled over so fast my cheeks were wet before I knew what was happening. "Ainsley loved them both. She was never supposed to know the things I had to tell her. Never supposed to carry the secrets I asked her to keep. All because of you and some bar room waitress." I wiped my cheeks and stepped toward him again. "How dare you criticize one single choice I made trying to clean up your mess?"

He opened his mouth to speak and I raised one hand.

"I love Francine because she is my baby." I gulped air and swallowed hard. "*Mine*. I fought for her. I fed her and rocked her and read to her every night. I gave her a home. A family. Her father's name. Two parents who love each other."

His eyes were green ice cubes. "I don't love you, SarahBeth. I don't even know you."

I stood strong, though I wanted to crumple, hearing the words actually come out of him. He didn't love me.

"I was going to take Violet to the hospital and leave her for social services to find. After I didn't need her to keep Francine company anymore. I had a plan. But then Ainsley found her."

"Ainsley wouldn't hurt a fly." Burt's hands went to his eyes. "She couldn't have hurt a defenseless little girl."

"Ainsley had a dark side you didn't ever want to see. She was stealing from us that summer before Francine was born, did you know that? Cash from the box in your desk, planning to run away from home. And then one day right before New Year's, she came out here to get some peaches and she heard that brat of yours banging on this door—I guess Violet figured out how to climb out of the crib and she was hollering about being afraid of the dark. Ainsley cut the lock and opened the door, and she found them. Francine and Violet. She stayed out here with them that day and waited for me. I thought she was painting."

Burt's eyes lost the kind of deep light people often don't get back once it dies as my words landed, and I couldn't even bring myself to feel pity.

"Ainsley didn't," he said. "She wouldn't have... she would've told me."

I rolled my eyes. "You think she would've confided in the man who cheated on her mother? Who tried to break up our family? Maybe you really didn't know her."

His shoulders dropped practically to his knees. "I know she had a kind heart. What did you tell her to get her to go along with this?"

I could almost feel a wall crumble in my heart as I looked at him. The man I'd loved for more than half my life. The man I had given my body and soul, to keep here with me. Every secret

I'd carried in the name of keeping Burt Godfrey happy was about to come out. What did it matter anymore, really?

My voice sounded cold, like a doctor telling someone they have some terrible disease. "I told her if she'd help me sell my pregnancy with Francine, I'd figure out a way for Violet to stay with us too. I couldn't, of course, but I thought I'd deal with that later. Maybe Ainsley knew I didn't mean it—she wrecked my plan to drop Violet at the hospital by telling the brat her name and that they were sisters. I worried. I prayed. And then that January, before I could come up with another idea, Violet got a cough. Didn't seem serious at first." I backed up one step when he stood up straight.

"Not serious?" Burt's question squeaked out on a whisper. "How can a toddler living in a damp, allergy-infested outdoor room have a cough that's 'not serious?'"

"It just kept getting worse. Ainsley asked about taking her to a doctor, but I put it off. I was afraid of what Violet might say in front of a doctor, and I was so close to being able to bring Francine inside. Then one night I came out here and found Ainsley holding Violet. Ainsley was crying. Violet wasn't breathing." I stopped, trying to shake off the memory of the anguish in Ainsley's voice. "Ainsley kept saying we murdered her baby sister by keeping her locked up out here."

"Why didn't she tell me?" Burt's hands went to his face.

"And split up her family when we had already let a child die to preserve it?" I scoffed. "Ainsley was far too logical for that."

He looked around the room, his nose wrinkling, before his eyes landed on me again, wide with shock. "You... this place... the smell... it was never the plumbing, was it?"

"You left me no options, Burt." I threw up my hands. "You and Ainsley set the game for me, I just played my hand. What else was I supposed to do? Of course I told Ainsley we had to hide the body or we'd both get into trouble. Ainsley insisted we hide it in here because she didn't want to bury her in the dark, she said Violet was afraid. She left a light burning in that room around the clock for years."

Burt's face crumpled. "I wondered about them all this time. Lila and I had a fight…"

"She told me. You didn't want to leave me, she said." The laugh that slid out of my throat tasted as bitter as it sounded.

"I couldn't leave all these children for one child. By the time I went back looking for her, she was gone, and I just thought she was so mad that she took Violet away so I couldn't see her after I stopped paying their rent." He shook his head. "Then about a year ago I started to wonder about Francine. She looks so much like Violet. I couldn't imagine how that was possible, but also I couldn't imagine how it wasn't." He took a deep breath. "I even thought about hiring a detective to find out what happened to Lila and Violet, just so I could sleep better. So I would know. I couldn't ask Cam, I reckoned, without risking word getting back to you, and every cop in five counties knows every other one, so I couldn't ask the police anyplace else without it getting back to Cam. And that got me thinking—this town—this whole county —is so small, I was afraid to ask anyone." He shook his head, meeting my eyes for the first time in a while and flinching at what he saw. "I couldn't risk you finding out if I was wrong. My God, I wish I'd done so many things different. I should've gone with Lila when she asked."

"Violet fought for air for days at the end." I spit the words, wanting to make him hurt the way his last words had hurt me. "She was miserable. And Ainsley thought it was her fault. Called herself a murderer in her darkest moments."

"If someone here is a murderer, it wasn't Ainsley." The disgust on Burt's face was so complete, every bit of love I'd ever had for him died right there.

"Ainsley gave your brat the germs," I said. "She came out here with a chest cold, because she thought I wasn't kind enough to Violet when she didn't come visit her. We were so close." I swallowed hard. "The look on her face when she told me she'd killed the little girl..." I shook my head.

"And you let her think that. Her last days on earth were spent thinking she'd killed a helpless child."

"I had no choice."

"You had many, SarahBeth. You just made the wrong one."

"I've made a lot of bad choices in my life, Burt. It seems you're near the top of the list."

"Stop it, both of you." Alexander's voice was low and tight from the doorway I hadn't even heard open. "You're just digging your holes deeper, saying things that can't be unsaid." My son's huge frame filled the shelter's squatty doorway, blocking out every bit of light.

"What did you hear?" I turned wide eyes on him.

"Enough to know neither of you understand anything about what's happened right under your roof." He stepped inside. "You're not even acting like you're on the same team. A family isn't that different than a football team. Papa, Momma is the coach, trying to do what she thinks is best for the team, even when she's wrong. Momma, Papa is like a quarterback, always most concerned with what's best for him. Ainsley..." He swallowed hard. "She was our center, protecting everyone, taking the hits herself so you two didn't have to. But she had her limit. I think she was going to tell someone about what happened to the little girl you kept in that room for so long. You kept her in there even after she was dead, Momma. I didn't want to think it was true, even though deep down in my gut I knew that smell didn't have anything to do with plumbing. We can just refuse to believe the truth when the truth is too hard, though, can't we? I think that's what Ainsley did, until she couldn't stand it. I went out to fish late one night in July and heard her, sitting by Baby Elizabeth's grave talking about how she couldn't stand the guilt anymore. I didn't want her to see me so I came up here. I looked under the tools and the body wasn't there."

"Oh, Alexander." I pressed my fingers to my lips, tears welling in my eyes as dozens of mangled dead animals flashed through my head. Of course. Alexander was the other person in our house capable of killing someone. And he'd thought Ainsley was going to expose my secret. Was he trying to protect me? "I moved Violet's bones. More than two years ago, after the tornado when y'all brought Meg in here, so no one would find them. Ainsley didn't have any evidence to back up her story. You didn't have to kill her, buddy. What did you do?"

"Me?" He stumbled backward, shaking his head. "Are you kidding? I didn't do anything. Wasn't it you?"

The door squealed open behind him, and Bethany ducked in, slamming it shut again. "Ainsley should have just buried this whole thing a long time ago." She dropped right into the middle of our conversation like she'd been listening outside, which I wouldn't put past her if there was a way to. "But she wasn't like us. Alexander's right, she talked to herself, or maybe to dead people, when she thought nobody was around."

So Bethany was listening. She had always been good at sneaking around unnoticed. And she was still talking. "I heard her in her room one night, late, a few months ago. She said being friends with Meg had made her see how wrong she and Momma were, because someone must have loved the little dead girl the way Meg loves Cory." Bethany hauled in a breath, her eyes cold and flat in the dim light. "Why would anyone let a dead person break up their family? Family is everything. You taught us that, Momma."

"You?" I wasn't even sure which one of us said it. Every pair of eyes that wasn't in Bethany's head went to her.

"Tell me y'all didn't know still. Are you serious? The sheriff straight said she was poisoned. Who cooks everyone's meals?" She reached into her pocket and held up a plastic bag.

"Are those cherry pits?" Burt squinted.

"Very good." Bethany smirked.

"We learned this in ag science," Alexander said, his eyes going wide. "Cherry pits, peach pits and apple seeds are... poisonous." He waved one hand in front of his face before it balled into a fist. "They have cyanide in them." The words came slowly. "Oh my God, Bethany."

"When you crush them," Bethany said, nodding like she was telling us she'd found a new recipe for meatloaf. "I put them in her eggs every morning. Easy enough when she always wanted hers different from everyone else's. All it did was give her headaches at first, until that last night when I put a ton of them in that sauce she liked for her chicken."

I turned wide eyes of my own on Burt. She didn't even sound sorry.

He was just as horrified as I was. And we both knew what had to be done now.

Burt stepped forward a split second before I did, and Bethany pulled his grandfather's revolver out of the back of her jeans and pointed it at all of us.

"Stay put, Papa," she said. "No one here is going anywhere until we've talked about a few things this family has ignored for too long."

FIFTY-TWO

Meg
October

"Meg, come on!" Alexander's voice sounded far away.

And annoying.

"Meg, come back to us." Was that Cam?

I didn't care. I was so tired.

"Cory needs you." They said that together, and I opened my eyes. Cold, dirty water spewed out my mouth and nose, burning until my eyes watered. I coughed, trying to sit up.

"Easy," Cam said, one hand behind my back.

Alexander sat back on his heels and tipped his face up to the sky. "Thank you," he said. Looking back at Cam, who was hunched over me as I vomited water into the tall grass next to the Godfreys' pond, shivering, he nodded.

"I'm glad y'all are okay," he said, standing. "If you'll excuse me, I have something to take care of."

"Did anyone find Cory?" I asked.

Alexander paused, shading his eyes and looking down at me. "I don't think he's in danger, Meg. I'll explain everything later. Just let me go do this now." Cam shot to his feet, but Alexander was already running.

"What in the hell was that?" Cam looked at Claire, who was watching me with big eyes. "Sweetie, do you know what he was talking about? Have you seen Cory today?"

She shook her head. "I just wanted to help Meg. I'm sorry."

"Don't be sorry," I said. "Do you know where your brother is going?"

She tipped her head to the side. "The shelter is the only thing that way."

"The shelter." I coughed again, fighting my way to standing up on legs that did not want to work for me. "The shelter. The back room." I pulled on Cam's hand. "We have to hurry."

"That's always locked," Claire called after us. "Momma worries."

I just bet she did.

That smell. The sketch. That rounded corner doorway. The little girl that looked so much like Francine.

Burt and SarahBeth had locked a child in that room and something terrible had happened to it. The thought of my baby being locked in there made me find strength in worn-out legs and breath in watery lungs.

"What's going on?" Cam ran alongside me, trying to grab my arm, but I shook him off.

"Did they have another kid? A girl, maybe after Daisy but before Francine?"

"SarahBeth lost a baby in her accident," Cam said. "People whispered about it in town for months."

I almost tripped. "Why would anyone gossip about something... like... that?" My lungs hurt, almost like they were cramping.

"You know how people are. Some said she fell on purpose because she didn't want another baby. Called her a murderer. Other people said Burt had a girlfriend. That he pushed Sarah-

Beth, trying to kill her. None of it provable, of course. Nothing to investigate, even. Just gossip. But the Godfreys stopped coming to church. Stopped sending their kids to school. New people who move in closer to town don't really know they exist now. They ghosted the whole county, kind of." He shook his head, stopping to bend and catch his breath just the far side of the barn. I did the same, scanning our surroundings.

I spotted Bethany outside the shelter. She stood there for a minute, her head tipped like she was listening at the door, then jerked it open and went inside. The sun flashed off something in the back of her pants.

"I'm good." Cam stood up straight. "You okay?"

Everything he'd just said swirled around what I knew about the Godfreys until I wondered if I really knew a single true thing about them at all.

Except one. Bethany was a selfish bitch. That, I'd bet my life on.

And if I was right about anything that was happening here, I might have to do that to save my little boy.

I took off again, my legs trembling with the effort.

"We can walk," Cam said. "It's right there."

"No, we can't," I called over my shoulder. "Bethany just went in there, and I'm pretty sure she's got a gun."

FIFTY-THREE

SarahBeth
October

I pressed my fingers to my lips. "Oh, Bethany."

"Don't you 'oh, Bethany' me. I was just trying to do the same thing you were doing. Keep our family together. And maybe prove to you two that I should get this place because I love it more than anyone else. This life, here on this farm, being a good wife and mother—it's all I've ever wanted. You both spent so much time and effort trying to force it on Ainsley and Alexander when they didn't even want it. Ainsley just wanted to clear her conscience so she could leave." Bethany jerked the gun at her brother. "And he doesn't want to farm, he wants to coach football."

"Bethany, you don't want to hurt anyone," Alexander said.

Did he hear her say that she murdered Ainsley because she wanted the farm? I didn't think it wise to say that out loud while she was waving that .45 around, though.

"I'm tired of trying the hardest and being the best, and still somehow never being good enough," she said, her face scrunching into a mask of despair and fury. "Just when Momma started to think I was better, that I wanted what she wanted, Francine came along and she's Momma's favorite now."

"Francine isn't—" Burt began, and I kicked him.

"Don't you dare," I hissed.

"She has a gun, SarahBeth," he said. "Tell the girl you love her."

"Bethany, you have always been the most like me," I said. "I don't have favorites, and I'm sorry if I made you think I do. But I love you very much. And I think you'd do a beautiful job running this farm."

"You're just saying that." She shook the gun.

"Am I?" I raised my eyebrows. "Hand me that and ask me again."

"Momma..." she sobbed.

Alexander lunged at her and grabbed the gun.

It went off, deafening in the small space.

Burt let out a strangled gasp, and I turned just in time to see the neat round hole in his shirt start to leak blood into the cloth.

The door opened before I could get to him. Burt slid down the wall to the floor and grabbed at the hole in his shoulder. Alexander, holding the pistol like it might bite him, shook his head, but wouldn't look at anyone.

From the doorway, with wide eyes and blue lips, Cam Blankenship pointed his gun at me and told me to hand Meg her baby.

I kissed Cory's small head and took him to Meg, looking around the shelter, my eyes landing on Claire and Daisy and Francine, who had followed Meg and Cam from the pond.

My family was everything to me.

Now I knew just how deep Burt's betrayal had been. Why and how Ainsley was dead. And how my hands were buried in every bit of it.

In trying to save our family, I had destroyed it.

I stuck my hands out and met Cam's disbelieving stare.

"If I'm going to jail," I said, all the hatred and anger that had boiled my blood just minutes ago replaced by chilly resignation, "at least I'm doing it with an unburdened heart."

FIFTY-FOUR

Meg
November

"You're sure I can't talk you into staying?" Cam shut the door of my truck and leaned in through the window.

"You're welcome to come with us," I said, laying one hand on his jawline, my words dripping regret. "This place has too many bad memories now, I can't shake them. Not even for you."

He poked his nose an inch from mine and stared into my eyes before he kissed me.

We'd spent one night together, the night after he arrested SarahBeth and Bethany Godfrey for murder. It was even more electric and magical than I ever could've imagined.

Five days later, with everything I wanted to take from Cottonwood County except this man packed in the back of my truck, that kiss was enough to make me forget my own name. His lips moved slowly over mine at first, growing more insistent as I buried my fingers in his thick hair, running the tip of my tongue along his lower lip until a growl ripped from his throat and he pulled back, his eyes bright and breath coming fast. "What are you doing to me? This has always been my home. I have a job here."

"Like they don't need cops literally everywhere." I rolled my eyes, putting both hands up before goodbye spiraled into another argument. "We're not going to cover anything here we haven't said in the past few days. I don't want to stay, you don't want to go." I sighed, swallowing the baseball that had somehow lodged itself in my throat. "This is how these things go for me. Probably for the best."

After the Godfreys had argued their way through confessions to multiple crimes with the sheriff standing right outside their bomb shelter that wasn't even fully soundproof, he'd made the news as far away as Kansas City for breaking open what the reporters were calling "The Trad Wife Murders," which I didn't really understand. But Cam said it was an internet thing and I counted myself generally happy to fail to understand those, so I ignored it.

"How could this be for the best, you leaving me?"

I laughed right in his face. "Did you hear SarahBeth and Burt? They were, to their own children and this whole county, the perfect example of married bliss. High school sweethearts, half a dozen kids, holding hands everywhere they went, sticking together through her terrible accident—and it was all a big lie. There's no such thing as true love."

"I would like the chance to prove you wrong about that." He ran one finger up my cheekbone. "Corrianna Blake of Vipers Hollow, Virginia, AKA Martha no last name I could locate of Whitney Falls, Arkansas, now Meg Whitney of Cottonwood County, Kansas."

I very nearly vomited in my lap.

"Breathe." Cam put his hands on my shoulders. Two beats later he shook me. "I meant that. Breathe."

I realized I wasn't and sucked in a deep breath.

"What did you just say? How?" I reached for Cory's seat. "Cam, I can expl—"

He laid one finger over my lips.

"I said that, not exactly the way I'd planned, but casually, because I want you to know that what destroyed the Godfreys was secrets: Burt's girlfriend, SarahBeth's lies, Ainsley's big dreams, Bethany's jealousy. And we don't have secrets, me and you. If you think we could keep it that way... well. I've been thinking."

Time itself stopped.

"About what?" It was a small miracle I got the words out.

He... knew. He knew all about who I was. If he had even found Martha, he had to know about my sister Emma—and that meant he probably mostly knew how and why I'd killed my own daddy.

Whitney Falls meant he knew about Mary and Tim and Sam Tomlinson and Charlotte—three of the four were dead, one of them because of me. But if he knew about Mary, he probably knew about Cory, too—that I hadn't birthed him myself. If he knew all that, chances were good he knew that Cory's real parents were not only monsters who didn't deserve my beautiful boy, they were also dead.

And he was saying he didn't care.

I didn't know what to do with that.

"I love you, Corrianna-Martha-Meg. I love that little boy. I read all the files, and I read them months ago, for the record. Ainsley asked me about a human trafficking ring in Arkansas that she had seen on the news, and I started poking around. Saw a photo of you in a church newsletter someone posted on Instagram with a woman who had those same violet eyes my little buddy does. Turns out, the boss is a pretty good detective with the right motivation." He thumbed a tear off my cheek and shook his head. "I knew you had been hurt—I could tell you felt what I felt that first night at dinner, and you just didn't want to let yourself feel it. The more I found out, the better I understood that you must be terrified of men in general, and one who wears a badge in particular. Right?"

I nodded. "I couldn't fall in love with you, Cam," I whispered. "I didn't want to hide who I was, but I couldn't stand the idea of you finding out and hating me, either."

His turn to laugh. "Hate you?" He tapped the end of my nose. "Here's what I think of everything I dug up about your life before you came here: your father was a disgusting excuse for a human being and you did the world a favor. The sheriff in your hometown isn't a fool—he knows that way better than I do, and told me himself that his only regret was not locking your father up before your little sister died. Mary McClatchy was literally the scum of the earth, and you've given my little buddy here a shot at much brighter future than he would've had if you'd left him behind to end up in the foster system after she died—of a pulmonary embolism, according to the coroner's report, in case you've been wondering."

My eyes fell shut, one nightmare laid to rest Mary was really and truly dead, and nobody thought I'd killed her. I sucked a deep breath through my nose and opened my eyes to find Cam staring into them.

"I don't even know what to think," I said.

He smiled. "I'm thinking I'd sure like to be part of whatever's next for you two."

"Even if it means moving?"

"Home is where your family is. My momma taught me that."

"Are we your family, Sheriff Cam?" My voice was soft, tears brimming in my eyes.

"I'd sure like for you to be."

My breath caught, hot tears spilling down my cheeks that Cam kissed away.

Things like this just didn't happen to me. Happy endings were for other people and TV shows.

"Well? Will you really have me?" His eyes were bright with excitement.

"I think I'd like that."

He rounded the hood grinning at me and climbed into the passenger seat. "So, where are we headed?"

"West hasn't worked out so well for me, so I thought maybe north. How do you feel about seeing Chicago?"

"Bigger than Kansas City," he said. "But if you're there, I will learn to love crowds and lines."

I pointed to the stack of canvases wrapped carefully in the back of the truck. "I know it's not New York, but I want to talk to galleries about her paintings."

He put one finger under my chin and tipped my face up to his, kissing me until I couldn't have told you what country Chicago was in for a million dollars. But I could feel the love he poured into that kiss, and it made my head swim in a way whiskey had never come close to.

"Somewhere, right this minute, Ainsley is smiling," Cam said. "I know you thought she didn't want us to be together, but I don't believe that's true now, if it ever even was."

More tears fell and I laughed, brushing at them. "I don't usually cry this much in a year. But I hope you're right. That she can see. I love the idea of her seeing her work hanging in a gallery in a big city."

"Chasing dreams." Cam pointed to the road. "Let's go do it."

"What dream are we chasing?" I asked as I started the truck.

"Is there a bigger dream than happily ever after?"

I smiled and pulled out of the drive, the *For Sale* sign bright white against the cream siding of the house in the review mirror.

"Happily ever after, Momma," Cory chirped.

Happily ever after. It had always been too much to hope for. Too much to risk.

But maybe it was waiting for us up ahead.

In a city the size of Chicago, I might even be able to use my real name.

A LETTER FROM LYNDEE

Dear Reader,

Thank you so much for coming along with me to Cottonwood County in reading *The Housewife Next Door*! I am so thankful every day that I get to go to my computer and create stories and characters, and readers like you make that possible. If you'd like to be the first to hear about my new releases, you can sign up using the link below:

www.bookouture.com/lyndee-walker

I was surprised when I got to the end of *The Pastor's Wife* and felt Martha had more story to tell. That book was supposed to be a standalone, but when I found out my editor agreed that Martha's story might not quite be over, I started thinking about where she went when she left Whitney Falls, who she became this time, and how she'd find her way as a young mom who didn't know anyone wherever she ended up.

As I worked, Martha became Meg to me—a whole other character showing me new and different bits of her heart and her past. A young woman who desperately didn't want to be like her own mother, but hadn't really had much of a role model for being a good mother in her life, either. I talked to my editor and we decided to let Meg's story unfold without mentioning Martha until that point came up organically in Meg's story.

I had planned for her to meet the accomplished veteran

mom on the next farm and then discover she wasn't the only person in this pocket of Kansas hiding dark secrets, but as I was writing away, it wasn't SarahBeth up on the hill saving the day with a copperhead near Meg's feet—it was her daughter Ainsley, a farm girl with big talent and big dreams who'd had all that squashed by secrets and guilt. So Ainsley became the surrogate sister Meg needed so desperately while SarahBeth became something more sinister than I originally imagined, pulling strings behind the scenes. And the one thing all three of them had in common was a desperate fear of being like their own mothers.

I had an absolute blast getting to know these complicated, messy women, and I hope you enjoyed their story. I'm so thankful to everyone who read and loved *The Pastor's Wife*—I have been thrilled and humbled by the things you all have said about Martha and Mary, and I hope you enjoyed your time with Meg and Ainsley just as much. I'm already working on the next book—with all new characters this time—and I can't wait for y'all to read it, too. Thank you so much for trusting me to tell you a good story.

With much affection,

LynDee

instagram.com/lyndeewalkerbooks
facebook.com/lyndeewalkerbooks
tiktok.com/@lyndeewalkerbooks

ACKNOWLEDGMENTS

I say this every time because it's true: so much work from so many brilliant people goes into every novel, and I am so thankful for everyone who had a hand in bringing this one to you.

First, many thanks to my editor, Lydia Vassar-Smith: for letting me run with this story, for trusting me to take you on a twisty ride, for your encouragement and advice, and for your unwavering support and faith in my work. It's truly a pleasure working with you.

My eternal thanks to my agent, John Talbot, for being not only a savvy literary agent but also a good friend. I'm very fortunate to have you in my corner.

My publicist, Jess Readett, for answering all my questions and thinking of so many fun ways to hook new readers into my stories.

I also want to thank the entire editorial and publicity staff at Bookouture for being so kind and welcoming on this book as well as *The Pastor's Wife*. There's not a better team in all of publishing, and I love that if you turn the page, dear reader, you'll see a list of everyone who worked hard to bring you this book.

I would never finish a book if it weren't for my amazing family, y'all, so all my thanks as always to Justin and the littles for picking up slack around the house and making sure my deadlines get met.

Last but never least, thank you to my amazing readers, the ones who jumped with me into a new genre here and the new ones who found my work because of Martha.

As always, any mistakes you may find are mine alone.

PUBLISHING TEAM

Turning a manuscript into a book requires the efforts of many people. The publishing team at Bookouture would like to acknowledge everyone who contributed to this publication.

Audio
Alba Proko
Melissa Tran
Sinead O'Connor

Commercial
Lauren Morrissette
Hannah Richmond
Imogen Allport

Cover design
Eileen Carey

Data and analysis
Mark Alder
Mohamed Bussuri

Editorial
Lydia Vassar-Smith
Imogen Allport

Copyeditor
Laura Gerrard

Proofreader
Jon Appleton

Marketing
Alex Crow
Melanie Price
Occy Carr
Cíara Rosney
Martyna Młynarska

Operations and distribution
Marina Valles
Stephanie Straub
Joe Morris

Production
Hannah Snetsinger
Mandy Kullar
Nadia Michael
Charlotte Hegley

Publicity
Kim Nash
Noelle Holten
Jess Readett
Sarah Hardy

Rights and contracts
Peta Nightingale
Richard King
Saidah Graham

Dear Reader,

We'd love your attention for one more page to tell you about the crisis in children's reading, and what we can all do.

Studies have shown that reading for fun is the **single biggest predictor of a child's future life chances** – more than family circumstance, parents' educational background or income. It improves academic results, mental health, wealth, communication skills, ambition and happiness.

The number of children reading for fun is in rapid decline. Young people have a lot of competition for their time, and a worryingly high number do not have a single book at home.

Hachette works extensively with schools, libraries and literacy charities, but here are some ways we can all raise more readers:

- Reading to children for just 10 minutes a day makes a difference
- Don't give up if children aren't regular readers – there will be books for them!

- Visit bookshops and libraries to get recommendations
- Encourage them to listen to audiobooks
- Support school libraries
- Give books as gifts

There's a lot more information about how to encourage children to read on our websites: **www.RaisingReaders.co.uk** and **www.JoinRaisingReaders.com**.

Thank you for reading.